HISTORICAL

Your romantic escape to the past.

Compromised With Her Forbidden Viscount
Diane Gaston

The Lady's Snowbound Scandal
Paulia Belgado

MILLS & BOON

COMPROMISED WITH HER FORBIDDEN VISCOUNT
© 2024 by Diane Perkins
Philippine Copyright 2024
Australian Copyright 2024
New Zealand Copyright 2024

First Published 2024
First Australian Paperback Edition 2024
ISBN 978 1 038 93536 6

THE LADY'S SNOWBOUND SCANDAL
© 2024 by Paulia Belgado
Philippine Copyright 2024
Australian Copyright 2024
New Zealand Copyright 2024

First Published 2024
First Australian Paperback Edition 2024
ISBN 978 1 038 93536 6

MIX
Paper | Supporting
responsible forestry
FSC® C001695
www.fsc.org

Published by
Harlequin Mills & Boon
An imprint of Harlequin Enterprises (Australia) Pty Limited
(ABN 47 001 180 918), a subsidiary of HarperCollins
Publishers Australia Pty Limited
(ABN 36 009 913 517)
Level 19, 201 Elizabeth Street
SYDNEY NSW 2000 AUSTRALIA

Cover art used by arrangement with Harlequin Books S.A.. All rights reserved.

Printed and bound in Australia by McPherson's Printing Group

Compromised With Her Forbidden Viscount

Diane Gaston

MILLS & BOON

Diane Gaston's dream job was always to write romance novels. One day she dared to pursue that dream and has never looked back. Her books have won romance's highest honors: the RITA® Award, the National Readers' Choice Award, the HOLT Medallion, and the Gold Quill and Golden Heart® Awards. She lives in Virginia with her husband and three very ordinary house cats. Diane loves to hear from readers and friends. Visit her website at dianegaston.com.

Visit the Author Profile page
at millsandboon.com.au
for more titles.

Author Note

When I was young, it was Zeffirelli's movie of *Romeo and Juliet* that first made Shakespeare accessible to me, and I've always loved the 1961 movie of *West Side Story*, which, of course, was a modern retelling of Shakespeare's play. The problem with both, though, is that these romantic lovers don't have happy endings. They die! (Well, in *West Side Story* only Tony dies.) I wanted to rewrite both and make the ending turn out right!

There was always a romance writer in me even before I knew it.

This book was inspired by *Romeo and Juliet*, but Anna and Will start out as enemies at first sight instead of lovers at first sight, and although they have a lot to overcome, they do reach that happily-ever-after. I insist upon that!

To my friend Anne
just because she deserves it!

Chapter One

Vauxhall Gardens,
June 1817

Viscount Willburgh wandered through throngs of shepherd-esses, harlequins, Roman gods and goddesses, kings and queens of old, clergymen and devils, and dominos of every colour, all under a blaze of a thousand lamps hung in the trees of Vauxhall Gardens. Even if the revellers of the pleasure garden had not worn masks and half masks, it still would have been impossible to tell a servant from a lord from a pickpocket. Anyone could pay a shilling to be a part of Vauxhall Gardens' masquerade.

Unfortunately his companions, lacking imagination like Will and the majority of men in attendance, had seen fit to don black dominoes with white masks. The two of them had disappeared into the throng of dancers in the Grove and Will had given up searching for them.

Why the devil had he agreed to this escapade in the first place? Attending a raucous masquerade at Vauxhall Gardens did not suit Will's nature at all. Vauxhall was all illusion and decadence, but life's reality was hard work and weighty re-sponsibility.

Even so, there was much he could see—The Cascade. The

rope walkers. The Chinese temple. He could even seek out the hermit in the farthest corner of the Gardens. None of it held much appeal. Affairs of state were plaguing his mind, especially after the Prince Regent's message to the Lords advising the continuance of the seditious practices.

Should Parliament approve suspension of habeas corpus? There was certainly unrest throughout the kingdom, but was that not to be expected? The price of bread was high. People were starving. Should not the Lords be doing something about feeding the people instead of taking their rights away?

The festive music of the orchestra and the crowd's gaiety did not sit well with such thoughts. Will edged his way to the relatively quieter Grand Walk, but a group of drunken carousers annoyed him even more.

Maybe a visit to the hermitage would do. At least it would be quieter down the Dark Walk, darker this night, because clouds covered the moon and stars, and the air carried the scent of impending rain.

The lamps in the trees that flanked the walk grew fewer in number, as did the promenaders, couples mostly, probably looking for a secluded nook for a private tryst. A wave of envy jolted Will. He'd never had much time for dalliances and, unlike his friends, had eventually concluded that amorous affairs of the temporary kind merely left him empty.

He ought to turn back. Find a boat to take him across the river. Avoid the rain.

He was about to do that very thing when he suddenly had the Walk to himself. Until some distance ahead of him a woman jumped from the trees. A man followed and seized her from behind. The woman cried out and struggled to get free, but the man covered her mouth and pulled her back into the darkness of the wood. Vauxhall was not all merriment; danger also lurked there.

Will sprang into action, entering the woods where he saw the man and woman disappear. The man was dragging her into a shelter, a private supper room designed for assignations.

Will charged the man, wrapping an arm around the man's neck, choking him. The man, dressed in a domino and mask like himself, released his prisoner. She fell to the ground. A fist to the man's face and a kick to his groin sent the fellow fleeing for his life. Will turned to extend his hand to help the woman to her feet.

'Are you injured?' he asked.

'Shaken a bit, is all.' She looked down at herself and gasped. 'Oh, dear!' The bodice of her dress was torn, revealing her shift and stays. Her hands flew to her chest.

'Come into the shelter,' Will said. 'We can put you back to rights.'

A lamp lit the shelter enough for Will to see she wore a red hooded cape and a plain blue cotton dress covered by a pinafore. Or it had once been covered by a pinafore. The pinafore and dress were torn at one shoulder and now were held in place by the woman's hand. Her eyes were a startling light brown, lighter than her hair, a warm brown shot through with gold where the lamplight caught it. She wore it down, as if she were a girl, not a woman. How old was she? Still masked she could be anything. A maid, a shopgirl, or even a harlot—although a harlot typically would not be struggling to free herself.

The shelter held a chaise-longue and a table upon which sat the lamp and a bottle of wine with two glasses, apparently arranged ahead of time.

The woman—girl?—turned away. 'I—I am remiss in not thanking you right away, sir. I cannot imagine what I would have done had you not assisted me.'

Will could well imagine what the man had planned for her.

But he focused on the practical. 'Do you have pins with you? To pin up your dress?'

'I do.' Still with her back to him she let go of the torn dress and lifted her skirt slightly to retrieve pins concealed in her petticoat. She set to pinning the bodice in place. 'If only I could see...'

'Turn this way,' Will said. 'I'll help you.'

She'd managed to cover herself. Will needed only to straighten the fabric to make it appear as if it had been stitched. He stood close to her, close enough to feel the warmth of her body and the scent of her—lavender and mint and sunny summer days. Of one thing he was certain—she was a woman, not a young girl. He had not been so close to a woman in a long time, certainly not in such an intimate situation.

'How do you know how to pin a dress?' Her words were breathless.

His breath accelerated, heating up the inside of his mask.

'I have a younger sister.'

The confounded mask. It made it difficult to breathe and even to see.

With an annoyed grunt, he pulled it off.

The woman jumped back. 'You!'

Will was puzzled. 'You know me?'

Her voice trembled. 'Oh, yes. I know you, Lord Willburgh.' She removed her own mask.

'The devil...' Will glared at her. No. Not the devil. 'A Dorman.' The name was poison on his lips. 'The Dorman whose father killed my father.'

She bristled. '*Your* father killed *my* father! It was your father who challenged my father to a duel!'

He countered. 'It was *your* father who seduced my mother!'

She lifted a brow. 'Was it?'

This animosity had not begun with Will's father's death. The Dormans had feuded with the Willburghs for generations, purportedly over ownership of disputed land. It had really started three generations ago, when Will's great-great-grandfather and that generation's Lord Dorman fought over a woman, the woman who became Will's great-great-grandmother. After that event the discord over the disputed land heated to a fever pitch. The fire was further fuelled by more romantic rivalry—Will's great-grandfather's affair with that generation's Lady Dorman, and most tragically for Will, the seduction of Will's mother by the current Baron Dorman's ne'er-do-well brother, who knew precisely what he was about. Will's father challenged that younger Dorman to the ill-fated duel.

They killed each other in that duel, a duel that changed everything for Will. At seventeen, he suddenly inherited a title, all its responsibility, and all the scandal that engulfed the family as a result. From then on—ten years now—Will's carefree

life as a young man had ceased. Life became nothing more than
Duty. Duty. Duty.

Staring at this Dorman woman brought it all back. All his
grief. All his anger.

Her eyes lit with fear and she backed farther away.

He did not usually allow that part of him to show. 'Do not
worry. I'm not going to kill you.'

Her voice turned low. 'What are you going to do?'

Will took a deep breath and slowly released it. 'I am going
to finish pinning your dress and escort you back to wherever
you should be.'

Will damped down his emotions and finished pinning the
pinafore. She leaned as far away as possible as he did so. Even
in his anger he experienced the allure of being so close to her.

He stepped back. 'That should pass, if no one looks too
closely.'

Without another word he walked to the door and put his hand
on the latch. She followed. As he opened the door, a bolt of light-
ning lit up the sky, followed by a crack of thunder.

And pouring rain.

Damnation.

He closed the door. 'We'll wait out the storm. With any luck
it will pass quickly.' He inclined his head to the chaise-longue.
'You may as well sit.'

She hesitated, looking wary, but she had nothing to fear,
even if she was undisputedly lovely. He wanted nothing but to
be rid of her.

She perched on the edge of the chaise as if ready to escape
at any moment.

He walked over to the table and poured himself a glass of
wine. 'Would you like wine?'

Again she hesitated, but finally responded by holding out
her hand.

He placed the glass in it and retreated to a corner to lean
against the wall.

Will's emotions waged a war within him. Again he remembered galloping across the land to try to stop the duel, arriving
just in time to hear the loud report of their shots and see the

smoke from their pistol barrels before both men fell. He rushed to his father. Blood poured from his father's chest which heaved with every struggled breath.

'Your duty now,' his father gasped before his eyes turned sightless and his body went limp.

Will gulped down the whole glass of wine and poured himself another. His father had often warned Will he'd be Viscount one day and his father must train him for it. But his father never had the time.

Never took the time.

Instead his father died foolishly and Will had to learn everything on his own at seventeen.

Rain battered the roof of the shelter and thunder continued to rumble. Will concentrated on the sound until the wine and the weather lulled him back to a semblance of calm.

He glanced at the Dorman woman, sipping her wine and patting her hair.

'Your hair stayed in place,' he said, breaking their silence and remembering how he'd admired it.

Her hand returned to her lap.

'Who are you supposed to be, anyway?' He gestured to her costume.

She glared at him. 'Red Riding Hood.'

He laughed. 'And you were almost caught by the wolf.'

She straightened. 'Or perhaps you are the wolf in disguise.'

'Not the wolf. Not your grandmother either.' He poured himself the last of the wine.

She pursed her lips, disapproving.

Disapproving his drink and accusing him of being the wolf? *Who does she think she is?*

Oh. Right. She was a *Dorman*.

He tossed back a defiant look. 'So what the devil were you doing alone at Vauxhall? That was flirting with danger surely.'

'I was not alone,' she countered. 'I was with my cousin and she met with—with—gentlemen of her acquaintance. Then we became separated.'

It was his turn to be disapproving. 'Two young ladies unchaperoned, then?'

She glanced away. 'I was the chaperone.'

Will laughed. 'That was a hare-brained plan, was it not? Like two sheep to the slaughter. I daresay there is more than one wolf prowling around Vauxhall.'

She gave him a direct look. 'I undoubtedly failed, did I not?'

'Undoubtedly,' he agreed, taking a sip of wine. 'Do you and your cousin often come to Vauxhall alone?'

'We were not alone. Lord and Lady Dorman and Lucius came, as well. They will wonder where I am. And I really must find Violet.'

He scoffed. 'Cannot the *gentlemen of her acquaintance* be trusted to keep her safe?'

Anna took another sip of wine.

She certainly was not going to tell *him* that Violet had tricked her into a meeting with Mr Raskin, the Season's most notorious rake, and his vile friend, the man who'd tried to carry her off.

Where was Violet? Was she in a shelter like this with Raskin? If so, Anna feared Violet needed no force to go with the man.

It had been Anna's responsibility to keep Violet from doing anything foolish. Lord and Lady Dorman counted on her for that and would blame her for Violet's behaviour.

Willburgh broke into her thoughts, his voice scathing. 'And where was your cousin Lucius while you two young ladies met gentlemen of your acquaintance at a Vauxhall masquerade?'

Lucius and Willburgh had been schoolmates at Eton, Anna knew, and briefly at Oxford. Until the duel. Lucius returned to Oxford then. Willburgh had not.

'I was not meeting any gentlemen!' she snapped. 'Lucius…' Wait. Why should she tell *him* what happened?

He made a derisive sound. 'Let me guess. Lucius abandoned you as soon as he was able.'

'He didn't *abandon* us,' Although Lucius had pretty much disappeared into the crowd as soon as they were out of sight of Lord and Lady Dorman.

Anna ought to have insisted they all stay together as Lord and Lady Dorman expected, but would Violet and Lucius have listened to her? They'd probably planned to abandon her all along without a thought about leaving her unprotected.

A familiar ache returned, the ache of being alone in the world, belonging nowhere to no one. She could almost hear the words of her father, Bertram Dorman, her beloved papa, after her mother died—'*It is just you and me now. And I'll never leave you.*'

Thanks to Willburgh's father, that was a promise her papa could not keep.

Anna's eyes stung with sudden tears. She'd loved him so.

And he was not even really her father, merely the only father she'd ever known. Her mother, on her deathbed, had confided that her real father had been an officer in the East India Company army, killed when she was a baby. Her mother married Bertram Dorman not even a year after and he was the only father Anna could remember. She'd adored him and he doted on her as if the sun rose and set upon her.

Anna blinked her tears away. She was lucky the Dormans became her guardians and allowed her to live with them. Otherwise she'd have been sent to an orphanage.

As they often reminded her.

She glanced at the man who was her rescuer. He leaned casually against the wall, his long legs crossed at the ankles, his arms across his chest. He was taller and more muscular than she'd thought, but then, she'd never before seen him up close. She caught the scent of bergamot and sandalwood that clung to him as she had done when he pinned up her dress. He'd been so gentle pinning her torn dress, although there was no doubt of his strength. He'd displayed it by easily dispatching her assailant. He'd frightened her only briefly when his anger flared.

The Dormans hated him and the other Willburghs because of that silly family feud, so Anna had never been this close to him. She'd spied him occasionally in the village and glimpsed him at some of the Season's society balls, but she'd given him a wide berth. Lucius had gone to school with him and perhaps something there made him particularly detest Willburgh, but Anna hated him because *his* father had killed her beloved papa.

This man was not responsible for that, of course. He'd been

little more than a youth at the time. But his was the face her
anger settled on.

At the moment Willburgh's head was bowed, as if he were
pretending she was not even there. That certainly did not help
appease her anger. To be thought of as being of no consequence
to anybody only angered her more.

She'd make him see her. 'Where were you bound when
my—my problem—detained you? Did I interrupt some important plans? Or were you merely wandering the Dark Walk
in search of damsels in distress?' Or was he planning to meet
some woman in a shelter like this?

He raised his head as if he had indeed forgotten her presence.
'I was on my way to see the hermit.'

'Alone?' She raised her brows.

He gave her a direct look. 'Like the hermit, I was seeking
escape from the crowds and the noise.'

Anna hated the crowds and the noise, as well. Indeed, she
was not overly fond of London and all the delights of the Season. Ordinarily being caught inside during a rainstorm would
have been a pleasantness.

'You—you do not like Vauxhall?' she asked him.

'I do not,' he responded.

'Then why come?'

He shrugged. 'I was talked into it.'

'Oh, really?' She let her voice drip with scepticism. As if
a man like him truly could be talked into anything he did not
wish to do.

Perhaps he'd been spurned by a lady companion—although
somehow that idea did not fit him.

He shifted his position and took a step towards her. 'I was
separated from my companions, as were you.'

She doubted he'd been left on purpose as she had been.

He laughed dryly. 'Perhaps it was fate. So I could rescue you
and be stranded here.'

She lowered her lashes. 'I am grateful to you.'

When she raised her head again their eyes met and their
gazes held.

Until he took a breath and walked over to the window and looked out. 'I think the rain has stopped. I'll escort you back.'

She rose and gathered her red cape around her. Neither of them bothered to put on their masks. They reached the door together, brushing against each other as Willburgh turned the latch and opened the door.

Only to see Lucius and Lord Dorman, also unmasked, standing right outside.

'Willburgh!' Lucius reeled back as if struck in the chest. He recovered, leaning forwards again to glare at Anna. 'You are with *him*? *Him*? How shameless can you be? With *him*!'

Chapter Two

Lucius's words slashed into Anna like knives.

'See here, Lucius—' Willburgh responded.

But Lord Dorman cut him off. 'Do you mock us, Anna? Disrespect all we have done for you? Of all men, you behave the trollop with this one?'

'She did not—' Willburgh began, only to be cut off again.

'Come, Lucius,' Lord Dorman demanded. 'Let us go back. I wash my hands of her.'

Anna stared in disbelief as they turned their backs on her and strode off.

'Make haste,' Willburgh said, but she was too stunned to move.

He seized her arm and pulled her through the door.

'It is not what it seems,' he called after Lucius and his father. 'You must hear me.'

Anna could hardly keep pace with Willburgh as he charged after Lucius and his father, their dominos billowing behind them in their haste. They did not even bother to turn around. She and Willburgh caught up with them at the Centre Cross Walk.

Willburgh released Anna and seized Lucius's arm. 'You will hear me!'

Lucius shrugged him off 'Hear you? We caught you in a compromising position. What else is there to hear? Do you think we do not know what you were doing?' He laughed. 'Here I thought you were stiff-necked like your father. Obviously you take after your mother—'

'How horrid—' Anna broke in, appalled that Lucius would say such a thing out loud.

Other costumed people were in earshot and several stopped to observe the spectacle. They were easily recognised, having forgotten their masks.

Willburgh glanced at the observers and back to Lucius and his father. 'Have a care. Let us discuss this privately.'

'You may follow us to the supper box,' Lord Dorman said.

The way to the Dormans' supper box led them through the first Triumphal Arch and directly across from the Turkish Tent.

Lady Dorman, dressed in powdered wig and fashion from a century earlier, stood as they approached. 'You've found her, I see.' She sounded as outraged as her son and husband. Evidently the news has already reached her, even in those few minutes. She glared at Anna. 'An assignation with the enemy. How could you, Anna? After all we've done for you.'

'There was no—' Willburgh tried, only to be cut off again.

Lucius faced him. 'We will hear no excuses from you! Reprobate.'

Lucius wore a red domino, lined in black. Somehow the red of his cape was unlike hers. Instead he resembled an image of the devil she'd once seen in the window of Humphrey's Print Shop. Lord Dorman wore white powder and a colourful silk coat and breeches, matching the era of his wife.

At that moment Violet walked up, Mr Raskin in tow. 'We have just this moment heard.' She, too, turned to Anna. 'Is that why you ran off, Anna, and left me all alone?'

Anna gaped at her. 'Violet!'

Violet turned her gaze to Raskin. 'I don't know what I would have done if dear Raskin had not found me!'

Raskin bowed. 'It was my honour, I assure you.'

No one asked where he and Violet had been.

Anna looked at them all in turn. She knew she was of no real importance to them, except in the ways they found her useful. As companion to Lady Dorman and Violet, for example. Someone to fetch for them or carry parcels. But she thought they would at least *listen* to her. She thought they knew her well enough to know she would not indulge in assignations.

Lord Dorman's voice rose. 'We cannot tolerate your cavorting with this—this—sworn enemy, of all people! It is unforgivable, after all we have done for you.' He rubbed his hands together. 'I wash my hands of you!'

Willburgh's voice was even higher. 'I demand that you listen to me. You are mistaken—'

Lord Dorman's face turned red with anger. 'I heed no demands of yours, sir. Out of my way.' He pushed past Willburgh and gestured to the others. 'We are leaving! Now.'

They filed by Anna, each pointedly refusing to look at her.

Even though she remained rooted in place, Lord Dorman turned back to her. 'You may not follow. You are no longer welcome in our home.'

Only Mr Raskin looked back, a smirk on his face. The others walked away without a backward glance.

Anna finally found her voice. 'Well, this is famous. What am I to do now?'

'Damn them,' a voice next to her said. 'Damn them all. *Dormans.*'

Willburgh. She'd forgotten he was there. He was the reason the family had so roundly rejected her. Had she been caught with Raskin's friend and truly compromised, they would not have been so outraged.

He returned her glance. 'Forgive my language,' he murmured. 'And I forgot you were a Dorman.'

She used her stepfather's name, she thought, but she was definitely not a Dorman.

She glanced away, her predicament becoming more real. 'What am I to do?'

He moved so he was in front of her and he caught her gaze. 'Is—is there not a friend I can deliver you to? Someone who would assist you?'

A friend? She'd had no opportunity to make friends. She

knew Violet's and Lucius's friends, but she would not dream of asking any of them to take her in.

'There is no one,' she told him with a helpless laugh. 'And I have no money. What I own is in the possession of Lord Dorman.'

'Well, I can give you money,' he responded.

A masked gentleman dressed as a harlequin strolled by, a grin on his face. 'You are in a fine pickle, are you not? Better you than me!'

'Get lost,' Willburgh snarled.

'Someone you know?' she asked.

He shrugged. 'I suppose. Good thing for him he wore a mask.'

People strolling by were slowing as they passed them and obviously talking about them. She'd always worried that Violet would someday be such an object of gossip and scorn. She never dreamed she'd be one.

'We should go,' Willburgh said. 'I've had enough of this place.'

They left the supper box and walked towards the Proprietor's House entrance, passing the orchestra, which had started playing again. Soon a tenor's voice rang out:

The lord said to the lady,
Before he went out:
Beware of false Lamkin,
He's a-walking about...

Willburgh said, 'We'll hire a hackney coach to take us over Vauxhall Bridge.' Vauxhall Bridge had opened the previous year. Otherwise they'd be crossing the Thames by boat. At the entrance he sent a servant to have a coach brought around.

Anna did not know his plan. Was he intending to drop her somewhere in Mayfair and leave her to fend for herself? She was afraid to ask.

As if reading her mind, he said, 'I suppose I could take you to a hotel.'

'A hotel. Yes,' she responded without enthusiasm. At least she'd have a place to sleep for one night.

The hackney coach pulled up.

'Take us to the Pulteney,' Will called to the jarvey.

The jarvey's brows rose knowingly and he answered with a smirk. 'Yes, m'lord. The Pulteney.'

What was this man thinking? The Pulteney was a very respectable hotel. It had been fine enough to house the Tsar of Russia and his sister a few years ago; it should be respectable enough for a Dorman.

Miss Dorman's cheeks flamed red at the driver's comment. She'd obviously understood the driver's reaction.

Will helped her into the coach. He sat in the backward-facing seat, his spirits sinking even further than before. He could not take her to a hotel, he realised. With the spectacle the Dormans created at Vauxhall, there was certain to be plenty of gossip already. If he took her to a hotel at this hour of the night, in the costume she wore, would that not make the situation look worse? Confirm what the Dormans believe happened? What everyone would believe happened?

'Miss Dorman, I do not think it advisable to take you to a hotel. I will tell the driver to take us to my townhouse.'

Her eyes widened in alarm. 'To your townhouse!'

'My mother is in residence. No one can make of it what it is not.' Certainly his mother would not jump to that erroneous conclusion. She knew a Dorman was the last woman he would be caught alone with.

Although that was precisely what happened. They were caught alone, unchaperoned, in one of the shelters at Vauxhall created for 'private parties.'

He stole a glance at Miss Dorman who was absently gazing out the window into the darkness. He admired that she did not go into hysterics, although she certainly had every right to do so. She'd said very few words since they were discovered, but he felt the terrible blow the Dormans inflicted on her. Accusing her. Rejecting her. Abandoning her. He sensed the aloneness they'd created in her. When his father died, Will had felt very alone, even though he'd had family and friends around him. He was alone in becoming the viscount, though. No one else shared that burden.

Will opened the window to call to the jarvey to take them to Park Street instead.

Will and Miss Dorman rode in silence until the hackney coach pulled up to Will's townhouse. He helped her out of the coach and paid the jarvey. As the hackney coach rumbled away, Will hoped no curious eyes were awakened to see him escort her into the house.

Bailey, his butler, roused himself from a chair in the hall. 'M'lord, forgive me. I must have dozed off.' He stumbled in surprise at spying Miss Dorman, who was a sight in her Red Riding Hood costume.

'You needn't have stayed up, Bailey,' Will said. 'But I am glad you did. This is Miss Dorman.'

'Miss Dorman?' The butler sounded even more puzzled.

Bailey was aware, as were all the servants, that the Dormans and Willburghs were sworn enemies. He was, though, an excellent butler and quickly schooled his features back to blankness.

'Can you wake up Mrs White?' Will asked. Mrs White was the housekeeper. 'We need a room made up for Miss Dorman. She will need night clothes, as well. And a dress for the morrow. And any other items essential for her care and comfort.'

'Right away, sir.' Bailey bowed in Miss Dorman's direction. 'Miss Dorman.'

She nodded in return.

In the light of the hall, Miss Dorman looked pale and fatigued, as if she might collapse in a heap at any moment.

Will took her arm. 'Come into the library. You can sit there. I should have asked Bailey for refreshment. You look like you are spent.'

'Thank you,' she managed.

He led her to a comfortable chair and lit a taper from the sconce in the hall, using it to light the library lamps. 'I can have Bailey bring tea later. All I have here is some brandy.'

'Brandy would be most welcome.' She sat on the edge of the comfortable sofa near the fireplace as if wishing to bolt.

He took the decanter from a cabinet and poured two glasses, handing one to her.

She took a sip. 'I should not be here,' she said.

'Lord and Lady Dorman left you no choice,' he countered. 'A hotel would be worse. It would only generate more talk.'

'They would not let us explain.' She held the glass against her cheek for a moment, talking more to herself than to him. 'Do they really think so little of me?'

Will's anger rose again. Yes. How dare they simply leave her like that? He drained his glass and poured them both another. 'I will call upon them tomorrow. I will make them listen. They will have to listen to me.'

The brandy was having no effect on him. Certainly not calming his anger. He paced the room.

Mrs White entered, still in her nightcap, robe wrapped around her thick waist. Bailey stood behind her.

'I am here, m'lord,' Mrs White announced. 'The room is being readied. Everything is being done.'

Will's shoulders relaxed. For the first time this night someone else seemed to take the reins from his hands.

She approached Miss Dorman. 'Miss Dorman, is it? I am Mrs White, the housekeeper. I will show you to your room. You look as if you need a nice rest.'

Bless the woman, Will thought. She knew nothing of what happened but was taking pity anyway. Neither she nor Bailey had asked any questions, even though, as old retainers, they well knew the animosity between the Dormans and the Willburghs. They'd been around when his father was killed by her father. Will owed them an explanation. Later, though.

Mrs White led Miss Dorman to the stairs, right across from the library door. At that moment, though, Will's mother appeared at the top of the stairs.

'I heard voices,' his mother said, then saw Mrs White and Miss Dorman. 'What is this?'

Anna looked up at the woman who, in her eyes, caused her papa to die.

She'd seen Lady Willburgh before at a distance, an always

elegant figure, still beautiful in her fiftieth year even in her nightcap and robe. How Anna resented her! She'd lured her papa into a seduction. If only he had resisted her.

'Who is this creature, Mrs White?' Lady Willburgh demanded. 'Why is she in my house?'

Willburgh came to the doorway. 'I will explain, Mother.' He climbed the steps to her. 'This is Miss Dorman who must stay the night as our guest.'

'Dorman!' Lady Willburgh's voice rose. 'Violet Dorman?'

'Anna,' Anna replied.

'The orphan?' The woman's voice was scornful.

Yes, Anna thought. Orphaned because of you.

Willburgh spoke. 'I will explain, Mother. But let Mrs White show Miss Dorman to her room.'

'I will not have a Dorman in my house!' she responded indignantly.

'It is not your house, Mother,' Willburgh said evenly.

Anna, still at the bottom of the stairway, lifted her gaze to the woman and tried to keep the animosity out of her voice. 'I am sorry to intrude, ma'am. Believe me, it was not by my choice.'

'Not my choice either!' Lady Willburgh sniffed. 'She cannot stay.'

'She *will* stay.' Willburgh took his mother by the arm. 'Come back to your room and I will explain.'

He escorted her away.

'Unhand me, Will.' His mother's arm felt surprisingly frail in his hand.

He led her to her bed and lit a candle from the fireplace.

'She is *his* daughter!' she exclaimed, standing her ground. 'How could you bring her here?'

Will faced her and made her listen while he told the whole story, starting with Miss Dorman's abduction.

When he finished, her eyes flashed. 'Those Dormans. They are nothing but trouble!' She glared at him. 'You should have left her to her fate! Likely she wanted that man to—to—'

'Mother.' Will admonished. 'What sort of man would I be

not to intervene? Besides, I had no idea who she was until we were in the shelter. And then it rained.'

She pursed her lips together.

'I will call upon Lord Dorman tomorrow,' he assured her. 'I will straighten this out. Do not fret another moment about it.'

He smoothed her covers and helped her sit on the edge of her bed.

She fussed with her nightdress. 'You say others heard Dorman's accusations?'

'I am afraid so,' he admitted.

Her eyes narrowed. 'Then there will be a scandal. More scandal, because of *them*.'

At the time of the duel, tongues had already been wagging about the younger Dorman's affair with Will's mother. The duel set the scandalmongers on fire. It had taken until he was old enough to take his seat in the Lords for it all to die down enough for his mother to show her face during the London Season.

'I believe we can nip the scandal in the bud. Try not to dwell on it.' It all depended upon Lord Dorman's cooperation.

He lifted the covers and his mother crawled under them. 'I will not sleep a wink, knowing a Dorman is under my roof.'

Will placed a kiss upon her forehead and tucked her in like his nurse used to do for him when he was very young. He blew out the candle and left the room, hearing her continue to grumble to herself about the Dormans.

Will understood that even knowing about this incident would have set his mother off. Any mention of the Dormans tended to do that. He'd never have mentioned it to her if only the Dormans had been reasonable, which, of course, they were not.

According to family lore, the Dormans had never been reasonable. The feud had existed for generations, beginning with that land dispute, land that abutted the Dormans' property at the Willburgh estate in Buckinghamshire. The land was potentially valuable, but, because of the dispute, it had gone undeveloped for over one hundred years. Before his father's death, Will had thought the dispute a frivolous one, surmising it only required some sort of compromise each side was too stubborn to propose. It was not the land but the death of his father for which

Will could never forgive any Dorman. Even *the orphan*, as his mother had called her.

He'd heard that Lord Dorman had initiated another search for a clear deed to the land. Well, now Will would be damned if Dorman would procure rights to it. Will would contest it with all his might. He'd also heard that the Dorman finances were precarious, no doubt due to the excesses of each family member, Lucius especially.

The hypocrite. Lucius was quick to accuse his cousin of indiscretion when it was widely known Lucius spent a fortune on his latest lady-in-keeping—and the other women he saw behind her back.

But Will must damp down these feelings. He must approach the Dormans with a cool head.

He continued down the stairs in search of Bailey to again explain the events of this terrible night.

Chapter Three

Lucius Dorman arose much earlier than was his custom and dressed more quickly, having been summoned by his father *in no uncertain terms*. He entered the breakfast room where his parents were already seated, stern expressions on their faces.

'Good morning, Father. Mother,' he said, gauging that his expression should not be too cheerful.

'About time you got out of bed,' his father barked. 'I swear you'd sleep the day away if you could.'

His father was correct. He'd much rather sleep all day. The night was so much more interesting, but then, he was like his father in that respect. And his mother. But it might be prudent not to make that point at the moment.

'I rose as soon as I heard you needed me, as I would do any time.' Lucius chose a slice of bread and ham from the sideboard. After the evening's festivities, his stomach was not in its finest shape. He poured himself a cup of coffee, adding much cream and only one lump of sugar and settled himself across from his esteemed father and mother. Why they were in a pet was beyond him.

Unless it had to do with the utter betrayal of his cousin. Cavorting with Willburgh. The insult was unbearable.

The Meissen clock on the mantle ticked loudly as he waited for his father to speak.

The man finally roused himself. 'Do you realise what a bramble bush you've landed us in?'

'I?' Lucius was affronted. It was all Anna's doing as he saw it—if that was to what his father referred.

'You know that we need that girl,' his father said. 'You will have to marry her.'

Lucius straightened. 'I'll do no such thing! I'll not marry the leavings of *Viscount* Willburgh. You cannot ask it of me.'

'We will need her money,' his father responded.

Lucius countered. 'I'll marry someone else rich.'

His mother smiled patiently. 'You know you cannot attract an heiress. Your father's title is not so elevated. A wealthy merchant's daughter you might manage, perhaps, and if you find one of those before Anna is twenty-one, you will not have to marry her.' She glanced away thoughtfully. 'Of course, Anna has aristocratic blood and that is very important. And she is so eager to please, she would make an acceptable wife.'

Anna's mother was the daughter of an earl, although the title was now extinct. The family was anything but prolific. All gone now, with only Anna left. The family's considerable fortune was bequeathed to her alone but only if she did not marry until twenty-one, only a few weeks away. If she married before twenty-one, her fortune would go to any children she might bear and with the same restrictions.

Lucius's parents had always let it be known to him that he might need to marry her. He hadn't minded so much—until seeing her with Willburgh.

'You expect me to marry the chit after she's been with Willburgh?' Surely they would not ask that of him.

'It pleases me no more than it does you,' his father responded. 'But we are in dire straits. We must cajole her back to us. If we can find her, that is. I've sent two of the footmen to search for her. We will have to concoct some story to counteract the scandal.'

His mother groaned. 'I am certain tongues are wagging as we speak.'

'She'll come back to us,' his father mused, mostly to himself. 'She has nowhere else to go.'

And she knew nothing of the fortune that awaited her at age twenty-one if she remained unmarried. Lucius's father had kept that information from her so she would feel even more beholden to the family for taking her in. Keeping the secret of her inheritance kept the whip in his father's hand. Besides, the allowance the family trust provided her was a nice boon for the rest of the family. Anna knew nothing of that either.

Lucius and his parents often laughed about Anna being his bride. They joked that she was their secret gold mine, only to be fully mined when she came of age. Lucius had no doubt he could charm her into marriage. He flattered himself he could charm any woman. Besides, it was not like Anna would have any other choices.

Although how the devil had she come into Willburgh's sphere? He must have targeted her somehow. Lucius burned with rage just thinking of Willburgh with her.

Willburgh, his most detestable enemy, had been ahead of him in school, as well as being ahead of him in almost every other way. In contests of strength. In success in his studies. In cleverness and courage. Lucius, though, had always bested him with women. That was why Willburgh seduced Anna, Lucius was sure. To thumb his nose at Lucius.

The droning voices of his parents interrupted these thoughts.

'You must secure her hand, Lucius,' his father was saying. 'Grovel to her if you have to. Put on that charm of yours.'

Lucius would never grovel! Not for Willburgh's used goods.

'Are you heeding your father?' his mother asked.

Lucius glanced from his mother to his father. He'd play along with them for the time being. And if he had to marry Anna, he'd find ways to punish her for letting Willburgh have his way with her.

'I will do as you say,' he told them. 'As I always do.'

Anna did not sleep well, even though the bed was more comfortable than her bed at the Dormans' townhouse, and the nightdress Mrs White provided her was woven of cotton softer than any Anna owned. Even the room was larger than her bed chamber and was beautifully furnished.

A pleasant but obviously very curious maid came to help her dress. Anna had no idea what, if any, explanation of her presence would be given to the servants, so she said nothing. The maid addressed her as Miss Dorman, so the girl knew that much—that she came from the camp of the enemy. The maid was trained well enough that she did not ask any questions of Anna, except regarding what was necessary to help her dress, but, even with that constraint, the girl was chatty.

'Mrs White said I was to bring this day dress for you,' the maid said. 'It was Lady Willburgh's, but she never wore it, really. Said the colour washed her out.'

Anna was to wear a dress of the woman who caused her papa's death? That held little appeal. It was a print fabric, fawn with darker brown vines, leaves and flowers on it. How the woman chose such a fabric in the first place was a mystery, but, at least Anna would not have to wear that awful Red Riding Hood costume. The dress needed stitching here and there to fit her. Anna, apparently, was slimmer than Lady Willburgh. 'Less womanly,' Violet would have said.

Violet.

Last night Violet could have spoken up for her, but, typically, she didn't. Violet usually found ways to blame Anna for her own transgressions. No doubt last night Violet had engaged in an assignation precisely like the one for which Anna had been falsely accused.

The maid piled Anna's hair high atop her head and managed several curls to cascade down, a far cry from the simple chignon Anna usually wore. Somehow the beige and brown of the dress complimented her nondescript brown hair and seemed to emphasise her light brown eyes.

When she walked down the stairs to the first floor a footman greeted her. 'Good morning, miss. They are waiting for you in the breakfast room.'

He directed her to a sitting room at the back of the house and opened the door. Willburgh and his mother were seated at a table. Both looked up at her arrival.

Willburgh rose. 'Miss Dorman. I see Mrs White has found you something to wear. Come have some refreshment.' His tone was devoid of emotion, neither welcoming nor repelling. 'I trust you slept well.'

Of course she did not sleep well! 'The room was very comfortable.' She nodded respectfully towards Lady Willburgh. 'Thank you for the dress.'

The older woman harrumphed. 'I loathe that dress. You might as well keep it. I'll never wear it again.'

Because Anna wore it?

The butler she'd met the night before attended her. 'What may I serve you?'

Anna did not think her stomach was up for the kippers and cold meat on the sideboard. Or even the blackberry preserves or sweet cakes. 'Some bread and butter will do,' she said. 'Thank you.'

After the butler placed the bread and butter on her plate and poured her a cup of tea, he left the room.

When Anna lifted the cup to her lips, Willburgh spoke. 'I will call upon Lord Dorman this morning.'

Anna took a sip and placed the cup back in its saucer. 'I will accompany you.'

His brows knitted. 'That would not be wise. Best to leave it to me.'

She shook her head. 'This is about me. For me, and I will hear what is said of me.'

Tossing and turning all night did not exactly help her decide a specific course of action. She still did not know what she should do.

But deep inside her, she knew what she would not do.

Lady Willburgh's hand shook. 'The scandal will be terrible.'

'Terrible for me, certainly,' Anna responded.

'And for our family!' Lady Willburgh shot back. 'No respectable mother will allow her daughter anywhere near Will after this! And the *ton* will take great delight in the fact that he has compromised *you*.'

Because they were enemies.

Anna faced the woman. 'I presume your son told you the truth of what happened.'

Lady Willburgh waved her hand. 'The truth. The truth does not matter. Society will much prefer the fiction.'

'Mother,' her son admonished. 'This is not helpful. I will go to Lord Dorman and fix this.'

'And I will go with you,' Anna added.

Henrietta Street, where the Dormans' London townhouse was situated, was only a few blocks away, a tad less fashionable and a bit smaller, which meant nothing to Will, but probably rankled Lucius Dorman. Lucius had always made such comparisons, a part of the rivalry between them, Will supposed. Although before the duel, Will had never paid much mind to Lucius, especially at school. Lucius was a nuisance, nothing more. After Will's father was killed, though, Will could not help but despise all things Dorman, including Lucius. It was only then that he noticed Lucius's lack of character, his shirking of responsibility, the excesses of his vices—gambling, drinking, and whoring. Lack of loyalty, too. Lucius had been vicious to his cousin—a Dorman—when he should have been protecting her.

Or was Will merely resentful of Lucius's freedom? Not that Will ever wished to be as dissolute as Lucius. But, after his father's death, Will never had a day without responsibility, never possessed a chance to simply do whatever he wished.

Now he must call upon the Dormans. He'd rather swim in a cesspool than call upon them, but he must.

He ordered his curricle, even though it made more sense to walk the short distance. Riding in the curricle lessened the chance his society neighbours would see him escorting Miss Dorman to Henrietta Street. They would know what that meant.

Will did not want her company on this errand, though. Better he discuss the issue man to man with Lord Dorman, distasteful as that was. Although if they resolved the matter this morning, he could leave her there and have no more to do with the lot of them. That was one advantage he could see. The only one.

Mrs White had somehow found a proper bonnet for Miss Dorman and a paisley shawl that complemented the dress she wore. She'd even found Miss Dorman a reticule. Why the woman needed a reticule was a mystery to Will. She had nothing to carry in it.

As they approached the Dorman townhouse, Will spoke to her. 'I will direct the discussion with Lord Dorman. It is best you leave it to me.'

'I cannot do that.'

He gaped at her reply.

'I will speak for myself. I believe I am the best judge of what I need.'

It was just like a Dorman to counter him.

Will shrugged. 'As you wish, but it will be a mistake not to allow me to handle this.'

They reached the Dorman townhouse and his tiger, who had been riding on the back of the curricle, jumped down to hold the horses.

Miss Dorman faced Will. 'Do you expect me to trust you to have my best interests at heart? How can I trust any of you?'

She had a point, Will conceded, but only to himself. Will *was* trustworthy, though. It was a point of honour with him and it did not matter if you were enemy or friend, if he gave you his word, he would keep it. When countless people depend upon you, like all the people who depended upon the Viscount Willburgh for their livelihoods, their food, clothing, and shelter, it would be dishonourable not to be trustworthy.

Since she was a Dorman, of course, he wanted to have the last word. 'I am a man of my word.'

'As any dishonourable man might say,' she added.

So much for having the last word.

Will climbed down from the curricle and extended his hand to help Miss Dorman.

He called to his tiger, 'Toby, walk the horses if they need it. I am not certain how long we will be.'

Will and Miss Dorman approached the door. Will sounded the knocker.

A butler answered. His face broke into a relieved smile when he spied Miss Dorman. 'Miss Anna! You are safe! What wonderful news!' He glanced at Will and frowned. Recognised him, no doubt.

Will handed the man his hat and gloves. 'Announce us, please. I wish to speak with Lord Dorman.'

The butler sputtered, as if uncertain of what to do.

Anna stepped forwards. 'Announce us, Sedley. We will wait in the drawing room.'

'Yes, Miss Anna.' The butler bowed and headed for the breakfast room where she presumed Lord and Lady Dorman would still be, lingering over their tea.

She gestured for Willburgh to follow her up the stairs to the drawing room.

They entered the familiar room, which for some odd reason seemed foreign to her. 'You may sit, if you wish,' she told Willburgh, but neither of them did.

Anna walked to a window and peered out to where Willburgh's tiger held the horses. From behind her she could hear Willburgh drumming his fingers on some piece of furniture. Anna's insides twisted in anticipation. What would it feel like to be in their presence again? After the things they'd said to her the previous night. After they'd walked away leaving her at Vauxhall Gardens alone?

Except for the company of the enemy.

The Dormans did not keep them waiting. After only a few minutes Lord and Lady Dorman burst into the room, followed by Lucius.

'Anna! My dear child! You've come home!' Lady Dorman embraced her.

Anna stiffened. An embrace from Lady Dorman was the last thing she expected.

Uncle Dorman also came to her, taking one of her hands in his. 'Our prayers have been answered. You are here. We are much relieved. I sent all the footmen out to search for you. Was it one of them who found you?'

'No one found her. We came on our own,' Willburgh said.

Her uncle ignored him and kept hold of her hand. 'I think

we went a bit mad last night. Were we not, Lucius?' He turned to his son.

'Indeed,' Lucius replied, although his voice was dry.

What game were they playing? Acting so glad to see her? Their words from the night before echoed in her ears. She believed in their rejection, not their welcome.

She pulled her hand away.

Dorman patted her on the shoulder. 'We will not speak again of your little indiscretion, my dear. Fear not.' He glared at Will. 'We know who is to blame.'

Willburgh stood impressively tall and strong as he faced Lord Dorman. 'You have no idea who is to blame, sir, as you refused to hear us. The only indiscretion was your own, sir, to unfairly accuse your niece. You will hear us now—'

Dorman waved his hand dismissively. 'Whose ever fault it was matters not, I assure you. The important thing is that our dear Anna is in the bosom of our family again.'

'You gave us such a fright!' added Lady Dorman.

'So you left her all alone at Vauxhall?' Will protested.

'Not alone, my dear fellow,' Lucius drawled. 'She was in *your* company.' He turned to Anna. 'I suppose you spent the night with him, Anna.'

Anna had heard rumours of Lucius's conquests of women—actresses and the like. How dare he accuse her of loose morals!

'She spent the night at my townhouse,' Willburgh answered Lucius. 'With my mother in residence.'

Anna's anger rose. Lord and Lady Dorman and Lucius offered no apology. No acceptance of their responsibility in the event.

'You gave her no other choice.' Willburgh sounded angry, now, as angry as she felt.

Lady Dorman put her arm around Anna. 'Come sit, my dear. I've ordered some tea.'

Her touch felt revolting. Anna pulled away. 'I prefer to stand.'

'Then come with me to your room,' the woman persisted. 'I am certain you are eager to change that atrocious dress. I suppose it was one of Honoria's.' This last was said in a disdainful tone.

Anna supposed Honoria was Will's mother.

'I will stay here until this is sorted out, ma'am,' Anna retorted.

'Here. Here,' Lord Dorman broke in. 'There is nothing to sort out. You are home. That is all that matters.'

She swung around to face him. 'Home? Home?' Her eyes flashed. 'The place I am no longer welcome? That was what you said last night, was it not, sir?'

The man's expression turned ingratiating. 'Now, now. You know I did not mean it. Heat of the moment and all that.'

'You called me a trollop.' Anna, her temper lost, turned towards Lady Dorman. 'You accused me of having an assignation with this gentleman.'

'But you did have an assignation!' cried Lady Dorman.

Ever since Willburgh's father killed her papa, Anna knew her welcome at the Dormans' was on thin ice. She coped by being of service in any way they required. She always knew they valued her only because she was useful as Violet's companion, someone they could trust to behave in a moral and upright manner and who could try to make Violet behave so.

It took nothing at all, though, for them to think the worst of her.

Violet appeared at the door. 'What is all this talking? You woke me up.'

Anna strode over to her. Violet could have defended her the night before. She knew Anna was not sneaking off to bed Lord Willburgh. 'And you, Violet. You said I'd run off when you of all people knew I'd done no such thing.'

Violet, still in her dressing gown, looked at her haughtily. 'But you did run off, Anna.'

Lucius broke into this confrontation, his voice placating. 'Anna, it makes no difference to us if you ran off or if you were enticed away.' He tossed a scathing look at Willburgh. 'You know how fond we all are of you. This family cannot do without you. It was merely who you chose to be private with that shocked and surprised us so. You cannot put yourself in a compromising position with a Willburgh and expect us not to lose our senses. But we forgive you. We care about you so very much that we do forgive you.'

'You gave us such a turn!' cried his mother.

Lord Dorman readily agreed. 'That is so.'

Violet Dorman rolled her eyes.

Anna was appalled. Not one apology. From any of them. Not one acknowledgement of the wrong they'd done her.

Violet's gaze swept over her parents and brother. 'Have you all become beetle-headed? She's been with *him*.' She pointed to Willburgh. 'You disowned her for good reason.'

Lucius took Violet's arm and led her a few steps away. 'We have welcomed her back *for good reason*,' he said, enunciating each word.

But Anna could not fathom what that reason might be, especially after all the horrid things they'd said to her the night before. It did not matter, though. Nothing would entice her to spend another day under their roof.

She drew an audible breath. 'Enough. I am done with this. I came to pack my belongings and leave. Please have a trunk brought to my room immediately.'

'Pack your belongings?' cried Lady Dorman. 'You are leaving?'

'Come now,' Lucius cajoled. 'Where will you go?'

Violet laughed dryly. 'Do not be a dunderhead. She's going with *him*.'

'You are correct, Violet,' If they persisted in believing the worst of her, Anna would not disappoint them. 'I *am* going with Lord Willburgh. You stated it all so publicly last night, right near the Turkish Tent in Vauxhall Gardens. Loud enough for everyone to hear. You said that I have been compromised with Viscount Willburgh. What other choice do I have?' She walked up to Willburgh and threaded her arm through his. 'What must a compromised lady do? I must marry him.'

Chapter Four

Will stiffened in shock. What the devil? Who said anything about marrying? She was the last woman in existence he would ever marry.

The Dormans reacted more loudly. Shouts of 'No!' and 'You must never!' and 'Traitor!' and 'Turncoat!' sounded in his ears.

This was not what Will had expected. He'd expected to see Lord Dorman alone. He'd expected Lord Dorman would listen to the account of what really happened, then the man would apologise to his niece and agree to her return. Once that was done Will expected they would discuss how to minimise the scandal they'd created.

He should have known the Dormans would muddle up everything.

In a guise of being reasonable, they'd persisted in blaming her. They still had not allowed Will to tell them what really happened. Instead they'd thought the worst and refused to acknowledge that they left that young woman at Vauxhall Gardens, alone and friendless.

Except for himself, that was. He was no friend, though. It was only because he was a man of honour that he'd not deserted her, as well.

This was how she thanked him? By threatening to marry him?

Well, he would see about that.

'You ungrateful wretch!' cried Lady Dorman. 'After all we have done for you, you betray us this way? Marrying a Will-burgh? You could do nothing worse!'

Will agreed. There could be nothing worse than a Willburgh marrying a Dorman.

Miss Dorman stood firm. 'The trunk to my room, please.'

Lord Dorman's face turned bright red and his hands were curled into fists. 'I will not allow you to dishonour our family in this manner. You will not marry him.'

Lucius scowled, but his expression suddenly brightened. 'Father. You can stop her. She is your ward. She cannot marry without your permission.'

Lord Dorman brightened. 'That is right. My permission.' He glared at his niece. 'I will never give my permission. You will never marry this Willburgh.'

Good. That much was settled.

She shot back. 'Then we will elope.'

No! Will cried silently.

'No!' Lord Dorman shouted. 'I'll keep you prisoner here. I won't let you out. I swear I won't.'

This was getting way out of hand.

Will held up a quelling hand. 'Lord Dorman, you will not keep her prisoner. That will make more trouble for yourself than you can imagine. Just have the trunk brought to her room so she can pack her things and leave.'

Will supposed he would have to take her back to his town-house and after that he did not know what he would do with her.

Amidst protests from the others, Lord Dorman summoned the butler and made the arrangement.

Will walked at Miss Dorman's side up the stairs. He was angry with her—angrier at the rest of the Dormans—but definitely angry at her.

'Don't get in a lather, Willburgh,' she whispered.

What did she expect of him? To be happy?

Marriage was indeed the usual solution when a gentleman compromised a lady. If the gentleman did not marry the lady, the lady would be ruined. Not much happened to the gentleman in such a case, though. But he and Miss Dorman could not marry. They despised each other.

They entered a small bed chamber, little more than a closet. Miss Dorman retrieved a key from a hiding place and unlocked a drawer in the dressing table.

She took out a small box. 'My mother's pearls and locket.' She slipped the box in the reticule.

A servant brought in a very small trunk and a maid came to help Miss Dorman pack a few dresses and other necessary items. She left a good deal behind.

'What about the other dresses?' The maid lifted a ball gown, the same one Will had admired her in weeks ago. Before he'd learned who she was.

'I do not want them, Mary,' Miss Dorman said.

The girl set it aside. 'But you've only four dresses!'

'They will be enough.' Miss Dorman looked around the room. 'I think we are done.' She turned to Will. 'What shall I say to do with the trunk?'

This was her plan; she should know, he thought, but said, 'It should fit on the curricle. We may need ropes to secure it.'

She turned to the maid again. 'Will you get one of the footmen to carry it down to the curricle and get ropes, if needed?'

'Yes, miss.' The maid curtsied and started for the door. Before she reached it, she spun around and rushed back to Miss Dorman, giving her a heartfelt hug. 'I will miss you, Miss Anna,' the maid cried. 'I do not know what it will be like without you!'

'Oh, Mary!' She returned the hug. 'I will miss you, too. You have been such a treasure.'

The girl rushed out of the room.

Miss Dorman gave the room one more look. 'I am ready.'

Will let her pass through the doorway ahead of him. 'Did you foresee all this?' he asked. It seemed well thought out.

She shook her head. 'No, but I knew I could never return. Anything would be better.'

Even marrying him, he supposed. But that would never do. Every day the mere sight of her would remind him that her father killed his father.

They walked down the stairs together. The Dormans appeared in the hall and yelled curses at them until they were out the door.

Will stood with her on the pavement as the footman and his tiger fastened the trunk on the back of the curricle.

'I will not marry you,' Will said through gritted teeth.

She responded without facing him. 'And I will not marry you.'

Now he was truly puzzled. 'Then why announce that you would—we would? To *them*?'

She smiled. 'Petty revenge, I'm afraid. Me, marrying you. Lord Willburgh. The enemy. They will be at sixes and sevens for days.'

Will could not help returning a smile. 'Well, it serves them right. If they'd had an ounce of sense, they would have listened to us and kept the whole matter quiet. We could have gone on as before.'

'I could never have gone on as before,' she said.

The trunk was secured and Will helped Miss Dorman into the curricle.

He called down to his tiger, 'I am driving back to Park Street. Not a far walk for you.' There was no room for the tiger to ride with them.

'I expect I will arrive there before you, sir,' the tiger, a small but spry man in his forties, responded. He set off on foot. Will signalled the horses to start moving.

'You are taking me back to your townhouse?' She sounded surprised.

'Until we can figure out what to do next.' Of which he had no idea.

'Take me to a jeweller,' she insisted. 'Or somewhere I might sell my mother's pearls and locket. So I have funds to find a room to let somewhere.'

'A room to let?' What the devil was she talking about now.

She stared ahead. 'I need money. My jewellery will give me funds until I can secure some sort of employment.'

Employment? What sort of employment could she find? Impoverished ladies might become a lady's companion or a gov-

erness, but this whole Vauxhall Gardens event was certain to
cause talk. Who would recommend her? Who would hire her?

He blew out a breath. 'You do not have to sell your jewels.'
She seemed to have pitifully few of them. 'I will give you whatever funds you need.'

She turned to him. 'I am not asking you to do that.'

He turned onto Duke Street. 'Believe me. The money is of
no consequence to me.'

As a youth he'd had little regard for money. There always
seemed to be an abundance of it, always more than he needed.
After his father was killed, though, he'd learned that finances
were not that simple. He'd managed to preserve his father's
wealth and to build upon it, but the lessons he'd been forced to
learn so quickly took their toll. At least he could honestly say
that supporting her would indeed be of no consequence to him.

There was more traffic on the streets than when they'd left
for the Dormans', men on horses, people in carriages, people
walking on the pavement. Mayfair was too much like the village back in Buckinghamshire. Small enough that everyone
knew everyone else, and they all could see that Lord Willburgh
drove Miss Dorman in his curricle.

When they pulled up to Will's townhouse, he noticed the
neighbour's curtains move. No doubt it would be noticed that
he brought her to his house, trunk and all. Toby, his tiger, was
indeed waiting to take the horses and as Will alighted, two footmen came out to get the trunk.

Will helped her down and they hurried into the house.

His mother was in the hall waving a newspaper in her hands.
'Did you see this? Did you see this? It is in the newspapers!'

He ought to have guessed. Spreading the tale word of mouth
was not enough. 'Well, let us go to the drawing room.' The butler was attending the hall. 'Bring some tea, Bailey.'

'We are ruined!' his mother wailed. 'What are we to do?'

He was not about to discuss it on the stairs.

They entered the drawing room.

Having just been in the Dormans' drawing room, Will could
not help but note the contrast. He'd resisted his mother's desire
to remodel the principal rooms of the townhouse. This room

remained much like it had been when he was a youth—before his father died—serene with its pale green walls, plasterwork and striped upholstery. The Dormans' drawing room was all that was new in garish shades of red, gold, and blue.

Will needed this serenity today.

'Mother. Miss Dorman. Please sit.' He gestured to the chairs and sofas. 'I cannot bear all of us pacing the room.' Like they had at the Dormans'.

Miss Dorman chose an armchair. His mother perched on the edge of an adjacent sofa, as far away from the young woman as possible. Will chose the sofa opposite his mother, placing himself in between.

'Here.' His mother shoved the newspaper into his hands. 'Read it.'

It took him some time to find it.

At Vauxhall Gardens last night, Miss D— was caught by her guardian, Lord D and his son, in a private assignation with their sworn enemy Lord W—. A loud altercation ensued, Lord D— leaving his ward with W—, disowning her.

That left nothing out.

But the truth.

'May I see it?' Miss Dorman extended her hand.

He handed the paper to her, pointing to where the words were on the page.

She handed it back to him.

His mother glared at her. 'This is all your fault! I cannot bear it.'

'Leave it, Mother.' He put his head in his hands.

He did not know what to do. What solution was a good one?

Miss Dorman spoke. 'I'll accept your offer of money. I will move away.'

'Oh, that will be lovely,' his mother said scathingly. 'Then everyone will say you disappeared because Will got you with child.'

'Then I won't move away,' she countered. 'We can pretend to be betrothed and after several months, I'll cry off.'

Society said a woman could break an engagement to be married, but if a man did so it would be considered a breach of promise.

Will brightened. 'That might work. My reputation might suffer a little, but the *ton* will get over it.' A man with a title and money rarely stayed outside the *ton*'s good graces for long.

Of course. *His* reputation might survive, but what about hers? With scandal, no funds, and no family to back her, what prospects would her future hold? She'd indeed be ruined.

He wished he hadn't realised this.

'It is not you whose reputation concerns me the most!' his mother wailed. 'No match you make will ever be as good as it would be without this scandal, but you will recover. A man always recovers. It is your sister I am worried about.'

His sister, Ellen, was sixteen, on the cusp of being presented to society and entering the marriage mart.

His mother's voice rose. 'She already suffers from the scandal your father created—this will put her beyond the pale. How will she ever make a good match now?'

He might remind his mother that it was her affair with Miss Dorman's father that started the whole thing. True, she'd only wanted to get his father's attention by inviting Dorman's addresses. Indeed, his father had noticed and the result was disastrous.

Bailey, the butler, appeared at the door with the tea service and a plate of biscuits. He set them on the table, then quietly spoke to Will. 'May I see you outside for a moment, m'lord?'

'Certainly.' Will rose, asking leave of his mother and Miss Dorman. He stepped outside the room. 'What is it?'

His butler pulled a piece of paper from his pocket and handed it to Will. 'One of the footmen discovered this handbill being sold.'

Will skimmed the paper. It was a scandal sheet showing a drawing of two people, looking vaguely like him and Miss Dorman, *in flagrante* and a very embellished account of what happened at Vauxhall Gardens.

'It was selling quite well, I am afraid,' Bailey said.

'Deuce.' It had taken no time at all for someone to profit from the event. Will inclined his head towards the door. 'I'll have to tell them before someone else does.'

He re-entered the drawing room.

'More bad news, I fear.' He showed them the scandal sheet.

His mother dropped her head into her hands. 'We will never recover from this! This is the end of all for us.'

Will walked over to the window and looked out. He knew what he must do. The clarity of it struck him like a blow to the chest. He ought to have known it from the moment he opened the door to Lucius and Lord Dorman at Vauxhall Gardens. Will must do what any gentleman of honour would do to salvage his reputation and the reputation of the lady. Miss Dorman herself had hit upon it. Only one way society would forgive this imagined transgression.

Will turned to Miss Dorman. 'We must marry.'

'No!' Anna shot up from her chair. She would not marry him. She would not! 'Just tell me where I might sell my jewellery. I'll find a room to let and trouble you no more.'

Was it her impulsive threat to marry Willburgh at her uncle's house that gave him this idea? That she was willing to marry him? She would never do so. She'd despised him for ten years, even without knowing him. If only she'd never met him!

If she had not met him, though, what would have happened to her at the hands of that vile creature at Vauxhall Gardens?

'Do not be foolish,' Willburgh said. 'Money from two pieces of jewellery will never be sufficient. You'll say you'll find employment. What employment? Who would employ you? You have no one to recommend you. Even a servant needs references.'

His words rang true, but she did not want to heed them. She lifted her chin. 'I will find something.'

He stood toe-to-toe with her, glaring into her face. 'Do you know the sort of employment left to a single woman of no means and no references? Such women walk the streets at night.'

Violet's governess had told them stories about streetwalkers, women reduced to selling their bodies in order to survive.

These were meant as cautionary tales of what can happen if a young lady does not protect her virtue.

But Anna had done nothing unvirtuous.

'Then pay to support me,' she snapped. 'You said the money would be of no consequence!'

'It would not be—' he began.

His mother interrupted. 'No, Will! You mustn't. Having her in your keeping will only cause more talk. Consider your sister...'

His face stiffened in pain. With his back to his mother, he spoke only to Anna. 'My sister. Ellen is sixteen. An innocent. Most of her life has been tainted by scandal. My mother is right. This does not affect only you and me. I must consider her.'

Anna knew of Ellen Willburgh, but never gave the girl a moment's thought. But she remembered herself at sixteen. So worried for what the future might bring. Could her hatred of the Willburghs extend to this innocent girl? Anna remembered the scandal the duel caused.

She could imagine ladies of the *ton* whispering together of how Willburgh had to send away that poor ward of Lord Dorman's, how it must mean there was a baby. After her papa was killed she'd overheard ladies whispering about him. She remembered suddenly that they'd speculated about her, too—and her mother. She'd made certain, then, to always behave with complete decorum.

Even so, the sins of one member of a family always tainted the whole family.

Anna raised her gaze, looked into Willburgh's face, and spoke in a pained voice. 'I do not want to marry you.'

'I do not want to marry you either.' His voice reflected hers.

'Must we elope?' she asked.

'Without your uncle's permission, it is the only way,' he responded.

Chapter Five

〰〰〰〰〰〰

They set off the next day in a post-chaise.

The decision to hire a post-chaise rather than take one of Willburgh's own carriages had been a topic of much debate, mostly with his mother—Anna's opinion was not sought, not that she had one in this particular matter, except that she'd rather not go at all.

His mother prevailed.

'Good gracious,' she had exclaimed. 'Is there not enough gossip? Someone is bound to recognise the crest on your carriage. They will know you are going to Gretna Green and soon it will be in papers all over the country.'

Anna doubted that much interest in them existed.

In any event, Willburgh, Anna's future husband, opted for the post-chaise. To make the changes at coaching inns as simple as possible, they each brought luggage small enough to carry by hand. Anna's portmanteau was reluctantly lent to her by Lady Willburgh and contained one change of clothing. Toby, the tiger who'd ridden with them to Henrietta Street two days ago, was the only servant to come with them. He rode on the outside of the chaise.

The fastest route apparently was the mail route. Mail coaches with their ability to travel day and night could make the trip in three days. Anna and Willburgh did not require that level of speed, however. It would take them seven days.

The longer the better, thought Anna. More time meant more of a chance to come up with a different way out of this predicament.

They had little conversation as the streets of London opened into country scenes and glimpses of small villages. Anna could not simply gaze at the fields and hedgerows they passed and pretend Willburgh was not with her, though. He sat next to her on the one seat and Anna could not ignore how tall and broad-shouldered he was. Every bump in the road pressed his body against hers. His long legs knocked into hers. His warmth and strength had its effect on her. When had she ever been so close to a man and for so long a time? And such a man. The sort who would turn heads wherever he went.

Except for short breaks to change teams and one longer one for a midday meal, Anna spent eight hours enveloped by Willburgh's presence, yet raging against being forced to marry him. It was exhausting and unsettling.

When dusk fell, they pulled into a red brick, thatched roof inn with a sign posted of a fox and hound.

'Where are we?' Anna asked.

'Northampton,' Willburgh responded tersely. 'We'll spend the night.'

An ostler opened the door of the chaise and Willburgh disembarked first. He turned and offered Anna his hand to assist her.

Her legs were stiff and aching from sitting, but she managed to descend from the chaise. Toby spoke to the stable workers then followed them carrying their luggage.

'Remember who you are,' Willburgh whispered to her as they entered the inn.

He had decided they should travel under false names to protect them from more gossip should the handbills and newspapers have reached this far.

'Welcome,' the innkeeper greeted them.

'I am Mr Fisher,' Willburgh announced. 'I would like two rooms. One for me and one for my sister. And accommodations for my coachman.'

The innkeeper's brows rose at the word *sister* and his mouth twitched. 'Very good, Mr Fisher. We can accommodate you and your *sister*.' The man cast a meaningful look at Anna. 'And your coachman.'

She managed to appear composed, pretending she hadn't noticed. It was discomfiting, to say the least.

Willburgh signed the register. 'May we arrange a private room for dining as well?'

'It will be done, sir,' the innkeeper said.

'We will freshen up and desire our meal in one hour. Will that be possible?'

Anna thought Willburgh sounded every bit a viscount in his imposing tone. The innkeeper had already tagged her as not being a sister; the man likely figured out Willburgh was not a mere mister.

'It will indeed, sir,' the innkeeper said. 'I will show you to your rooms directly. Do you need servants to attend you?'

Willburgh turned to Anna. 'You will likely desire a maid to assist you at bedtime. Do you want assistance now?'

'No,' she replied. 'I will manage.'

The innkeeper gave them rooms right next to each other. Toby carried their luggage to the rooms and excused himself, assuring Willburgh all would be ready in the morning to continue their trip.

Anna luxuriated in the sensation of being entirely alone, away from Willburgh—except she could hear him moving around in the other room. She sighed and walked over to the basin to wash her hands and face and ready herself for dinner.

Will paced his room trying to release the pent-up tension of being cooped up in the chaise for long spells of time. And sitting next to Miss Dorman.

He was well aware of crowding her, though she did not complain and did not try to shirk away. Her scent filled his nostrils, and it was impossible to miss the loveliness of her profile, the soft femininity of her figure, especially when his body was jostled against hers. His senses were filled with her. How was he to endure a week of this close proximity?

A lifetime.

He shook off that thought. It did no good to think about marrying her. He'd learned after his father's death that it was best to think about the next task in front of him. The enormity of the whole picture always froze him in place.

He washed his face and hands and shaved the stubble off his chin, brushed off his clothes and waited until an hour had passed, then left his room to knock on her door.

'I am ready,' she said.

They ate a typical coaching inn meal of mutton stew and bread and drank ale instead of wine. Perhaps after she retired for the night Will would come down to the public rooms and have something stronger. They hardly spoke.

They'd hardly spoken to each other all day. What was there to say, after all? They both knew they did not want to marry.

But Will forced that thought away. Handle the next task. Only the next task.

He escorted her back to her room after dinner. A maid awaited her there to attend her.

At her door, he said, 'We'll leave early in the morning. Breakfast at seven. Order a maid to wake you early and help you dress.'

'As you wish,' she responded.

As soon as her door closed Will returned to the public room and ordered a glass of whisky. And a second.

The next day of travel was much like the first. Passing towns and villages. Stopping to change teams. Enduring the close quarters and desolate silences. As the sun dipped lower in the sky, they entered a town larger than the ones they'd passed through.

Will broke the silence. 'We'll stay the night here.'

'What town is this?' Miss Dorman looked out the window with some interest instead of blankly staring at nothing in particular.

'Loughborough,' he responded.

'Loughborough?' Her interest seemed to increase. 'The Loughborough where the Luddites attacked the lace factory?'

'Yes.' He was impressed that she'd heard of it. As a member of the House of Lords Will had been completely informed. 'The attackers came from Nottingham, not from Loughborough. They attacked the watchmen, destroyed fifty-five frames, and burned the lace.'

Their chaise passed by a three-storey building with the name *Heathcoat and Boden* on it. The building looked empty and neglected.

'That is the lace factory, I suppose.' Miss Dorman gestured to the building, an imposing structure made of the same red brick as their inn the previous night. She added, 'I do not know to whom I should owe sympathy. The owners and workers in the factory or the men whose livelihoods disappeared because of the machines.'

'There was a great deal of suffering on both sides,' Will agreed.

They stopped at the Old Bull Inn and their evening was much like the previous one, although their discussion of the Luddite attack and the economic hardships that spawned it gave them conversation across the dinner table. Miss Dorman asked many questions and seemed interested in hearing how the Lords had discussed the situation. They debated the suspension of the Habeas Corpus Act which allowed persons to be imprisoned without bail, in Will's view the most important issue of the day.

The third day brought them into Nottingham and led to conversations about Robin Hood and debate about stealing from the rich to give to the poor and whether there had indeed been a Robin Hood or had he been a fictitious legend.

In addition to being almost irresistibly alluring, Miss Dorman was also an intelligent woman of good education and thoughtful opinions. Many of the young women thrown in his path to court had little to say of substance at all. Miss Dorman told him she, along with her cousin Violet, had been given typical lessons in proper behaviour, stitchery, piano, and other feminine skills. She also loved to read and had been permitted to read whatever was in Lord Dorman's library.

As long as she was in no one's way.

When Will settled down to sleep that night, he allowed himself to be a tiny bit hopeful about marrying her. Perhaps there could be something more between them than the grievances of the past.

Will had just fallen asleep when a knock on the door awakened him. It was Toby, looking alarmed.

He gestured for the man to come in. 'What is it, Toby?'

'Sir.' His tiger was out of breath. 'I was in the public rooms having a pint when three men came in, asking the innkeeper and others if there was a Lord Willburgh staying here. I believe it was young Mr Dorman, sir. And a fellow he called Raskin and another fellow.' He swallowed. 'I lay low in case they'd recognise me, but they wouldn't. That sort don't take notice of men like me. Any road, I decided I'd better tell you right away.'

Lucius. Looking for him. Planning to thwart their elopement, Will was certain. He was glad he'd used a different name, but they'd figure out who Will and Miss Dorman were quickly enough. Dorman had obviously guessed that they would head to Gretna Green using the quickest route, the mail route.

Will would be damned if he'd allow Lucius to stop him.

He paced the room, thinking, then stopped and turned to his groom. 'Here's what we will do, Toby.'

The knock on Anna's door woke her. It took a moment for her to remember where she was. And why.

She went to the door. 'Who is it?'

'It's Will. I need to talk to you.' He used the name his mother called him. Will. He'd never done that before.

'One moment.' She hadn't packed a robe but did have a shawl, so she wrapped that around her, almost covering all of her shift, which she wore to sleep in so as not to pack a nightdress. She opened the door.

He was dressed more like his groom than a viscount. Before she could ask why, he burst into the room and shoved a dress at her. 'Put this on. We have to leave now.'

How dare he order her like that. 'Leave? What time is it?'

'I do not know,' he answered. 'Five, perhaps. Heed me. Lucius is here, staying in this inn. And Raskin and some other fellow. My groom heard them asking for us.'

Anna felt the blood drain from her face. 'Lucius? Why would he?'

'It foxes me,' Willburgh replied. 'To stop us, can be the only reason. We have to leave. Are you able to dress yourself?'

Would Lucius truly want to stop her? Why? After the things he said to her—that all the Dormans said to her—why were they not glad she was gone?

'I am able to dress myself,' she responded. 'But why this dress?' The dress was plain, like a maid's dress.

'Toby has hired a man and woman to impersonate us. One of the ostlers agreed to do it. With his wife. This is her dress. They will dress in our clothes, carry our luggage, and ride in our post-chaise. Toby will go with them. With any luck Lucius will believe they are us.' He shoved a cap into her hands. 'Wear this, too.'

'But I need things from my portmanteau,' she protested.

'We'll purchase whatever we need. It is a market day, I'm told, so all we need should be available.' He made it sound so easy. 'Hurry. I'll wait outside your door.'

Good thing she'd left anything she cared about in London at Willburgh's townhouse.

Anna dressed as quickly as she could. Fixed her hair in a simple chignon, covered it with the cap, and opened the door.

He gestured her to come with him. They walked quietly down the hallway and the stairs and out into the yard. Willburgh's groom was waiting for them. He and Willburgh spoke again about the arrangements and the groom directed them to the market square.

As they set off, the sun was sending its first rays into the new day. Even though it was June there was a breeze that chilled the air. The market was not open, of course but they found a place to sit out of the wind. They sat on the stone pavement which sent cold right through Anna's clothes.

She shivered. 'The first item I wish to buy is a shawl.'

Willburgh gazed at her. 'You are cold.' He changed positions. 'Here. Come sit in front of me. I'll warm you.'

He sat cross-legged so that she wound up sitting on his legs instead of the cold stone. He leaned her back against him and put his arms around her.

His body did indeed warm her, but also sent a strange thrill throughout. Her cheeks flamed. It was scandalous for him to hold her like this, but since they were dressed as they were, the few people who arrived to set out their wares paid them no heed. When the food booths opened Willburgh bought them loaves of brown bread and hot salop, a sweetened sassafras tea.

'I've never tasted such things,' Anna remarked. 'They are lovely.'

Willburgh smiled, which only made his handsome face more handsome. 'I am glad.'

By the time they'd finished eating and returned the wooden bowls to the vendor, more and more booths were filling with wares. They wandered through them until discovering one selling shawls. Some were beautiful paisley shawls worthy of a Bond Street shop, but Anna chose a plain woollen one in a brown shade not unlike the dress Lady Willburgh had lent her.

Had that only been three days ago?

'Good choice.' Willburgh nodded.

'The plan is to not be noticed, correct?' she responded.

'You have grasped it.'

Surprisingly, his approval pleased her.

Next they purchased two portmanteaux, one for each of them and spent another hour or more finding toiletries and used clothing. In the end they looked very much like a labourer and his wife and nothing like Viscount Willburgh and the lady he was to marry.

They sought respite in The Bell Inn, right on Market Square.

'What now?' Anna asked as they sat drinking tea and eating pasties. 'How do we proceed?'

'That is what I am turning over in my mind.' He pulled out a map and a copy of *Cary's Coach Directory*, two items he'd just purchased. He laid the map on the table. 'We should not follow the mail route, that is certain.'

Using the mail route must have been how Lucius almost found them.

'We'll stay east.' He pointed to the map. 'It will take longer, but we can avoid Lucius and his companions that way.' He looked up. 'There was a third man with Lucius and Raskin. I wonder who he was.'

She curled her hand into a fist. 'A—a companion of Raskin's abducted me. Could he be the third man?'

He blinked in surprise. 'I assumed that man had been a stranger. He was someone Raskin knew?'

'I was not given his name.' Her heart pounded with the memory. 'I do not think I was supposed to.'

'Lucius knew him as well?' His voice deepened.

'I cannot say.' She glanced away. 'I would hate to think Lucius would…'

But she feared both he and Violet had set her up. Perhaps without knowing what the man would do or perhaps it was their idea of a joke. Lucius did seem to know precisely where to find her after the rain.

What horrible men they all were. So unlike this man whom she'd called her enemy. Even though he despised her, he'd protected her. And was doing so still.

She met Willburgh's gaze again and held it.

Chapter Six

W<small>ILL</small>'s anger flamed. He'd half a mind to seek out Lucius and show the man precisely what he thought of him. With bare fists, preferably. The lady seated across from him surely did not deserve such treatment.

She was proving more game than he'd anticipated. Uttering not one word of complaint the entire trip, even through this morning's trials. Not a word about wearing plain clothes, nor of giving up her own dresses. He knew she could not be happy about any of this.

He needed to get back to the task.

'How we should travel, I cannot decide,' he said, breaking the silence that followed talk of Lucius. 'Whether to hire another post-chaise, or take the stage coach, or even purchase a vehicle and horse.'

Her brows rose. 'You have enough funds with you to purchase a vehicle and horse?'

He cocked his head. 'I might arrange it.'

At that moment a youth approached their table. Will glanced up at him.

'Are you Mr Fisher, guv'nor?' The boy could not have been more than fourteen.

Willburgh looked at him suspiciously. 'Who asks, if you please?'

If Willburgh wished to portray a labourer, he sounded precisely like a viscount.

'Name's John.' The boy gave a little bow. 'I am to tell you that the gentlemen have gone.'

Willburgh nodded, but still looked askance. 'And why did you think I was Mr Fisher?'

The boy pointed to the hat Willburgh had placed on the chair next to him. 'M'brother's hat. M'brother's the one you hired to be you and his wife to be your wife.'

Miss Dorman winced when the boy called her Will's wife.

The boy went on. 'Yer groom paid me to find you after he left with m'brother and the gentlemen left soon after.'

Willburgh relaxed. 'Thank you, John.' He reached in a pocket and pulled out a coin to hand to the boy.

The youth took it and wrapped his fist around it. 'If you do not mind me asking, sir, if you have any other work to be done? I'm good around horses and I'm clever in a pinch, if you get my meaning.'

Willburgh stared at him, obviously thinking.

Finally he said, 'I have need of a groom to accompany us the rest of the way to Scotland.'

The boy hopped from one foot to the other. 'I am your man, sir. I can be a groom. I've been around horses all m'life. M'father was an ostler. And m'brother.'

Willburgh gestured to a chair. 'Sit, John, and hear what I have in mind.'

The boy sat. Willburgh called to the servant to bring the boy some tea and a pasty, which the servant brought right away.

When the servant was out of earshot, Willburgh said, 'I wish to hire another post-chaise, but to take a different route to Scotland. I do not want those gentlemen to know where we are or where we are heading. They must not find us.'

'Do not worry, guv,' the boy said after biting into the pasty. 'M'brother will fool them.'

'Can you assist in hiring the post-chaise? Or any available vehicle?' Willburgh asked.

'Yes, sir,' the boy replied, his mouth full. 'But if you do not mind me saying, you are not dressed like riders of a post-chaise usually are dressed.'

'Because labourers would not hire a carriage like that,' Miss Dorman broke in. 'We will have to dress more prosperously.'

So she and Will returned to Market Square and the clothes dealers and found clothes that were not too rich, nor too poor. John, Will's new groom, went to talk to the head ostler at The Bell Inn, to hire a carriage for them.

By noon Anna and Willburgh were riding in another post-chaise with their luggage secured and Willburgh's new groom, John, on the outside. The forests made so famous in the Robin Hood legends gave way to rolling countryside with stone fences and sheep grazing. They also glimpsed tall chimneys of smelt mills and spied mining villages.

The seat to this carriage was more spacious so Anna did not have to sit with Willburgh's body touching hers, except when the road caused the carriage to ram them together. Perhaps she was getting used to it, because it did not bother her as much as before.

They had more conversation than before, as well, conferring on the route they were taking, commenting on what they saw outside the carriage window. By sitting in the Lords, Willburgh knew things, such as the state of the mining industry, the challenges to farming, the hardship the war had caused some of these villages, the fomenting of unrest in the country. Anna liked learning of such things.

At dusk they entered Sheffield, a town unlike any Anna had seen before, dirty, grimy, its streets ill paved. It was a town full of industry, known for making cutlery, the place silver plate was created, a lead mill, a cotton mill. Smoke. Poverty.

And yet they passed by a beautiful church with a tall spire.

Willburgh seemed as aghast at the conditions as Anna was.

'I will remember this town,' he murmured, although she did not think he was speaking to her.

The chaise pulled into the King's Head Inn and ostlers

jumped to tend to them. John carried their luggage like a proper groom, although he did not have the livery. Anna thought that befitted the roles they were playing—shopkeepers, if anyone asked.

They entered the inn and met the innkeeper who asked their name.

'Oldham,' Willburgh said.

'Mr and Mrs Oldham,' repeated the innkeeper handing the register to Willburgh.

Anna waited until they were standing in the room and John and the innkeeper had left. 'You put us in the same room!'

He faced her. 'It is best.'

'It is not best for me!' she scoffed. 'We are not married yet!'

'Heed me.' He sounded angry now, too. 'We have Lucius and—and his disreputable friends chasing us. Maybe there are others. This is better for our disguise. Besides, this town looks dangerous. I can protect you.'

'I can take care of myself,' she huffed.

They went to dinner in silence.

Anna declined a maid even for after dinner. He left when she was readying herself for bed. Only one bed in the room. Where was he going to sleep? He had better not take any liberties with her. When they were married, she'd endure it, but not now.

Although his arms around her that morning to keep her warm were extremely pleasant. Even thrilling.

She needn't have worried, though. When he returned to the room she pretended to be asleep. He approached the bed but all he did was remove a blanket. He stripped down to his shirt and drawers, a sight she could not help watching. She also watched him settle into a chair, his legs on another chair, the blanket around him.

How was he to sleep in that position? And, even if he could sleep, how would it be for him to feel cooped up in the carriage all day tomorrow?

'Willburgh?' she cried softly.

He startled at the sound of her voice. 'What?' He tried to

straighten in the chair, scraping the one that held his legs on the wooden floor.

'You cannot sleep on that chair,' she said. 'I should. It will fit me so much better.' She sat up to trade places with him.

'You will not sleep on the chair.' His voice was firm in the darkness, the sort that brooked no argument.

She argued anyway. 'You will be miserable and cross in the carriage. Not to mention aching bones.'

'No matter. You will not sleep on the chair.' His voice grew louder.

She persisted. 'The floor, then. I should do nicely on the floor with a blanket and pillow.'

He sat up. 'Are you daft, woman? I would not take the bed and leave you on the floor or a chair or wherever else you contrive. Leave it.'

'As you wish, then,' she retorted in clipped tones.

Anna lay back down under the covers, turning her back to him, but the creak of the chairs every time he moved kept her from sleeping. It was impossible to endure another person's discomfort. Totally against her nature.

She rolled over to face him. 'Willburgh?'

'What now?' he snapped.

She could not believe what she was about to say. 'This bed is big enough. We can both sleep in it.'

His silence was palpable.

'I have given up propriety, if that is your concern.' She swallowed. 'They took that away from us days ago.'

'Propriety is not the only concern,' he responded, his voice quieter.

She forged on. 'You must not touch me, though. I draw the line there.'

The chairs scraped and she watched him stand up. Blanket in tow, he walked towards the bed. She scooted to the far side tucking some of the bed linens around her like a shield. The bed dipped as he climbed in. They were face-to-face for a moment before they each rolled away. Anna was more awake than before, acutely aware of the warmth of his body so near to hers, of the cadence of his breathing. Of the scent of his soap and of him, now becoming so familiar to her.

Of that strange thrill she'd experienced when his arms were around her that morning.

When Will woke the next morning his arm was around her and she was nestled against his chest. His first impulse was to push away from her, but he checked himself in time, not wanting to wake her.

And she felt so good against him, so soft and round and smelling like the lavender water they'd purchased the day before.

He closed his eyes and tried to bring back the memory of pistols firing and his father falling to the ground. Her father stood a moment longer, a look of triumph on his face, before he, too, collapsed. The emotion of that day came back, but when he opened his eyes he could not attach any of it to her.

He did not mind her company. Could no longer blame her for their predicament. No. It seemed as if they were facing this together. The two of them against the world.

Her eyelids fluttered and soon he was looking into her eyes, the colour of a fine brandy, still warm and sleepy. Her eyes widened, though, and she pulled away from him. He moved away as well, climbing out of the bed and gathering his trousers.

She rose and wrapped her shawl around her. They'd replaced the drab brown one they'd chosen at first with this muted green one, embellished with embroidered flowers. Neither of them spoke until they were dressed and ready for breakfast.

Before they sat down to eat, Will sent a servant to alert John to ready their carriage. They breakfasted in a private dining room, attended by one servant girl.

When they were alone, she broke their silence with each other. 'Did you sleep well?'

He felt his face flush. He actually had slept better than any night since Vauxhall Gardens. Even before. 'Quite well,' he responded. 'And you?'

Her eyelids fluttered. 'Very well.'

The stiffness between them was unlike when they'd started this journey, but Will missed the growing ease between them.

The servant returned. 'Mr Oldham, your groom wishes to inform you the carriage will be ready within an hour.'

'Thank you,' Will replied.

After the servant left, the silence between him and Miss Dorman filled the room again.

Will broke it. 'I was thinking that we should agree on how I should call you, should I need to use a name. I do not wish to slip and call you Miss Dorman.'

She looked up at him over her cup of tea. 'I cringe when you say Dorman. Call me Anna.'

'Anna,' he repeated, liking the sound on his tongue.

He ought to tell her to call him Will. But, no. Not yet.

Travel the next two days and nights was as pleasant as could be expected. John proved adept at finding the equipage needed when the post they hired could not continue any longer. Some carriages were more comfortable than others, but Miss Dorman—Anna—was as uncomplaining as ever.

Their days were filled with the changing scenery. Fields. Mountains. Lakes and rivers. Villages and towns of all sizes, each with its unique character. Their nights grew more comfortable. They shared a room and a bed and slept snuggled next to each other.

As much as Will tried to tell himself their physical closeness was no different than it had been when he'd used his body to warm her in Nottingham, his senses demanded more. In the darkness he was consumed with the desire to join her body to his, but he'd somehow kept to his promise. He held her but no further liberties. Will did not know what their nights would be like after marriage; he could only trust that eventually he could make love to her the way his body demanded. That she seemed to welcome his arms at night and smiled at him more during the day, fed that trust. He could almost believe their marriage could be more than tolerable. It might even bring great pleasure.

Then he'd remember who she was and how it came to be that they shared a bed together. Then hope vanished.

They'd spent those two nights first in Skipton; then, Orton and before Will knew it their latest post-chaise was pulling into the Bush Inn in Carlisle. The Scottish border was less than ten miles away.

This was the most vulnerable part of their journey thus far, though. They were back on the mail coach route where they'd sent their decoys. If there was anywhere to encounter Lucius and his companions, this would be the place.

'We'll stay in the carriage until we know,' he told Anna.

'And be ready to leave quickly if Lucius is here.' She was always quick to comprehend.

Will sent John to make enquiries and to look around the inn and stable yard. He'd seen Lucius, Raskin, and the other man back in Nottingham. He would recognise them.

Not more than a half hour later John walked back to the carriage with none other than Toby!

'Toby is here,' Will prepared to exit the carriage.

'I hope that is good news,' she said as he helped her out.

John spoke straight away. 'Those gentlemen are not here.'

'But they are waiting for you,' Toby added. 'At the border.' He turned to Anna and tipped his hat. 'G'day, miss.'

'I am glad to see you are in one piece,' she responded.

They settled into a private dining room Toby had arranged. Refreshment was ordered and Will, Anna, and Toby sat down to plan the next step while John saw to their luggage.

Toby filled them in on his part of the journey.

He and John's brother and the wife managed to remain a few hours ahead of Lucius. They avoided the coaching inns that the mail coaches used but once had to make a run for it when Lucius showed up asking for them. They reached Gretna Green before they were discovered, but since they had no information of Will and Anna's plans, there was nothing Lucius could learn from them.

'Mr Dorman was hopping mad, too,' Toby said. 'Cursing and pounding his fists. The ostlers ordered him to compose himself or leave. Right before I slipped away, I heard him say they would wait for you at the border and hire more men to stop you. I wouldn't put it past him to have followed me, though, so you cannot stay here.'

Will spread his maps on the table. 'Then we must find another way. Another route. Gretna Green is not the only Scottish town where we can marry.'

It was too late in the day to try to make it into Scotland if they had to go farther out of their way.

'We could take another day,' Anna said. 'Find the next best place to cross the border west of here. No matter what, I do not want to encounter Lucius.'

The map showed a route to a village called Canonbie that was right over the border but east of Gretna Green.

'What if they guess we have gone east? Canonbie would be the first place they would look.' Anna pointed to a town marked a bit north of there. 'We should go a little farther still. Here, perhaps.'

She pointed to Langholm.

There was a knock on the door and John entered.

He was out of breath. 'A post boy coming from Mossband told me a gentleman was looking for Lord Willburgh's groom, supposedly who'd been on horseback. That'd be you, right?' he asked Toby.

'Me.' Toby frowned.

Will started to fold up the maps. 'John, get us something to take us out of here right away, but we won't leave from the yard. Meet us somewhere.'

'There's another coaching inn on this street,' John said, although how he knew, Will could not guess. 'The Angel Inn. I'll run ahead and get something from there. You can meet me there.' He started for the door.

'Wait,' Will said. 'Let us make them think we are staying the night here. I'll procure a room and you can make a pretence of taking the luggage there. Then go to the inn. We'll meet you at the other inn as soon as we can sneak out of here.'

'I'll stay here,' Toby said. 'If they find me, I'll make it seem you are here, as well.'

Will and Anna went with John to arrange the room. Will went so far as to order dinner and paid for it all right away. After John brought the luggage and left, Will and Anna were out on English Street within a half hour. Will carried their luggage.

By the time they made it to the inn, John had a post-chaise ready for them and they set out east for Brampton, a market town about nine miles east of Carlisle. They pulled into a white stucco inn, The String of Horses.

Thwarting whatever plan Lucius had for chasing them to Scotland drove out of Will's mind the realisation that he would be married on the morrow. *Focus only on the next task.* When he settled in the bed next to Anna, though, the thought came back to him, both with anticipation and misgiving. What would bedding her be like next he lay beside her?

For that alone he hoped he'd keep Lucius at bay.

Chapter Seven

$\mathcal{A}$nna woke as the first rays of daylight shone through the window. This would be her wedding day.

She gazed at the sleeping face of the man who would be her husband. It was a handsome face, almost boyish in repose. It had also become a familiar one over these few tumultuous days since he removed his mask at Vauxhall Gardens.

But she did not know him, really. She knew the Dormans' version of him, especially Lucius's version. A haughty man. A selfish one. One who could not be trusted. That version had been ingrained in her over the last decade.

Ever since his father killed her papa.

She supposed she could call him haughty, but could that merely be his anger over being forced to marry her? He was not selfish, though. His own interests seemed to never count in any action he undertook. That was true from the moment he rescued her in Vauxhall.

Could he be trusted? All she could say was he'd not given her any reason not to trust him.

If only she could forget what his father did, she might even look forward to marrying him. She knew the *ton* would consider him a catch. He was a viscount, after all.

He murmured in his sleep and rolled over. Anna slipped out

of the bed without disturbing him. She padded over to the wash basin and poured fresh water. Taking advantage of his sleep, she washed herself as thoroughly as she could and splashed on the lavender water. Its scent calmed her. Reminded her of her mother. Of when she had a home, when the three of them, she, her mother, and her papa lived together in an exotic house in India. She remembered the warm breezes, the scent of spice in the air. And her mother's lavender water.

She was a far cry from that idyllic childhood. When her mother caught a fever and died, Anna and Papa took the long trip to England, where she'd been told she was *from*, but had never set foot. She'd lost everything but Papa and, then, within a year, she'd lost him, too.

That wound was still painfully deep.

Blinking away tears, she dried herself and checked to see if Willburgh was still sleeping. She changed into a clean shift and put on her corset, tying her strings as best she could. She'd been wearing the same dress since Nottingham, but the night before had unpacked her only other dress, a carriage dress of dark blue. Most of the wrinkles were out of it this morning. Such a dress would have been fashionable over five years ago. It was made of corded muslin which gave it the effect of white fabric with thin blue stripes running on the bias. Its collar nearly touched her chin, but the buttons down the front made it easy to put on herself. The ribbon sash at her natural waist made it particularly old-fashioned.

Anna held her breath as she put it on, hoping it would fit. She released a relieved sigh when she was able to button every button. She checked herself in the dressing mirror. The sleeves were a bit too long and the bodice a little loose, but it would do.

Willburgh's voice came from behind her. 'The dress looks well on you.'

Anna turned around, surprised he was awake and even more surprised at how pleased she was at the compliment. 'I did not know you were awake.'

'I just woke up.' He swung his legs over the side of the bed and continued to gaze at her. 'You made a good choice on that dress.'

It would not do to grin in gratification of his words, but she could not suppress a small smile. 'It is hardly *à la mode*.' Lady Dorman and Violet would have perished before wearing such a garment.

As he rose from the bed, Anna's memory flashed with how warm and comforting it was to sleep next to him. As if she were not alone in the world.

Would they sleep together as a married couple? Would he wish to perform the marriage act with her? Her senses flared at that thought. Did that mean she wanted him to or she did not want him to?

While he washed and shaved and dressed, she brushed out her hair and, to be a bit fancier, braided it first before winding it into a chignon. Not that it mattered, though. She covered her hair with a bonnet.

Willburgh had arranged a private dining room for their breakfast. The less they showed themselves the better, in case Lucius had tracked them this far. John reported that there had been no sign of them, however.

After a quick breakfast they were again on the road, this time on the final leg of their journey. John called down to them when they neared the Scottish border. Anna held her breath. Both she and Willburgh scanned the surroundings to see if Lucius would appear or if anyone would try to stop them, but their passing the border was uneventful.

Willburgh turned to Anna at that moment. 'We've made it to Scotland.'

She could not tell if he were pleased or disappointed. 'Willburgh, this is what we must do, is it not? We have no choice, do we?'

He looked deeply into her eyes. 'We have no good choices. This is what we decided was the best of them.'

She held his gaze. 'I am sorry it has come to this.'

Will glanced away.

Was he sorry? When he woke that morning and watched her buttoning her dress and looking at her image in the mirror, he'd been aroused by the intimacy of the sight and the situation. She was lovely and he wanted nothing more in that moment than to remove that dress and take her back to bed. As the coach rumbled on, though, the old feelings of resentment and frustration crept back in. He was not marrying by choice. He was marrying the enemy.

By noon they entered Langholm, the destination they'd chosen. Most of its buildings were built of a grey stone that lent the town a dismal, depressing air. What's more, the sky was also grey and the air heavy with signs that rain was imminent.

How fitting that rain should have forced them together both now and at Vauxhall.

When they pulled into the Crown Inn, fat droplets started to fall. John went off to sort the post-chaise and the luggage, Will and Anna dodged raindrops to dash into the inn.

And found nobody.

Will paced the hall, waiting for the innkeeper to appear, to no avail. This was exasperating. 'Where is the innkeeper?'

Laughter sounded from another room. Will followed it with Anna right behind him.

They entered the tavern where a half dozen men were drinking, three seated and two leaning against a bar behind which one was wiping a glass. Every single one of them turned their heads to look at them.

The man behind the bar gestured for them to approach. 'Well, now, I dinna hear you enter the inn. I'm the innkeeper. You'll want a room, I expect.'

'We do.' Will wasted no time. 'We also want to be married—'

Collective laughter responded to that.

'Do y' now.' The innkeeper thrust out his hand for Will to shake. 'Name's Armstrong. There are plenty of us Armstrongs about, so they call me Armstrong of the Crown.' The man laughed as if he'd said something funny.

'A pleasure, Mr Armstrong,' Will accepted the handshake. It would have been an impudence for Armstrong to presume such familiarity of a viscount, but the man could not know Will was a viscount. That had been the whole point of their disguises. 'Can you please tell us where we might find someone to marry us?' Will's patience was wearing thin. Better to get this over with as soon as possible.

The man came out from behind the bar, with a bottle and two glasses. 'Come sit and have a drink and I might tell you.'

This was annoying, but so the Scots could be to Englishmen. Will pulled out a chair for Anna to sit. He sat next to her. Chairs scraped as everyone turned to face them.

Was an Englishman such a novelty? In a border town?

Armstrong poured them each a glass. 'Have a whisky.' He waited for them each to take a sip. 'Now, for a guinea each for my friends here and me, I'll tell you what you want to know.'

Will had been told to expect to show his coin to anyone even peripherally involved in a Scottish wedding. He reached in his pocket and paid the outrageous amount.

'Who is it who is after being married?' the innkeeper asked.

'We are.' Will gritted his teeth.

Armstrong rolled his eyes. 'I meant your names, lad.'

All Will wanted was directions to where to find someone to marry them, but he felt he had no choice but to play along.

'I am Neal Willburgh.' He gestured to Anna. 'This is Anna Dorman.'

Anna spoke up then. 'Anna Edgerton. I am Anna Edgerton.'

Will gaped. This was the first he had heard of this. 'Not Anna Dorman?'

'No.'

The innkeeper quipped. 'Have the two of you met, by any chance?'

The room broke out in laughter.

She wasn't a Dorman? Not a real Dorman? Something loosened inside Will, like a knot untwisting.

The innkeeper went on. 'And I gather the two of you are of age.'

'I am twenty,' Anna said.

'Twenty-eight,' Will added, pointing to himself.

Armstrong grinned. 'And you truly want to be married?'

One of the men seated at the other table shouted, 'Heed what you are doing, lad! Before it is too late!'

The others laughed.

The innkeeper chuckled, but turned to Anna. 'Miss, do you truly want this man to be your husband?' He spoke as if it was a poor idea indeed.

'Yes,' said Anna.

Will's patience was lost. 'Perhaps you could merely tell us where we might find someone to marry us?'

The innkeeper held up a hand. 'Do you truly want her as a wife?'

'Do not do it!' another patron called out.

'Yes, I want to marry her,' he snapped.

'And nobody's forcing you?' the man asked.

Anna looked as if she was suppressing a smile. 'No one.'

Will was less amused. 'Of course no one is forcing us. Can you direct me to the proper person—'

The other men snickered.

'First I must fetch a piece of paper.' The man disappeared behind the bar again.

To bring them directions, Will hoped.

When Armstrong returned he placed the paper on the table along with an ink pot and pen. 'Fill this in, my lad and lassie. As soon as I sign, and two of these witnesses sign, you are married!'

The room broke out in guffaws and the innkeeper filled everyone's glass from the bottle. 'Let's drink to their health!'

Will glanced at Anna whose eyes were sparkling. 'You guessed.'

'Not at first.' She smiled.

Will dipped the pen in the ink pot and filled in his name. He handed it to Anna.

'We do not fuss about in Scotland,' Armstrong explained. 'All you need is to be of age and to declare you want to be married of your own free will. Simple, eh, lad?'

Will managed a smile. 'Simple indeed.' He downed his glass of whisky and the innkeeper poured him another.

All the signatures were completed and the paper returned to Will. He folded it and placed it in his pocket. He was not certain if what he felt was relief or bewilderment. He downed the second glass of whisky.

'I'll record it in my ledger, as well,' Armstrong said.

The other men came up and clapped him on the back, giving him various warnings about married life.

'Do as she says, whatever she says,' one man told him. 'Won't never go wrong.'

The others groaned at that one.

They were more gallant towards Anna, bowing to her or kissing her hand, all of which she accepted with good humour.

John entered the tavern, looking stunned at the revelry. 'I've brought your bags, sir.'

Will managed a smile. 'Congratulate us, John,' he said. 'We are married.'

Anna smiled through the impromptu celebration. The Scots in the tavern seemed very ready to be joyous and their merriment was infectious. The whisky helped as well, its warmth spreading through her chest and making her mellow.

She was glad it was done, the marriage. No more uncertainty. The die was cast. She was even happier at her impulsive reclaiming of her name. Her real name; the name given at birth.

She'd used the Dorman name since a baby, her mother had explained. Now, after how the Dormans had treated her, she was glad to claim another, even for only a few minutes.

Because now she would ever be a Willburgh, the name she'd once learned to hate. Armstrong poured her another drink. The lovely whisky floated all her tension away, all the tension of the last ten days when her life again changed for ever. She watched the Scotsmen tease Willburgh about being a married man and about not knowing her name. It made her laugh.

The innkeeper wagged his eyebrows. 'I ken it is time to show you to your room.'

The other men hooted.

Anna finished her third glass of whisky and stood. And swayed. 'Oh. Goodness,' she said. 'I felt dizzy for a moment.'

The innkeeper pushed Willburgh towards her and he put his arm around her to steady her.

'Follow me,' the man ordered. He turned to John who had also consumed a glass or two. 'Bring the bags.'

'Yessir. They're in the hall.' John walked ahead of them.

In the hall, Armstrong had Willburgh sign the register. 'Be sure to write Mr and Mrs Willburgh,' he bantered.

When they started up the stairs, the man looked over his shoulder. 'I'll be giving you the best room in the inn.'

Anna's legs felt like jelly. She held on fast to Willburgh's arm. Behind her John tripped on a step and dropped their portmanteaux.

'Pardon,' he said.

The room was tucked away at the far end of a hallway. Armstrong opened the door with a key and they entered. Anna noticed a large bed with four carved posts and an intricately carved headboard. It was made of the same dark wood that panelled the tavern. There was also a dressing table and other tables and chairs.

Armstrong lit a fire in the fireplace and took John by his collar and pushed him out of the room, closing the door behind the two of them.

'I think you had better sit.' Willburgh guided her, not to a chair but to the bed. He sat her on the edge. He unlaced her half boots. 'Your shoes are still wet.'

And it still rained. She could hear the rain patter against the window.

'It was a funny wedding, was it not?' Her head felt so light. In fact her whole body felt as if it might easily float to the ceiling.

'If we are married, perhaps you should call me Will.'

Anna took his head in her hands and lifted his face, looking into his eyes. How had she never noticed his eyes were a piercing blue?

'We are married, Will.' She blinked. Gazing at him left her feeling giddy inside. And wary. Was he happy about being married to her?

Of course he was not.

Chapter Eight

Will was drawn closer to her, closer to tasting her lips, but she pulled her hands away as if she'd touched a hot poker.

As the innkeeper had led them up to the room, Will's excitement grew. He knew what Armstrong and his friends teased him about. They expected him to consummate this marriage. Post haste.

And he wanted to consummate this marriage. He was on fire to do so. The whisky had stripped away all his resolve. His mind could not keep hold of family enemies and duels and death. All he could think of was how she felt in his arms at night and how that delight promised greater delights. Now that he could bed her. Should bed her. Wanted to bed her.

He'd drunk too much and so had she.

He slipped off her half boots and stood.

'I know what is supposed to happen between a husband and wife,' she said, slurring her words. 'And I know you do not want to do it. You did not want to marry me, but you had to and you are angry at me. You do not like me. *Sins of my father* and all that.' Her upset was building with each word.

He sat beside her and turned her to face him. 'You, Anna, have had too much whisky.'

She lifted her chin. 'I've only had three.'

He nodded. 'Three.' That was sufficient for her good sense to fail her. 'And I have had a great deal more than that. I know precisely what we should do.'

'What?' She sounded combative.

He took off his coat and waistcoat and pulled off his boots. 'We should rest.'

She blinked at him. 'In bed?'

'In bed.'

A grin grew on her face. She tried to unbutton her dress, but could not manage it. Will was not certain he could either, but he managed the first one, then the next. Excitement grew inside him. Arousal.

He undid all her buttons and pulled the dress over her head. She turned her back on him. 'Unlace me,' she murmured.

He managed to untie her laces and she slipped out of her corset. He recalled how she felt wearing only her shift and he yearned to rid himself of that flimsy barrier, to throw off his shirt and feel her naked skin against his.

But he wouldn't. Instead he lay her down in the bed and moved next to her, to hold her like he'd done the past two nights.

With a sigh she settled against him. And fell asleep.

When Will woke the room was dark except for the glow of the coals in the fireplace. They'd slept until night apparently, the whisky and the several days of acute stress knocking them out. The day before was a blur, but he remembered one thing. They were married.

They'd thwarted Lucius's efforts to stop them and they were married. They'd achieved that goal. Never mind that it was a goal neither of them wanted; it was still a goal achieved. He was glad of that.

He tried to recall the wedding ceremony, but it was a jumble, possibly because he had not known it was happening until it was all done.

She'd caught on much before him. She was clever. Uncomplaining.

And not a Dorman.

Will laughed at himself for being glad of that.

He rose from the bed and poured some water to rinse the foul taste from his mouth. Another gift from the whisky, along with his foggy mind. He turned to look for a lamp or a candle to light before he crashed into something and woke her. Lord, he was hungry. They had not eaten since breakfast. Perhaps there was a lamp on a table.

There was a table right inside the door, in a particularly dark corner. He gingerly felt his way to it, hoping he would not topple a chair or something in its path. He groped the surface of the table. His fingers touched a candlestick. Excellent. He groped his way to the fireplace and rubbed his hand on the mantle. A taper, as he expected. Will lit the taper from the one glowing coal in the fireplace and touched it to the candle, blinking as the flame came to life.

He could now see the room better. To his relief, the candle illuminated a plate of bread and cheese and a teapot on the table by the door. He placed the candle on the table and helped himself to a piece of hearty oat bread and a generous slice of Caboc cheese.

He poured a cup of tea and gulped it down, not bothering with milk or sugar. The tea was tepid. Will did not care. He poured himself another cup and drank it, as well.

The refreshments had not been there when they first entered the room, Will would swear. That meant Armstrong or someone else must have come into the room while they were sleeping. That was distressing. Someone had entered and he did not wake.

What if it had been Lucius?

Lucius was no longer a threat, though. Will and Anna were married.

Will helped himself to more bread and cheese and washed it down with a third cup of tepid tea.

Anna stirred and Will turned towards her, just able to make out her face.

Her eyes opened. 'Willburgh?'

'Will,' he corrected. Who else did she expect?

'Will,' she repeated. 'I could not see you in the dark. What time is it?'

'I am not certain.' There wasn't a clock in the room, not that he'd found at least. 'Middle of the night.'

She sat up and groaned. 'My head aches.'

Why did he feel disquieted around her suddenly? Why sound so churlish?

He tried to soften his voice. 'That's the whisky.'

She pressed her fingers against her temple. 'How much did I have?'

'Plenty.' He'd lost track of how many times his glass was filled. 'You said three, I believe.'

She sighed. 'I don't remember that. I don't remember coming up to this room. Did we miss dinner?'

'We did,' he responded. 'Are you hungry? There is bread and cheese and tea.'

She groped around until finding her shawl. She wrapped it around her and walked over to him.

He pulled out a chair for her. 'Have a seat and I will cut you some.'

'Some tea first please.' She sat in the chair. 'My mouth is so dry.'

He poured her tea and handed it to her. 'It is no longer hot.'

'I do not care.' She drank it as quickly as he had done.

He cut her a piece of bread and a slice of cheese and sat across from her. She ate as eagerly as he had.

She took a sip of her second cup of tea and lifted her gaze to his. The candlelight softened her face. She looked vulnerable. And alluring.

'Did—did we—?' she asked.

He knew what she meant. 'No. We didn't.'

She glanced away. 'I—I want you to know that I will understand if you do not want to. I—I know you did not want this marriage. I know you may not want to bed me.'

Will's first impulse was to snap back at her and accuse *her* of not wanting to bed *him*, but she looked so forlorn, he pushed that impulse away, remembering her growing distress the day before, saying that he did not like her and that he blamed her for her father's actions. He did like her—or was growing to.

He lowered his voice. 'We are man and wife. To think of

what we wanted before is useless now. I expect us to have—marital relations.'

She faced him again.

He went on. 'We—we do not have to—to consummate our marriage tonight, though. I make you a promise that I will not touch you until you are ready.'

She peered at him. 'I cannot tell if your words mean you want to or you do not want to, because I certainly do not wish it if it is abhorrent to you.'

He met her eye. 'It is not abhorrent to me.' Good God, his body was already humming with desire for her.

She glanced away again. 'I—I am not sure if it is abhorrent to me.'

Who might have discussed such matters with her? Young women might have such instruction right before their wedding day. No one would have had that conversation with her, though.

'What do you know of it?' he asked.

She gave a wan smile. 'Cautionary tales from the governess. Titillating tales from some of the maids. I know what happens.' Her brows knitted. 'I believe it must give pleasure, otherwise would men seek it out so; would women engage in affairs?'

That was an intelligent deduction. 'I will do my best to give you pleasure, Anna.' He meant that. 'Whenever you wish to try.'

She inhaled a deep breath. 'Tonight? Best not to wait, I think.'

Will stood and extended his hand.

Anna put her hand in his and let him lead her to the bed.

Her knees trembled. She was afraid, yes, but it was a fear she was eager to face, much like when she was young and afraid to ride horses but wanted to more than anything. Of course, riding a horse was exhilarating, something that gave her great pleasure. Could she trust that the marital act brought pleasure? Having heard a description of what happens between the man and the woman, and having seen animals copulate, she could not imagine pleasure from it. Perhaps it would merely be gratification from conquering the fear.

When they neared the bed, he swooped her into his arms

and gently placed her on it. Anna felt giddy. It was so unexpected. So playful.

She'd not imagined that Willburgh could be playful. She sat on the edge of the bed and watched while, in the same playful spirit, he removed his trousers. Only his drawers remained. She was used to seeing his drawers. He'd kept them on when they'd shared a bed.

She smiled. 'Did you fall sleep in your trousers?'

'I must have.' He took off his drawers, as well.

Now he wore only his shirt, but it covered his body nearly to his knees.

He undid the ribbon at the collar, but paused and his expression sobered. 'We may do this clothed or not. What do you prefer?'

She hardly knew. Except, once she'd learned to properly mount a horse, she'd wanted to gallop.

'Unclothed,' she said.

He crossed his arms and grasped the hem of his shirt. In one fluid motion, he lifted the shirt over his head. He was naked.

Anna could not take her eyes off him.

'Have you seen a man unclothed before?' He tossed the shirt aside.

'I've seen statues.' But statues did not prepare her for this male physique.

He was broad-shouldered with rippling muscles all the way to his waist, like a statue of Hercules she'd once seen in Lord Lansdowne's house. His waist was narrower, though, and his skin was spattered with hair and glowed in the dim light in a way cold marble could never do.

Would she ever tell him that he compared favourably with Hercules? She doubted it, but it made her smile.

Standing naked in front of her, he twirled a finger in her direction. 'And your clothes?'

Her breath came faster. She wore only her shift.

'I'll take it off for you, if you like,' he murmured.

She'd never heard his voice sound like that. Like a purring cat. It added to the thrill.

'Very well,' she managed.

He came closer and took the thin fabric in his hands, easing it up her legs. As his hands came close to her female parts, her body seemed to throb. She wriggled, freeing the garment from beneath her. He'd moved slowly before, but now pulled the shift over her head as swiftly as he'd removed his shirt.

His gaze swept up and down her body, his blue eyes darkening.

The modiste that dressed Lady Dorman and Violet and altered their castaways for her always complained that her breasts were not large enough to fill a dress properly and that she was too tall. She was not round and luscious like Violet.

'I am a disappointment, I know.' She scooted onto the bed and covered herself with the bed linens.

He peeled them away. 'Not a disappointment at all.'

He was being kind.

He climbed in the bed next to her and she rolled on her side to face him.

Her nervousness returned and she could hardly get a breath to speak. 'How do we start, then?'

How was he to start? Will wondered. How was a man to give a woman her first experience of the marital act, especially when she'd been forced to marry?

It had been a long time since he'd lain with a woman, but the lack had not overly bothered him. There always seemed to be too much to do and too much required of him to pursue any amorous adventures like his old schoolmates were fond of doing, the friends who'd convinced him to go to Vauxhall Gardens that night.

That lifetime ago.

His head might not have felt the lack of female company, but his body certainly did. He'd kept it in check the three nights he'd shared a bed with Anna.

But just barely.

Now, with barriers gone and expectations high, his body wanted nothing more than to surge on, the fastest and hardest that he could go.

But he would not do that to Anna.

Their truce was fragile. The trip to Scotland had given them time to become acquainted with each other. She proved herself more intelligent, more resourceful and more forbearing than he ever would have imagined. And she seemed as willing as he to see if they could make something good out of this forced marriage.

He could ruin that by rutting like some bull in a field of cows.

Which was precisely what his body wanted to do.

Will began carefully by touching her cheek. She tensed, but he simply stroked her skin with the back of his hand. She relaxed. He put his hand on the back of her head and lowered his lips to hers.

Gentle kiss, he told himself. *Barely touch her.*

When he moved away, she sighed.

'I'm going to touch you,' he said. 'I'll tell you what I'm going to do before I do it.'

She nodded.

'You can tell me to stop any time.'

She nodded again.

He stroked her cheek again and her neck and slid his hands down her arms.

'Now your breasts.' He started by stroking the skin above her breasts.

'They are too small, I'm told.' Her voice was forlorn.

He guided her face so she would have to look him in the eye. 'Your breasts are lovely.' He covered one with his hand. 'See? They fit perfectly.'

She laughed. 'Now you are making sport of me.'

He made her look at him again. 'No, I am not.'

He caressed her breasts again, but instead of relaxing her, her back arched and eager sounds escaped her mouth.

Could she be aroused?

'A kiss,' he murmured and placed his lips on her nipple, then dared to taste it with his tongue.

She writhed in response, but she did not say no.

He continued caressing her, running his fingers down her abdomen, sweeping his fingers down her legs. The force of his arousal intensified, becoming more and more painful and demanding by the moment. He could not wait much longer.

'I must prepare you now,' he told her. 'If you feel you are ready—'

'For goodness' sake, Willburgh,' she rasped.

'Will,' he corrected.

'Will,' she repeated. 'I am not made of glass. Gallop already.'

He eased up enough to look at her. 'Gallop?'

'I meant I am ready.' She pulled him down.

That was all the permission he needed. He moved atop her and she opened her legs and arched her back. He knew she was unschooled in this; her body must be doing its own demanding. His body urged him to thrust into her, but he had enough restraint to go slow. When his male member touched her, she flinched, but immediately rose to him.

'This—this might cause you pain,' he managed.

'I assure you, I will deal with it,' she responded.

As you wish, he thought. He wanted to give her pleasure this first time—or at least not cause her too much pain. He eased himself in slowly.

She gasped and tensed around him. He moved slowly at first, creating a rhythm that she quickly matched. They moved faster and faster together.

Galloping, he thought, right before crossing the border between reason and desire.

Anna had not thought it would be like this. She had not imagined the want, the need, that propelled her forward, to ride with him as far and as fast as he could take her. Into some unknown place that she suddenly was desperate to discover.

His kiss had surprised her with its gentleness. His touch had soothed and excited her. His consideration of her, though, unsettled her. When, since her papa had died, had another person been concerned about how she would feel?

The only sound in the room was the clapping of their bodies coming together and their gasping breaths. His thrusts came faster and with more force, but that only intensified the need inside her. That first stab of pain quickly became inconsequential in light of the ride he was taking her on. She did not know the destination, where want and need would be fulfilled.

But she wanted to get there as rapidly as possible.

When her pleasure burst, she cried out. She had not expected this.

His came right after. He tensed and trembled inside her. Spilling his seed? It must be.

The next moment he collapsed on top of her and rolled off to lie beside her, panting.

'So that was all?' she said, as if disappointed.

'What do you mean, "that was all?"' he shot back, rising enough to glare at her.

Anna laughed. 'I am jesting with you. It was really quite—' How to describe it? 'Quite nice.'

He lay back again. 'Nice. That is damning with faint praise.'

'Indeed it is not,' she countered. 'If so, I would be implying it had fault.' She turned to face him. 'And it really was quite perfect.'

Her gaze captured his and held, perhaps saying more than words could convey.

He closed the distance between them and touched his lips to hers again, as gently as he had done before, but not tentative. Affirming.

He tucked an arm around her and pulled her against him. His skin was warm against hers and slightly damp. With her head against his chest she counted his heartbeats. And reprised every moment of the lovemaking in her mind. He'd been her enemy for so long, but now she could not imagine any other man touching her, kissing her, joining with her.

She pressed her lips to his skin. 'A fortnight ago would you have dreamed you would be here? With me?'

When he responded she felt the words rumble in his chest. 'I would have wagered a fortune against such an idea. I would have lost.'

She dared another question. 'Are you sorry about it?'

He laughed. 'Not at the moment.'

Chapter Nine

The next morning Will woke when sunlight poured in the window. He glanced at Anna, still asleep, looking young and innocent and beautiful.

He'd bedded her. Twice. And had found it a profound experience, so why were his emotions in a jumble this morning?

He closed his eyes, but instead of sleep, visions of his father's duel with her father flew into his mind. He again saw them lifting their arms and firing, the smoke bursting from the barrels of both pistols. His father fell, his shirt turning red with his blood.

A mere fortnight ago, Will could go weeks without remembering—reliving—that scene. Since that night at Vauxhall he'd relived the memory nearly every day. Was he doomed to think of it every time he looked at her? He was married to her. Bound to her for the rest of their lives.

But he had not relived the memory the day before. Or the past night. That was a puzzle. From the moment he married her, in that manner so casual he almost missed it, he'd been caught up in revelry. Making love to her had been—he had no words to describe it. Only that he'd felt—whole. As if he did love her and wanted to marry her. As if they belonged together.

But her father killed his father.

The memory returned.

He rolled over in bed and sat up, too restless to remain there.

She woke up and stretched. 'Good morning,' she murmured and he remembered the delights of the night they shared together.

He remembered how good it felt to touch her, to teach her about lovemaking, to make it comfortable for her, to make certain to give her pleasure. Gazing at her and remembering, he wanted to repeat the experience.

But it was madness to care for her. To actually like her. To want her comfort and happiness. Her father killed his father.

But no. The day before she'd given a different name.

'Tell me something,' he said as he picked up his clothing from the floor. 'Tell me why you said your name was Edgerton.' His voice had an edge to it.

She covered herself with the bed linens. 'The man who fathered me was named Edgerton.'

'He was not Dorman?' He put on his drawers.

'No.' There was tension in her voice.

Because he was sounding churlish, no doubt. 'But you were called Dorman. Lucius's cousin.'

'It was the only name I knew.' She paused. 'Until my mother told me my real name. On her deathbed.'

Will knew her mother had died when Dorman and she came to stay with Lord and Lady Dorman.

Her expression turned pained. 'My mother told me about Edgerton. She'd been married to him before she married Bertram Dorman.'

He tried to mollify his tone. 'What happened to him?'

'He died,' she said. 'When I was a baby. He was a soldier in the East India Company army. He was killed at Seringapatam. In the battle.'

'In India?'

'In India.' Her voice was taut, as if her words were difficult to speak. 'That was where I was born and lived until my mother died.'

How little he knew of her. She'd been born in India? Lived there before coming to the Dormans? Of course, he'd been at

Oxford at that time and had been totally absorbed in his own interests and desires.

'I called Dorman Papa,' she went on. 'He was the only father I knew. When my mother died, I was afraid, because I did not really belong to him. I dared not talk to him or to anyone about it. What if he would leave me as well?'

The Bertram Dorman Will knew of was reputed to gamble and drink to excess. Worse, he was a womaniser who loved to toy with a woman's affections, as he had done with Will's mother. Her fears had merit.

'A vile man,' Will muttered as he completed dressing.

She got out of bed and put on her shift and corset before speaking again. 'He was not a vile man,' she said with feeling. 'He was generous and fun and kind to me. It was a blow to learn he was not my father. A worse blow when he was killed. I will not hear ill spoken of him!'

Will would not hear him praised. 'He seduced my mother.'

'The Dormans said your mother seduced him!' she cried. 'I do not care. He was good to me and when he died I had no one.'

Will could not stop himself. 'You obviously had the Dormans.'

She turned her back to him, stepped into her dress, pulled it up, and buttoned it.

She faced him again. 'Eventually Lord and Lady Dorman decided I could stay, but after my—my papa—was killed, it was not a certainty. You might say I was *allowed* to live with the Dormans. They found many ways to let me know I was there only out of the goodness of their hearts.

The Dormans had always let Anna know she did not truly belong there, but lived with them at their whim. Did she belong anywhere, to anyone?

Last night, when Will so gently and daringly made love to her, she'd felt perhaps she'd found where she truly belonged. This morning, though, he became like the man with whom she'd been caught in the rain at Vauxhall. Disagreeable. Disdainful. Despising her.

She put on her stockings and sat at the dressing table to comb her hair into some semblance of order. She could hear him moving around behind her but she was hurt and angry and wished he would leave.

She plaited her hair, wound it into a chignon and covered it with a cap. Married women wore caps, did they not? Even if married to a disagreeable man.

He became so quiet that she wondered if he had left the room. She jumped when he did speak, but his voice was still clipped.

'Forgive me,' he said. 'I spoke unkindly.'

She turned around to look at him and their eyes met. Her senses leapt at the sight of him. She could not help it. How was she to guard her emotions when the mere sight, sound, and scent of him affected her so?

Perhaps he apologised out of duty. He'd married her out of duty, had he not? Had he made love to her out of duty? No. No. That must have been real. It had to be real.

A knock at the door broke into her thoughts.

'Who is it?' he asked.

'The maid, sir.'

He glanced at Anna as if to ask if the maid should enter. She nodded.

'Come in,' he called through the door.

The maid looked no more than a girl. She wore a crisp, clean apron and a plain dress.

'My da—Mr Armstrong—sent me to tell you there are three gentlemen to see you.'

She was the innkeeper's daughter, then.

'Gentlemen?' Will frowned. 'What are their names?'

'I do not know, sir,' the maid replied. 'My da dinna tell me. They are *English*, though.' She spoke the word *English* as if it left a bad taste in her mouth.

'Is it Lucius, do you think?' A new worry. Anna shoved Willburgh's manner aside. Who else could it be? 'Or perhaps Toby or John?'

'Not Toby or John,' he replied, his brow knitted. 'They would not dress as gentlemen and there would not be three of them.' He turned back to the maid. 'Tell them I will come directly.'

'Yes, sir.' The maid curtsied. 'Da says they will be waiting in the tavern.' She left the room.

Anna's heart raced. 'It must be Lucius. And—and—what if the other one is—is *that man*.'

'The one who abducted you? Why do you think so?' he asked.

'I—I am just afraid that he is. The man spoke to Raskin before Raskin disappeared with Violet.'

'Raskin and Violet ran off together?' Willburgh's expression darkened. 'I will see what they want.'

'Wait.' She hurriedly put on her half boots. 'I will go with you.'

Will thought it unwise for her to go. If it was Lucius and the others, they were likely up to nothing good. But after he'd acted so churlish towards her, he could not deny her wishes.

He did not like himself very much at the moment. She'd done nothing to deserve his ill manners. Her behaviour had been faultless this whole trip. She deserved better than him snapping at her.

He suspected it was not memories of his father's duel that made him pull away from her. He knew she was not at fault. God help him, though, he was petty enough to be glad she was not really a Dorman. The man who fathered *her* was not the man who killed his father. He could no longer use that as an excuse.

What was it, then? Was it that he'd told himself—and his mother when she pushed—that he was not ready for marriage. He needed to master being a viscount first and he was far from perfecting that role. It consumed him. He did not want to be like his father, so enveloped in other duties that he neglected a duty to a wife.

He opened the door for her and the two of them walked down to the tavern.

When they entered, Armstrong was behind the bar.

He broke into a grin at the sight of them and wagged his brows. 'Well, well, well. Mr and Mrs Willburgh, good morning to you.'

How pleasant it was to be greeted by a friendly face. 'Good morning, Armstrong. I hope you are well.'

'No' too poorly, thank you.' He winked at Anna. 'And you, Mrs Willburgh? How do you fare?'

Anna's cheeks turned pink, but she smiled at him. 'No' too poorly, sir.'

Armstrong laughed.

'I understand we have visitors,' Will said.

The innkeeper frowned. 'That lot. *English*, y'know.' He sounded just like his daughter.

'We are English, you realise,' Will reminded him.

'Aye,' Armstrong cocked his head. 'But there are English and then there are *English*.'

Will thought he could agree with that statement, although he'd been acting the disagreeable type to Anna.

'I put them in the private dining room,' Armstrong said. 'So they won't upset the guests.'

His hand swept the room, but only three men were seated at a table who might have been disturbed, the same three men who had been present at the wedding and celebration after.

They all lifted their glasses and Will gave them a friendly wave.

He turned back to Armstrong. 'Show us the way.'

Armstrong draped a towel over his shoulder and led them to the dining room door and opened it.

Will stepped in before Anna.

It was Lucius, Raskin, and another man seated at a table, tankards of ale in front of them. The third man, Will recognised as one of Lucius's old schoolmates. Millman. Millman was precisely the sort of degenerate who would force himself on a lady. Will clenched his fist, wanting nothing more than to plant it in Millman's face.

They looked up, but none of them stood.

'This is a surprise,' Will said, although he was not surprised. 'You are a long way from London. What are you doing here, Lucius?'

Lucius looked from Will to Anna. 'I see we are too late.' He looked daggers at Anna. 'We came to bring you home, Anna. Where you belong. But you have betrayed the family thoroughly,

I see. With a Willburgh. You've had your Scottish wedding, I presume.'

'I have.' Anna lifted her chin. 'But you have it wrong, Lucius. I am where I belong now. It was you, your parents, and Violet who betrayed *me*.' She glared at Raskin. 'You and Violet left me alone at Vauxhall, so you are a part of it as well, Raskin.'

'Me?' Raskin put on an innocent face. 'I would never do such a thing.'

Millman leaned on the back two legs of his chair, smirking at everyone. Before Will knew it Anna walked around the table and yanked the back of his chair. The man fell sprawling to the floor with a loud crash.

Well done, Anna, Will said to himself.

He had to admit he liked that fire in her.

'That is for what *you* did,' Anna cried.

The man protested as he fumbled to his feet. 'I did nothing.'

She leaned into his face. 'I know what you did. What you tried to do.'

His face turned a guilty and angry red. He lifted his hand as if to strike her, but Will was there in a flash. He seized the man's arm and twisted it behind his back.

'See here!' Lucius protested.

Gripping the man closely, Will spoke into his ear. 'You stay out of my sight, Millman. And if I hear of you repeating with any woman what you tried to do to *my wife*, I'll be coming for you.'

Millman scurried out of the room.

'Not too hospitable of you,' Raskin drawled.

Will whirled on him. 'Do not get me started on you.'

'There you go, Willburgh,' Lucius piped up. 'Always throwing around your superiority. Here we've raced across the country, trying to save Anna from you, and this is how you treat us.'

'Your efforts would have been unnecessary if your father would have cooperated,' Will said. 'Or if any member of your family had had the decency to listen to her.'

'It was dear Anna who did not cooperate,' Lucius countered. 'Who would not listen. We were willing for her to come back to the family with all forgiven, but look how she thanked my parents for all those years of taking care of her. Marrying the enemy.'

Anna broke in. 'Do not speak of me as if I am not here.'

Lucius made a conciliatory wave of his hand.

Anna's eyes flashed and she pointed towards the door. 'You both left me with that worm. And then your parents abandoned me altogether. I want nothing to do with you.'

Lucius gave a slimy smile.

'This is a waste of our time,' Will said. 'Come to the point of why you wanted to speak to us. You could have guessed you were too late to stop us.'

'Oh, yes.' Raskin sneered. 'That delightful barbarian, Armstrong, told us.'

Lucius stood. 'You are right, Willburgh. Although I cannot believe I am saying that. This is a waste of time. I only wish I could be there when you both discover just how foolish this elopement was.' He glowered at Anna again. 'My dear, you will regret choosing a Willburgh.'

Raskin rose as well and gave them an exaggerated bow. With one final glare Lucius and Raskin left the room.

Anna lowered herself into a chair. Her knees were shaking with anger.

Willburgh leaned against the back of another chair. 'You were magnificent, by the way.'

She glanced at him.

Some of the anger inside her could be laid at his feet.

But he did defend her.

She took a breath. 'It was *him*, was it not? Millman?'

'Guilt was written all over him,' Willburgh responded. 'Lucius and Raskin knew his reputation. Everyone did. And yet they left you with him?'

'Lucius had left already, before Raskin came with—with *him*.' She pressed her fingers into the table. 'After Violet and Raskin disappeared, he approached and offered to escort me back to my aunt and uncle. Well, you know what happened after that.'

Willburgh blew out a breath. 'I hope we are rid of them for

good.' He pushed himself away from the chair and walked to the window.

It seemed he stood there a long time, before he turned back to her. His expression had softened. 'Shall I arrange breakfast?'

Any appetite she'd possessed had been swallowed up with emotion—starting with her waking to a colder Willburgh. 'If you so wish.'

'I do wish. I am famished.' His brows rose. 'Are you not hungry?'

She shrugged.

'We should eat. I'll let Armstrong know.' He left the room.

When the door closed, she moved the tankards of ale to a sideboard. She did not want to think of whose hands and lips had touched them. She opened a window as if to release the room of their every essence.

The air was crisp and clean and a breeze did its job of scouring out old smells. The sky was a vivid blue, a beautiful day so in contrast with her mood.

What had Lucius meant when he said she and Willburgh would discover what a mistake this elopement was? Had Willburgh already discovered the mistake?

Willburgh returned with two generously large bowls of porridge. He ate greedily, precisely how you'd expect a famished man to eat. Anna forced herself to eat a spoonful or two, and it sparked her hunger. She finished the whole bowl and looked up at him, waiting for him to make some scathing remark.

Instead, he asked, 'Do you wish to travel back today?'

Be trapped in a post-chaise with him?

Her answer must have shown on her face, because he quickly answered his own question. 'No travel today, then.'

She felt her cheeks flush. She'd thought she was more skilled at hiding her thoughts. 'Did you wish to start back?' she asked.

He held up a hand. 'Believe me, I have no need to be cooped up in a small carriage if it is not absolutely necessary.'

So he did not want to be trapped with her either. Yes. Their lovemaking must have been a fluke.

She rose and walked over to the window.

He joined her. 'What would you wish to do if you could do anything?'

Her mind went blank. Who'd ever asked her such a question since her papa died?

She flung it back to him. 'What would you do?'

He stared out the window for a moment before speaking, 'It is a fine day for riding.'

She gaped at him. Again her face betrayed her.

He smiled. 'Ah. You agree with me.'

She turned away. 'It is impossible. We have no horses. No saddles. I have no riding habit or proper boots or a proper hat.'

He cocked his head. 'We are in a large enough town. What did I hear Armstrong call it? *Muckle Toon*. Such problems might be easily remedied in a town of this size.'

She peered at him. 'I do not understand what you mean.'

'Anna.' He met her gaze. 'I have the funds. We merely purchase what we need.'

Willburgh was true to his word. He purchased everything they needed.

A visit to a bank provided the funds. Mr Armstrong directed them to where they could find what they needed. Armstrong even knew a horse breeder with stock to sell.

Willburgh purchased *three* horses. *Three*, when he probably had a stable full of horses on his estate.

Anna found it difficult to fathom.

It took the rest of the day and visits to several establishments to accomplish everything else. Anna was able to see much of Langholm and to assist in each aspect. Goodness! Willburgh even sought her counsel on selecting the horses. She picked the horse she would ride. Imagine. Before this she'd ridden whatever steed Violet or Lucius did not want to ride.

Anna selected a lovely and very sweet grey Highland pony she named Seraphina. Willburgh chose a brown pony for John and a bay dun for himself. Anna named his pony as well as John's. She could not resist naming Will's Armstrong and John's Crown, after Armstrong's inn. Amazingly, they had no difficulty finding saddles that fit them, a riding habit that fit her well enough, and boots, hats, and gloves.

As they left the last shop, Willburgh said, 'I was thinking. Since we purchased the horses, we might as well ride them as far as we are able. Would you agree? We could ride them all the way to London if we so desired.'

She stared at him, astonished. Not to be jostled in a post-chaise with no room to move? Instead to be on horseback in the fresh air? Every day?

Again her face must have shown her thoughts.

He smiled. 'There it is, then. We ride all the way to London if we like.'

'Is it what you desire?' she asked.

He was confusing her again. Why would he go to such lengths merely to please her? He had turned kind and generous again. Like the night before. Why would he do so, when he woke so unhappy with her?

It must be that this was what *he* wished to do. She just happened to desire it, as well. That would make sense.

The day, really, in spite of how it started, had been a joy.

They ate dinner in the tavern and all the men who had been there the day before, the ones who witnessed their wedding, were gathered there again. It felt like they were among old friends.

And then the day was over.

And they were faced with going to bed.

Chapter Ten

When they readied for bed, the air was filled with tension, such a contrast to how the day had been after they'd rid themselves of Lucius and his cohorts.

Will could not remember when he'd last had such an enjoyable day not spoiled by some burdensome task or another hanging over his head. How could he feel guilty for giving himself over to the pleasure of the moment, when she'd been giddy with excitement when choosing her horse?

'A horse of my own!' she'd cried. 'I've never had anything so grand!'

His chest had burst with joy at her words.

And why should he not feel joyful? Purchasing whatever they wanted—whatever *she* wanted—had been a delight, even more of a delight, perhaps, than their passion-filled night before. Will did not want these feelings to end.

Now that they were back in the room in the inn, though, it was as if all his disagreeableness of the morning had returned.

Will wanted the joy back.

Anna climbed into bed much as she'd done when they stayed at the other inns and he'd promised not to touch her. Will joined her. He moved close to her, spooning her in front of him. But her body did not quite melt under his touch as it had the night before. She felt distant even though she was in his arms.

He gathered his courage and whispered in her ear, 'I want to make love with you again. Will you permit it?'

He felt her muscles tense, but she said, 'If you wish it.'

'I do wish,' he replied with feeling. 'But only if you wish it, too.'

She needed to share in the pleasure, like when they'd purchased the horse, or it meant nothing.

It seemed a long time before she answered. 'I wish it.'

He removed his drawers and threw them aside. She sat up and he lifted her shift over her head. One candle was still burning, bathing her lovely skin in a soft glow. His need for her flared, but he touched her carefully, relishing in the silkiness and warmth of her skin.

She was not indifferent to his touch, stirring beneath his fingers. He leaned forward and placed his lips against hers, hoping he could erase the words with which his lips had wounded her. She softened.

They lay down then, but he contented himself with the pleasure of stroking her skin. What harm to give himself to this pleasure? To give her this pleasure as well? They had no difficulties to face, no plans that needed to be made, and none of his duties back home could press him here. Was this not what he'd once lost? To simply enjoy himself?

His body's needs grew stronger and her response urged him on. He rose above her and entered her with ease. Her body was ready and it felt like a welcome, like forgiveness. All Will could think at the moment was that he loved her and was glad he was married to her.

In the next moment his primitive urges drove all thought and emotion from his mind. He moved faster and faster and she met him, stroke for stroke. Together they came to the brink of pleasure and carried each other over it. He felt her release burst and his followed. He slid off her and held her in his arms. They did not speak. Eventually her breathing became even. She was asleep.

Sleep came later for him as he savoured the joy for as long as he could.

* * *

They rose early in the morning and dressed for riding. While they ate breakfast John saw to the horses. Their portmanteaux had been exchanged for saddlebags, now all packed and ready to go.

Mr Armstrong insisted on wrapping up bread and cheese— and three bottles of cider—for their trip. He and his daughter and the tavern regulars were there to wave them off as if they were old and dear friends.

Will helped Anna onto her horse, but turned to shake Armstrong's hand before mounting his own.

'Thank you, Armstrong.' He handed the man his card. 'If I may ever be of service to you or your family, write to me.'

Armstrong glanced at the card. 'I'll be a—you are a lord?' He turned to his friends. 'The lad's a lord!'

'G'wan!' they cried.

Will clapped him on the shoulder. 'Do not hold it against me.'

Armstrong shook his head in disbelief. 'First one I met who wasn't *English*.'

Will laughed. 'I am English but, from you, I will take that as a compliment.'

Armstrong turned to Anna. 'So you are a lady, then, lass?'

Anna smiled graciously. 'Ever since you married us, sir.'

Armstrong waved his arms. 'Be off with ye before I charge you an extra guinea or two for the room.' Will had already paid him generously.

They said their final goodbyes and were on the road.

As the inn receded in their sight, Anna said, 'I believe I will miss them.'

Will thought she said this more to herself than to him but he responded, 'As will I. They were decent people, the lot of them.'

It was another fine, clear day, not too hot for June. A perfect day for a ride and Will was determined to enjoy it.

John rode a few feet behind Will and Anna. Will rode next to her, but they did not talk much.

It was difficult to endure her distant silence, especially since he wanted her to share in the freedom from all responsibility

that he felt. On this ride back to London, they could take all
the time they wished. They could indulge every whim without
any care. He'd be patient with her. He could not expect Anna
to trust he would not turn churlish again merely because he
felt the opposite.

He was determined to be amiable, though.

'You ride well,' he said as they left the town and entered the
countryside.

She turned to him and he was gratified to see her smile. 'I
enjoy it.'

He smiled, as well. 'Then I am glad we are making this trip
on horseback.' He wanted to keep the conversation going. 'We
should make it to Carlisle by noon, I should think.'

Their first destination was Carlisle, to find Toby.

She merely nodded.

Once out of the town they rode past fields rich with crops and
green pastures dotted with sheep or cattle. Stone fences or thick
hedgerows crisscrossed the lands. Will wondered how many of
the barriers were a result of the Clearances, where large land-
owners took over the land, driving off the tenants whose animals had grazed over the pastures for generations.

Another topic Will met with ambivalence. He also was a land-
owner who needed to increase the productivity of his farms,
but he could not help feeling more was owed to the common
people who were displaced.

There was nothing he could do about it at the moment,
though. He filed such thoughts away for a later date and merely
relished how beautiful was the land.

Anna took in a deep breath of the crisp countryside air. Coils
of tension deep inside her since Vauxhall Gardens loosened a
bit. The scenery itself was calming. To be riding, even at this
sedate pace was a joy. She was already in love with her pony,
who seemed completely at ease.

She glanced at the man riding beside her, so tall and comfortable in the saddle. She smiled to herself. He looked too big
for his Highland pony although the animal seemed perfectly
content to be carrying him on its back.

She thought of the night before. His lovemaking had been as gentle and kind as the first time, and she'd given in to the pleasure of it. He'd been exceptionally kind the whole of this trip, but in a sudden instant he'd turned back into the enemy—antagonistic, disagreeable, churlish—much like he'd been when they first removed their masks at Vauxhall Gardens. She did not know what to trust. The kind man or the ill-natured one?

At least riding her lovely pony amidst the beauty of the countryside and breathing the fresh country air mollified her emotions. She could forget for long stretches of time that he might not be the strong, handsome, loving man that first night of lovemaking—and the one following—promised him to be.

Whatever he was, though, the die was cast and she must lie in the bed she'd made for herself. Or what had been made for her.

They reached Carlisle when the sun was high in the sky. Noon or near to it, and they found Toby at the Bush Inn where they had left him. With him were John's brother and his wife, Lottie.

Willburgh requested a private dining room and they gathered there as equals for refreshment and to trade tales of their separate experiences.

'You should have seen when the gentlemen discovered us was us,' John's brother, Adams, said. 'The one was hopping mad.' He grimaced. 'They thought they could get the better of me, but I was bigger and stronger.'

Anna gasped. 'Did they fight you? Did you get hurt?' She had not wanted anyone to come to harm because of her.

John's brother grinned. 'No, ma'am. They did some pushing and shoving, but I put a stop to that right off.'

His wife gave him a proud look.

'I am so very grateful to both of you,' Anna said.

The brother's wife waved her words away, then said, 'I have your dresses packed for you.'

Anna touched the young woman's arm. 'I would like for you to have them, Lottie.' They had come from the Dormans and Anna did not want them anyway.

Her eyes brightened. 'Thank you, ma'am.'

Their meal was leisurely and pleasant, but as it went on, Will-burgh asked Adams, 'Are we keeping you from your work?'

The young man shrugged. 'The stable let me go. But you paid me plenty. We'll be all right and something will come up.'

Willburgh looked towards Toby. 'We should have something at Willburgh House, do you not think?'

Toby nodded. 'Looks to me like you have three more horses need tending to. An extra hand will be welcome.'

'And there is always need for an extra pair of hands in the house.' He glanced at Lottie. 'If you like. It means leaving your home, though.'

'This isn't our home, sir,' John said. 'We came for the work.'

'We'll gladly work for you, m'lord,' his brother said.

While they discussed arrangements, Anna watched Will-burgh. Here was another surprise. Such a generous offer. He hadn't been required to make it; he'd paid them well, after all. He offered them security.

When the horses were rested and their repast over, she and Will returned to the road. Toby, Adams, and his wife were to travel by coach directly to Buckinghamshire where Willburgh's country estate was located. Anna knew the house and property, of course. She'd glimpsed it many times while riding with Vio-let and Lucius. It was grander than Dorman Hall, the Dormans' country house. The Dormans' property abutted Willburgh's at that parcel of wooded land to which each claimed ownership. Part of the feud between the families.

When she and Will left Carlisle behind and were back in the open countryside, Will had ridden ahead. Anna urged her horse to catch up to him.

'Willburgh?' she called.

He turned around and waited for her. Her horse came to Willburgh's side.

He smiled—a bit sadly, she thought. 'It's Will,' he said.

She felt guilty for deliberately not calling him by his pre-ferred name. 'Will,' she repeated. 'I wanted to say—' She didn't know how to say it. 'I wanted to say that it was good of you to hire John and his brother and wife.'

His smile brightened. 'A mere trifle.'

She remained next to him, while John rode behind. She made an effort to talk to him, to comment on the sites they passed or the other travellers on the road. They avoided the busy routes with their wagons of goods and speeding coaches. They were no longer dependent upon coaching inns and post horses and could stop and rest their horses at any village inn they wished. They rode the smaller roads and were often the only ones in sight. It was quiet and peaceful and her coils of tension loosened even more.

They stopped at one such village inn to spend the night, registering as Mr and Mrs Willburgh. Their room was small and Anna's legs were aching from the day in the saddle. The bed, though, was comfortable enough to make love. After Anna again experienced that exquisite burst of pleasure, she relaxed in Will's arms. The wall she'd constructed over her heart cracked a little. Anna fell asleep as the crack allowed a glimmer of hope to seep into her heart.

The next day Anna's heart opened a little more, each time Will treated her or someone else well. He was truly the best man she'd ever known and her heart leapt at the mere sight of him.

The frantic travel by post to reach Scotland could not have been more different than the leisurely return trip. They stopped as often as they wished or whenever the horses needed rest. They avoided the larger towns but happily explored whatever smaller village they fancied, villages with names like Newbiggin, Bollington, and Goosnargh. When staying at inns, Will always signed them in as Mr and Mrs Willburgh and no one questioned that. They wore ordinary clothes and rode ordinary horses and were simply assumed to be ordinary people.

On fair days they picnicked by clear blue lakes and explored crumbling ruins. They rested in the inns on rainy days, playing cards and making love during the day. When the roads were dry and the air was fine, they let the horses gallop, the wind tugging at her hat. It felt like flying.

Anna told Will about India, about her *ayah* and the other beloved servants she left behind, about the sights and sounds and smells. Will regaled her with stories about his school days, about the mischief he and his friends engaged in, about the oddities of his tutors. They remarked on what they saw along the road and the people they met. At night they let their bodies speak and the lovemaking only got better and better.

Throughout the trip neither of them spoke about fathers or duels or Dormans or duties or even what arriving in London would bring.

After almost a fortnight, though, they faced the end of their idyll. The roads became thick with wagons, horsemen, and carriages. The fields and woods and tiny villages gave way to factories and workshops and crowded tenements. Finally they reached the neat streets, shops, and townhouses of Mayfair where passers-by dressed in fine fashions eyed them with curiosity and dismay. Anna suddenly saw herself through their eyes. Her clothes, full of the dust of the road, were the worse for wear after almost two weeks of travel.

When they turned onto Park Street, Anna's spirits sank. They were at the end. At the door of Will's townhouse.

Anna, dirty and shabby, looked like she ought to be using the servant's entrance; Will, like a labourer seeking work. John appeared more like his companion than his groom.

Will helped her dismount and John held the horses while Will sounded the knocker. Bailey answered the door.

The butler's shocked expression quickly became composed when he welcomed Will's return and quickly summoned a footman to tend to the horses and another to collect their bags.

Before leaving her pony, Anna stroked the horse's neck. 'Thank you, Seraphina, for carrying me so far,' she murmured.

She was rewarded with a nuzzle back.

Anna reluctantly stepped away. 'See she's taken good care of,' she pleaded.

The footman bowed. 'Yes, m'lady.'

Anna blinked. Right... *M'lady.* She was Lady Willburgh now.

Will introduced John to the footman. 'He is our new groom,' Will explained. 'Show him the stables and introduce him to the head groom. He is to be welcomed and given every consideration. Let them know. He can be in charge of these horses.'

'Yes, m'lord,' the footman said.

Anna approached John before he was led away. She clasped his hand. 'Thank you, John. You must let us know if you need anything at all.'

'I will, ma'am,' the youth said.

Will escorted Anna into the hall where the butler eyed her with some distress. She hoped it was merely due to her dress.

'Bailey, you saw John, our new groom,' Will said.

'I did indeed, sir,' the butler replied.

'Check on him later, if you will,' he went on. 'I want to make certain he is treated well. He was invaluable to us.'

How like Will to be concerned about John, Anna thought. The young man *had* been invaluable to them.

'I will, sir,' the butler replied. 'And Toby? Is he with you?'

'I sent him on to Willburgh House.' He handed Bailey his old hat and worn gloves. 'Is my mother at home?'

'She retired to the country a few days after you left, m'lord,' Bailey responded.

'Probably for the best,' Will said, as if to himself.

Anna could just imagine what her new mother-in-law would have thought of her present appearance.

'Are there rooms ready for us?' Will's voice sounded different. Like a viscount's. He even stood differently. Stiffer. With an air of command.

Had her affable, relaxed new husband disappeared?

'Yes. Your room and the one adjoining it for the viscountess.' The butler looked a little disturbed. 'Some of the servants have the day off, it being Sunday and we did not know to expect you today, but I will find your valet, sir, and a maid to tend to—to the viscountess.' He turned to Anna. 'The belongings you left here are in the room, unpacked, m'lady.'

At least they'd thought of her.

'Very good, Bailey.' Will spoke before Anna could acknowledge him.

Will offered his arm and walked with her up the stairs to the bed chamber that had been Lady Willburgh's. His mother must not have been pleased at being so displaced, Anna thought.

'There is a connecting door to my room.' Will opened it to

show her. 'Is there anything I can do for you before a maid appears?' His voice sounded so formal.

Anna looked around at the beautifully decorated room. How could his mother not resent her use of it?

'I will not need you.' She echoed his formal tone.

What she did need was for it to be only the two of them in a simple room in an inn, helping each other, not waiting for valets and maids. Those days—and nights—would never return.

She removed her hat and pulled off gloves, placing them both on a chair. Still feeling like an intruder, she opened drawers and discovered her clothes were indeed there, as Bailey had said. She took out a clean shift and corset. It would be glorious to change into them. It would be glorious to clean off the dirt of the road.

In a corner of the room behind a spectacular hand-painted screen was a lovely French wash stand with ornate marquetry. Inside its cabinet were soap and towels. The pitcher was filled with water. It did not matter to Anna if it was fresh or not. She stripped off her riding habit and underclothes and washed the dirt of travel off her body. It would be lovely to wash her hair as well, and even to have a tub bath, a nice long tub bath with nice hot water. Would it be offered to her? she wondered.

Or could she, now Lady Willburgh, simply order it done?

This she could not imagine.

After she dried herself and put on her clean shift and stockings, there was a tap at the door.

'It is the maid, m'lady.' It was the chatty maid who had served her before. She entered the room carrying Anna's saddlebags. 'I've brought your luggage. Mr Bailey also said I was to help you dress or whatever you wish me to do. I'm not a lady's maid, though.'

'You helped me well enough before,' Anna said. 'What is your name?'

'I am Hester, m'lady.' Hester was little more than a girl, smaller than Anna with a riot of blond curls escaping her cap.

Anna nodded. 'Hester, I found my underclothes, but I have not yet found my dresses.'

The girl walked over to the wall covered with Chinese wallpaper. She found knobs cleverly blending in with the wallpaper and opened a cabinet, a clothes press built into the wall. 'Your dresses are in here, m'lady.'

Anna could not help but laugh. 'I would never have found them.'

'Which dress, ma'am?' Hester asked.

Anna glanced inside the cabinet where three dresses were neatly folded on shelves, one of which was the dress Will's mother gave her. She selected that one.

'This is the one Lady Willburgh gave you,' Hester exclaimed. 'I must say it looked better on you than it did on her.'

'It wasn't her colour,' Anna said diplomatically. She touched her hair. 'Before I dress, I should like to brush my hair. I have a brush and comb in the bags over there.'

Hester went to the dressing table and opened a drawer. 'There is one here, as well.'

Anna joined her. 'Someone thought of everything.'

'His Lordship wrote a letter saying you would come soon,' Hester said. 'He told Mr Bailey to tell Mrs White to make sure you had everything you would need.'

Anna had not known that.

'But you need more dresses,' Hester added as Anna sat at the dressing table and she removed the pins from her hair. 'You don't have nearly enough.'

When her hair was arranged, the maid said, 'Before I forget, I am to tell you to meet His Lordship in the drawing room when you are ready.'

Yes. She'd be meeting *His Lordship*, not her Will.

Chapter Eleven

Will sat at his desk in the library, piles of mail and other papers in front of him. It would take an age to attend to it all. A quick riffling through the pile showed many notes from his peers in the Lords. Two or three letters from his mother. Bills from various shopkeepers. Letters from the managers of his various estates. A summons to come see his men of business. Charities seeking donations. Relatives seeking funds. Relatives writing to chastise him for compromising Anna. Others warning him not to marry her.

He wanted to chuck the lot into the fireplace and watch it burn to ashes. He wanted to be with Anna, free to ride down country lanes, explore new villages, revel in the delights of sharing her bed. His mind refused to focus, yet all this correspondence was vitally important. Countless people depended upon him meeting his responsibilities.

His idyll was over.

Staring at the endless piles was achieving nothing, though, and he'd told Anna to meet with him. Will left most of the letters unopened and walked out of the library to go to the drawing room where Bailey was just setting down a tray of tea, biscuits, and sandwiches.

'Thank you, Bailey.' Will took two of the sandwiches off the tray. 'I did not realise how hungry I was.'

'I suspected it, sir,' the man replied.

Will sank down in one of the chairs. 'Before you go, tell me. What has it been like here?'

'Well, sir.' The butler straightened. 'About as dreadful as one could imagine.'

Will groaned. 'Tell me.'

'The printers seemed to be attempting to outdo each other. Several handbills were released embellishing the tale. Some made you out to be a terrible villain, preying on an innocent. One could have been written by Lord Dorman, all about how his ungrateful ward betrayed the family by consorting with you, merely to hurt them.' He dipped his head. 'I saved them for you. They are on your desk.'

They must have been at the very bottom of the piles.

'Your mother received some nasty letters,' he went on. 'And all the invitations she'd received hitherto were withdrawn.'

'She was wise to leave town, then.' And Will had been glad she'd gone.

His feelings towards his mother were ambivalent at best. Although he'd resolved not to ignore her as his father had done, he did not believe she was wholly innocent in the affair that caused his father's death even though she attempted to paint herself as ill-used. Especially when she tried to manipulate him to get her own way. She was often the most burdensome of his chores.

Bailey added, 'She was quite distressed.'

As well she would be. Will was glad he and Anna were spared that at least. It would all die down now they were married.

'Is that all, sir?' Bailey asked.

Will stood and walked over to the cabinet. 'Is there brandy here?'

'There is, sir.'

Will opened it and took out the carafe of brandy and a glass. 'Then nothing more. Thank you, Bailey.'

The butler bowed and left the room.

Will poured himself a glass of brandy and drank it in two

swallows. He wished he had taken Anna straight to Dover and hopped on a packet to the Continent. Think how exciting it would be to explore France, Italy, Spain, and Greece with her?

If only he could. He'd merely neglected his duties for three weeks and his work had turned mountainous. Payment for choosing enjoyment over a rush back to duty.

He poured himself a second glass of brandy.

Anna entered the room.

It had been almost two weeks since Will had seen her dressed in anything but her riding habit, a simple dress—or her shift. She took his breath. She wore that dress his mother gave her, the one that complemented her colouring so well. Her skin glowed with the health a week spent in fresh air would do. Her light brown eyes captivated him. She looked stunningly beautiful.

All he wanted was to take her in his arms and carry her back to his bed chamber. And remove that lovely dress.

Instead he stood. 'There is tea. And refreshments.'

She gestured to his glass. 'What are you drinking?'

He lifted the glass and peered at it as if noticing it for the first time. 'Brandy. Would you prefer a glass?'

She looked at him with questions in her eyes, but merely said, 'Please.'

Did she realise he sought out brandy when stressed?

He put his glass down and turned to the cabinet to get one for her. 'Is the room and service meeting your satisfaction?' Lord. He sounded stiff-necked.

She took the glass from his hand. 'Of course it is.' She spoke with a touch of irritation.

At him, he supposed.

She lowered herself into a chair. 'Hester has been a help.'

Will sat, too, and passed a plate of sandwiches to her. 'I am glad. She is a good worker.'

He took a couple of biscuits and berated himself. This was not what he wished to say to her. It was as if they were strangers again.

His thoughts were consumed with her. How was he to accomplish all that needed doing?

She sipped her brandy and seemed to be watching him carefully. 'Hester tells me I need a new wardrobe.'

He remembered the urgency of their purchasing old garments from the market in Nottingham as well as the pleasure of shopping for her riding habit in Langholm. Think how delightful it would be to comb the second-hand clothing shops on Petticoat Lane with her.

But, no. A viscountess must have her clothing made by a modiste.

'Buy whatever you want,' he said. 'Have the charges sent to me.'

'And a new riding habit?' She smiled wanly.

'Of course. A new habit.' He answered automatically, thinking how deprived of enjoyment he felt not to be ordinary enough to shop on Petticoat Lane.

A minute later he realised she'd meant him to remember how excited they'd both been when the garment fit her. The moment had passed.

He also realised he'd answered her exactly how his father answered his mother when she attempted to talk to him about something she desired to buy. '*Buy whatever you need,*' his father would say, as if he'd wished not to be bothered.

Or maybe his father was simply preoccupied by work. Will could understand now. Will was overwhelmed at how much he needed to do.

But somehow his father never seemed to yearn to be free of responsibility. When his father said duty comes first, he almost always sounded glad.

Anna finished the glass of brandy. She might as well have been alone. Will was preoccupied. He was also almost formal with her, more like he'd been those first days when they were nothing but enemies. It was as if he'd turned from being her Will of their travels into the viscount as soon as they crossed this house's threshold.

She put her glass on the table. 'What is it, Will? You are not attending.'

He shook his head as if dislodging more important thoughts.

'Forgive me. You said a new habit. New clothes. I could unearth the name of my mother and sister's modiste, but you may not want to use her.'

'I'd rather not,' she admitted. 'I certainly do not want to use Lady Dorman's modiste.'

'No, indeed,' Will looked distracted again.

She tried again. 'Will, what is wrong?'

He met her gaze. 'Wrong? Nothing.' But he finished his brandy and stood. 'I am sorry to do this, but I must leave you.' He seemed in a hurry to do so. 'I need to tend to a desk full of correspondence in the library.'

'Oh.' He was leaving her alone? 'Is there anything I might do to assist?' Anna wanted his company, even if he seemed a million miles away.

He shook his head. 'You are free to do as you wish, though. If you need anything, call a servant.' That felt like a dismissal. 'I will see you at dinner.'

He left.

He left? How could he leave her so abruptly? Not that he seemed like much company the last few minutes. What had happened?

The room turned deadly quiet except for the ticking clock. She must do something at the moment or go mad.

She placed the empty plates and the glasses on the tray that held the untouched tea things. She could at least carry the tray down to the kitchen.

As she descended the stairs to the lower floor and emerged in the hallway to the kitchen, Mrs White, the housekeeper, met her. 'M'lady! I was coming to you. You are not to be carrying trays. I will take that.' She almost pulled the tray out of Anna's hands.

'I thought I would help,' Anna explained. 'I knew some of the servants had the day off.'

At the Dormans' she'd often perform servants' tasks when asked.

'You are not to help, m'lady,' the housekeeper scolded. 'You must ring and we will come to see what you need.' The woman started to walk away.

'Mrs White?' Anna called. 'What were you coming to see me for?'

'The dinner menu. I will meet with you in a moment.' She turned away again.

'Shall I follow you?' Anna called after her.

The housekeeper turned back. 'Goodness, no.' Her voice softened. 'Lady Willburgh never came down to the kitchen. I will come to you.'

'Where shall I meet you?' asked Anna.

Mrs White looked a bit pitying. 'M'lady, you must tell me where you wish me to be.'

There was nowhere in this house Anna felt comfortable. 'Would the bed chamber do?' She could not call it *her* bed chamber.

'That will do nicely,' the housekeeper said. She bustled away with the tray.

Anna paced the bed chamber until the housekeeper came. There was very little to discuss about dinner, as it was obvious Mrs White and the cook knew precisely what they wished to serve.

'What else might you need, m'lady?' Mrs White asked as she readied to leave the room.

'Nothing at the moment. Thank you.' What she really needed and wanted was a return to the gambol of the past two weeks with Will.

After the housekeeper left, Anna paced the room again, until she could stand it no longer. She wanted to be with Will even if he was busy. She'd go down to the library and park herself there. Read a book. Or even better, assist him.

She descended the stairs and entered the library without knocking.

Will stood. 'Anna!' He did not sound overly glad to see her. 'I was just about to come to you.' He straightened a pile of papers on his desk. 'I just this moment learned I must leave you. Lord Lansdowne and Lord Brougham have sent for me to meet them and others at Brook's. There is to be a vote tomorrow to suspend habeas corpus. It is important we discuss the matter beforehand. I must go.'

'You must go now?' she asked.

'I must.' He straightened another pile.

'And you will be gone tomorrow?' she managed.

'Tomorrow. Yes.' He hurried past her. 'I am sorry. I will miss dinner. And I may be late. These things take time.' He turned back to her. 'Choose any book you like. The library is yours.'

And he was gone.

And she was alone.

She stood at the window and watched him rush out of the house and hurry down the street.

The vote on habeas corpus was important, she knew. It protected citizens from imprisonment without proof that they had committed a crime. The government thought its suspension would help control the unrest that was fomenting across the country and to prevent the sort of revolution France had endured.

If Will had simply spent a few minutes talking with her about it, Anna might be more forgiving of his abandoning her. She'd have felt important to him, not excluded. Instead, it seemed like he'd been eager to be away from her.

She was mystified at this change in him, but had she not experienced this once before? He'd become haughty and disagreeable the morning after their wedding. She was mystified but also angry. She had done nothing to deserve this treatment, to be left alone with virtually no regard for her feelings. She might as well be back with the Dormans for all the consideration she received from him.

One thing was different, though. She was not entirely powerless. She was Viscountess Willburgh now and a viscountess could sometimes have her way.

Anna turned on her heel and strode out to the hall, but it was unattended at the moment. She wasn't about to ring bells and wait, no matter what Mrs White thought of her. She marched down to the lower floor and found Mrs White and Bailey conversing in the servants' hall.

'M'lady,' Mrs White began. 'I said you must ring—'

Anna interrupted her. 'I did not wish to wait for bells. This is what I want. I want a bath. As soon as it might be accomplished. I want to wash my hair. Bring dinner to my room when it is convenient and I do not care what Cook fixes. She need not fuss. Anything will do.'

Without waiting for a response, Anna turned around and hurried off, before her emotions exploded. On her way to her bed chamber, she stopped by the library and pulled three books at random.

'*Choose any book*,' he'd said, as if that made amends.

Anna's bath was arranged right away and Hester attended her. Since Anna was not intending to leave her room, she dressed in night clothes afterwards. She sat at the dressing table while Hester combed the tangles from her hair.

The maid remarked, 'M'lady, your hair curls nicely.'

'Curls?' Anna remembered that this maid had arranged curls in her hair before, when Anna had first stayed here.

'Yes, m'lady. Especially if you bunch it up in your hands as it dries.' Hester took a lock of Anna's hair and demonstrated. 'See? It curls.'

Indeed when she released her hair, the curls remained. Anna was used to pulling her hair straight, although she did remember having curls when she'd been a little girl.

Hester bunched up another lock of hair.

'You made my hair curl before,' Anna remarked.

'Those weren't what I call curls. Want to see curls?' Hester removed her cap. 'See my hair? It is too curly. But yours will be nice curls.'

'Hester, your curls are lovely,' Anna said.

The girl sighed. 'More like a trial, ma'am.'

Hester's good-natured company was giving Anna some comfort. She certainly needed it.

'Hester, you said I need new clothes. Do you know where I might find a good modiste? I do not want to use the one the Dormans used.'

Hester sniffed. 'You certainly can do better than that one. My cousin says she is not very skilled and she charges too much. And she is not really French.'

Anna suppressed a laugh. 'I suspected that. Your cousin knows her?'

The maid stopped with the comb in mid-air. 'My cousin sews for a modiste who dresses the daughters of merchants and cits. She wants to have her own shop someday.'

'Do you think your cousin might sew for me?' Anna asked.

Hester dropped the locks of hair she was bunching. 'Do you mean that, m'lady? I'm sure she would love to. My goodness! She'd be making clothes for a viscountess!'

'I'm not sure she would want to advertise that it was me,' Anna responded. 'Not with the scandal, but Lord Willburgh would pay her well, I am certain, especially if she could make some clothes quickly. Could she see me tomorrow, do you think?'

Hester put the comb down and bunched more curls into Anna's hair. 'I could go to her now and arrange it. If I have permission to leave, that is.'

'Who should I speak to arrange permission for you?' Anna asked.

Hester giggled. 'M'lady, you need not seek permission. If you say I can leave, I can leave.'

The meeting at Brook's dragged on until near midnight. Will might as well have missed it. He could barely attend to the discussion let alone contribute. His mind was filled with Anna. He missed her company. His body ached for her.

This would not do. He needed to pay attention in meetings like this. He needed to contribute.

Lord Lansdowne offered him a ride home in his carriage and Will was forced to continue their discussion as the carriage made its way to Park Street.

How was he to go on? He had his responsibilities. His duty. He could not spend his hours mooning over her like a lovesick calf.

The carriage stopped and a groom opened the door. With

Lansdowne still making one more point, Will paused before climbing out and bidding the man goodnight.

He entered the house. The hall was being attended by a sleepy footman who took his hat and gloves. Everything was dark and quiet.

Will hurried directly upstairs to his bed chamber, catching his valet dozing in a chair.

'Beg pardon, sir.' The man jumped to his feet.

'No need,' Will responded. 'It's late, I know. Is everyone asleep?' He meant had Anna retired or was she waiting for him?

'I expect so, sir,' The valet helped him off with his coat and boots.

'I'll tend to myself from here, Carter,' Will said. 'You can go to bed.'

'Very good, m'lord.' Carter bowed and, carrying Will's coat and boots, left the room.

As soon as he left, Will went to the door connecting his room with Anna's. He opened it a crack and listened, but all was quiet. There was a light, though, so he entered. It was a candle on a table near the bed, burning itself almost to a nub.

It left enough light, though, to see that Anna was in bed, eyes closed, breathing evenly.

'Anna?' he whispered, but she did not stir.

He stood watching her for a long time, yearning to strip off the rest of his clothes and join her, but reluctant to disturb her peaceful sleep. Eventually, he turned around and returned to his own bed chamber.

Anna opened her eyes and watched him walk away.

She'd already heard a clock strike twelve so she knew it was later than that. Had he thought her asleep? Why did he not come to her anyway?

It wounded. And angered her.

If he had only joined her in her bed, she might have forgiven him for staying away so long. Instead he walked away.

She rolled over and hugged a pillow, but sleep did not come easily.

Chapter Twelve

⤜⤛⤜⤛⤜⤛

The next morning Will woke early, acutely aware that he was alone in the bed, alone for the first time in over a fortnight. He missed her. He greatly missed her.

His valet was as prompt as ever in appearing to help him dress. Will had half a mind to send Carter away and see if Anna was still abed. Perhaps there was still time to make love in the morning like they'd done on their journey, but if he did that he'd keep his valet waiting and the maid serving Anna might have to wait, as well. Will made it a point of honour to be considerate of the servants and to appreciate the services they performed for him.

So he let his valet dress him, and as soon as Carter left, Will went to the connecting door. He opened it and listened, but all was quiet. He walked in as quietly as he could.

The bed's linens were smoothed and everything appeared neatly in order.

She had arisen early. Earlier than he.

He hurried down to the breakfast room and found Anna there, sipping tea and reading the *Morning Post*. She wore the same dress as the day before, the one his mother had given her, but her hair had been transformed into cascading curls that framed her face and bounced at her slightest movement. He was entranced.

She looked up. 'Good morning, Will.' Her voice was flat. And chill.

'Good morning.' What was he to say to her?

He wanted to tell her she looked beautiful. Wanted to beg her forgiveness for leaving her alone the day before and tell her they could spend this entire day together. But that would mean neglecting some correspondence that must be answered this day and missing the meeting his men of business had deemed of the greatest importance. Afterwards he must make his way to the Old Palace of Westminster for the House of Lords session and the vote. His day was filled.

He gestured to the newspaper. 'I arranged to have a notice of our marriage put in the papers.' One of the tasks he'd accomplished the previous day. 'It will be printed tomorrow.'

She lowered the newspaper and simply stared at him. Or perhaps *glared* was a better word, although no specific emotion seemed to be reflected in her expression.

None that he could read, at least. He selected his food from the sideboard and sat across from her. 'I am afraid I will be gone most of the day today.'

She stared at him again, pausing before she spoke. 'And what shall I tell Cook about dinner?'

He hated his reply. 'I will not be here for dinner.'

She returned to the newspaper.

By the time Will finished his breakfast, he'd convinced himself her coolness towards him was a good thing. He needed to do his work and the sooner she realised that took precedence over everything else, the better. His could not be a life of enjoyment and spontaneity. The mountain of papers on his desk was testimony to that.

Because he wanted what he could not have. The freedom to enjoy her company.

Before Will settled down to his pile of papers, he wrote out letters with his seal indicating that the shopkeepers could bill him for any purchases Anna made. He could have had Bailey or one of the footmen bring her the letters, but he chose to deliver them to her himself.

He found her in her bed chamber, surprising her, apparently.

'Will!' She shut the drawer she'd been looking through. 'I—I did not expect to see you.'

He handed her the letters. 'Show these letters at any of the shops,' he told her. 'They will allow you to purchase whatever you like.'

She took them from him. 'Thank you,' she said in a low voice, but raised her head to meet his gaze. 'Because I will need clothing quickly, I expect to be asked to pay more than what is customary.'

He held her gaze and felt his resolve waver. He wanted to take her in his arms. Instead he said, 'Cost does not matter. Buy what you like.'

A faint smile flitted across her face. 'As you have often told me.'

He wished she'd not reminded him of their time together shopping. He'd never had such pleasure spending his money.

He hesitated a moment, still gazing at her, but then glanced towards the door. 'I have work to do,' he said. 'I wish you a good day.'

He left.

Will holed himself up in the library, putting pen to paper, hardly looking up until he heard voices in the hall. He rose and walked to the door, opening it a crack to see Anna and the maid leave by the front door. From the library window he watched them walk down the street. It lowered his spirits even more.

By noon he was forced to stop working on his correspondence and called for his carriage. As he climbed in he thought he ought to have told Anna to take the carriage. He could have caught a hackney coach. Too late.

His coachman drove him to Fleet Street and the offices of his men of business. Whatever they'd deemed so urgent wound up taking a little more than an hour. He had time to kill until he must appear at Westminster. He strolled up and down the street waiting for his carriage and stopped when a shop window caught his eye.

The shop was Rundell and Bridge, goldsmiths and jewellers to the king.

He went inside. Until this moment he'd not given it a thought. Anna had no wedding ring. He'd fix that forthwith.

The next morning Anna's humour was improved. The meeting with Hester's cousin had been unexpectedly diverting and productive. Anna even left with two new dresses she could wear right away. She and Hester also managed to buy two hats, three pairs of gloves, several pairs of stockings, and countless ribbons. They'd even gone to a tailor to be fitted for a riding habit and to a corset maker.

Hester and her cousin devised a brilliant way for Anna to build a complete new wardrobe quickly. Her cousin would ask as many modistes as she could think of if they had any dresses that were not paid for or not finished for any reason. If they would be of a near size to Anna's, Hester's cousin would propose buying the dress for her unnamed customer. Then the cousin and her seamstresses would alter the dresses so they would not be recognisable as the originals. 'So m'lady wouldn't be talked of for wearing someone else's discards,' Hester's cousin explained.

As if she would not be talked of for other reasons, Anna thought.

After Anna dressed and Hester arranged her hair she examined herself in the mirror. The pale lilac dress complemented her well. She looked the best she'd ever looked in her life.

Not that Will would notice.

He hardly took the time to say hello to her. What plans would take him away this day? she wondered.

This morning Will arrived for breakfast first. He stood when she entered the room.

She managed, 'Good morning.'

He stared at her, finally saying, 'Is that a new dress already?'

'It is.' Although the pleasure of it was diminished by his lukewarm response. 'Do you approve of it?'

His gaze flicked up and down her body. 'I do approve. You look very well in it.'

That was better, but not by much.

'Did you manage to buy all you needed?' he asked.

'Not in one day.' She sat across from him. 'I did order a new riding habit, though.'

He sat, as well. 'Very good.'

Even mention of riding did not elicit more from him.

She'd heard of marriages like this—or perhaps read of them in a novel—the courtship all filled with declarations of love only to turn into coldness or abuse after the wedding.

But she and Will had no courtship and she was confident he would never hurt her, at least not in a physical way.

After filling her plate, the footman left the room.

Will rose. 'I bought something for you.'

'Oh?' She poured her tea.

He walked over to the chair next to hers and took a small box from his pocket.

He placed the box in her hand. 'You should have had this on our wedding day.'

Anna opened the box and gasped. It was a ring. A beautiful ring with one large diamond in the centre and smaller ones encircling it. The diamonds were set in a gold band fashioned in a floral filigree design.

Her eyes flew to his face.

He took the ring from its box and slipped it on the third finger of her left hand.

Her heart beat so fast it took a long while before she could speak. 'You—you should not have—it must have cost a great deal—'

He continued to hold her hand. 'I wanted you to have it.'

She was awed. 'It is beautiful, Will.' Even more so because he troubled himself to buy it for her.

He smiled. 'Now our marriage is official.'

She leaned over and kissed him on the cheek. He gazed at her and reached up, touching her cheek so gently it sent waves of sensation throughout her body. She yearned to have him share her bed again.

He moved back to his original seat and handed her the *Morning Post*. 'The announcement is in it.'

She scanned the page until she found it.

'Does the wording suit you?' he asked.

'It seems adequate,' she responded.

She was more puzzled than ever. Right when she'd resolved herself to think him turning cold, he did something so lovely. Buying her a ring. Why was he so cold and formal with her? Why did he not come to her bed?

Bailey entered the room. 'Pardon, sir, this missive just arrived for you. The messenger said it was important. He awaits your reply.'

Will read it. 'Tell the messenger I will come within the hour.' Bailey left.

Will handed the message to Anna. 'This is from a man at Coutts Bank. It is about your trust.'

She looked up in surprise. 'My trust? I have no trust.'

'He says that you do and insists that I call upon him immediately.'

She perused the message. 'There must be some mistake. How would I have a trust, when I have no money?'

Will stood. 'I will go right now.'

She rose, too. 'I will go with you.'

'Women are not typically expected to go to—'

Was he going to say women were not welcome at Coutts? She cut him off and was adamant. 'I will go with you.'

'Very well.' He started for the door. 'I will call for the curricle.'

Within a half hour Will's curricle was brought around. He was surprised to see who held the horses.

'Toby, you are back from the country.' Will helped Anna into the seat and climbed up himself, taking the ribbons.

'I am, sir. All is well there.' He jumped into the groom's seat.

Anna turned towards him. 'How are John's brother and his wife settling in?'

The groom shrugged. 'As best they can. You know how it can be if you're from a different place.'

More to worry over, thought Will.

As they reached the Strand, Will wondered at the urgency of the summons to Coutts. What could be so urgent? And why did Anna know nothing about a trust in her name?

'Could the trust have been set up by your relatives?' Will asked her.

'My mother said we hadn't any relatives,' she replied.

'But there was your father.' Perhaps this was about her father.

'None on my father's side, my mother said. Or on her side.'

They passed Somerset House and St Clements and pulled up in front of Coutts Bank. Toby jumped down and held the horses.

Will helped Anna down. 'I do not know how long we will be,' he said to Toby.

'I'll walk 'em if need be, sir,' the groom replied.

Will escorted Anna into the building. He announced himself to the attendant at the door. Several men within earshot turned to look when they heard 'Lord and Lady Willburgh.' Anna was the only woman present.

'We are here to see Sir Edmund Antrobus,' Will said.

'Lord Willburgh,' the attendant said too loudly. 'Yes. Follow me. I am certain Sir Edmund will see you.'

As they followed the man, Anna whispered to Will, 'We are attracting a great deal of notice.'

'I can see,' Will responded.

They had to wait only a few moments for Sir Edmund, who was one of the partners at Coutts, second in importance to Thomas Coutts himself. To come without an appointment and be seen right away? What did it mean?

Sir Edmund bowed to Anna. 'Lady Willburgh. It is a pleasure. I did not expect you.'

'Indeed, sir?' responded Anna. 'This apparently concerns me.'

'Yes. Yes.' He gestured to some chairs. 'Please do sit. May I serve you tea?'

'Thank you, no.' Will glanced at Anna who shook her head. 'Tell us. What is of such importance?'

Sir Edmund did not sit until they both took their chairs. 'It was the announcement of your marriage that prompted me to contact you, sir. From the—um—information made available to us before this, we did not know for certain that you would be married.' That information being from the handbills, he meant?

'I must say that I would have strongly advised you to consult with us before taking that step—'

'Why would we consult with you?' Will asked.

'Why? Because of the trust.' He looked dumbfounded.

'What trust?' The man was making no sense.

'Why, Lady Willburgh's trust,' Sir Edmund said.

Anna spoke up. 'I have no trust!'

Sir Edmund turned to her. 'Oh, but you do, my dear lady. It was set up by your grandparents.'

'But I have no grandparents!' she cried.

'No.' Sir Edmund gave her a sympathetic look. 'Not now, because they died shortly after your poor mother. Your grandfather set this up before their deaths.'

'So what of this trust?' Will asked.

Sir Edmund turned back to him. 'What have you heard of her grandparents?'

'Nothing,' Will replied.

Anna broke in. 'That is because I know nothing!'

Sir Edmund continued to address Will. 'The grandfather was Norman Lyman, a nabob. Made a fortune in India, then retired to Croydon in Surrey. It broke their hearts when their only daughter eloped with that soldier, especially when she went with him to India. Her parents disowned her, but settled some money on her when she had the child.' He inclined his head towards Anna.

Will glanced at Anna. Her face was pinched with distress. No wonder. Sir Edmund told it in a manner so oblivious of her feelings.

Sir Edmund went on. 'Then Edgerton died and she married Dorman. Mind you, this is all before her twentieth year.' He grimaced. 'Dorman must have been the only Englishman to lose a fortune rather than make one in India. He went through her money like water through a sieve.' Sir Edmund chuckled. 'Dorman begged Lyman for more money after she died, but Lyman set up the trust instead, providing the child with an allowance, but no more.'

Will interrupted him. 'So Lady Willburgh inherits this trust?'

'No,' Sir Edmund said. 'That is why I wished to see you. To explain.'

'Then tell us.' Anna's voice was strained.

'Well,' Sir Edmund went on. 'The Lymans did not approve of either of the marriages. They blamed their daughter's age. They were determined to prevent the same mistakes being made by their granddaughter.' Again the man gestured to Anna as if Will would not know to whom he referred without pointing her out. 'So the will has a stipulation. If the heir marries before age twenty-one she forfeits the inheritance entirely and it reverts to her children when she dies, with the same stipulation and so on.'

Will leaned forwards, unwilling to believe his ears. 'Do you mean there is a fortune to be inherited, but Anna—Lady Will-burgh—cannot inherit because she married—'

Anna broke in. 'I will be twenty-one within months.'

Sir Edmund attempted to look sympathetic. 'I am afraid you do not inherit, but your children, if you have any, will.'

'And what happens if she does not have any children?' Will asked, his voice rising.

'Then it defaults to a charity. I would have to look up which. The Church, I believe.'

Will turned to Anna who looked as if she was struggling to control her emotions.

'How much of a fortune is this?' Will asked.

Sir Edmund held up a finger. 'I looked it up this morning after I read the marriage announcement. Ninety-six thousand, five hundred and thirty-six pounds.'

Will saw Anna grip the arms of her chair. It was an astounding figure. Enough wealth to live very, very well.

Will swallowed. 'Is there any property?'

Sir Edmund shook his head. 'As the will directed, the property was sold upon the death of both Mr and Mrs Lyman.'

Will glanced at Anna again. She looked about done.

He felt a knot twisting in his stomach.

She would have been only a month away from a fortune large enough for her to live on her own terms no matter how much gossip flew around her.

If only he hadn't married her.

Will stood. 'There is nothing else to say.'

Sir Edmund rose, as well. 'We will continue to manage the trust and you are certainly welcome to ask for an accounting at any time.'

Will offered his hand to Anna. She let him help her from the chair, but she did not look at him.

Sir Edmund walked them to the lobby. 'You must tell us if you have children, of course. Each child will receive fifty pounds a year.'

'Fifty pounds,' repeated Will.

'Yes,' responded Sir Edmund. 'Each child—as long as they do not marry before age twenty-one.'

'But not me,' Anna said, her voice wounded.

'Oh, but you received it,' he said. 'Did you not know?'

She shook her head.

'Was it paid to Lord Dorman?' Will's tone was tense.

'Well, he was her guardian.'

So Dorman knew all this and did not tell her? Will fumed.

Sir Edmund's hand covered his mouth. 'We gave him the money not two weeks ago.'

Will's lips thinned. 'We were married by then.'

Sir Edmund nervously wrung his hands. 'I suppose we should try to get the money back.'

'It belongs to the trust,' Will responded.

They reached the lobby. Sir Edmund bowed politely, bade them farewell and quickly turned away, hurrying back to his desk.

Will and Anna walked outside.

'Anna—' Will began.

She interrupted him. 'I want to go back to the townhouse.'

He did not know what to say to her. It was his fault they married so quickly. They could easily have waited for her to come of age. What had he done?

Chapter Thirteen

Toby came with the curricle and Will helped Anna into the seat. She could not speak. She felt as if someone had struck her in the face.

Betrayal. More betrayal.

By the Dormans, certainly. They could have told her she was an heiress. They could have let her know that she was not wholly dependent upon them. Fifty pounds was a great deal of money, enough for her clothing, pin money, food. She'd never been a burden on them.

Her stepfather—Anna could no longer think of him as her papa—could have told her, too. Why had he not if he'd truly cared for her?

Even her mother. Why had she not told Anna about her father and her grandparents long before she died?

And these grandparents she'd never known—they betrayed her, as well. They sent money after she was born, true, but they'd cruelly rejected her mother when she married her father. How her mother must have felt, no more than sixteen years old, to be shunned by her own parents? What if they had helped her instead? Maybe her father would not have had to stay in the army. Maybe he would not have had to go to India. Maybe he would still be alive. Her mother, too. Maybe she would not have caught the fever that took her life. Maybe Anna could have had a family who loved her.

And if her father had never died and her mother never married her stepfather, perhaps her stepfather could have found someone he truly loved. Maybe he would not have dallied with Will's mother and the duel would never have taken place. Perhaps Will's father would still be alive and Will would not have been so wounded.

She glanced at him. He was totally in control of the horses and was driving them skilfully through the busy traffic on the Strand. His expression was grim, though.

And why would it not be? Because of her he was trapped into a marriage that had been completely unnecessary.

Those days on the ride back to London were mere illusion. They were pretending they led other lives, lives without care, lives in which they could be happy, but all the while they'd not known the mistakes they were making.

The curricle pulled up to the Park Street townhouse. Will helped her down and she immediately rushed into the house. She passed the footman who attended the hall and hurried up the stairs to her bed chamber. The bed chamber that should have remained Will's mother's. She removed her shawl, her bonnet, and her gloves and flung herself onto the bed.

But she would not let tears fall. Some hurts were beyond weeping.

There was a knock at the door and Hester entered. 'Oh, my lady. Pardon me. I did not think you were napping.'

Anna sat up in the bed. 'I wasn't napping.'

Hester was clearly excited. 'I came to tell you that my cousin finished another dress and she has located several others for you to look at if you can come for fittings tomorrow.'

At least the search for a complete wardrobe was an exciting distraction. Even though she could have afforded three wardrobes if...if...

Anna blinked away those tears she refused to have fall. 'I am certain I can go to a fitting. Will you be able to accompany me?'

'Goodness.' Hester laughed. 'We'll merely tell Mrs White you need me.'

Anna managed a smile. 'Then let us go in the morning.'

Will sat at his desk and tried to look through the mail that had arrived that day. When he could not concentrate, he paced the room.

It was no use. He strode out of the library and into the hall.

'My hat and gloves,' he said to the footman. 'I'm going out.'

'Yes, m'lord.' The footman rushed off and returned in a trice. Will put them on. 'I shouldn't be gone long.'

He walked the few blocks to Henrietta Street and sounded the knocker at the Dorman townhouse.

When he was admitted by their butler, he demanded, 'I wish to see Lord Dorman.'

'One moment, m'lord,' the butler said.

Will cooled his heels in the hall until the man returned. 'Lord Dorman will see you.'

The butler led him to the same drawing room where Will and Anna had spoken to him before.

'Lord Willburgh,' the butler announced.

Will faced them all. Lord Dorman, Lady Dorman, Lucius, and Violet. None of them looked pleased to see him. None of them rose when he entered.

'What now, Willburgh?' Lord Dorman snapped.

'I have been to see Sir Edmund Antrobus at Coutts.' Will did not need to tell them Anna had come with him. 'I know what you have concealed from Anna all these years, what you knew when we called upon you before.'

Lucius laughed. 'Did I not tell you the elopement was foolish?'

Will glared at each of them in turn. 'Do you know how exceptionally cruel it is to have deprived Anna of her rightful inheritance? What sort of gentlemanly behaviour is that?'

Again it was Lucius who spoke. 'We did nothing of the sort. It was *you* who deprived her. By compromising her. By eloping with her. We tried to stop you. Why do you suppose I tore off to Scotland?'

'Do not say so, Lucius,' Will shot back. 'A word from any of you would have stopped it.' He turned his glare to Lord and Lady Dorman. 'And how badly done of you to conceal the truth of her fortune? She had a right to know. You made her believe she was accepting your charity. Her expenses were paid and you knew it.'

'She cost us more than a paltry fifty pounds!' Lady Dorman cried.

Violet laughed. 'It is such a joke, though, is it not? She was only a few short weeks from being rich.'

Lucius grinned at her.

Will regarded them all with disgust. 'I do not know more detestable people than you lot.'

Lord Dorman half rose. 'See here, Willburgh. I will not be insulted in my own house. You may leave.'

Will turned to go, but turned back again when he was in the doorway. 'I wonder how well a handbill will sell with the story of how Lord and Lady D fraudulently kept fifty pounds belonging to the trust when they knew Anna was married and they were not entitled to it?'

Lucius vaulted from his chair. 'You would not dare!'

Will gave them a sinister smile. 'Oh, wouldn't I? Give me the name of the printer you used for the handbills you had printed—'

'We won't tell you!' Lady Dorman was red-faced with anger.

Will kept his smile. 'Thank you for confirming that suspicion.'

'Why you—' Lucius came at him, but Will walked out before he even got close.

That evening Anna half expected Will to have arranged some meeting or other so he would miss dinner, but he didn't. She'd hoped to eat alone in her room again. She really did not wish to see him, to see the disappointment on his face. For marrying her.

Hester had convinced her to wear the new dress for dinner and to put her pearl earrings in her ears. It pleased the young woman, so Anna did as she requested. The dress was a Sardinian blue silk, but what Anna loved about it was that Hester's cousin had replaced the full sleeves with white satin inset with lace. She'd added matching lace to the neckline and at the hem. It was versatile as well, appropriate for afternoon or for less formal events such as the theatre or dinner parties.

Not that Anna expected to be invited to dinner parties.

Besides the fact that Will was not going out, the dinner was already planned. Mrs White had dutifully consulted with Anna on the menu that morning which meant, really, teasing out what dishes Cook wished to prepare.

Morning seemed so long ago. Before their visit to Coutts.

Will had just stepped out of the library door when Anna entered the hall.

'Will,' she said, feeling she must greet him.

'Anna,' he returned.

They walked into the dining room together. The long table had been set with a place at each end, far enough away from each other that Anna might as well have dined alone.

Will frowned when he saw it. 'This seems odd.'

When Anna dined with Will and his mother, they'd been seated on each side of Will who sat on the end.

Bailey was attending the room. 'Is there a problem, sir?'

Will twirled his finger. 'Move the settings so we sit closer to each other.'

Bailey moved Anna's place to a chair adjacent to Will's.

As soon as they sat, wine was poured and soup was served.

Having Bailey in the room and a footman bringing the food put even more of a damper on conversation than had become typical with them. What did they have to say to each other that they would not mind the servants knowing? Surely nothing about the fortune she'd lost.

How was she to ever get through this?

'Were—were you able to address the piles of papers on your desk?' she asked. Might as well pretend to be a viscount and viscountess having a quiet meal at home—Pretending worked so well on their ride back from Scotland.

'Everything urgent is done,' he replied.

They fell silent for a while, except for the sounds of their chewing and swallowing and the crackling of the chandelier above them.

Will looked up from his plate and took a sip of wine. 'Your dress is quite nice. One of the new ones?'

'It is,' she replied. 'Hester's cousin sent it over today.'

His brows rose. 'Hester's cousin is the modiste?'

'No, she is a seamstress,' Anna responded. 'She sews for a modiste, but she is helping me and, I must say, she's ingenious about it.'

'Is she?'

Anna did not have any illusions that Will was truly interested in dresses or the cousin of one of his maids, but she described how clever Hester's cousin was in gathering a brand-new wardrobe for her. It passed the time until the meal was almost done.

As they were finishing their pudding, Will said, 'Hester's cousin ought to have a business of her own. There must be others who need clothes quickly or at less cost.'

'She is very clever,' Anna agreed.

'Have Hester come speak to me,' he added. 'Perhaps her cousin merely needs some investment to get started.'

Anna gaped at him. He truly was an extraordinary man.

When the meal was done they retired to the drawing room for tea. As soon as Bailey left them after bringing in the tea service, Will went immediately to the cabinet in the corner of the room and took out the decanter of brandy. Tea simply would not do for him, not after the day they'd had.

He held up a glass and gestured an offer of brandy.

'Yes. Please,' she replied with feeling.

He poured them each a glass and handed hers to her before seating himself in a chair near hers.

This had been one horrible day. First the visit to Coutts, then the one to the Dormans. That had been foolish. Useless. Although he did confirm that they were behind some of the printing of the handbills.

That had not surprised him.

He should not have called on Dorman, but he'd been so angry

he had to do something. He needed to get a hold on his emotions or he'd never be clear-headed.

He glanced at Anna sipping her brandy, looking abstracted. No need to tell her about calling upon the Dormans and distress her more.

But he had to say something about what they'd been through. 'What Sir Edmund told us. It does not change anything.'

He meant he would still do his duty by her, try to make her life as pleasant as possible. He understood, though, that it must change how she felt about this marriage. About him. She must resent him for pushing the idea of marriage. How could she not?

She took another sip. 'It does change things,' she insisted. 'It makes everything worse.'

He had to agree with her. He'd not rescued her. He'd not saved her reputation. If he'd simply agreed to what she wanted—to live free from the Dormans—she'd have a fortune in a few weeks and then could do whatever she wished.

He finished his brandy and poured another one. 'If we had waited a few weeks...'

'You would be free,' she finished for him.

She had it wrong. 'No, you would be free,' Will said. 'You would be a wealthy heiress.'

Anna emptied her glass and extended it for Will to refill. She put it to her lips and let the amber liquid warm her mouth and chest.

She stared into her glass for a long moment before raising her eyes to his. 'What is it about me that no one saw fit to tell me about this will?'

He didn't answer, but she did not really expect him to.

She twirled the glass in her hand. 'I thought my stepfather cared about me. But if he did why did he not tell me I could be rich someday?'

'Perhaps he thought you were too young,' Will responded.

'I was ten. That seems old enough to me.'

'Perhaps he would have told you in time.' If he'd not first been killed by his father, she figured he meant.

It had been a long time since Anna had thought about that

and she'd rather not think on it now. 'Lord and Lady Dorman should have told me, then.'

He nodded. 'Indeed they should have.'

She fell silent, sipping her brandy. When she finished it, she placed the glass on the table next to her.

'No one was honest with me,' she said with feeling. 'My mother was not an orphan. I was not a charity case that the Dormans needed to care for. Even my pa—' She stopped herself when a sudden thought intruded. She turned to Will. 'Did my stepfather keep me with him because of the money?' Did he not care for her at all? Had anyone besides her mother cared for her?

Will looked at her with what seemed like sincere sympathy, but could Anna trust in him? Did he truly care for her or was he merely trying to be kind? He changed so unpredictably even before this revelation—that he need not have married her at all. It was nonsensical to believe he would not resent her.

An ache grew in her heart that all the brandy in the world could not soothe. She wanted him to love her. Desperately wanted it. Because he was truly the finest man she'd ever known and, briefly, she'd felt cherished and safe in his arms. As if she belonged with him always and yet their being together was merely a fluke. A mistake.

A mistake that need not have happened. She felt sick with grief. The magical life of her early childhood, her unhappy life as a Dorman, the illusion of a home with Will, all were lost to her. What was she to do?

Anna stood, unable to contain her emotions any longer and not wishing to impose them on Will. 'I should like to retire now. If you will excuse me.'

'Of course.' He rose to his feet and appeared for a second as if he thought he must accompany her. She did not want him to, not out of obligation.

She walked out alone.

Chapter Fourteen

The next day's visit to Hester's cousin was not as diverting as the one before, but Anna made an effort to hide the swirl of emotion that threatened to consume her. Odd how she could both actively engage about the dresses and, at the same time, puzzle out how she was to go on in her marriage.

These two young women were filled with enthusiasm about providing her with a wardrobe the likes of which neither of them could ever afford. Yet so much could go wrong for them. What if Will refused to pay for the dresses? What if he let Hester go without a reference? Will, of course, would do none of those dishonourable things, but other men did. Anna remembered Lady Dorman's modiste insisting on payment before making another gown for her. Or Lady Dorman nearly turning out one of the maids because Violet accused her of stealing an item Violet had merely misplaced.

Anna was so much luckier than they were. And luckier than many other women who'd been forced to marry. Will might not care for her; he might resent her, but he would never shirk his duty to her. She would always have everything she needed.

Except those glorious times when they were simply Mr and Mrs Willburgh.

She squared her shoulders and lifted her chin as Hester and

her cousin altered the dress to fit her. It was a muslin carriage dress in pale yellow with a matching spencer of corded silk. The lace that had festooned the original dress had been removed when Anna deemed it much too fussy.

After the fittings Anna and the two cousins visited several other shops and Anna purchased hats and gloves and scarves. Anna found a beautiful paisley shawl that Hester's cousin said would match all her new clothes. They even stopped at a shoe-maker's shop to order shoes and a bootmaker where Anna was measured for some very fine riding boots and walking boots.

By the time Anna and Hester returned to the townhouse, it was late afternoon and Anna had spent a great deal of Will's money. She'd taken him at his word and he'd better not complain.

They stepped into the hall, the poor footman tasked with carrying their packages stumbling in behind them.

Will appeared in the doorway of the library. 'I would speak with you, Anna.' He sounded grim.

Anna turned to the footman. 'Please take the packages up to the bed chamber.'

'I had better go with you,' Hester said to the young man.

She gave the footman attending the door her hat and gloves and followed Will into the library.

He didn't ask her to sit, but put a handbill into her hand.

'A new handbill. Out today,' he said.

She read it immediately.

The handbill spoke about how she had lost her inheritance by only a month by marrying Will. It went on to make up a story about a violent fight between the two of them because he'd caused her to lose a fortune.

She crushed a corner of it in her hand. 'How did they even know of this?' She looked down at the handbill again. 'They must have known we spoke with Sir Edmund. Would Sir Edmund have told them?'

Will had a pained expression. 'Not Sir Edmund. Me.'

'You?'

'I called upon Lord Dorman yesterday,' he admitted. 'They were all there. I didn't tell you—'

She searched his face. 'But, why? Why call upon them?'

He averted his gaze. 'I was angry at them for what they'd done to you.'

Or what they'd done to him, perhaps. Getting him trapped into marrying her.

She felt sick.

On her shopping spree, she'd seen boys hawking handbills. Were those handbills about her? She'd also spied people staring at her and whispering behind her back. Shopkeepers' brows rose in recognition when they learned her name.

It was discomfiting to be talked about, to have one's personal affairs exposed to all.

'I am sorry, Anna.' Will's voice turned low.

She tried to shrug it off. 'Nothing to be done about it now.'

'We should go to the country,' he said. 'Leave London. We never should have come here in the first place.'

She looked at him. 'What about your duties in Parliament?'

He paced in front of her. 'I'll have to shirk that responsibility. In any event, I might prove a distraction from the real work that must go on.'

Surely they were not that important.

'We can leave tomorrow morning,' he went on.

A full day in a carriage with him? Anna imagined silence between them. And distance, trying not to sit too close. Like that excruciating first day on the trip to Scotland.

Before she fell in love with him.

'Very well.' She spoke firmly. 'But I want to ride. I want to ride Seraphina.'

He seemed to consider the idea. 'Have you your new riding habit?'

She shook her head. 'I'll wear the old one. I do not care. They can print a handbill about it, if they like.'

'Very well,' he said. 'We'll ride the ponies. It is not more than forty miles. We should be able to reach Willburgh House before dinner.'

They rose at dawn and were ready to leave an hour later.

Anna suspected the town servants were happy to see them

go. She'd invited Hester to come with her and be her lady's maid, but Hester declined. She had family in London…and there was a certain footman in the house four doors away she had her eye on.

Anna would miss her.

Hester had mended and brushed her riding habit so that it looked as good as it could. Putting it on was like reuniting with an old friend. And like being enveloped in happy memories.

Hester promised to ship the new riding habit and all her new dresses to her when they were done. She had all the accessories they'd purchased and four dresses to take with her, including the blue one which could be worn at an evening party or even a ball. Anna did not think there would be any of those, though.

True to his word, Will rode his Highland pony even though Anna was certain he had a finer horse he could have ridden. Anna rode Seraphina and John accompanied them on the brown pony.

Just as they had done when leaving Scotland.

Will's coachman would carry both Anna's and Will's trunks as well as Bailey, the valet, and the two footmen. The other grooms, including Toby, would bring the curricle and the other horses Will had stabled in Town. Luckily Will said he and Anna needn't stay with the carriages. They could ride as freely as they'd done before.

Except the pall of reality shrouded the journey. They'd been run out of town by gossip.

It was nearly five o'clock by the time they reached the wrought iron gate that led to Willburgh House. When Anna had been a girl, she'd passed by this gate and glimpsed the house a few times. The Dormans had filled her ears with disparaging remarks about the unfashionable baroque architecture and inferior red brickwork which they said had been made on the estate itself.

John dismounted to open the gate and closed it again after they passed through. The avenue leading to the house was lined with lime trees standing like soldiers on review. Off to one side she glimpsed an octagonal dovecote. On the other side, she could barely see a small lake behind cultivated landscaping.

As Anna rode closer, the house appeared even more impressive. Certainly it was not of the classical style that Lady Dorman insisted was the height of good taste, but it had tall, paned windows in abundance, a lovely symmetry and its red brick showed well, with Corinthian pilasters setting off the centre of the house from the two wings at its side.

Will slowed until his horse was next to hers. 'You've seen the house before?'

'Not properly,' Anna responded.

'What do you think of it?' He sounded uncertain.

'It is very pleasing,' she answered honestly. And daunting.

A satisfied smile flitted across his face and he rode ahead again.

John followed a little behind Anna. 'That's a big house, m'lady.'

She turned her head to answer. 'It is indeed.'

They'd given no forewarning of their arrival so undoubtedly the household would be in a dither. Will's mother was supposed to be in residence. What sort of reception would Anna receive from her? Anna doubted it would be welcoming.

Shouting could be heard from the house as they rode closer. Servants began to pour out of the doorway and line themselves in order of precedence to receive the return of their viscount. And their new viscountess.

Her appearance was certainly not typical of a viscountess, in her worn, ill-fitting riding habit that she was so fond of. She hadn't thought ahead about it.

Too late for regrets.

Will rode up to the front of the house and one of the footmen promptly took the reins of his pony, giving the animal a quizzical look. A servant Anna assumed was an under-butler spoke to Will as she reached the house. The servants were all eyeing her, but trying not to appear to be doing so. Anna knew she looked a fright and the expressions on the maids confirmed it.

Will quickly took her in hand and presented his staff to her, their names washing through her mind like water through sand. How was she to remember them all?

One face was familiar. John's brother's wife, who smiled shyly at Anna.

'My double!' Anna shook her hand. 'It is good to see you again, Lottie. I hope you are well and happy here.'

The young woman's smile faltered. 'I am quite well, ma'am.' She did not answer Anna's second question.

John stood awkwardly with the ponies who seemed to receive the same disapproving looks as Anna had. Will noticed and introduced John to them.

He called over John's sister-in-law. 'Would you like to take John to your husband, Lottie? Tell the others that John is to care for these ponies.'

Anna's heart lurched. How good of him. To notice John. And to care.

He rejoined her at the door. The under-butler opened it and they entered a fine panelled hall, the painted ceiling two stories high depicting some classical scene and leading to an arcade of marble columns. But Anna could not take it all in. In the hall stood Will's mother looking like thunder and a very pretty young girl who looked sixteen. Will's sister, she presumed. Will walked straight to them.

'Mother.' He gave her a dutiful peck on the cheek.

'You could have let us know you were arriving today,' she complained.

'No, we could not,' he said casually, then turned to his sister with a grin. 'Hello, Lambkin.' He took her in his arms and swung her around. 'I've missed you.'

Anna approached Will's mother. 'How are you, Lady Will-burgh?'

The older woman looked her up and down, but rather than return the greeting, turned to her son. 'This is very inconvenient, Will. You have put the house in an uproar.'

'We do not require a fuss, Mother,' he responded, leading his sister over to Anna. 'Let me present you to my wife, Anna.' He presented his sister proudly. 'My little sister, Ellen.'

Anna, still stinging from Lady Willburgh's blatant rebuff, smiled. 'I am delighted to meet you, Ellen.'

'Why are you dressed that way?' Ellen asked, eyes wide.

It was so spontaneous and what everyone else must have wanted to ask that Anna laughed. 'These are the only riding clothes I had.'

'There is a tale about that,' Will interjected. 'We'll tell you all of it later.'

'Did you really elope to Gretna Green?' the girl asked.

'Not Gretna Green,' he responded. 'But we did elope to Scotland.'

The servants filed back in and hurried to their tasks. One footman held their saddlebags awaiting instructions. The housekeeper, whose name Anna could not remember, stood a few steps away. She was a formidable, thin-lipped woman with narrowed eyes that seemed to miss nothing.

'What rooms should we prepare, ma'am?' the housekeeper asked Lady Willburgh.

Will answered. 'We will occupy the lord and lady's chambers, Mrs Greaves.'

'As you wish, my lord,' she replied. 'It will take some time, though, to ready the lady's chamber. In what room do you wish us to put Lady Willburgh's belongings?'

'You mean the Dowager Lady Willburgh's belongings,' he corrected. 'Lady Willburgh's belongings will be placed in the lady's chamber.'

The housekeeper and Will's mother exchanged glances. 'I did understand you, sir.'

Anna was to displace Will's mother again.

Will blew out a breath. 'Really, Mother. Could you not have selected another room before this?'

She sniffed. 'I would have had you told us when you were coming.'

Anna broke into this. 'Please. At the moment all I need is a place to tidy myself and change clothes.'

'You may use my room,' Will's sister offered.

'Excellent idea, Ellen,' Will said. 'Will you show Anna where it is?' He gestured to the footman to follow them.

Ellen led her through the marble columns to an impressive oak staircase. 'My room is on the second floor,' she said. 'Mama's room—the one you will have—is on the first floor. They both face the garden, which you will like.'

When they entered her room, the huge windows revealed a lovely garden and park.

The footman waited at the doorway. 'Which...bag...m'lady?'

Anna indicated which was hers.

The footman brought it in and turned to leave.

'Would you summon my maid, please?' Ellen called after him.

One of the footmen helped Will change from his riding clothes to home attire. When he was done he asked the man to have his mother meet him in the parlour and to have tea served there. Now Will was seated in one of the more comfortable chairs in the parlour, eyes closed, weary from the long ride.

He heard his mother enter and rose.

'Really, Will,' his mother began. 'I am much put out with you, coming with no warning like this. This whole quagmire has taken a terrible toll on my nerves and it does not help that you spring all this on me without even a how do you do.'

Will was too weary for this. 'You make too much of it, Mother.'

She presented her cheek and he kissed it.

She glanced around and sighed. 'Do I need to ring for tea?'

He gestured for her to sit. 'I have already arranged it.' She selected a chair and Will sank back into his. 'Tell me how you have been,' he said. 'How are matters here?'

She fussed with her skirt. 'Well, it has been difficult to manage without Bailey. And Ellen has asked me why you had to marry if you had done nothing wrong. What was I to say?'

'What did you say?' he asked.

'Only that it would ruin all of us if you did not marry.'

'That was the truth of it.' Right. There had been some urgency to marry—to prevent the scandal from affecting Ellen. But they could have waited. Should have waited.

He certainly was not going to tell his mother that they need not have married at all.

His mother rubbed her brow. 'I cannot bear it that you had to

marry into *that* family?' She gestured in the general direction
of the Dorman property which abutted theirs, albeit acres away.

'Actually she is not a Dorman.' Perhaps it would ease his
mother's nerves to know this. 'She had a different father. Her
mother was widowed before marrying Dorman.'

She averted her face. 'That is not what he told me,' she said
in a barely audible voice.

'What did you say?' Will demanded.

She faced him. 'That is not what Bertram Dorman told me.
He said she was his daughter.'

The will proved her parentage, if necessary, but Will believed
Anna even before that.

He waved a hand. 'It does not matter. We are married and
we must make the best of it.'

'I know.' She sighed again. 'I just wish it were different.'

'We all wish it were different,' he said.

At that moment Anna and Ellen appeared in the doorway.
Anna's face told Will she'd overheard him.

He stood. 'Come sit, Anna. We've ordered tea.'

She nodded a greeting to Will's mother who said, 'Well, you
look better.'

Anna did indeed look better than the travel-weary rider she'd
been. She looked beautiful.

'Thank you for the compliment, Lady Willburgh,' Anna replied.

Will directed her to the sofa and he sat beside her, briefly
touching her hand as he did so. She moved her hand away.

Ellen sat facing them. 'You said you had a tale to tell about
eloping. Tell it now, Will!'

He glanced at Anna, not certain if she'd wish their story told.
He'd no intention of telling all of it anyway.

Not about their passion-filled nights and joyful days.

Anna's expression was impassive.

He was saved for the moment by the under-butler bringing
in the tea. Without consulting Anna, his mother poured for everyone.

Will took the opportunity to directly ask Anna. 'Shall I tell
of our adventure?' He tried to keep his voice light.

'As you wish,' she replied, giving away none of what she really might wish.

Still, Will went ahead and told the tale anyway, starting with how Lucius tried to stop them and how they foiled him.

'Do you mean that groom and maid that turned up here, when, honestly, we had no work for them? They pretended to be you? You let them wear your clothes?'

'They did a fine job,' Will insisted. 'It was not until Lucius saw them that he realised they were not us.'

'And you wore old clothes that were once worn by who knows who?' his mother continued sounding outraged.

Will ignored her and continued from where he left off, telling how they detoured to Langholm and how Armstrong, the innkeeper married them.

'Anna caught on right away,' Will said. 'But I confess, I was married before I even realised.'

Ellen laughed. 'So clever of you, Anna!'

His mother huffed. 'How dreadful! No proper vows at all. And in a tavern!'

'It suited us,' Will said. 'Did it not, Anna?'

Anna picked up her cup of tea for a sip. 'It was perfect,' she said. Her ring caught the light from a nearby lamp and sparkled. At least she was still wearing it.

'What is that on your finger?' his mother asked.

'My wedding ring,' Anna replied.

'You wore that ring in Scotland?' His mother sounded horrified.

'I bought it in London two days ago,' Will responded.

Ellen broke in. 'You didn't explain why you were riding today or where those funny horses came from.'

Will made a quelling gesture with his hand. 'We are just coming to that part of the story. And those are not "funny horses." Those are Highland ponies. I bought them so we could ride home.'

His mother shook her head. 'Who ever would want to ride that distance?'

Anna spoke up. 'It was my request. As was riding today.'

Will told about their riding back to London, which explained

Anna's riding habit, even though his mother continued to purse her lips in disapproval. Telling of those days filled him with melancholy. It brought back the pleasure of their nights together, the joyfulness of their days, and how freeing it had been to not be a viscount. Anna's head was bowed during this part of the story. Was she remembering too? Or was she thinking that she need not have married him and that he was responsible for all of London knowing why.

He glanced at his mother, the very picture of incivility. If he wanted to assign blame for them marrying so quickly, he could give some to his mother.

But he knew the blame rested on him.

At that moment the coach carrying their trunks and Bailey and the footmen arrived. Will excused himself to be certain all was in order.

'More commotion.' Lady Willburgh sighed and turned to Anna. 'I suppose we must find a maid to attend you, although I do not know who that will be. I assumed you would hire your own person from London.'

Anna did not miss the criticism in Lady Willburgh's statement. 'There was no time,' she explained.

She was still reeling from hearing Will's words—'*We all wish it were different.*' They should not have surprised Will's mother. The woman had always made it very clear she was not happy that Anna had to marry her son. Anna even wished she had not married Will, did she not?

No. What she wished was that they could again be simply Mr and Mrs Willburgh traveling from Scotland indulging their every whim.

Loving each other.

'Let her use my maid,' Ellen suggested.

Yet another sigh from Lady Willburgh. 'I suppose that will do, although it does put an extra burden on the girl.'

All Anna wanted at the moment was to be alone, unattended by anybody. 'I do understand that the unexpected nature of our arrival has created problems for you, Lady Willburgh. For that I am sorry, but I assure you, I do not need much assistance. I do not need to be moved into the lady's chamber right away. Any room will do.'

Lady Willburgh waved a dismissive hand. 'It is too late for that. Mrs Greaves already has the servants tearing my room apart.'

'At your son's direction,' Anna clarified. 'Not mine.'

Ellen passed the plate of biscuits to Anna who selected one.

'What was Scotland like?' Ellen asked. 'Did you meet Highlanders and Jacobites?'

'She has been reading novels,' Lady Willburgh explained in an exasperated tone.

Anna set her biscuit on her saucer. 'I do not know if we met any Highlanders. We were only in the Lowlands. We might have met a Jacobite or two.' Those, like Armstrong who disdained the English. 'But they did not say that they were. They seemed indistinguishable from the sort of people you would see in a tavern in England, except they spoke like Scotsmen.'

'I certainly hope *my* daughter does not see *anyone* in a tavern!' huffed the girl's mother.

Anna regarded Lady Willburgh over her cup of tea. Would she not say one favourable thing?

The woman was still a beauty, even as she must approach fifty years. Her full head of hair still had more blond in it than grey, and the only lines on her face were at the corners of her eyes. Her daughter had the same dark hair as her brother, but had inherited her mother's flawless skin and delicate features.

In contrast, Anna had always been told her own looks were 'passable'—this by Lady Dorman and Violet, primarily. Indeed, her hair could only be called brown and her features were too big for her face. And she was taller than was fashionable and lacked sufficient curves.

For this alone she could understand Lady Willburgh's disappointment in her. At least, though, she knew precisely where she stood with the woman. She surely could never be duped into thinking Lady Willburgh cared about her.

Unable to think of a polite way to escape, Anna asked Ellen what books she had read. Anna had read many of them and Ellen delighted in discussing all aspects of her favourite nov-

els, which seemed to include those of the author of *Waverley*.
No wonder she asked about Highlanders and Jacobites.

'Wait until you see our library,' Ellen exclaimed. 'There is
none like it in all of England!'

'I should like to see it,' Anna responded.

Ellen turned to her mother. 'Mama, may I show Anna the
library now?'

Lady Willburgh waved her hand. 'Do. I need some solitude
for my nerves.'

Chattering all the way, Ellen led Anna up the oak stairway to
a drawing room that was panelled with the same sort of wood
that was on the staircase. Once in the room Ellen stopped.

Anna looked for another doorway. 'Where is the library?'

'Here!' Ellen swept her arms to encompass the whole room.
She laughed at Anna's confusion and rushed around the room
somehow opening the panelling to reveal bookshelf after bookshelf.

Anna smiled. 'What a surprise!'

Ellen twirled around. 'It is my favourite room.'

Anna thought it might become her favourite room, as well.
She was reasonably certain that Lady Willburgh did not spend
much time here. The room also seemed to be absent a desk—
unless it, too, was hidden behind panelling—so Will probably
did not spend much time here either. And if Ellen was her only
company?

At least she did not convey disappointment or disapproval.

Chapter Fifteen

Will's valet could be trusted to unpack for him, but he thought he ought to make certain Anna's trunk would be taken care of. He doubted his mother would do it. He'd hardly said more than two words to the housekeeper about it before his estate manager sent word that he needed to speak to Will urgently.

The manager's office was in an outbuilding. Will took the back stairs and went out one of the doors leading to the garden. He crossed the lawn to the building. The door was open and he saw the manager seated at a desk, looking at a paper.

'Parker?' Will entered the office. 'You need to speak to me?'

Parker, a robust man with thinning hair and a restless energy, was only a few years older than Will. His father had been estate manager when Will's father was alive and his son learned the job at his side.

He rose and strode over to Will, extending his hand to shake. 'Good to see you, Will. I hear you've managed to scandalise all of London and get married. My best wishes to you and your wife.'

Will accepted his hand, the informality normal between them. They'd grown up together as boys and Parker had always looked out for the younger Will.

Parker went on, 'My apologies for asking for you when

you've hardly set foot in the place, but there are a few things that best not wait.'

They sat while Parker detailed several problems and they discussed the solutions and made the needed decisions. That done, Will rose to leave and Parker walked with him to the doorway.

'One more thing,' Parker said. 'I thought I'd give you warning. Jones and Keen have complained to me that they do not know what to do with now two new grooms, since you brought another one today.'

Jones was the stable master; Keen, the head groom.

Why was this so difficult? 'Surely there is enough work to keep two more men busy. There are three new horses to tend, after all.'

'Seems that one of the men heard that Adams and his wife came from Lord Dorman's London house to cause trouble here.' Parker explained.

Will pressed his hand on his forehead. 'That is nonsense. Who would say such a thing?'

'I wouldn't be surprised if it was one of the Dorman servants who told him that,' Parker said. 'They've heard all the London gossip just as we have.'

Will shook his head. 'It could not be further from the truth. John, Adams, and Lottie prevented Lucius Dorman from thwarting the elopement.'

Although if Lucius had succeeded, then Anna would have been able to inherit her fortune.

'Walk with me to the stables,' Will asked. 'I'll speak to Jones and Keen.'

They walked the distance to the stables where there was plenty of activity since the carriages and horses had arrived. Will noticed right away that the Highland ponies were unnecessarily tucked away in the farthest stalls. He could just glimpse John and Adams tending to them. Toby was sitting nearby.

Will strode through the stable to purposely greet the two brothers, Parker in tow. Will did not bother to ask how they were settling in, because he knew the answer. Instead he asked Adams if the accommodations for him and his wife were adequate.

'They'll do, sir,' the young man said unenthusiastically.

'They were given a room above the stables,' John said. 'It's separate from the other men, but only by a wall.'

Will turned to Parker and frowned. 'That was the best you could do?'

'I left it to Keen, sir,' the manager said.

'Well, we must do better,' Will insisted. 'Find them a little cottage. I know we have some vacant.'

'Yes, sir,' Parker said.

'Thank you, sir,' Adams said.

Keen, apparently having heard that the Viscount was in the stables came bustling through. 'Welcome back, sir,' the man said.

Will did not mince words. 'I do not like what I see here, Keen, nor what I've heard. I expect these two men and Adams's wife to be treated in a fair manner. They are not spies from the Dorman estate. Quite the reverse.' Will inclined his head towards Toby. 'Toby can tell you all that they have done for me and for my wife. I expect you to make certain every man knows the truth.' Will did not usually show his anger so plainly. 'If in the future there are any rumours about the Dormans or about my workers, I want to be informed immediately.'

Before he walked out, he made certain to shake Adams's hand and to clap John on the back. He knew every worker in the stables was watching him and he wanted them to know these two men were in his favour.

Will and Parker went on to the carriage house and imparted the same information to Jones, the stable master. When Will finally returned to the house it was time for dinner. He didn't feel like changing clothes for dinner, but did not want to risk coming to the table smelling like horse.

His valet helped him make quick work of dressing for dinner. Afterwards he knocked on the door connecting his room to the lady's chamber, hoping to find Anna. When there was no answer, he opened the door and entered the room.

It appeared that all his mother's things had been removed, but Anna's trunk still sat in the middle of the room. Had it even been unpacked? Will did not want to snoop that far.

Instead he went to the drawing room where his mother typically waited for dinner to be announced. Anna was there. And his mother.

He greeted them all and walked over to the carafe of claret. He noticed Anna did not have a glass.

'Would you like some claret, Anna?' he asked.

'I would,' she responded.

He poured and handed the glass to her.

He turned to his mother. 'Mother?'

'I have some.' She lifted her glass.

He frowned as he poured his own claret. Had his mother not offered any to Anna?

He went to sit by her. 'I was called away,' he said. 'How has it been for you?'

He hoped to hear that his mother had graciously shown her around or had made certain her room was readied for her.

Instead Anna said, 'Your sister was kind enough to show me your library. Very unusual.' Her tone was polite. Disguising much.

He was dismayed. 'Yes. It is unique. You must feel free to treat it as your own.' He wanted her to feel welcome. She was bound to him. He had spoiled her chances to determine her own fate, had she become an heiress. It was his duty to do right by her.

He hated being so formal with her. They'd not been formal at all on their ride back from Scotland. He wanted to tell her what was on his mind—how John and Adams and Adams's wife were treated for one thing—but it felt like a wall between them, one made of molasses perhaps because he felt like he could slog through it with time and effort.

At least he hoped so.

Ellen came rushing in. 'Am I late? I was afraid I would be late.'

She and Will did a pantomime of her asking for claret and him pouring her only a short glass.

Their mother took a sip of her wine. 'Had Betty been delayed in helping you?'

Ellen looked puzzled. 'No. Why would she be?'

'I thought—' She inclined her head towards Anna. 'I thought she might have been busy.'

'Oh,' Ellen exclaimed. 'Anna said she did not need Betty.'

Their mother lifted a brow. 'Indeed?'

Anna smiled graciously. 'As you can see, I did not change clothes so I needed no maid.'

Their mother formed a stiffer smile. 'I did notice.'

Bailey appeared at the door. 'Dinner is served in the dining room.'

'The dining room?' Will was baffled. 'For only the four of us?'

His mother stood. 'I thought you would desire a formal dinner for your first...' Her voice trailed off so he didn't know to what *first* she was referring.

He offered Anna his arm and she accepted it. If his mother wished to be formal than he would lead the party to the dining room with Anna on his arm. His mother and sister would need to follow.

In the dining room the long table was set oddly, with Will and Anna at each end and his mother and Ellen on each side at the table's centre. At least it seemed odd to Will, because conversation was more difficult, nearly impossible between Anna and him. So the dinner was a stress to him and he worried that it was even worse for Anna. If not for Ellen's conversation, it would have been unbearable.

After dinner Will hung back while Anna, his mother, and Ellen retired to the drawing room for tea.

He stayed only to speak with Bailey. 'The table setting was not comfortable. It put us all at a distance from each other.'

'It was as your mother requested,' Bailey explained.

'I realise that,' Will said. 'But we do not need the long table.'

'I offered to remove some of the leaves, but your mother—'

Will put up his hand. 'Say no more. I understand. But do remove the leaves for tomorrow's dinner. We do not need them unless we have guests.'

'It will be done, sir.' Bailey bowed.

Will left to join the others in the drawing room, but only his mother and Ellen were there.

'Where is Anna?' he asked.

Ellen answered him. 'She begged off, saying she was fatigued from the journey.'

He was losing patience with his mother's unwelcoming treatment of Anna. 'I hope you sent Betty to attend her.'

'She said she did not need Betty tonight,' his mother responded.

He sat facing his mother. 'You need to be more cordial to Anna, Mother. No matter what you wish, I am married to her and she is my wife. This will not change.'

'I am very cordial to her,' his mother protested.

'No, you are not,' he countered. 'I expect you to do better.'

His mother pursed her lips and did not respond.

'I'll do my best,' Ellen added.

He had not been faulting her. He smiled at her. 'I know, Lambkin. I can count on you.'

He stood and excused himself.

His valet was surprised that he had come to the room so early. Will told him he wished to retire. When the man finally left, Will went to the door connecting his room with Anna's. He opened it a crack.

The room was dark and it was clear she was in bed.

He closed the door again and returned to his room.

The next morning Anna woke early and, having no confidence that a maid would come to assist her, dressed herself. She made her way down to where she supposed the breakfast room would be, somewhere near that small sitting room she'd seen when first arriving.

A footman with a dour expression pointed to the proper room. She entered and was the only one there.

After a couple of minutes the footman reappeared. 'Breakfast is still being prepared, ma'am. We are not accustomed to serving so early.'

Goodness. Did she hear disapproval in the footman's voice? 'I am well able to wait,' she responded, her tone sharper than usual. 'I will learn these things in time, but this is my first morning here.'

Which ought to have been obvious to the young man.

He did not respond directly to the statement but asked, 'Would you like tea or coffee?'

'Tea, please.'

She expected him to ask what she preferred for breakfast, but he bowed and left.

It seemed like she waited a lot longer for tea than she had even at the Dormans' when it was only her making the request. She was considering going on a search of the kitchen when the door opened and Will entered.

He looked surprised to see her. 'Good morning.'

'You've been riding.' She could tell. He carried the scent of the out of doors on him.

'I have,' he admitted. 'I usually ride in the morning when here. Take a look at the land.'

He might have asked her to ride as well, knowing how much she loved it. She averted her gaze, not wanting to reveal her disappointment.

He glanced around the room and frowned. 'Has no one seen to your breakfast?'

'One of the footmen is seeing to it.' She did not tell him that she'd been waiting nearly half an hour.

One moment later the door opened and in came footmen carrying warming dishes of red herring, baked eggs, and sausages, bowls of porridge, and plates of bread and cheese. One footman brought a pot of coffee, cream, and sugar and poured for Will. Last came Anna's tea. The under-butler asked Will what he wished to be put on his plate.

'Serve Lady Willburgh first,' Will told him.

The man dutifully asked Anna.

'Bread and cheese and an egg, please,' she responded.

When they both were served, the servants left and they were alone.

Will leaned towards her. 'How was your night, Anna?'

Lonely, she wanted to say.

But if she revealed how much she yearned for him next to her in bed, he might do so out of duty. She had no wish to be bedded out of obligation.

'I slept well enough,' she answered perfunctorily.

'You retired early,' he went on. 'I feared you might be ill.'

She felt many things—lonely, estranged, unwelcome. Angry—but not ill. 'No,' she told him. 'I am not ill.'

They ate in silence until Will said, 'You know if there is anything you need, you have merely to ask?'

Ask who? she wondered. The servants? His mother? Him? At least if she asked him, he would see to it. It would be his duty.

Very well. She would ask. 'I would like a tour of the house and grounds. So I know my way about.' And she would not have to wander around to find where she was supposed to go. 'Who should I ask to show it to me?'

He didn't answer right away. 'I will give you the tour.'

She'd expected him to assign Bailey to the task, not himself. She did not know what to say.

'We can begin after breakfast,' he went on. 'If that suits you.'

Heaven help her, she could not resist his company even if he offered it out of duty. Even if he was *disappointed* she was here at all.

When they were finished eating, Will stood and extended his hand to help her up. 'Where would you like to start?'

His tone turned stiff and formal, but the warmth of his hand in hers seeped through her whole body. She was disturbed by this visceral reaction.

'You know the house,' she managed.

'We'll start on this floor, then.'

He walked her through the sitting room where they'd first gathered with Lady Willburgh and Ellen, to another sitting room, to the dining room where he told her about the ancestors whose portraits were on the wall. He pointed out that the huge painting of fruits and nuts, oysters, and a lobster was by a Flemish artist and had been in the family for over a hundred years.

On the other side of the hall was a drawing room that led to another room filled with classical statues and a bust of Pitt and other important men. Beyond the sculpture room was Will's office.

'My duties require me to spend a great deal of time here,' he said.

The room was dominated by a large desk stacked with papers and ledgers. Behind the desk were shelves of books and other ledgers. It was saved from looking dismal by the large windows opening onto the beautiful garden outside and two comfortable chairs facing the fireplace. Above the fireplace was a portrait of a young man with powdered hair and a blue velvet coat with a red collar. She stared at it. It resembled Will.

'My father,' Will muttered, turning away from it.

She wished she hadn't stared at it. The mood grew sombre instead of merely stilted.

'Shall we tour the first floor?' Will strode to the doorway.

Anna hurried after him.

He explained who the portraits were on the stairway. There were four. His grandparents. His mother—dazzlingly beautiful as a young woman—and another of his father, older this time. Would Will look as stern as this, in ten or twenty years?

She'd seen the drawing room before, of course, but Will pointed out some special family items there. A Pembroke table and some ribbon-back chairs, both by Chippendale and acquired by his grandparents. This most formal room had the plasterwork and pale colours of years ago when Robert Adam's neoclassical style was popular. The Dormans had preferred the more modern furnishings, brighter colours on the walls and fabrics, tables and cabinets of ebonised wood or embellished with gold paint or Egyptian details.

They toured the library. She thought Will almost looked pleased that it captivated her. There was also a lovely music room brightened by the windows with a pianoforte, a harp, and a chest she presumed held sheets of music.

'Do you play?' he asked.

'A little.' She'd learned along with Violet, but never had as much time to practice as she wished.

'Use it whenever you like.'

He showed her his room, but he said little about its adornments or furniture. For some reason, Anna felt the spectre of his father strongly there. She wondered if he'd moved into the room without changing what his father had left.

They walked through the connecting doorway to her room.

He glanced at the bare walls. 'There were paintings I wanted to tell you about, but my mother has had everything taken out of the room.' He frowned. 'I'll have some more paintings brought in to be hung. There are several in the attic.'

'May I select them?' Anna asked.

He looked surprised she'd asked. 'Of course.' He then noticed her trunk, still in the middle of the room where the footman had left it.

'What is your trunk doing here? Did you not call for a footman to take it away?'

'It is not unpacked yet,' she responded.

He countered in a chiding tone. 'You must ask the maids who attend you to unpack for you and see the trunk stored away.'

'No maid attended me,' she replied.

'Why not?' He sounded disapproving.

'Betty was assigned the task, but I did not want her to do it,' she told him.

'Why?'

'It was clear she found it a burden.'

'*She* found it a burden?' He turned to face her. 'You are the Viscountess, Anna. They are employed to meet your needs.'

'Really, Will,' she shot back, annoyed now. 'My first days here I should order the servants about?'

'Unpacking your trunk was hardly an unreasonable demand,' he responded.

Should she tell him that the servants already displayed a reluctance to help her, if not animosity towards her? Following his mother's lead, no doubt.

'I prefer to tread carefully,' she said instead.

He shrugged but added. 'You need a lady's maid to attend you.' He still sounded as if he was admonishing her.

She agreed. 'I do, but I should very much want a lady's maid to want to serve me.'

They left this room to go up to the second floor. Muffled voices came from one bed chamber.

Will inclined his head towards that door. 'My mother.' There was an edge to his voice. 'That is the room she selected. It used to be mine.'

The door to a different room opened and the maid, Betty, appeared. She sent a guilty glance towards Anna and Will before disappearing around the corner.

'The servants' stairs are back there,' Will explained.

Ellen walked out of the room Betty had left and stopped abruptly upon encountering them. 'Good morning! What are you doing?'

Will gave her a playful, endearing hug, making Anna's heart ache. Towards his sister, he acted like her old Will. 'I'm showing Anna the house, Lambkin.'

Anna smiled. 'The grand tour.'

'Oh.' The girl's brow creased. 'I am famished or I'd come with you.'

'Join us later,' Anna told her. Ellen was the only person in the household with whom Anna felt welcomed.

'I will!' Ellen hurried to the stairs.

Will smiled as he watched her disappear, then his expression sobered. 'Shall we continue?'

Was showing her the house merely another chore for him? He seemed to be taking little pleasure in it. Or was it her company he disliked?

Perhaps he could not get over the disappointment of marrying her when he had not really needed to.

They toured the children's wing and some guest bedrooms. He pointed to the door leading to the servants' rooms at the top of the house.

'That is about everything.' He headed back to the stairway.

All? 'What about below stairs? The kitchen and the rooms around it?'

His brows rose. 'You want to see that? My mother never goes down there.'

Lady Dorman never went down to the kitchen either. 'I would like to see it.' Anna wanted to know what the servants' areas were like.

'Let us use the servants' stairway, then.'

Chapter Sixteen

They reached the lower level of the house where the servants' hall, the kitchen, scullery, still room, housekeeper's room, butler's pantry, and such were located.

Will greeted each servant they encountered by name and presented them to Anna. Anna was certain each one of them greeted her suspiciously and with disfavour.

Mrs Greaves, the housekeeper, appeared and stuck to them like a plaster to a wound. She was deferential and cordial to Will, but cool and curt with Anna, and her demeanour was mirrored in all the others they encountered.

Did Will notice? She was not sure he had.

When they toured the laundry, which was in a wing off the kitchen, Anna found Adams's wife there. 'Lottie! I am surprised to see you in the laundry. I thought you worked in the house.'

Lottie curtsied. 'Mrs Greaves moves me around, ma'am.'

Will's brows furrowed. 'Is this the best place for you? What work did you do in the inn?'

'Tended the rooms, mostly, sir,' she responded. 'I helped serve in the tavern some, as well.'

'But not the laundry?' he asked.

'No, sir. Not the kitchen either.'

He touched her arm in a reassuring manner. 'I am certain

the house needs you more than the laundry. We will speak to Mrs Greaves.'

'Thank you, sir.' She curtsied again.

He nodded in acknowledgment. 'Did your husband tell you we are locating a cottage for you?'

'We are grateful, sir.'

'What was that about a cottage?' Anna asked him when they left the laundry.

'I was not satisfied with the rooms they were given over at the stable,' was all he said.

They walked up the stairs and back to the hall.

Will gestured towards the door. 'I must meet with Parker, my estate manager, who is in one of the outer buildings. He is expecting me.'

'Do those buildings include the stables?' she asked. 'I would like to know how to find the stables.'

He hesitated. 'You can accompany me, then.'

'Thank you,' she replied. 'I will just get my hat and shawl?'

'I'll wait here.'

Anna dashed up the stairs and retrieved her shawl, still packed in the trunk in her room. She put on her hat and was out the door again, approaching the stairs.

Voices sounded from the floor above. Anna stepped out of sight.

It was Lady Willburgh. 'Remember, she is a Dorman and can be up to no good for us here.'

'Do not fear, my lady,' Mrs Greaves responded. 'We will take our direction from you.'

Anna's stomach dropped. She had suspected Lady Willburgh wanted to make her feel unwelcome. To what end? What choice did any of them have that she was here? Certainly Anna had none.

A wave of loneliness washed over her. She was the outsider here just as she'd been the outsider at the Dormans'.

Ellen seemed happy enough to have her here, but Anna would not ever put that sweet child in the middle of this muddle. The only others she knew—John, his brother, and wife—possessed even less power than she. Anna would not risk them being damaged, not after they'd helped so.

No, she was alone, as alone as she had ever been.

She listened to be sure Mrs Greaves and Lady Willburgh had retreated and, squaring her shoulders, strode back down the stairs.

Will paced the hall waiting for Anna.

Why had he volunteered to show her the house? He had mounds of work to do and he was already late to see Parker.

He simply could not resist the chance to spend time with her. He was proud of his house, his heritage and it did not want to cede the pleasure of showing it off to her to anyone else. But they were so distant from each other, as if a wall had been erected between them that was too high and too thick to breach.

That news about her lost trust sounded a death knell on their marriage.

He should tell himself it was good they were distant. He could get his work done then.

But watching her descend the stairs with that special grace of hers took his breath away. She was strong, not delicate and did not pretend to be otherwise. Her lovemaking had been strong, as well. It aroused him to think of it and he thought of it far too often.

Like right now.

'I'm ready,' she said as she reached the bottom step and wrapped the shawl around her.

He offered his arm, knowing he'd be affected by her touch. 'We can leave by the garden door. It is quicker.'

When they stepped out into the fresh country air, Will was proud anew at the beauty his grandfather and father created in the gardens and grounds. A great expanse of green lawn, a formal garden behind the house, and pathways leading to the picturesque gardens beyond.

'What do you think, Anna?' he asked.

'About the gardens?' She took in the view. 'Lovely.'

'Perhaps tomorrow I'll give you a proper tour of them.' Could they find in that cultivated wilderness a respite from what separated them? Could he get over himself? He feared he was the wall between them.

The outer buildings were beyond the gardens and the stables, past them.

She'd been quiet through most of the walk, but suddenly spoke. 'You told Lottie that *we* will speak to Mrs Greaves on her behalf. I hope you meant you would do it.'

That was what was on her mind? 'I will, if that is what you wish.'

'Good. Mrs Greaves will have to listen to you.'

Will had chided Anna about not seeking the servants' assistance, but when they toured below stairs, he noticed how the house servants reacted to Anna. If they believed Anna was a Dorman spy like they'd thought of the Adamses, he'd have to set them straight.

Anna went on. 'I want to look for a lady's maid for myself from outside the household. Perhaps from some agency in London.'

He thought that was best, too. 'Whatever makes you happy.'

She averted her face but not before he spied a cynical smile on her lips.

'Will! Anna!' Ellen ran to catch up to them. 'Did you finish the tour of the house?'

'We did,' Will said. 'I'm on my way to meet Parker.'

Ellen turned to Anna. 'Would you like me to show you the garden? I'll wager I can show you places Will doesn't even know about.'

'I'll wager you can't,' Will quipped.

'Will was going to introduce me to the estate manager and show me the stables,' Anna said.

'Oh, you can meet Parker any time.' She pulled on Anna's arm. 'Let me show you the garden, then we can go to the stables.'

Anna had the grace to turn to Will raising her brows in question.

'Go with Ellen,' Will said, disappointed to lose her, even though he ought to be relieved. He could get back to work. 'I'll see you both at dinner.'

* * *

That evening dinner was a bit more comfortable for Anna. For one thing, the table had been made smaller so she was not banished to the far end.

When Lady Willburgh saw the room, though, she'd exclaimed. 'Who did this? The room is unbalanced with the table that way!' She shot a scathing look towards Anna.

But Will answered, 'I ordered it, Mother. As long as it is only the four of us dining, it stays this way.'

His mother had pursed her lips, but she said no more. Ellen, who was becoming more dear to Anna, carried the conversation again, chattering about her and Anna's tour of the garden and asking Anna all kinds of questions about her impression of the house.

Lady Willburgh asked Will about Lottie and if it was his place to involve himself in the running of the house. Obviously she'd heard from Mrs Greaves of his request that Lottie be used in the house. Will answered that as long as he was Viscount he could involve himself wherever he wished.

Lady Willburgh said little after that and was quiet even when they'd finished dinner and had retired to the sitting room for tea.

'Play cards with me, Anna,' Ellen begged.

After some hesitation, Anna replied, 'Oh, very well. What do you want to play?'

Ellen opened a baize-covered card table. 'Piquet?'

'Piquet.' Anna pulled up a chair. 'Although I warn you I am not very good at it.

It did not help that Will watched them while he sipped his brandy. It made her heart beat faster and she lost attention to the cards.

After losing the second game to Ellen, Anna declared a desire to go to bed. 'Before I lose another,' she said, smiling.

Will stood. 'I'll go with you.'

Her heart skittered even faster.

As they walked up the stairs, he asked, 'Do you want a maid to attend you?'

'It isn't necessary,' she responded. Actually she'd rather he helped her, like he'd done in those first days of their marriage.

'I promise we'll find a lady's maid for you,' he went on. 'I'll write to an agency tomorrow.'

She thought she would be the one writing.

He opened her door but stopped her from going in right away. 'May I come to you later?' he asked softly.

She searched his face. His eyes looked sincere and a bit wary. 'If you wish,' she replied, wary as well.

They made love that night, but in a sad way, it seemed to Anna. As if they both mourned the loss of joy they'd once shared together. Their pleasure came, though, but to Anna it seemed melancholy. Still, she wanted him in her bed. Perhaps with time they could regain some of what they'd lost.

The next morning Anna woke when the first light of dawn was peeking over the horizon. Will was gone.

Her spirits plummeted. Once again she'd let herself believe he cared about her, but once again she was alone. Was he using her like a bandalore, reeling her in, then rolling her away, over and over?

She rose from the bed and donned her riding habit. She plaited her hair and tucked it into the old hat she'd worn on the travels. The footman attending the hall was dozing. She did not wake him but walked past him and through Will's office to the doors to the garden.

A milky mist carpeted the lawn and swirled at her feet as she hurried to the stables, hoping at least one of the grooms was awake. When Ellen showed her the stables she merely pointed to them; they never walked close to them.

The doors to the stable were open and, to her relief, several grooms were at work. She spied John and hurried over to him.

'Could you saddle Seraphina for me?' she asked.

The other grooms eyed her curiously—or perhaps suspiciously. When Seraphina was saddled and ready, John helped Anna mount her. Anna leaned over and hugged the pony's neck.

'I am so glad to be riding you,' she whispered.

As she rode out, Will walked in.

'Anna!' He looked surprised.

She took in a breath. He was at his most handsome, in comfortable riding clothes and boots, almost like he'd dressed on their travels. And the sight of him brought back the night before, the lovemaking she'd so desperately missed.

She blinked, unable to meet his eye. 'Good morning, Will.'

He paused before responding. 'Wait. I'll ride with you.'

Every morning the next week Anna rose early to ride. Sometimes Will rode with her. She never waited for him, but, more often than not, he left the house when she did and they walked together to the stables. They rode together, then, too, rarely talking more than necessary. For Anna, though, it increased the pain. Riding together had once been her delight, but now a reminder of what must have been an illusion.

It was clear to her he rode with her out of obligation, what was expected of him.

He no longer joined her at night, which only intensified the pain.

His days were busy otherwise and she rarely saw him after breakfast until dinner. Lady Willburgh and Mrs Greaves continued to run the household without involving her and any time Anna tried to broach the subject with her mother-in-law, she was put off. Lady Willburgh often kept Ellen busy at her side, as well.

So during the day, Anna was very much alone. She occupied herself by reading or walking in the garden. Or tidying her room, because she did not have a lady's maid and had not yet received a response from the agency she'd written to.

Anna was accustomed to taking care of herself, so this was not a huge hardship. Requesting the service of a maid when she needed one continued to be difficult. Her requests were never promptly filled unless Lottie was available, but Lottie could do little more than clean her room and take her clothes to the laundry and bring them back.

A trunk carrying her new clothing from London had arrived the day before. Anna had not fully unpacked her first trunk and she debated whether she should make a fuss to be given some help in unpacking this new one. This one included her new riding habit. Discovering it made her rather sad.

She was laying the riding habit across her bed when Will stuck his head in the doorway. 'I have an errand in the village. Is there anything I might do for you there?'

She closed the trunk's lid. 'I would like to come along.'

He paused as he always did when she asked for something from him. 'Very well. I am leaving within half an hour.'

Anna made certain she was ready on time and soon they were on the road in the curricle, with Toby riding on the back. Anna had not visited the village since the scandal and elopement. She supposed the villagers knew all about it. They certainly knew more about the generational feud between the Willburghs and the Dormans than did members of the *ton* in London.

She sighed at the thought of facing them.

Will noticed. 'What is it, Anna?'

She regretted revealing that much to him. 'Nothing of consequence. The villagers know me and will have knowledge of all the gossip.'

He glanced at her. 'Perhaps they will simply wish us well.' He turned his eyes back to the road. 'They will also want the Viscountess to spend money in their shops.'

Oh, yes. She carried a title now. One would not know it by how it was for her at Willburgh House.

The village was about five miles from Willburgh House and it took them less than an hour to reach the familiar streets and buildings that she had not seen since accompanying the Dormans to London months ago. Will stopped the curricle in front of the mercantile shop. Toby hopped down and held the horses. Will helped Anna climb down. She left him to his errands and entered the mercantile shop.

The shopkeeper there knew her from when she lived with the Dormans. He was welcoming and eager to assist her. Other customers in the shop nodded politely and did not leer or whisper behind her back as they had in London. But then, she was the Viscountess Willburgh, the highest-ranking woman in the area.

After making her purchases in the mercantile shop, Anna walked towards the milliner. She needed a hat with a wide brim to shield her face from the sun when she took her walks. The village milliner always had such hats for sale.

Before she reached the shop, she spied a familiar figure seated on a bench, her head in her hands.

'Mary?' Mary was Violet Dorman's lady's maid, the maid who'd been so helpful in packing her things that awful day.

The young woman looked up. 'Oh, Miss Anna!' She dissolved into tears.

Anna sat down next to her. 'What troubles you? Tell me.'

If Mary was in the village, then the Dormans were back in the country. Anna was not happy about that. It also meant that Violet was near.

The maid leaned against Anna as she wept. Passers-by were noticing and looked concerned, but Anna could not worry about that now.

Finally Mary spoke with shuddering breaths. 'Miss Dorman gave me such a scold! She pushed me out of the shop and told me to stay out of her way!'

Anna had seen many of Violet's outbursts. It used to be her task to calm Violet down.

'I—I tripped and knocked against her,' Mary said. 'I did not mean to!'

'Of course you did not,' Anna responded soothingly. 'She should not have lost her temper with you.'

'She is losing her temper all the time now!' cried Mary. 'They all are! I wish you were back, Miss Anna. It was better when you were there. Now all they do is yell at each other! I hate it there! I don't want to go back!'

Mary was distraught or she would never be saying such things to anyone, especially Anna—Anna who was now in the enemy camp. Mary never talked about the family. Anna was fond of her. She was young but sweet-tempered and talented at her job. She loved clothes and hairstyles and all of it.

'I wish you were still there, Miss Anna.' The maid whimpered.

Anna put an arm around her. 'It is Lady Willburgh now, you know.'

Mary straightened. 'I beg your pardon, miss—I mean— ma'am.'

An idea was forming in Anna's mind, one that grew stronger by the moment.

She faced Mary. 'What if—? What if you came to Willburgh House? I am in need of a lady's maid. You could work for me.'

The young woman's jaw dropped. 'Me? Work for the Willburghs?'

Anna knew what she meant. They'd all been trained to consider the Willburghs the enemy.

'It might be difficult at first,' Anna admitted. 'The servants will see you as a Dorman. They will not be welcoming, but there is one young woman there who is also new and she will look out for you. As will I.'

Mary gaped at her. 'Do you think I could?'

'I would like you to work for me.' That was the truth. It would be like having an ally there.

Mary's eyes grew wide. 'Will it not cause trouble?'

Anna laughed. 'A great deal of trouble in both households, but you know I will not scold you or push you and I will not let the others in the house mistreat you. Lord Willburgh will deal with any fuss the Dormans make. They cannot force you to stay.'

The young woman glanced away and back again. This time her expression appeared resolved. 'I'll sneak away and walk to Willburgh House. Do you not think that a good plan?'

'We will have to follow up with a letter, but that will work well enough.' Anna hoped anyway. 'Come whenever you can.' Anna stood. 'Now I am off to the milliner.'

Mary's expression turned grave. 'Miss Dorman is in there.'

Anna patted her hand. 'All the better.'

Anna did encounter Violet in the hat shop. The shop girls took notice.

Anna decided to be cordial. 'Good day, Violet. I hope you are well.'

Violet's eyes flashed before she turned away without a word.

The cut direct. Anna expected no less from Violet, who no longer outranked her. If that did not put Violet in a rage then certainly stealing her lady's maid would.

Yes, Violet would be in a rage.

Chapter Seventeen

～～～～

Will finished his errands and waited with the curricle. He, of course, had been treated well by the villagers. He could only hope that Anna experienced the same.

His senses flared when he saw her approach, laden with packages, her face glowing with excitement, wearing something he'd not seen much of lately. A smile.

Her smile fled when she saw him. 'Am I late?'

He reached for her packages. 'Not at all.' He stowed the packages beneath the seat and a hatbox behind it. 'You had some success shopping I see.'

'I purchased what I needed.'

The stiffness between them returned.

He helped her onto the curricle and climbed in beside her. Toby let go of the horses and hopped on the back.

'I have something to tell you.' Her voice sounded different.

He lifted his brows.

She settled herself in the seat. 'When we are out of the village.'

Will drove through the busy village streets until the traffic cleared and the village buildings receded behind them.

He did not want to wait longer. 'What do you need to tell me?'

'Well.' She sounded cautious. 'As I left the mercantile shop I saw Mary sitting on the bench. Mary, Violet's lady's maid. She helped me pack my trunk that day in London.'

'Wait. *Violet's* lady's maid.' He shot her a glance. 'The Dormans have returned from Town?'

'Yes. Apparently they are not very happy. Mary said they are arguing all the time.'

Will frowned. 'They usually do not leave Town until later in the summer. I wonder what brought them back?'

'She did not tell me the reason.' Anna shifted in her seat.

Will's mind whirled. Had the Dormans come to cause trouble for them? He had enough to contend with without that.

She continued. 'Apparently Violet had a fit of temper and pushed Mary away. Mary wished she did not have to go back with Violet—'

Or had Dorman left too many debts in London? Will had heard rumours about gambling losses.

'So I offered her the position of lady's maid. For me.'

Will almost pulled on the reins and halted the horses. 'You did what?'

'I hired her to be my lady's maid.' She spoke as if it were the most normal thing in the world.

'No!' His voice rose. 'I'll not have a Dorman servant in my house. That is like putting the fox in with the hens. No.'

'Will.' She spoke very deliberately. 'I hired her. I am not going to tell her no. She is going to come to Willburgh House and I am not sending her away.'

Was she mad? 'I absolutely forbid it.'

'You *forbid* it?' Her voice was raised now. 'You forbid it? You told me I could hire my own lady's maid. I choose to hire Mary.'

'I said you could select from an agency. Not from the Dorman household.' The two sets of servants were as hostile to each other as the families were.

'I do not recall that conversation.' Her voice was clipped.

'Hear me now,' he said. 'You are not hiring a Dorman servant as your lady's maid.'

'Hear *me* now,' she countered. 'You may be *disappointed* in marrying me, but recall that I had as little choice in the matter as you did.'

Disappointed in marrying her? He'd never said that to her!

Then he remembered she'd overheard him say something like that to his mother.

She pointed to his hands. 'You hold all the reins.' She held up her reticule. 'You possess all the money. I am completely at your mercy. If I had refused to marry you, you would have gone on much as you do now. Perhaps your sister would have suffered, because she is a woman, too, but not you. So if you refuse to allow me this one request, I have no power to change the decision. Does that seem fair to you? I was as innocent of any indiscretion as you were, but this time it is not society who turns its back on me, it is you.'

That arrow hit its mark. 'You do not understand what is at issue here.'

'I do not understand?' Her eyes shot daggers. 'I know all about the silly feud over land. And you forget that I loved my—my stepfather. So do not tell me I do not understand. It is you who do not understand. I lost everything. I even lost a fortune I never knew I had. You lost the opportunity to select your own wife. I am asking for one thing for myself. To help Mary. I know her. She has no family. She has few choices as do I. If she becomes my maid, she has something. She has me to watch out for her. If she does indeed leave the Dormans' house, as she plans to do, and you refuse her, she cannot go back.'

Arrows. Daggers. He was full of pain. He did not want to hurt her or the poor maid, but this was an unreasonable request. Was it not? She should have asked him before she made the offer.

They spoke no more during the rest of the trip. When he pulled up to the door of Willburgh House, she did not wait for assistance. She climbed down from the curricle herself and hurried inside just as the footman was opening the door. Toby jumped down and took the horses in hand.

Will was frozen for a moment. Then he directed the footman to gather Anna's packages and to deliver them to her bed chamber. He did not go inside but turned to walk away from the house.

* * *

That evening Anna sent word she had a headache and would not be at dinner. Will knew better what was troubling her. When he retired for the night, he peeked into her room to try to talk some sense into her. She was in bed and still. He had to assume she was asleep or that she wished he'd go to the devil.

She simply did not understand the rift between the Dormans and the Willburghs. Could a servant from the other house ever be trusted? Or would they betray the family to their rivals?

He ought to have told her more about what happened to Adams, John, and Lottie simply because of a rumour that they were Dorman spies. Perhaps then she would have realised why they could not hire a Dorman servant as her lady's maid. *Especially* as *her* lady's maid. Of all the servants, the lady's maid and the valet were most likely to become privy to the private affairs of their employers. What could happen if that servant told all to the enemy?

No. He must stay resolved. She must accept that he knew best in this matter.

Will did not have a very restful night's sleep, though, tossing and turning and continuing to see Anna's outraged expression and hearing her tell how wrong he was.

But he wasn't wrong.

He dared to knock on her door and enter her room early the next day, thinking to catch her before she rose to ride. Maybe they could talk about this in a more civilised manner on horseback. Today, though, her curtains were drawn and she sat in the dark staring into the fireplace.

'Are you not riding today, Anna?' He tried to sound like yesterday's angry words had never happened.

'I am not riding.' She did not even look at him.

He opened his mouth to tell her how ridiculously she was behaving, but he closed it again. He could sense her despondency as if it were an open, bleeding wound and he had no wish to hurt her further. Instead he turned around and made his way out of the house and over to the stables.

John had the white Highland pony saddled and ready for Anna.

'Lady Willburgh is not riding today,' Will told him.

'She is not?' John was surprised. 'I do hope she is not ill.'

'Not ill.' But sick at heart, he feared.

Will started across the field feeling aimless, but soon realised he was riding to the disputed patch of land where his property bordered the Dormans'. Sheep were grazing in his field, their bleats sounding like conversations between them.

Anna would have laughed at them, he thought.

In the distance he saw something moving. As he rode closer he could see it was not a sheep but a small, thin young woman carting a very large sack, so large that she was almost dragging it.

He knew instantly who it was and rode to her. 'Mary, is it?'

She dropped the sack and gave him a wary, frightened look as if he might be the devil himself. 'My lord.' She curtsied.

She looked very young and vulnerable standing below him, reaching for the sack again and clutching it like it contained all her worldly belongings.

Which it probably did.

How much courage must it have taken for her to make this trip, to sneak away in the dark and know she could never return? How much faith in Anna, as well.

'You are headed to Willburgh House?' Where else might she be going?

'To Lady Willburgh,' she responded. 'I—I am to be her lady's maid.' She caught herself and lowered her head. 'If it please Your Lordship, that is.'

He dismounted. 'We've been expecting you,' he heard himself saying. 'Let me relieve you of your burden.'

Had he gone daft now?

Tossing the bag onto his horse, he gestured for her to proceed on her way and fell in step with her. She was shy and frightened and very determined and nothing like a Dorman spy might appear.

'I—I am grateful to you, m'lord,' she stammered. 'Miss Anna—Lady Willburgh, I mean—was always very kind to me. It will be an honour to be of service to her.'

He asked her about her family. Her parents when they had been alive had worked for the Dormans so she worked for them, too, but, she told him, she'd always liked Anna the best. And now the family did nothing but argue and Miss Dorman had become very prone to scolds and slaps across the face.

'M'lord,' she asked as the house came into view. 'Will you ask your servants not to hate me?'

That was a shaft to his heart indeed. 'I will. But you must come tell me if any of them treat you badly.'

'Oh, no!' she exclaimed. 'I could never do that. I would never tell on them. It just isn't done!'

The young maid might do very well here after all, Will thought.

Anna sat at her dressing table combing out her hair, although why she bothered she could not say. She had no intention of leaving this room all day.

Desolation threatened to engulf her. It was one thing for Will to distance himself from her, but it was quite another for him to think he ruled her.

Although what was marriage but a woman ruled by a man? By common law a husband and wife were one person, although that never meant they were equal. A woman's property and fortune became her husband's upon marriage, and any children born to them belonged to the husband. So Will could rule her and she had no recourse.

It was just that their early days and fleeting moments afterwards had convinced her that Will was different, that he wanted to respect her, wanted her to have some say in what happened to her. It was shattering what he said to her about hiring Mary. '*I absolutely forbid it.*' How could she ever again trust his kindness when he could be so cruel?

But then, how could she trust anyone really? They all betrayed her eventually.

As she tugged at a knot with the comb, she remembered the pleasure of Will brushing her hair. And the pleasure of his lovemaking. Tears stung her eyes and she blinked them away.

She'd thought he loved her. He did not love her any more than the Dormans did. Or, perhaps, any more than her stepfather had. Will's mother loathed her and the servants loathed her. She was surrounded by people who despised her.

She put down the comb and lifted her chin.

Well, she could not care that they all despised her. She had done nothing wrong, nothing to deserve their ire. She'd hold her head up and go toe-to-toe with any of them.

The door opened and Will stuck his head in. 'Anna?'

She did not want to see him! She turned away.

'I've brought you a maid.' He made it sound like this would be welcome news. 'To help you—'

How dare he!

She swung around. 'I told you I did not want a—'

Mary had entered her room. 'G'morning, Miss Anna—I mean, Lady Willburgh.'

Anna jumped from her chair and rushed over to the young woman. She wrapped the maid in a hug. Not how a lady treated her lady's maid, but Anna did not care. She was so happy to see her.

Her gaze caught Will's. He stood in the doorway smiling and her heart swelled at the sight of him. He had brought Mary to her! He had given her something that she wanted, simply because she wanted it, even though he'd been thoroughly against it.

He took a step back. 'If you will pardon me, I must speak to a few people about our new lady's maid.' He addressed himself to Mary in the kindest voice possible. 'We'll get you settled.'

Anna wanted to pull him back to embrace him, to tell him how grateful she was, but he left too quickly.

Mary stared at where he'd disappeared. 'My goodness, Miss Anna—I mean, m'lady—I don't know why Miss Dorman and Mr Lucius said he was such a villain. Lord Willburgh was ever so kind to me.'

'He is a very kind man.' Anna blinked back tears of happiness. She took Mary's hand in hers and squeezed it. 'I am so glad you are here, Mary.'

The maid looked around the room with its two trunks in the middle of the floor and complete lack of embellishments. 'It is a pretty room, but not fancy at all, is it?'

'You can help me decorate it,' Anna said, her spirits brightening considerably.

'Perhaps I might unpack your trunks for you first.'

Will did not relish the task of telling the household about the new lady's maid. He expected them to react as he had; his mother, worse. He would tell her first.

He climbed the stairs to his old room, her new bed chamber.

Ellen caught him in the hallway. 'Good morning, Will.' She frowned. 'What is it? Has something happened?'

His expression must have given away his trepidation. 'Oh, Lambkin. I am about to cause an uproar.' He explained it all to her—except for the angry discord he'd made Anna endure.

'Violet's lady's maid?' Ellen shook her head. 'The uproar is going to be at the Dormans', I should think.'

'I'm afraid our servants will not be happy to have her,' he confessed.

She seemed to consider that. 'Probably not, but think how nice it is for Anna to have someone familiar to her as her lady's maid.'

He gave his sister a hug. 'Thank you for saying that.'

'I'll encourage Betty to be kind to her,' she said.

'That would be very good.' He took a bracing breath. 'Wish me luck. I am going to tell Mother.'

Her eyes widened. 'Good luck.'

He knocked on his mother's door and heard her tell him to come in.

He opened the door. 'Good morning, Mother.'

Luckily she was alone, seated by her window, sipping a cup of chocolate. 'You never visit me in my room.' She glanced around. 'Such as it is. What is it now?'

He told her.

Her expression turned thunderous and she gripped the cup handle so hard he feared it would break.

'No, Will.' She spoke through gritted teeth. 'This is unacceptable. Willburghs never hire Dorman servants. You know that.'

'Anna chose her, Mother,' he said.

'Well, she might have considered my nerves.' She put her

cup down and fussed with the collar of her morning dress. 'You know how distressing it is for me to have anything to do with the Dormans. They killed your father, remember!'

His anger flared. 'If you wish to add Father's death to the discussion, do not forget to include the part you played in it.'

'Oh, that is too cruel!' she wailed. 'It is unfair of you to say this to me. You know how completely I was taken in! That is why I despise the Dormans so. Look how ill they treated me.'

Oddly he hadn't specifically thought of his father's death when he'd forbidden Anna to have this servant as her lady's maid. He'd reacted to the generations-long feud, the conviction that Willburghs and Dormans did not mix. He hadn't been reliving the duel every time he looked at Anna, as he'd feared.

But he thought of his father dying in his arms now and sadness engulfed him. Sadness. Not anger.

He hardened his voice to his mother. 'This little maid did not kill my father. Neither she nor Anna had any part in that. Anna wants her to be her lady's maid. She knows her and feels comfortable with her. Anna has the right to choose her own lady's maid, after all.'

'We could find one she might like from an agency,' his mother pleaded. 'Anyone but a Dorman servant. Tell her she may have anyone she chooses from an agency. You can insist upon it.'

Obviously he would not insist. Could not insist. Nor had he been able to turn away that young maid. It had made him hate himself that he thought to even try.

He answered his mother. 'I will not insist Anna do something against her wishes. It would be cruel to her and to that maid for me to insist. Anna has made her choice and I will support it.' He raised his voice and spoke even more firmly. 'I will also expect the servants to accept this young maid. I will not brook anyone treating her ill. That includes you, Mother.'

'I will have nothing to do with her!' his mother cried. 'This is all your fault. If you hadn't compromised a Dorman we would not be in this fix! You have ruined everything!'

'Perhaps I have, Mother,' Will countered. 'But remember

these decisions are mine to make, not yours, not anyone else's.'
Such was the burden of being viscount.

'Mark my words, Will. That maid will do nothing but report
all our business back to the Dormans. You've let a spy into our
household.'

Will simply left the room.

Ellen waited in the hallway. 'I heard that.'

He blew out a breath. 'I wish you had not.'

Her expression was all sympathy, though. 'Would you like
me to come with you when you tell the servants?'

'Yes.' As Viscount this was his problem alone. But he had an
idea of what he would face and really felt the need of support.
'I'd be grateful if you would,' he told Ellen and straightened his
spine. 'Let us do that now.'

Chapter Eighteen

Lucius Dorman was lounging in the drawing room while his mother and Violet sat whispering together on the sofa. Violet was in a snit because no one could find her maid and she was threatening to send the girl packing. Lucius could not care less about the maid. He was fuming about Willburgh and Anna. He'd heard rumours in the village that they were getting along very well. Humph! The very least Willburgh could do after thwarting all of Lucius's plans was to be miserable. There must be some way to make the man suffer. Apparently the loss of Anna's fortune meant nothing to Willburgh. Or maybe to Anna

The loss of Anna's fortune meant a lot to Lucius. It would have paid his debts and his father's debts and set them up rather nicely.

He and his family had botched things rather thoroughly, Lucius had to admit, but he'd been so furious to find Anna with Willburgh that all rational thought went out of his head. Not that he held a *tendre* for her, exactly, but she was supposed to be his family's ticket to the lap of luxury and Willburgh had foiled that plan.

The thing was, what to do now? How to get revenge on Willburgh and Anna and restore the family fortune?

Lucius was still musing over this problem when his father stormed into the room waving a piece of paper.

'This was just delivered. From Willburgh House!' He flung the letter at Lucius. 'Read it!'

Lucius read aloud.

'Dear Lord Dorman,
I write to you this day to inform you that I have hired the maid Mary Jones to be Viscountess Willburgh's lady's maid—'

Lucius looked up. 'Well, that solves the mystery of where Violet's maid disappeared to.'

He read on:

'I assure you, Dorman, that I will assume the payment of any wages you owe Miss Jones, so there will be no need for you to correspond with her or to concern yourselves with any of her affairs.

Lady Willburgh and I realise this loss in your household is very sudden and we regret any inconvenience it may cause you. I am confident that you realise what an improvement in status this is for Miss Jones and that you will forgive her need to leave without notice.

Yours, etc.

Willburgh'

'Improvement in status.' Lucius threw the letter down in disgust. 'That is just like Willburgh to lord it over us.'

Violet nearly vaulted out of her seat. 'Anna has stolen Mary from me! She cannot do that! Mary is *my* lady's maid.'

'What a dirty trick!' their mother cried. 'Anna goes too far. She's completely crossed over to the enemy.'

'Papa,' Violet begged. 'You must do something! Get her back!'

Their father shook his head. 'I can do nothing! The maid was free to leave her employment at any time. She had better not ask us for a letter of reference, however. I'd make certain no one would hire her.'

Lucius vowed he'd get back at Willburgh and Anna somehow. He'd make them regret ever trifling with the Dormans.

After Mary helped Anna dress and unpacked her trunks, Anna left the maid in the hands of Ellen's lady's maid, who seemed cordial enough, and went in search of Will. To thank him.

She hurried down the stairs, through the hall and the sculpture room to Will's office.

She walked in without knocking.

He was not there.

His desk was still stacked with papers and ledgers and now two chairs also had papers on them. Poor Will! He intended to tackle this all himself? Even Lord Dorman employed a secretary. Mr Bisley. A thin, intense man who seemed delighted to spend his days with papers and ledgers much like these.

She smiled to herself. Perhaps Will could hire Mr Bisley away from Lord Dorman.

She made her way back to the hall and asked the footman there, 'Do you know where Lord Willburgh has gone?'

'To see Mr Parker, the estate manager, ma'am,' the footman told her with only a hint of the usual antipathy.

'Thank you so much,' she replied, climbing the stairs again. She'd have to wait until Will returned.

As she reached the landing, a voice from above her demanded, 'I would speak with you, Anna.'

It was Will's mother. Calling her by name? It must be the first time.

Anna made no reply until she reached the floor. 'Yes, Lady Willburgh?'

Will's change of heart had filled Anna with renewed strength. She'd stood up to him! And he'd done right by her. At that moment Anna felt she could do anything.

Even face her mother-in-law.

The older woman's eyes flashed. 'My son tells me you have

manipulated him into hiring a maid—a lady's maid, no less—from the Dormans. I will not have it.'

Anna should have expected this. '*You* will not have it?' she retorted.

'I insist you send the girl packing. This very instant!' She stomped her foot for emphasis.

Anna burned with anger which she could barely keep in check. 'I will not do that.'

'You will do that!' Lady's Willburgh's face flushed. 'Our family cannot have a Dorman servant in our household. She'll be privy to all our affairs!'

Somehow Anna knew Lady Willburgh did not include her when she said *our family*. 'This is my household, too, and, as Will's wife, I am family. I have every right to select what servants I wish. Mary Jones stays.'

'You wretch!' the older woman cried. 'I knew you were a Dorman. Manipulative! Selfish! Like the lot of them. I wish that Will had never married you! You have disrupted all our lives.'

Anna could hold her temper no longer. 'I may be a *disappointment* to you, Lady Willburgh. I may be a disruption, but I am not a Dorman! What I am is Will's wife, whether you like it or not. I am the Viscountess. I have allowed you to run the house, because I did not wish to take everything away from you. Your room. Your title. I thought you would be generous enough to teach me how to manage the house and gradually pass the responsibilities on to me, but instead you accuse me of being manipulative and selfish when you know I did not choose any of this! I *am* a part of this family now, however. In fact, I am second only to Will, and you must accept this.'

Lady Willburgh's lips thinned and her chest heaved.

Anna went on. 'From now on Mrs Greaves will take instructions from me, not you. I will plan the menus. I will instruct the servants. Me. Not you. You are the dowager. I am Lady Willburgh. If I make mistakes, then it will be because you decided to oppose me rather than help me.'

Will's mother seemed to collect herself. Her eyes flashed. 'You are nobody in my eyes! A clever maneuverer, I would say. You tricked my son into marrying you—'

Anna shot back. 'You know that is not true. You were the one who said we should marry. You are no better than the Dormans. Creating your own version of how you prefer to see things rather than the way they are.'

The older woman's face turned red. 'Do not compare me to the Dormans! I am nothing like them! My son will not allow you to speak to me that way! You might have tricked him into marrying you, but I will not give over the running of this house until he tells me to and Mrs Greaves will not listen to you. My son will not hear of you usurping my authority.'

'We will see about that!' Anna whirled around and strode down two flights of stairs, through the hall and out the door. Her anger propelled her along, to the outbuildings and Parker's office.

She walked in without knocking.

Both Will and Parker looked up, stunned by her entrance.

She was panting. 'I need to talk to you right now, Will.' She walked out the door again.

He followed, looking alarmed. 'What is it, Anna?'

She paced in front of him, still so angry she could not stand still. 'Your mother!'

Will released an exasperated breath. 'What has she done now?'

'She has insisted I get rid of Mary!' Anna cried.

'Wait. What?' He pressed his fingers to his temple. 'I spoke to my mother about this. And to the servants, as well.'

Anna went on. 'She said I had no right to hire her and that I manipulated you and that *she* will not have it—' He glanced away and Anna was not certain he was listening. 'She also accused me of being selfish and a disruption!'

Will nodded, rather absently, Anna thought. 'Let's walk back to the house.'

She wrested her temper under control as they neared the house. 'I never wanted a feud with your mother. I know I am nothing she would choose for you to marry, but I will not be accused of it being my fault.'

He blew out a breath as he opened the door off the garden. 'Why does this have to be so difficult?'

Anna flared again. 'I am not being difficult! I have tried to deal fairly with your mother! I know this is a hard change for her!'

They entered his office.

She swept her arm across the room. 'And this, Will. Really. All this paper!' She could not stop herself now.

'What has my work to do with it?' he snapped.

'Nothing at all,' she shot back. 'It is just that—I came looking for you, to thank you properly for hiring Mary. When I came in here—well—I never see you asking anyone for help. Any other gentleman of means would simply hire a secretary!'

He halted and looked like he was seeing the piles of paper for the first time.

He shook his head. 'One thing at a time. I'll speak with my mother.'

But she was not sure what he would say to his mother. He might take her side, for all Anna knew.

Or he might support her, like he did in hiring Mary.

'I should tell you,' she added in a calmer tone. 'I lost my temper with your mother. I told her I was taking over all her duties.'

'Taking over her duties,' he repeated absently. He straightened. 'I will speak with her now.'

'Thank you, Will,' Anna said.

She truly hoped this would be something for which she'd be thankful.

Will found his mother in a sitting room on the other side of the house. Mrs Greaves stood near her chair. The two had obviously been talking.

'Will, thank goodness you are here,' his mother said, reaching up from her chair to clasp his hands. 'Has *she* spoken to you? Did she tell you she threatened me? She threatened to turn me out of my home!'

Will pulled his hands away. 'Cut line, Mother.' He glanced at Mrs Greaves who suddenly was examining the Aubusson carpet. 'I have had enough of this.'

His mother blinked.

Will towered over her. 'Heed me now, Mother, because you

will not be given a second chance. You will treat Anna respectfully. She is the Viscountess now, not you. She has every right to take over your duties and to hire whatever servants she wishes.'

His mother turned away.

'Look at me, Mother,' Will demanded. 'A kind thing would have been if you'd taken Anna under your wing and taught her how you've run the house, but you and Mrs Greaves have shown yourselves to be unkind. That will stop now. You will respect Anna's wishes even if they disagree with yours. You will not interfere or obstruct. If she asks for your help, you will help her. Or—'

'Or what?' she asked defiantly.

'Or you will live in the dower-house.' He turned to Mrs Greaves. 'You, Mrs Greaves, will work cooperatively with Lady Willburgh and her lady's maid and you will instruct all the servants to do the same. If I hear of any of them disrespecting my wife or her maid or causing any sort of trouble, they will be terminated and you with them.'

'But—but I cannot control—' the housekeeper stammered.

'If you cannot control your servants, then perhaps you are in the wrong job.' He glared from one to the other. 'You two have made difficulties where none needed to exist. You will stop doing so right now.'

'It's that Dorman maid she hired,' his mother protested. 'She's causing the difficulties!'

Will gave a dry laugh. 'Come now, Mother. The girl has not been here even a full day.'

'The Dormans sent her to spy on us,' cried his mother. 'It is the Dormans' fault.'

'That excuse will no longer work.' He glared at her. 'Your choice, Mother. Be decent or be gone.'

Anna was not privy to what Will said to his mother, She did not see either of them until dinner. Lady Willburgh was much subdued and avoided any direct looks at either Anna or Will. When she did speak, Anna had the sense of a great deal of anger repressed, but she did not toss any of the barbs towards Anna that had been her custom.

Something had changed. Even the servants she encountered cast their eyes down at her approach and spoke carefully to her. What had Will said to them?

He spoke little, though. If it had not been for Ellen the dinner would have resembled a wake. The girl's happy mood and cheerful conversation lifted the pall over the rest of them.

After dinner Anna excused herself early without offering any excuse.

Mary came to her after finishing her meal with the other servants. 'Do you want me to help you get ready for bed?'

'I do not need much help,' Anna replied, but let the girl untie the ribbons of her dress and slip her out of it.

Anna washed herself and donned her nightdress before sitting at the dressing table and taking the pins from her hair. Mary skipped over to help her.

'How have things been for you today?' Anna asked.

Mary smiled. 'Betty has been such a help to me and she even fixed it so we can share a bedroom. Was that not nice?'

'What of the others?' Anna was not worried about how Betty would treat her.

Mary turned pensive. 'I am not sure. Mr Bailey was nice. Nobody else said much to me at the meal, but they were not mean to me.'

'And Mrs Greaves?' Greaves's treatment was perhaps the most important.

'I admit she scares me a little.' That Anna could well understand. 'She just told me what to do and things like that.'

No one had chided her for being a Dorman servant? That must have been Will's doing.

Mary put away her dress and bid Anna goodnight, but Anna did not retire. Instead she sat up listening for Will to come up the stairs and open his door. She heard his mother and Ellen come up before she heard Will's door open. She hurried to the connecting door and opened it a crack. It was Will's valet.

She left the door open a crack and waited some more until finally Will's footsteps sounded on the stairs and in the hallway. She could tell it was Will, because the footsteps sounded burdened and weary.

She'd been so angry at him that morning—until he brought her Mary—and now she felt such sympathy. He'd obviously faced his mother and that could not have been pleasant.

A wave of guilt washed over her. The Willburgh household had probably been running smoothly and comfortably until she came to disrupt everyone.

She'd planned to go to Will that night, to crawl into bed with him, tell him how grateful she was to him. Make love with him.

She quietly closed the connecting door and walked back to her bed. Alone.

The next morning Anna rose as early as usual. She was half-way dressed when Mary came in the room.

'Miss Anna—m'lady, I mean! I did not think you would be up so early. I am so sorry I was not here.'

'Mary, I did not think to tell you,' Anna responded apologetically. 'I am so used to rising on my own, but, now you are here, you can help me put on my new riding habit.'

With Mary's help she dressed quickly and was out the door and on her way to the stables. She hoped she was in time to catch Will.

From a distance, she spied him entering the stable door and she quickened her step.

The grooms were used to both of them riding at this hour and had the horses ready. Will typically rode his thoroughbred and Anna always rode Seraphina. By the time Anna entered the stable, Will was already mounted.

He nodded a greeting.

She looked up at him. 'May I ride with you a little, Will?'

'I'll wait for you outside,' he said.

Her heart beat faster as she mounted Seraphina quickly and rode out the door.

They headed in the direction of the farm fields.

'I want to check on the planting,' he explained.

Why had she not realised before? Will did not only ride in the morning for pleasure. He rode to oversee the work on his land.

They went awhile without talking. Finally Anna said, 'I

gather by the mood at dinner last night and the behaviour of the servants, that you supported my keeping Mary?'

He shrugged. 'It was the right thing to do. You ought to select the servants you want.'

'That is what you told your mother?' She wanted to keep him talking.

'That and more.' He did not look at her, but kept his eyes straight ahead, on the road. 'I also addressed the managing of the household. I apologise for being remiss. I thought my mother would take care of that. Show you how to run the household. Help you. I thought she would know her place.'

'She is very strong-willed,' Anna said.

He laughed. 'Indeed.'

'What did you say to her?' she asked.

Still looking straight ahead, he answered, 'I told her she'd better stop this foolishness or I'd send her to the dower-house.'

'You didn't.' Goodness! Anna truly had caused a disruption. 'Your poor mother! First I boot her out of her bed chambers and next out of her own home.'

'Not you,' he said. 'Me. Anyway, she can stay if she behaves herself.'

Now her mother-in-law would be required to stand on pins and needles because of Anna.

They reached some of the fields where farm workers were already at work.

'Good,' Will spoke more to himself than to Anna. 'We are catching up.'

When they returned to the house, they entered by the garden door.

'I had an idea,' Anna said, as they walked through his office. 'I thought perhaps I could help you with your piles of papers. Perhaps organise them for you or put things in ledgers.'

He paused contemplating the array of work before him.

'Until you hire a secretary, that is,' she added. 'You really should use some of your money that way.'

His brow furrowed. 'My father did not have a secretary.'

'That does not mean you couldn't have one.' She swept her hand over his desk. 'In any event, I would like to help.'

He paused again, then answered, 'Come to me after breakfast.'

Chapter Nineteen

The next few days were at least productive for Will, even though he felt far from composed.

Anna turned out to be very efficient and organised and quicker than he at performing some of the more tedious tasks, like putting all the receipts and bills in order and recording the expenditures in the ledger. He hated to admit it, but she rather proved a secretary would be useful.

For certain some eager younger son would not be as distracting. Will had the greatest difficulty concentrating when Anna was present. He was distracted by the way the sunlight from the windows illuminated her face and put streaks of gold in her hair. When she moved to shelve a ledger, or bent over to pick up papers that fell, or simply stretched the kinks from her neck, he was thrown into memories of stroking her skin or moving inside her.

He took to using the time she worked to meet with Parker and the other men who helped run his estate, especially his dairy manager. Their dairy cows were older and producing less milk each day. His manager found a farmer, not too far away, who had two young dairy cows for sale. The farmer agreed on Will's offer to buy them. They fixed on the morrow to make the purchase.

Will hoped his absence would not cause any difficulty. He mostly hoped his mother would continue behaving herself. She could cause a good deal of trouble even though he'd only be gone a day. He knew that Anna had asked his mother to be present in her meetings with Mrs Greaves. He did not know how that was going. In any event, he hoped his mother knew he was serious about sending her to the dower-house if she caused any more trouble.

Having Anna's new lady's maid was turning out better than Will expected. Mrs Greaves must have reinforced what Will had told the other servants himself so they'd been civil to her.

At least he did not have to worry about Ellen. She was always so refreshingly happy.

Will walked back from Parker's office and entered his office, knowing Anna would still be there. She sat at a table near his desk writing figures in a ledger. She looked up and smiled, which always reached right into his very essence.

He sat in a chair near her. 'I will be accompanying Parker and the dairy manager to that farmer I told you about, the one selling the cows.'

'Oh?' She turned to face him. 'When?'

'Tomorrow.'

'How long will you be gone?' She looked disappointed.

'Only a day.' He tried not to get distracted by how lovely she looked in her dress, even though she wore an apron over it to protect it from the ink. 'But we'll leave very early and are likely not to make it back before dinner.'

'Is there anything you would like of me in your absence?' she asked.

Will feared that if he indulged in what he'd like of her, he might forget all about cows and ledgers, and everything but her. And then what would happen?

He glanced around the room, more orderly now that Anna had helped him, but still stacks of papers, things to attend to. All would tumble like a house of cards.

He pretended he'd been thinking of her question. 'I believe you know enough what to do.'

* * *

Anna did not ride the next morning, but rose even earlier, wanting to see Will off. She'd arranged an early breakfast for him and insisted he eat something before he left. She also had Cook pack them some bread and cheese for later in the day.

He was dressed for riding, the attire that reminded her of their travels, even though this coat and breeches were impeccably tailored and of the finest quality cloth. Merely seeing him dressed this way always filled her with longing for what they so briefly shared. Things were more comfortable with him than they had been before their altercation about Mary, but she still feared he treated her well out of duty.

'You did not have to rise so early, Anna,' he said to her, still cool and distant.

'I wanted to.' Even if he did not want her to.

When he'd hired Mary against his own wishes, Anna had hoped it would bring them closer. It seemed like such a loving thing he'd done, just because she wished it. Then he'd allowed her to help him in his office. Should that not have brought them closer?

He simply spent most of the time out of the room, claiming other tasks and all the time her heart ached to be with him.

She'd forged a sort of truce with Lady Willburgh, but she had no illusions that the woman had any less dislike for her. Mrs Greaves and the other servants were overtly more solicitous of her, but she hated that fear of losing their employment made them that way. Even Ellen, who she thought might become a friend, seemed to prefer her solitary pursuits to spending time with Anna.

She was as alone as she'd ever been—except for Mary. Mary was the one ray of sunshine that made the rest tolerable.

And it had been Will who'd brought Mary to her. It simply made her love for him grow to even more painful proportions.

She watched him while she sipped her tea, her handsome Will, her champion, the husband who must still regret marrying her.

Anna asked him a couple of questions about his paperwork merely to dispel the silence between them. When he finished breakfast she walked with him to the hall. Outside the front door a groom waited with his horse.

When Parker and the dairy manager rode up, Will turned to her and she hoped for some sign he might miss her, at least a little. For a moment she thought she saw some softness in his eyes, but he merely put on his hat.

'I will be late returning. After dinner,' was all he said.

She knew that already. 'Safe travels, Will,' she told him.

He nodded and went out the door.

Anna climbed the steps to the drawing room which looked over the road to the house. She watched him ride away until she could see him no more.

'Safe travels, my dearest Will,' she whispered.

That afternoon Anna felt too restless to sit and write figures in ledgers. She missed Will, even though he was probably happy enough to be absent from her. She put away her pen and ink and called for Mary to help her change into her riding habit.

Riding Seraphina would calm her down. The pony always did.

It was a lovely day with blue skies and white clouds like cotton wool. The sun was high in the sky brightening the green foliage and wild flowers and warming the air. Anna rode aimlessly and found herself at the edge of Will's property, near the land that had been the source of the Willburgh feud with the Dormans. Because of the feud the families had never resolved the land's ownership, it was left uncultivated; the wooded areas, untended. Such a waste.

How like this land Anna was, caught in some unresolvable place, belonging to no one. Left to her own devices. Untended.

She rode Seraphina carefully through the wooded part of the property. The thick green foliage parted only enough to allow shafts of sunlight to pierce the ground where ferns and flowers of the underbrush bloomed white and purple against the green. The cawing of the rooks protecting their rookeries broke the silence.

Anna could almost forget her anguish in this wild, but peaceful place.

As she rode on, the rooks' cries faded into the distance, but the blackbirds, chaffinches, and robins took over the song. Then suddenly she heard human voices.

Through the trees she could see them. In a clearing. Embracing.

Ellen and Lucius.

Anna gasped.

They parted and Lucius walked Ellen to her horse. He lifted her into the saddle and pulled her down for a light kiss on the lips. She laughed and turned her horse to ride away.

Anna backed Seraphina deeper into the woods until she knew she would not be seen, then she turned and rode faster to escape the woods and intercept Ellen.

Ellen and Lucius.

At least she knew now why Ellen preferred solitary afternoon pursuits. That embrace. That kiss. No wonder Ellen seemed so incandescently happy lately. She fancied herself in love.

With Lucius.

No doubt he had manipulated her into thinking so. To toy with her? To achieve some revenge upon Will or Anna herself? Why would he do such a despicable thing?

Anna waited on the path she knew Ellen must take to return to the house until she saw her sister-in-law approaching her.

'Hello, Anna,' Ellen cried cheerfully. 'I did not know you would be riding, too. We could have ridden together.'

Anna decided not to spare words. 'I saw you with Lucius.'

The girl inadvertently tugged on the reins. Her horse faltered. 'I—I do not know what you mean.'

'I saw you with Lucius,' she repeated while Ellen regained control of the horse. 'I saw him take liberties with you. You were in the glen at the edge of the woods. I know what I saw.'

Ellen's horse was next to Anna's now. Ellen, on a taller horse, leaned over and touched her shoulder. 'Oh, Anna! Do not tell Will. Please do not tell him.'

'That you've been secretly meeting Lucius? How long has this gone on?'

'Oh…' Ellen's eyes took on a dreamy look. 'Five days. We are in love, Anna.'

In love?

Anna could believe Ellen thought so, but Anna knew Lucius better. He'd either manoeuvred to encounter her or had taken advantage of an accidental meeting. Whichever it was, Lucius was up to no good.

'Ellen, do you realise how improper this is?' Anna spoke insistently. 'You cannot be meeting a man alone like this. Think of your reputation. You will be ruined. I have already seen him behave in ways with you more compromising than what happened between Will and me. Look at what happened to us.'

'You had to get married.' Ellen sounded petulant now. 'But you were not in love, Anna! Lucius and I are in love.'

'I know Lucius.' Anna persisted. 'He is not in love with you. He is dallying with you. You are a conquest, nothing more. He is merely using his charm on you.'

Anna knew Lucius to be very capable of trifling with a woman's feelings or even of seducing her, but he usually confined himself to opera dancers and actresses, not respectable young ladies who'd not yet been presented. Not the sister of his biggest rival.

Ellen pursed her lips together and lifted her chin.

'You must heed me,' Anna insisted. 'This puts you in great peril. You must not see him again. He is not a man of good character. He will ruin your reputation and walk away from you.'

'He would never do that!' Ellen cried. 'I told you. He loves me. He told me all about the other women, but he has never met anyone like me. He said I make him want to be a better man.'

Lucius knew what to say to get what he wanted. Ellen had fallen for his nonsense and was being primed for—what? Complete ruin?

She needed to be protected from him.

'What if I do tell Will?' Anna asked.

'You can't tell Will!' Ellen pleaded. 'He will become angry with me and pack me off to some school somewhere! You do not know how angry he can become.'

Did she not?

'Then will you agree to stop meeting Lucius?'

The house was coming into view. They did not have much farther to ride before reaching home.

'That is my bargain,' Anna stressed. 'You stop meeting Lucius or I tell Will exactly what I saw.'

Ellen glanced away.

Anna pressed her. 'Ellen, you must agree. Believe me, I will do what I say. I'll even encourage Will to send you away if that is what it takes to save you from Lucius.'

Ellen rode a little ahead of Anna and did not answer for what seemed like several minutes. When she finally slowed enough to allow Anna to catch up to her, she said, 'Very well. I'll stop seeing him.'

Was she telling the truth? Anna hoped so. In any event she would keep a close eye on her sister-in-law.

Anna did not find sleep easy that night. Half of her was listening for Will to safely return; the other half wrestling with her promise not to tell Will about Ellen meeting with Lucius.

She regretted making that agreement. Will really ought to know. He'd want to protect his sister. Anna had no doubt Will would do anything for his sister.

He'd married Anna because of Ellen, had he not? To save her from a scandal that could ruin her chances to make a good match. What Lucius was up to could be so much more ruinous to Ellen's reputation.

She resolved to tell Will, no matter her promise to Ellen. It might make Anna one more enemy in the household, but it seemed the only decision that let her settle down to sleep.

Just as she was drifting off, Will returned, making more of a clatter than she'd heard him make before. She rose from her bed intending to tell him about Ellen right away when she thought better of it. Let him rest. Tomorrow would be time enough.

The next morning Anna thought she would catch Will when he went on his morning ride, but he'd told the grooms he wasn't riding today. It was disappointing. Talking while on horseback always seemed to go better between the two of them, but he was probably tired and needed the rest.

On her solitary ride she returned to where she'd seen Ellen and Lucius the previous day. Not that she expected to find them, but more to reassure herself that she indeed must tell Will. She would catch him at breakfast.

But when she came back in to the house through the garden, he stood waiting at the office door.

'I would speak with you, Anna.' He looked thunderous.

She was taken aback. 'Now?' Before she changed her clothes?

'Now.' He stepped aside to let her in the room.

She'd been proud of how she'd left his office the day before. Only two piles of papers needing correspondence on his desk. The ledgers neatly set in order on the bookshelf and the unrecorded receipts hidden in his bottom desk drawer. Had he noticed?

His angry glare made her doubt it.

And it roused her anger, as well. Why this change in him again?

She turned to face him. 'What is it, Will? What is so pressing that I cannot change out of my riding habit and into clean clothes?'

'The devil with clean clothes,' he shot back. 'I will tell you what is pressing. Our trip to purchase the dairy cows—the ones we needed so much—was wasted because someone outbid us.'

Anna was puzzled. 'That is unfortunate, but...'

'But nothing!' He glared at her. 'Do you know who outbid us? The bid we offered privately?' He didn't leave her a chance to answer. 'Lucius Dorman.'

'Lucius?' This made no sense. 'Lucius never bothered with tasks like that.' Something made even less sense. 'Why yell at me for something Lucius did?'

His eyes flashed. 'Because the farmer said Lucius knew of our bid, knew to offer more.'

'But how did Lucius know—?'

Will raised his voice. 'I will tell you how Lucius knew! *Your maid* told him.'

'Mary? No.' Impossible. 'Mary could not have told him! When would she have done so?'

He started pacing in front of her. 'She obviously slipped away.'

'I refuse to believe it!' Mary would never have done such a thing.

'One of the grooms saw her. With Lucius,' Will insisted.

'It couldn't have been!' Anna countered. 'It must have been somebody else.'

Will clenched his fists. 'He said it looked like Mary Jones. Who else could it have been? She came to spy on us. Just as I feared.'

'Mary is no spy!' She could not be. If Mary was a spy, then it meant even sweet, timid Mary had betrayed her.

'She goes, Anna,' Will glared into her eyes. 'I cannot have a Dorman spy in this house. She goes today!'

'No!' Anna straightened her spine and met his gaze with a blazing one of her own. 'I do not believe for one minute that Mary acted as a Dorman spy. You are judging her unfairly.'

'This is precisely why I did not want to hire her,' he said, leaving the rest unspoken—that Anna had insisted.

She ignored that. 'Think about it, Will. How would a lady's maid even know about the purchase of dairy cows?'

'You must have talked to her about it.' His glare turned accusing.

She gave a sarcastic laugh. 'I did not talk about dairy cows with my maid.'

'Then she found the letters in the office,' he asserted.

That was possible, Anna supposed, but very unlikely. 'Why would she go in your office?'

His voice grew louder. 'To find out our business so she could tell the Dormans.'

'No. Not Mary. It could not have been her!' Anna shot back.

He raised his brows indignantly. 'Are you are accusing one of my grooms, who has been in my employ for years, of lying?'

'Not of lying.' He was twisting her words. 'Of being mistaken.' She turned towards the door. 'Come with me back to the stables. Let's ask this groom. I want to hear for myself.'

Chapter Twenty

Will strode out of the room with her and they walked briskly to the stables.

He wasn't sure why the poaching of dairy cows angered him so. He knew they would find others eventually. It was because it was Lucius who had done it.

In a way he blamed himself. He knew it was not a good idea to hire a Dorman servant. He knew what would happen. The servant would talk and the Dormans would know all their private affairs and would interfere whenever they could. Will wanted the Dormans out of their lives. He wanted rid of the foolish rivalry that was a credit to neither of them.

Instead, he all but invited a Dorman into the most private parts of his home. All because he could not convince Anna he knew best in this matter and, as a result, he could not refuse her.

Well, this time he intended to stand by what he knew was right. The Dorman maid had to go.

He would not be heartless, though. He'd give the girl a good reference and plenty of money for a new start. But she would never be able to spy on him and his family for the Dormans again.

When they reached the stable Will asked for the groom who'd told him about seeing the maid with Lucius. The man was out in the field and it took several minutes for him to be brought back to the stables. While they waited, Anna stood apart from Will. She stood with her arms crossed and refused to look at him.

The groom finally hurried over to him. 'You asked for me, m'lord?'

Anna joined them, then.

'Yes,' Will responded. 'Would you please tell Lady Will-burgh about seeing the maid with Mr Dorman?'

The groom turned to her. 'I saw them. You see, one of the horses got spooked and ran off and I tracked him into that part of the woods. And I saw them through the trees.'

'Are you certain it was Mary Jones, my new lady's maid?' Anna asked.

'Well, yes,' the groom replied. 'I think so anyway.'

'Did you see her face?' Anna persisted.

'Well, no, ma'am.' He looked sheepish. 'She wore a red cloak, but it looked like your maid, ma'am. She was with the young Dorman.'

'Thank you,' Anna said.

She walked out.

Will caught up with her.

'That was not proof it was Mary.' She spoke firmly.

Will had to admit, the groom was less convincing this time. 'Who else would it have been?'

'Not a maid who's only been here a few days and has been busy learning her tasks.' She quickened her pace.

Will stopped her outside the garden door. 'It does not mat-ter, Anna. I can never trust her now. I cannot have the worry that whatever I do or say might become known to the Dormans and be fodder for their mischief.'

'But she's done nothing wrong!' Anna cried.

Will needed to hold fast to his position. 'I never wanted a Dorman servant here in the first place. She's an outsider. She needs to go.'

'An outsider?' Anna sounded outraged. 'Like me, do you mean?'

'A Dorman outsider,' he clarified.

'Oh?' Her brow lifted. 'You mean someone who spent years in the Dorman household because she had nowhere else to go?'

He caught her point, but needed to stay firm. That was one thing his father did teach him. To be firm. 'This sort of betrayal never happened before your maid came. I simply cannot have her here. She must go.'

'No!' She pleaded now. 'She will have no place to go. I will not let you be so unkind to her. I will not let you!'

Will felt her pain and regretted being the cause. 'I've no intention of being unkind, Anna.' He lowered his voice and spoke kindly. 'I'll pay her generously and provide her with good references. I will also give her time to make arrangements, whatever time you see fit. Will that do?'

Her eyes narrowed. 'It will not do. But you will not listen to reason.'

'I'm not debating it, Anna.' He was getting impatient now. 'I am serious. And I will not change my mind. So leave now. I'm done talking.'

Leave, because he was not feeling very good about the decision, but could not waver.

Anna opened the garden door and rushed in, so angry at him she could not see straight. She hurried up to her room. Mary was there, putting her clean laundry in drawers.

The maid's eyes grew wide. 'Miss Anna—ma'am—what is wrong? You look upset!'

'Oh, Mary!' Anna turned to her, her only ally in this house, but she needed to know for herself. She looked directly into Mary's eyes. 'I need to ask you something. And I want you to be very honest with me.'

'Of course I will, m'lady.' She looked earnest. And wary.

'I need to know if you have met with anyone from the Dorman house and if you told them anything about us. About Willburgh family business. Anything, even something small.'

Mary looked as if Anna had struck her. 'I would never, Miss Anna. Never. Why would I do such a thing? When you've been so kind?' Her eyes filled with tears. 'Who said I did?'

Anna could not bear to tell her it was Will. 'That does not

matter. Is there any way someone might have seen you with someone and thought it was a Dorman or a Dorman servant?'

A tear rolled down Mary's cheek. 'Do you mean here in the house? I haven't been anywhere else, except maybe in the yard. I don't want to talk to anyone from there!'

That was what Anna thought, but she had been fooled so many times before and Mary could have slipped away when Anna was helping Will in his office.

'I don't talk about what I hear, not to anybody,' Mary went on, her lip quivering. 'Am I being sacked?'

Anna enfolded the girl in her arms. 'What will become of me?' Mary wailed.

Anna knew that pain, that panic. She'd felt it many times before.

'Do not fear,' she reassured the girl. 'I will not allow anything bad to happen to you.'

But Will had been adamant and Anna had no power at all. She never did.

Anna was shocked at Will's unreasonableness and his sudden anger. He was completely unwilling to consider any other explanation of the events. He'd made up his mind it was Mary, merely because Mary had been a Dorman servant. An outsider. Well, Anna was an outsider, too. How could she trust that he would not be unreasonable with her as well? And how was she to predict when he'd erupt in these irrational outbursts?

Mary helped her change out of her riding habit. After Anna had washed off the dirt of the road and donned a day dress, she calmed a little. Only then did it strike her that she'd not told him about Ellen. Well, she certainly was not going to tell him now, not when he was in this unreasonable mood.

She felt the blood drain from her face. Anna knew who had told Lucius about the sale of the cows! It had been Ellen. It was Ellen the groom saw and mistook for Mary. They were about the same height and figure and who would ever believe a Willburgh would secretly meet with a Dorman?

Could she tell Will? He'd been so angry at her when he suspected Mary; how angry would he be if he knew it was his own sister who spilled family business to the enemy? And how much angrier still to discover she fancied herself in love with that enemy?

But she had to tell him. Ellen's future was at stake. When, though?

Will expected Anna to isolate herself in her room and avoid him and the rest of the family. That was her typical behaviour when upset. Instead she seemed to spend a lot of time with Ellen who had somehow contracted a spell of the blue devils. Anna's company did not seem to help Ellen's mood, though.

Will knew what troubled Anna, but Ellen's Gordian knots were a mystery. Just the other day she'd been full of cheer. Now she acted like she'd lost her best friend. And it was clear her best friend was not Anna. Ellen seemed as peeved at Anna as Will was.

From his office, he overheard an exchange between Ellen and Anna in the hall.

'I'm not going riding,' Ellen said petulantly. 'I'm going for a walk.'

'I'll go with you,' Anna responded.

'I do not want you to go with me,' Ellen cried. 'I'm just walking to the road and back.'

'To the road and back. Alone.' Anna sounded sceptical, but why would she care?

'Very well, not alone,' retorted Ellen. 'I'll take Betty with me. You can watch from the front of the house if you like.'

'I will,' Anna said.

Will checked and that is what they did. Ellen walked with Betty and Anna watched them closely.

The whole incident did not make sense to him. What did Anna care if Ellen took a walk alone? Ellen was used to walking and riding alone. He refused to ask Anna, though. He'd only spark another argument.

That night's dinner was tortuous. Anna spoke little and avoided talking to him, and Ellen was sullen. Only his mother seemed pleased, possibly because it was clear something had happened between him and Anna.

Anna excused herself after the meal was done. In the drawing room afterwards Will was alone with his mother and Ellen. Will decided to ask Ellen about the walk.

'I overheard you and Anna arguing about you going for a walk,' he began. 'What was that all about?'

His mother perked up in interest, presumably because this was about Anna.

Ellen looked distressed for a moment, but quickly composed herself. 'I do not know why she all of a sudden does not think I should walk alone. I've walked or ridden alone a lot since she's been here. I refuse to heed what she thinks. She has no authority over me.'

'Indeed she does not,' their mother readily—and somewhat happily—agreed. 'She is behaving very oddly, I must say.' She turned to Will. 'Are we to expect this always?'

'I do not know,' he responded.

His mother leaned towards him. 'You know how much I hate to pry—' Oh, yes, his mother *never* interfered, *never* pried. 'But what did happen between you and Anna to make her behave so oddly?'

He supposed he owed her an explanation. He picked the easiest one. 'We had a disagreement about her lady's maid.'

His mother looked smug. 'I told you that girl would be trouble. What did she do?'

Will took a sip of brandy. 'Remember I told you we were out bid for the dairy cows?'

She nodded.

'It was Lucius Dorman who outbid us.'

Ellen's head perked up.

'Lucius Dorman!' his mother cried.

'Someone tipped him off,' Will went on. 'I believe it was Anna's lady's maid and Anna insists it was not. But who else would have done it?'

'Indeed,' his mother agreed. 'I am certain you are correct. I told you that maid would spy on us. You might have listened to me.'

Ellen broke in. 'The cows were that important?'

'Not the cows,' Will explained. 'It was that our personal family information was told to a Dorman. We cannot have that. We cannot trust them.'

'Indeed we cannot,' his mother expounded. 'So Anna takes the maid's side against us? That is disloyal!'

'This is because of the feud,' Ellen said with derision. 'The feud that you think is so important.'

'It is important.' His mother shook a finger at Ellen. 'Remember that feud led to your father's death.'

Ellen sobered. 'No one ever told me how.'

Remind Ellen of Father's death, Mother, thought Will. *That will cheer her up.*

Her mother eagerly explained, 'Because of the feud, your father and Bertram Dorman, Baron Dorman's younger brother—Anna's father—fought a duel and they killed each other.'

'Anna's stepfather,' Will corrected.

'Stepfather, then,' sniffed his mother.

'How come they fought a duel over the feud?' Ellen persisted.

Will broke in. 'Because they were foolish.'

Ellen did not need to know of her mother's fling with Bertram Dorman. That certainly would not cheer her up. He could at least count on his mother not to tell her that.

'And the feud was about that land?' she asked.

'Yes. The disputed land.' That was all she needed to know.

'Well.' Ellen stood. 'I think it is all very silly!' She walked out.

At the moment Will agreed with her. How much havoc over generations had this feud created? Was he perpetuating the havoc?

Had the feud not existed would Bertram Dorman have bothered to seduce his mother? Would his father have fought a duel with anyone but a Dorman? Would the Dormans have acted so outraged when Will was caught in the rain with Anna? Nothing good ever came from the damned feud.

A few days ago he would have hoped that marrying Anna would turn into the one good thing that came from the feud, but look how that hope was dashed.

That night Will could not sleep.

His head told him he'd been right when he'd refused to hire

the Dorman maid. So now he was right to let her go, was he not? He'd expected trouble and trouble came. Was that not right?

Anna's arguments on behalf of the maid were compelling, though. They nagged at him.

Who else could it have been? No one else made sense. He wanted Anna to see his way, though she seemed determined not to.

Everything seemed wrong. What tortured Will the most was he feared he was wrong. Was he the one who made a mess of everything?

He heard the door connecting his room to Anna's open and he turned to face it.

She was framed in the doorway. 'Will? Are you awake?'

'I am awake,' he responded.

'I would speak with you,' she said. Not *may* she speak. She was not asking for permission but making a command.

He rose from the bed as she walked towards him, the flame of the candle in her hand illuminating her face, her curls loose around her head like an aura, her nightdress flowing as she walked, giving him glimpses of her womanly shape beneath. He was naked save his drawers and he yearned to pull off her nightdress and feel her warm, smooth skin against his.

Suddenly it seemed like there was no air for him to breathe, only this otherworldly spectre coming closer and his desire growing stronger. Was she his weakness?

He managed to answer her. 'Then speak, Anna.'

She stopped a mere three feet away. 'I have a plan that will remove Mary in mere days and will avoid further *disruption* to the family.' She emphasised the word *disruption* and sounded sad, but resigned.

It had been a word he'd used, he realised. 'What is the plan?'

She took a breath. 'Mary will leave here, but I will leave with her.'

'What?' Will was shocked.

She held up a hand. 'Hear me out.' She placed the candle on a nearby table and faced him again. 'Before we decided to marry, we'd contemplated you simply supporting me, giving me enough money to live on.'

That had been what she'd wanted, and if they'd done that, she'd have wound up wealthy. His fault she wasn't.

She went on. 'It was what we should have done all along. Set me up with some sort of settlement or stipend or something—nothing extravagant—and I will take Mary as my maid. We can live very simply, except I should like to afford to keep Seraphina.'

No! He wanted to protest. She would leave him? Wanted her horse, but not him? No!

'Where would you go?' he asked, keeping the emotion out of his voice.

She shrugged. 'Oh, I don't know. Perhaps a village near Reading. Reading sounds like a nice town.'

Reading? With its iron works and a ruined abbey? What could appeal there?

'Reading,' he repeated. 'You want to leave and take the maid and go to Reading.'

'And Seraphina,' she added. 'It solves everything, do you see? Think on it.' She picked up the candle again and turned to walk away, but paused and spoke over her shoulder. 'Except I've not given you an heir. I do regret that.'

The mention of an heir sent his mind back to tangled sheets and passion and pleasure unlike he'd ever experienced before. That was what he wanted back. That and the easy camaraderie they'd once shared.

She walked back to the door, a silhouette now, even more spectre-like. As she walked away his spirits plummeted even deeper than before. He was left feeling a dislike of himself that rational thought disdained.

And beyond that, emptiness.

The next day Anna avoided Will.

It was too painful to be near him, not because of his temper, but because she loved him so. He was a good man on the whole, trying to do the right thing by everyone. Everyone but her.

When he brought Mary to her, Anna thought it the most loving act, even though she could not say he loved her. It bitterly disappointed Anna, though, that Will could so cruelly take Mary away, with such baseless accusations. He might wrap her banishment in gold ribbons, but it was the fact of being unwanted that was so deeply wounding. How could Will do that? How could he not see that Anna needed to make Mary know that she was wanted, that she belonged somewhere and that someone cared for her? Could Will not see that Anna needed him to tell her she belonged with him, that he wanted her, cared for her?

Anna might be a disappointment to him, but, in this, Anna was disappointed in Will. It was best she and Mary leave.

At the moment, though, Anna had Ellen to worry about. She stayed close to Ellen the whole day and still agonised over whether she should tell Will about her and Lucius. Even though Ellen had given Anna her word that she would not see Lucius again, every instinct told Anna she could not trust Ellen not to slip away and run to him.

So when Ellen went to the library to select a book, Anna selected a book. When Ellen settled in one of the sunniest parlours to read, Anna sat in the same room with her own book.

Anna had selected one volume of *England's Gazetteer* to read of the places she and Mary might settle. She'd not set on Reading for certain, but mentioned it to Will so he'd know she was serious about leaving. Reading was as good a place as any.

The more she read of other villages and towns, the more her spirits dipped. Living in this area since her childhood made it familiar to her. She was used to the village, the church, the people. Even more, Anna had come to love this house. Even in the short time she'd lived in Willburgh House, it felt more like home than Dorman Hall. At Dorman Hall she'd been treated as if she were Violet's lady's companion instead of a member of the family. As if she did not truly belong.

She glanced over at Ellen who was gazing out the window instead of reading her book. Those first days here Anna had hoped she and Ellen could be friends. Now Ellen despised her.

Ellen glanced over at her. 'You do not have to watch me every second, Anna. I gave you my word I would not see Lucius. Do you not trust me?'

'I would like to trust you,' Anna answered.

Was it useless to keep such a close eye on Ellen? When Anna left, Ellen could continue her secret trysts.

That was why Anna must tell Will. So Anna's word could not be trusted either, could it?

Lucius would lose interest eventually, of course, but it was the harm he could do to Ellen beforehand that Anna worried about. No, Anna would have to tell Will and tell him soon.

But not today.

In the meantime Anna could try to convince Ellen that Lucius was not of good character.

'Let me tell you a little more about Lucius,' she said to Ellen. 'About the kind of person he is.'

She told Ellen about Lucius abandoning her at Vauxhall and leaving her to the mercy of his friend, Millman, and exactly what Millman tried to do to her.

Ellen listened with a defiant expression. 'You cannot convince me that he knew Millman would try to molest you.'

Actually Anna did not believe that of Lucius. 'No, but he remained friends with him after he knew what happened.'

'Are you sure?' Ellen countered. 'You were not with him after Scotland.'

'True, but I would wager any amount of money that Lucius would care more about his friendship than about what the man tried to do to me.'

'By then he was probably very angry at you,' Ellen said. 'You ran off and married Will. That was like a betrayal to him. That silly feud, you know.'

Anna did not know what to say in response.

Ellen rose and faced her. 'I cannot bear to be inside this stuffy old house for another moment. I am going for a walk.'

Anna opened her mouth to say she would walk with her.

Ellen waved her hand dismissively. 'I do not want your company. I will take Betty. We will walk to the road and back and you can watch from the front of the house like you did before.'

'I will be watching,' Anna said.

Chapter Twenty-One

After another tension-filled dinner that evening Anna retired to her room and had Mary help her get ready for bed. She'd hardly slept the past two nights. She hadn't told Mary about needing to leave. Why upset the girl until Anna had all the details set? Mary was happy here at Willburgh House, Anna could tell. Betty had become her friend and the two could be found together at every spare moment. Let Mary have her friendship for as long as possible.

When Mary left her, Anna crawled into bed and burrowed beneath the covers, but, instead of sleep, Anna's emotions spilled over and she wept. She'd held back tears long enough, and now the dam had broken. Her grief at all she'd lost—especially Will—flooded her. When she finally slept, though, her sleep was peaceful and deep.

Until she was jarred awake by someone shaking her, telling her to wake. 'M'lady! M'lady! Wake up!'

She opened her eyes.

Betty and Mary stood over her.

'You must wake up, m'lady!' Betty cried.

Anna sat up. 'What? What has happened?'

Mary held the candle while Betty shook her shoulder, a breach of proper servant behaviour, but Betty was distraught.

'She's gone, m'lady!' Betty cried. 'Not long ago. Maybe half an hour? Less.'

Anna brushed the hair out of her eyes. 'Who is gone?'

'Miss Willburgh!' Betty cried.

'Ellen?' Anna straightened, wide awake now.

'She's run away!' Betty stifled a sob. 'She took some clothes! What shall we do?'

Anna bounded out of bed. 'We must go after her!' She turned to Mary. 'Quick. My old riding habit!'

Mary shoved the candle into Betty's hand.

Anna ran to the connecting door to Will's room, burst in his room and in the dim light, found his bed.

'Will! Wake up!' She shook him like Betty had shaken her.

He shot up so quickly she jumped back.

'What is it?' He seemed even more awake than she was.

'Ellen has eloped!' she said. 'I'll explain later. We must go after her! Right now.'

He got out of bed, wearing only his drawers. Betty had followed her and lit a candle in his room.

'Get dressed now!' Anna cried. 'Hurry!' She ran back to her room.

While Mary helped her dress, Betty explained. 'She told me not to tell, but on those walks, she left a letter for someone in a knot in a tree that was on the road. Then yesterday she found a letter there for her.' Betty shook her head. 'That's all I know. Do you think that has something to do with her running away?'

'I'm sure it has,' Anna responded.

Betty went on. 'I thought something was up so Mary and I got up early. The clock struck four. She was in bed then, but something seemed strange so we went back and she was gone. We could not have been more than a quarter hour. Or a half hour.'

Perhaps she'd been dressed and ready to leave but pretending to sleep. But with the letters, there was no doubt that she planned this.

Will came into her room as she was putting on her boots. She gave quick embraces to both Betty and Mary and rushed out with him.

Their clatter on the stairs roused the footman monitoring

the hall. He was barely awake when Will called to him. 'Tell no one we've gone!'

Then they were out the door hurrying to the stables. By this time the first rays of dawn had appeared on the horizon, enough to light their way.

'She's been meeting Lucius in secret,' Anna explained. 'And Lucius has convinced her she is in love with him. I thought I stopped it, but they were passing letters on those walks. I think he is planning a terrible revenge. I think he is eloping with her!'

'Lucius!' Will growled. 'I'll kill him.'

Will's anger alarmed her. 'We just need to stop them in time.'

When they reached the stable door and opened it, Will's voice boomed. 'Grooms! Now! To saddle horses!'

He'd already picked up the saddles and brought them to the horses when John and Toby appeared, hastily.

'Saddle Anna's pony and my thoroughbred,' he ordered and turned to Anna. 'My thoroughbred is the fastest.'

The two grooms asked no questions, but made quick work of it. Will and Anna were soon mounted and ready to ride.

'Be ready if I need you,' Will shouted to John and Toby. 'I do not know how long it will be.'

Will galloped off and Anna followed him. He had the gate open for her by the time she reached it and he was standing in the middle of the road, looking down.

He looked over at her and pointed. 'They went that way.'

He remounted.

'Ride ahead, Will,' she told him. 'I'll come as fast as I can.'

Will needed to keep his wits about him.

He needed to conserve his horse's strength. How long before he could catch up to them? He didn't want his horse blown.

Will was reasonably sure Lucius and Ellen were headed to Aylesbury to a coaching inn. The tracks looked like Lucius drove his curricle. Lucius was not likely to take his curricle all the way to Scotland.

If Scotland was where he intended to go.

Will would not let himself think of the alternative—to merely

ruin her thoroughly. Just in case, Will kept his eye on the road
to make sure their trail did not turn off this main road.

As Will rode, the puzzle pieces fell into place. While he and
Anna were working together on his papers and ledgers, Ellen
was happily riding or taking walks alone. Meeting Lucius. It
was Ellen, not the poor maid, who'd told Lucius about the sale
of the cows, probably innocently, but still… Had it not occurred
to her that Lucius would take advantage of the information?
Why had she allowed the maid to take the blame?

Anna discovered this and was making certain Ellen did not
meet him again. That was why Ellen turned sullen and why she
turned against Anna.

Everything fit.

What a fool Will had been. He'd been as much a prisoner of
the feud as Lucius was, as their ancestors were. Would he have
been so unfair to Anna, if not for the feud? Would he have been
so harsh on poor Mary Jones? Would Lucius have bothered to
trifle with a respectable sixteen-year-old?

He must have ridden at a good pace for at least an hour.
They'd started out in near darkness and now the new day had
dawned. Sheep appeared on the hillsides, birds sounded in the
bushes and took to flight when he rode by. He saw farm workers making their way to the fields. The road was still empty
of traffic, though. He was not too far from Aylesbury. Another
hour, perhaps. He wanted to overtake them before they reached
the town. It would be the very devil to find the coaching inn at
which they would stop.

Will finally spied a vehicle in the distance, but it was coming towards him. As it got closer, he could see it was a farm
wagon carrying hay and pulled by a sturdy farm horse. A griz-
zled man drove the wagon and a young boy sat next to him on
the wagon's bench.

When Will came close enough, he asked them, 'Did you pass
a gentleman and lady in a curricle, by any chance?'

'I did, sir.' The man answered in a very unhurried manner.
'Thought it odd they were up so early, but you can never tell.'

Will could barely contain himself. 'How long ago did you
see them? Are they far? Are they still on this road?'

'Oh, they were on this road all right. Not too many side roads worth bothering with around here.'

'How far?' Will pressed.

'Not too far.' The farmer turned around in his seat and gestured to the road behind him. 'I passed them just over this hill here. Not too many minutes before seeing you. You can't see over the hill but if you could, you'd see it is not too far.'

'What is your name, my good man?' Will intended to send him a reward for his help.

'Name's Begum,' the farmer replied.

'Thank you, Begum.' Will rode on increasing his speed.

He did not see them over the hill but galloped over the next hill.

And he saw them!

He gave his horse its head and he closed the distance between them.

Lucius turned at the sound of Will's approaching horse. 'Blast it! It's your brother.'

He drove his horses faster, but Will caught up and brought his horse next to one of the curricle's horses. He took hold of the reins. Lucius stood up and thrashed Will with his whip, but Will kept hold, slowing his horse and the curricle.

Ellen pulled on Lucius's coat, yelling, 'Stop! Stop!'

There was a tiger riding on the back, a youth barely breeched who looked terrified.

With the curricle stopped, Will seized the whip and pulled it. Lucius kept his grip, but lost his balance and tumbled out of the seat onto the road.

Ellen shrieked, 'Lucius!'

The tiger had the presence of mind to hop off and run around to hold the horses. Will dismounted and was striding towards Lucius as he was getting to his feet. As soon as Lucius stood, Will pulled his arm back and punched him in the face. Lucius spun around and fell again.

'Will, no!' Will was close enough to the curricle that Ellen pounded him with her fists. 'Don't hurt him.'

Lucius got to his feet again, rubbing his chin. 'Always the brute, Willburgh,' he snarled.

'That's what you deserve and more,' Will shot back. 'Good God, man. My sister is only sixteen years old!'

'I'm old enough to know my own mind!' cried Ellen. 'We are to be married! Just like you and Anna.'

'That's it, isn't it, Lucius?' Will approached him again, fists clenched. 'The perfect revenge. I married Anna and your family could no longer steal her fortune, so you take my sister. Did you not realise that I could prevent you from having her dowry?'

Lucius raised his own fists but backed away. 'You wouldn't do that, though, would you, Willburgh? You'd never deny your sister. I'll bet her dowry rivals Anna's wealth.'

It didn't, but Ellen was worth a sizable amount.

'Stop this talk of money!' Ellen cried. 'Let us be on our way!'

'He's not taking you to Scotland,' Will told her. 'You are coming home.'

'No!' She closed her arms over her chest. 'We love each other and we will be married.'

'No you won't!' Will advanced on Lucius and threw another punch.

This one Lucius dodged. He was clearly trying to avoid Will.

'You will let me marry your sister,' Lucius said. 'Unless you want a scandal that goes beyond all scandals. A scandal so terrible your sister will be ruined.'

'By God if you've violated her!' Will charged him and seized the front of his coat, lifting him off the ground and thrusting him away.

Lucius fell again but laughed. 'Not *violated* because she was willing. Very willing and there are consequences for being willing.'

'I was willing!' Ellen insisted. 'Very willing.'

Will's anger surged so high his vision turned red. 'You've got her with child!'

'Do not insult me, Will!' Ellen cried. 'Of course he did not get me with child.'

Lucius laughed again. 'No, I am not that depraved, but you know the truth matters little to a London gossip rag.'

Ellen looked perplexed. 'What are you talking about, Lucius?'

Will took a step towards Lucius again. 'I swear I would gladly kill you!'

Lucius walked to the other side of the curricle, with Ellen in between Will and him now. 'You would not kill me, Willburgh,' he said. 'Not unless you could do so with honour. Would you like to kill me with honour?'

Will was so angry he could not think. He raged, not only about Lucius Dorman running off with his sister, but about all the Dormans had done to Anna, what they'd done to his father. And even his mother. Will was engulfed in his emotions. Reason had fled.

Lucius reached under the seat of the curricle and took out a box. 'Here is how you can get your revenge with honour.' He lifted up the box. 'These are my duelling pistols. I challenge you to a duel for the honour of your sister.'

'I accept,' Will said.

Anna knew she was near to catching up with Will. And with Ellen and Lucius. The farmer in the wagon told her. Already she felt relieved. Will would stop them. He would save Ellen from making a terrible mistake.

She rode Seraphina a little faster.

When she came over the crest of the hill she saw the curricle and horses stopped in the road. She glanced to the right and gasped.

In the field, two men stood back to back and began to pace away from each other.

Will and Lucius.

A duel.

'No, no, no, no, no,' she cried.

She urged her horse into a gallop, sailed over the hedgerow on the side of the road and, right when both men turned to fire, rode straight in between them.

The sound of the shots exploded in her ears. Seraphina squealed and toppled to the ground, throwing Anna off. She landed hard in a heap.

She could see the field. Saw Lucius run over to Ellen, seize her by the waist and run towards the curricle. They were getting away! Will ran towards her, calling her name. Seraphina writhed on the ground near to her and incongruously a youth in livery stood stunned a few feet away.

Will reached her just as she regained her breath. He slid to the ground. 'Anna!'

'I'm—I'm not hurt,' she managed, hoping it was true. She sat up. 'Go after them, Will.'

Lucius and Ellen were in the curricle, driving off.

'I'll come back for you.' He ran to his horse.

Anna crawled to her pony. 'Poor Seraphina.' She stroked the pony's neck.

To her surprise, Seraphina rose to her feet. She'd been certain the pony had been shot. Anna gripped her mane to help her stand, as well. She checked the pony all over, felt its legs for breaks, but found none. There was a gash on the horse's shoulder, not very deep, not even bleeding much.

'Poor Seraphina!' Anna laughed in relief. 'The shot just startled you.' She turned to the liveried servant, recognising him as Lucius's tiger. 'Nick, is it? Come help me mount.'

The poor lad roused himself enough to come to her side and help her into the saddle. She rode away leaving him befuddled and alone. They'd come back for him, but she didn't have time to reassure him.

Chapter Twenty-Two

Will rode as fast as he dared. Lucius was driving his horses at a dangerous pace. Ellen looked like she was hanging on for dear life.

If anything happened to her, how could Will forgive himself? He'd managed everyone and everything into complete disaster. He could not have possibly made more mistakes.

The road was rough in some places where rain and wagon wheels had dug ruts. The curricle bounced and shimmied over the surface and Will feared it would simply come apart.

When the road made an abrupt turn to the left, Will held his breath.

The curricle horses scrambled to keep their footing. The curricle tipped onto one wheel which hit a rock in the road. It flew in the air and Ellen's screams filled Will's ears. The curricle crashed onto its side tossing Lucius onto the road. Ellen hung on while the horses dragged the curricle several feet. Will caught up and brought the horses under control.

He helped a shaking Ellen to the side of the road, seating her there, and ran back to Lucius's still body.

Had Will succeeded in killing him? God, he prayed. Please. No.

'Is he dead?' Ellen wailed. She rocked back and forth.

Will felt for a heartbeat.

And found it.

'He's alive.'

But Lucius was unconscious. He'd hit his head when he fell. What's more, his shoulder looked broken. Will eased him onto his back and held him up, hoping to ease his breathing. Lucius moaned when Will moved him.

'Ellen!' Will called. 'Find something in the curricle to elevate his back.'

She simply rocked back and forth.

'Ellen!'

But she was insensible. What was he to do?

At that moment, though, Will saw Anna riding towards them. Intrepid Anna. He should have known he could count on her.

Before she could ask, he said, 'He's alive. Unconscious, but alive. Can you find something to put behind his back?'

She rode over to the curricle and dismounted. First she went over to Ellen and spoke quietly to her, putting a comforting hand on her shoulder. Then she dashed to the curricle and ran back to Will carrying a blanket and Ellen's portmanteau which had fallen out.

Will propped Lucius up and, after making certain he was as comfortable as possible, got to his feet and embraced Anna.

'I am sorry for it all, Anna.' His voice cracked. 'All my fault. All my fault.'

'Nonsense,' she murmured. 'You are not responsible, but we need to figure out what to do.'

He released her. 'Yes. Yes. Help me turn the curricle.'

Anna held the horses, while Will tried to set the curricle on its wheels, which seemed intact. Lucius had purchased a high-quality vehicle so that made sense. It would roll if Will could only set it to rights.

But he could not do it, not after several tries. He sat down near Lucius to catch his breath.

'Maybe tie one of the horses to it and have them pull?' Anna suggested.

Will nodded. It was a good idea.

He tied his thoroughbred to the curricle and led him away, but they still could not set the curricle back on its wheels.

'Should I ride for help?' Anna asked.

'We're about halfway between Aylesbury and home,' Will said. 'I do not know which way you should go.'

Anna looked towards Ellen. 'I'm worried about her, too.'

Ellen had curled herself into a ball and was shaking. Lucius moaned and tried to stand up.

Will went over to him. 'Stay down, Lucius. You are injured. Best not to move.'

Lucius shoved off Will's attempt to help him. 'Guh 'way,' he slurred. 'Hate you. Always did.'

He went down on his knees and vomited, clutching his injured shoulder as he did so.

Will eased him back against the blanket and he moaned in pain.

What was best to do? They could wait for the ordinary traffic to come down the road, but Will was afraid they needed help sooner. He was reluctant to let Anna go for help, though. She'd suffered a fall, too. She said she was not injured, but he was not sure. The horses were getting restless. Lucius's horses were already spooked. Who knew what might set them off again?

'Someone's coming!' Anna cried.

Two men on horses approached from the direction in which they'd come. One of the men had Lucius's tiger riding behind him.

Will stood. 'It is Toby and John!'

They rode up to him.

'We thought it best to come after you, m'lord,' Toby said. 'In case you needed help.'

With Toby and John's help, they soon righted the curricle and sorted out the horses' harnesses. They put Lucius and Ellen in the curricle with John driving. The tiger rode John's horse.

'Let's take them back home,' Will said.

He rode next to Anna. 'Are you certain you are not injured?'

She smiled at him. 'I will probably ache tomorrow, but, no— nothing broken.'

They rode a while in silence.

Will spoke, needing to tell her and to hear himself speak aloud. 'I was angry enough to kill him. Angry enough to agree to the duel.'

'Stealing Ellen away was reprehensible,' she said.

She did not reproach him for it? Will could not believe it. 'When I turned to fire—in that instant I saw my father's duel—I could not do it, Anna. I could not fire at him. I deloped.'

She looked over at him but he could not read her expression. Was it understanding? Admiration? He could not believe either one.

'Maybe that's the only thing I got right,' he murmured.

John called back to him. 'The gentleman's delirious!'

Will rode up to the curricle.

Anna watched him.

Will ordered Ellen to hold on to Lucius. When she did not respond, he rode closer so she could not fail to see him. 'Buck up, Ellen!' he demanded. 'He needs you. Hold on to him!'

She did as she was told.

Anna was filled with emotion.

Will was doubting himself, blaming himself, and yet he was handling all of this. Her heart burst with pride for him, but also ached with his suffering. She wished she belonged with him, because she loved him. If anyone was at fault for all that happened it was Anna. Her presence had caused him and his family all this trouble.

The ride back was fraught with tension and seemed endless, but finally they neared the gates of Willburgh House.

Will sprang into action again. 'Toby, ride to the village. Get the surgeon. Bring him here. We will take Dorman to the house.'

Toby nodded and galloped off.

To Lucius's tiger Will said, 'Ride to Lord Dorman. Tell them their son is injured and they must come.'

The youth cried, 'Yes, m'lord!'

The household must have been watching for them, because the door opened before they pulled up. Lady Willburgh took charge, immediately having Lucius carried to a guest room, and taking Ellen under her wing while listening to Will's explanation of what happened.

Anna was not surprised that she went unnoticed. She did not need anything, after all. She went to her room with Mary who helped her to quickly wash and dress in clean clothes.

It was Anna who was there to greet Lord and Lady Dorman and Violet, to fill them in on what happened. She took them up to Lucius's room.

The surgeon arrived and examined Lucius thoroughly. He was most concerned about the injury to Lucius's head. It was bad enough for Lucius to go in and out of consciousness. If Lucius survived the night, the surgeon said, his chance of recovery was good, but the next twenty-four hours would be crucial.

Lady Willburgh and Will told the Dormans they were welcome to stay. They could use the drawing room to rest when not with Lucius. Or they could sleep in the guest bedrooms. Lady Willburgh said refreshments would be provided for them.

The Dormans said they would stay in the drawing room for the whole day and night. Anna went to the kitchen herself to make certain Cook would be prepared for the extra guests. Mrs Greaves was there.

'Lady Willburgh gave those directions already, ma'am,' Mrs Greaves said.

For once Anna did not resent being usurped by her mother-in-law. 'She thought of everything,' Anna said with true admiration.

'Yes, m'lady,' Mrs Greaves agreed.

Would Anna ever be able to do even half as well as Lady Willburgh, if she stayed? Anna wondered.

Anna walked back upstairs and decided to check in the drawing room in case she might be useful there. When she approached the door, she heard Will's voice.

'I know this is not the time, Dorman,' he said. 'But I want you to know that I believe it is time to settle the land dispute. If you want the land, I can deed it to you. If you would prefer funds, we can negotiate a sale of sorts. Do not tell me now, but think on it when Lucius's health improves.'

Lord Dorman's voice quavered, 'Do you think he will improve?'

Anna peeked in the room to see Will put a comforting hand on Lord Dorman's shoulder. 'I think Lucius is strong. And he certainly is determined. He'll get better.'

Violet came down the stairs. She had a handkerchief in her hand and dabbed at her eyes.

She stopped when she saw Anna.

'How is he?' Anna asked.

Violet blinked before answering. 'The surgeon said he dislocated his shoulder. He put it back in place, but it must have hurt.'

'Must have been hard to witness, as well.' Anna gestured for her to come in the room. 'I'll pour you a cup of tea.'

When Violet saw her father, though, she ran into his arms and wept into his chest.

Will walked over to Anna. 'Come. Let us leave them alone.'

She walked out with him. 'You haven't changed your clothes, Will.'

He was still in the clothes he'd hastily put on before dawn. His face was shadowed with a growth of beard, making him look like a drawing of a pirate she once saw in a book.

He looked down at himself. 'I suppose I should change. That must be why Carter is hovering. Waiting for me.'

She walked with him to the door of his bed chamber. 'I overheard you talking to Lord Dorman about the disputed land.'

He looked surprised, then nodded. 'I want to be rid of it. The dispute, that is. By any means.' He smiled down at her. 'You did well today, Anna. Except for charging into the middle of a duel—'

She interrupted. 'I wanted to stop it.'

He nodded. 'I know.' He lightly touched her cheek. 'You might have saved my life. And I know you saved Ellen's.' He glanced towards the stairway. 'Maybe even Lucius's.'

Lucius's life was saved. By the next day the surgeon declared him out of the woods, but warned that he must stay put. He would need rest and quiet to completely recuperate. So his stay at Willburgh House stretched to a fortnight.

Anna did not press to leave while Lucius was there. That was enough of a disruption in the family. Her leaving would merely be another one.

It was a very odd two weeks. A member of the Dorman family—or all of them—visited almost every day. Having endured this crisis together, the animosity between the families seemed to dissipate. Will had been true to his word and ended the dispute over the land. He paid Lord Dorman an exorbitant sum for a clear deed to half of the land. Anna suspected it was the sum that would cover Lord Dorman's debts. Certainly that must have eased a great deal of stress in the Dorman house.

Anna was extremely impressed with Lady Willburgh's cordiality to the Dormans. She was especially kind to Lucius who, after all, had tried to elope with her sixteen-year-old daughter. The maids told Anna that Lucius had apologised to Lady Willburgh and to Will for his behaviour. He especially apologised to Ellen, confessed that he'd manipulated her out of a desire for revenge upon her brother, and that she was indeed too young to contemplate marriage with anyone.

Anna avoided Lucius as much as possible, but when she was in his company he seemed changed. He was courteous. Subdued. Completely lacking in sarcasm.

Ellen had changed as well, but in a way that made Anna sad. Her youthful joy and exuberance disappeared and it seemed like she spent as much time alone as Anna did.

Even though the venom that had permeated Anna's relationships with her mother-in-law, sister-in-law, and Will was eased with the more pressing issue of having to attend to the Dormans, Anna felt separate from them all. As if she'd already left. Even though Will was unfailingly polite and kind to her, he also seemed to treat her as if she'd already left.

Except for that one brief moment when she'd reached the site of the curricle accident, the intimacy they'd so briefly shared was not repeated.

They'd still not told anyone else that Anna was leaving, but when Lucius was almost ready to move back to Dorman Hall, and summer was nearing its end, Anna decided it was time for her to leave. Soon harvest would make more work for Will and she wanted to make this least burdensome to him.

That afternoon Will answered a knock on his office door. It was Anna.

She never came to the office, not since he'd accused her maid of spying for the Dormans. His desk was rapidly returning to the chaos it had been before she'd briefly become the secretary he had yet to hire to help him deal with it.

'Anna!' Will stood. 'What may I do for you?'

She glanced down at his paper-strewn desk, but quickly lifted her gaze back to him. 'I wish to talk with you, is all, Will. For a moment, if you do not mind.'

'Not at all.' He hurried from behind the desk. 'Sit. Shall I call for tea?'

'No. I shouldn't be so long.' She let him lead her to the sofa and chairs.

She sat on the sofa. He chose a chair facing her and felt a cloud of doom engulf him.

She arranged her skirts before speaking. 'I thought this might be the proper time to plan my—my departure.'

Will lowered his head, knowing she'd be able to read his expression. 'There is no hurry, Anna,' he murmured.

'This seems like a good time, though,' she said.

Will's chest began to ache, making it hard to breathe. 'What were you thinking?'

She took a breath. 'I think Mary may want to stay here. Will you be able to keep her on?'

'Of course she may stay.' He dared to reach over and clasp one of her hands in his. 'You don't have to leave either, Anna. You may both stay. Everything is different. I have changed.' He glanced away. 'Or I hope I have. I strive to do better.'

She regarded him with a look of tenderness on her face. 'Oh, Will. Do not take this on as your fault. I've been the disruption. We both know so.'

He knew no such thing. One could just as easily say she was the solution to all the family problems.

She went on. 'We were never meant to be together. Neither of us chose it, remember?'

He may not have chosen it then, but he did now. He wanted to be with her. 'We could keep trying.' He swallowed. 'I want to keep trying. I want you to stay.'

Anna's eyes filled with tears.

'It is no use. I want to leave,' she said.

The first part was true enough; the second a lie. She wanted to stay more than anything, but she was convinced she would only cause more unhappiness. Things were better, because, in so many ways, she was already gone.

He released her hand and spoke sadly. 'If that is what you truly want.'

He was sad now, she thought, but he would be happier without her. She was sorry she did not give him an heir, but how dangerous it would be to make love with him again. She could never leave if they joined together again, flesh to flesh, climbing to that incomparable peak of pleasure.

He cleared his throat. 'But I insist you travel to where you want to live to see if you truly like it. You may wish to live elsewhere.'

He was not arguing with her. Did that make her happy or despondent? She did not know.

'Very well,' she responded. 'I will make a trip to Reading first before arranging to move there.'

'I must accompany you,' he added. 'Since I am paying, I must be certain it is worth the money.'

That made sense. Besides, it would give her more time with him. 'I—I have another request,' she said. 'A silly one, I am sure you will think,' she said.

'What is it?' He seemed to brace himself.

'Might we ride to Reading?' she asked uncertainly. 'On the Highland ponies? Like we did leaving Scotland?'

Like those happy days, did she mean? The ache in his chest grew stronger. 'We can do that.'

Chapter Twenty-Three

They left in two days, telling everyone Will had business in Reading and Anna was accompanying him. They were simply wished safe travel; no one seemed to think anything more about it. Will's estate manager questioned it, but Will told him the business was personal and Parker accepted that. If anyone thought it odd that they rode Highland ponies to Reading, no one said so to them.

They left without fanfare, mounting the ponies and starting on their way. John accompanied them, but after a while, he rode ahead to arrange accommodations for them. Anna and Will rode side by side.

They did not have the beautiful weather that had graced them on their long ride from Scotland. The sky was overcast and the day was one of the warmest of the summer. Reading was a good day's ride and Anna told herself to savour the trip, no matter the weather. It was time with Will and she'd soon be saying goodbye to him for ever.

Will was not pushing the pace, which suited Anna. Mid-morning they stopped at an inn to rest the horses and have some refreshment, but the weather was not improved when they started on their way again. They did not talk much, reminding Anna of those first days when they travelled to Scotland.

Her mind kept wandering to the glorious days and nights she shared with Will on the trip back from Scotland. Especially the glorious nights when everything seemed full of promise. Anna would be alone again. Alone, because she would not be with Will.

The grief of it overwhelmed her. Tears rolled down her cheeks. She slowed enough to ride a little behind him so he could not see. She swallowed the sobs, not wanting him to hear her weeping.

She'd doomed herself with this foolish notion of moving away. At least if she'd stayed at Willburgh House she could see him every day. All she wanted to do was turn around and gallop with him all the way back...home.

She felt a drop on her cheek that was not a tear. Soon more drops fell.

Will turned in his saddle. 'It is about to pour! Look for shelter.'

They rode faster as the raindrops increased.

Finally he pointed. There in a nearby field was a shelter. They left the road and crossed the field to a wooden structure, open on one side, probably meant for exactly this use—shelter from a sudden rainstorm. There was room for the two ponies and them. They dismounted and dried off the horses as best they could and took off their hats and gloves. There was some hay to keep the horses entertained including a bale that they used as a bench.

Anna was acutely aware of the nearness of him. She had not been so close to him since the day of the curricle accident when he embraced her.

He laughed softly.

'What makes you laugh?' she asked.

'The irony of it,' he responded. 'Our first meeting was in a rainstorm and now...' His voice trailed off.

She gazed through the rain across the field. 'This is unlike Vauxhall, though, is it not?'

'And it seems a long time ago,' he said.

'Not even three months.' She turned to him. 'Do you know what else is amusing?'

'What?' he asked without any humour at all.

'Today is my birthday.'

He frowned. 'I should have known that.'

She shrugged. 'I never told you the day. It lacks any importance now.'

'Because I lost you your fortune,' he said.

Impulsively, she grasped his hand. 'Do not think that way, Will,' she pleaded. 'We did not know. Before the Dormans became such *nice people*—' she said this with sarcasm '—they did a very bad thing. A series of bad things.'

He leaned back against the wood of the wall. 'I cannot conjure up the same level of rage as before, but I doubt I will ever trust any of them.'

She sighed. 'They make it easy to blame everything on them. But I made so many mistakes that I regret.'

He sat up straight again. 'You? No. What mistakes did you make?'

She averted her face. She could not speak the biggest mistake. Insisting on leaving. Not accepting Will, his mother, his sister, as the people they were, and staying with them.

He leaned back again and closed his eyes. 'It was me, Anna,' he murmured. 'I let my hatred for the Dormans colour everything. Be my excuse for everything. The truth is I've never forgiven my father for dying in that duel and leaving me to deal with all his duties when I didn't know how. I still don't know how. But then I fought a duel, as well. Was there anyone so foolish?'

She gathered up the skirt of her new riding habit and turned her whole body to face him. 'But you didn't fire at Lucius.'

'I almost did,' he countered. 'I might have killed you.'

'You chose to delope,' she reminded him. 'You made that choice before you turned, didn't you?'

She moved next to him and put her head on his shoulder. 'The duel was my fault, to be honest. I should have told you about Ellen and Lucius right after I caught them.'

He scoffed. 'And might I have done worse then?'

She threaded her arm through his and laced her fingers with his. 'I wish I could do everything all over again.'

He clasped her fingers in his. 'Do you?'

* * *

Will savoured this closeness they fell into, like a habit they'd acquired on the road from Scotland. He liked feeling her hand in his again, liked the easy conversation, the feeling that they were alone in the world, just the two of them. They had everything but the joy of those days.

He did not want to break the spell. 'I'll wager you wish you'd refused to marry me. Think on it. You'd have your fortune today.'

'No,' she said. 'That was not what I was thinking.'

He turned to face her. 'What, then?'

She pulled her hand away and sat up. 'I wish—' she began, then waved the words away.

He wanted to press her, to insist she tell him whatever it was, but, no. That might drive her away. He wanted to bring her closer.

She rose and stood at the open side of the shelter. 'The rain is slowing. Nobody to stop us here like at Vauxhall. We should be able to resume the trip soon.'

'I do not want to,' Will muttered under his breath.

She spun around. 'What did you say?'

'Nothing.' He waved a hand as if to erase his words.

She stepped towards him. 'No. I heard you say something. What was it?' Her voice was turning sharp.

The last thing Will wanted to do on this trip was argue with her. He tried to sound flippant. 'I said I did not want to.'

'Did not want to, what?' she asked.

'Resume the trip.'

She searched his face as if trying to figure it out. 'I did not mean to leave the shelter now.'

'Neither did I.' He inhaled, getting courage. 'I meant I do not want to resume the trip. I do not want to take you to Reading.' He rose and held her by the shoulders. 'I do not want you to live elsewhere. I want you to come home. I love you, Anna. I've been too foolish to always show it, but I've loved you since Scotland.'

She looked up at him, not speaking, until he thought he'd

made another terrible blunder. He must release her. Must let her go.

He could not read the expression on her face, but he'd guess it was tenderness.

'Oh, Will!' she exclaimed. 'I have loved you just as long. I want only to stay with you always.'

It took a moment for her words to register. Then he smiled. He whooped with joy, picked her up and spun her around.

And kissed her.

'Then let's go home,' he said.

'I have a better idea,' she said. 'Let's go on to Reading. Meet John as planned. Let's spend the night there, like we did on the way back from Scotland. We can ride home tomorrow.'

He grinned. 'You called it *home*, Anna. Yes, my love. Tomorrow we go home.'

Epilogue

Buckinghamshire,
July 1819

They were all finally home to Willburgh House after a long Season in London—Anna, Will, his mother, and Ellen who'd made her come-out now that she was eighteen. No riding back from London this year for Anna. She was expecting their second child in November. Their darling son, Will's heir, named Henry after Will's father, was a healthy fourteen-month-old who'd accompanied them to London because neither Will nor Anna wished to be parted from him. It made the entourage to London and back more complicated, but they refused to consider leaving the child in the country with only his nurse. They travelled in three carriages. Anna, the nurse, and Mary in one; Lady Willburgh and Ellen in another because Anna's mother-in-law's nerves could not tolerate a crying, fussy toddler filled with energy. The third carriage held the other servants—and Will's secretary. Will rode, the lucky man.

Lucius rode with him. He just happened to be riding back to Dorman Hall at the same time and met them on the road. He kept Will company, although Anna suspected it was Ellen's company he most desired when they stopped for the horses and took refreshment.

Ellen had plenty of suitors for her first Season, many invitations, many social outings, but no offers she wanted to accept. Lucius was not one of the suitors, but he often found time to speak with Ellen when they happened to be at the same entertainments. His attentions could be described as brotherly, if you could imagine Lucius as behaving brotherly. The accident did seem to alter him, though.

Lucius continued on his way when they finally arrived at Willburgh House. Little Henry was wailing and flailing his arms and legs as they all piled out of the carriages. Nurse ran him into the house.

'Good gracious! What a racket!' Lady Willburgh huffed as she entered the hall and handed her hat, shawl, and gloves to the under-butler.

'He has good lungs,' Will told her.

Ellen laughed.

She'd not quite returned to the girl she was at sixteen, but some of her *joie de vivre* had returned. Anna thought she was wise not to feel compelled to marry at eighteen. Look at what happened to Violet, who'd married Raskin, the poorest choice of a husband Anna could imagine.

Not so her Will. Anna wrapped her arm through his and he responded with a hug. Will was the best of husbands.

He kissed her. 'How was the last part of your trip?'

Anna savoured the warmth and scent of him. 'I think you heard. Your son indeed has good lungs and great stamina. He is tired and hungry, I expect.'

'Poor you and Nurse,' he responded. 'But how are you?'

They started up the stairway together.

She touched her swelling belly. 'The baby kicked whenever the road was too bumpy.'

When they got to the doorways of their rooms Will pulled her inside his and kissed her properly and thoroughly and made her wish it was time to retire rather than time to dress for dinner.

'I missed you,' Will murmured.

'You could have shared our carriage,' she replied. 'There was room.'

He laughed. 'I believe I'll content myself with spending more time with you now we are home.'

She leaned against him and felt the beating of his heart beneath her ear. 'Yes.' She smiled. 'The whole family is home.'

* * * * *

The Lady's Snowbound Scandal

Paulia Belgado

MILLS & BOON

Born and raised in the Philippines, **Paulia Belgado** has worn many hats over the years, from office assistant, flyer distributor, singer, nanny and farm worker. Now she's proud to add romance author to that list. After decades of dreaming of seeing her name on the shelves next to her favorite romance authors, she finally found the courage (and time—thanks, 2020!) to write her first book. Paulia lives in Malaysia with her husband, Jason, Jessie the poodle and an embarrassing amount of pens and stationery art supplies. Follow her on X @pauliabelgado or on Facebook.com/pauliabelgado.

Books by Paulia Belgado

Harlequin Historical

The Marquess's Year to Wed
The Lady's Scandalous Proposition
Game of Courtship with the Earl
May the Best Duke Win

Look out for more books from Paulia Belgado coming soon.

Visit the Author Profile page
at millsandboon.com.au.

Author Note

Christmas is my absolute favorite time of the year, and I'm so thrilled that I was asked to revise my outline for *The Lady's Snowbound Scandal*, originally pitched as a reverse-dollar-princess story, into a holiday-themed book. Since this was going to be about a coldhearted robber baron who finds love, Ebenezer Scrooge would have been the easiest character to base the hero on, but then I never like to do things easy. So, I thought, why not use another infamous Christmas-hating character from literature and give him a love story? I sent this outline to my editor with the working title of *You're a Mean One, Mr. Smith* (which probably would never have gone past the legal department).

Of course, writing a historical romance set during Christmas meant diving deep into Victorian holiday customs. I quickly found out that the Victorians (and Queen Victoria and Albert) popularized many of the modern holiday traditions we know today, like putting up Christmas trees, sending cards and Christmas crackers. Also, Charles Dickens's *A Christmas Carol*, published in 1843, was said to have popularized eating turkey on Christmas Day, as previously most families had goose.

I hope you enjoy reading Elliot and Georgina's story as much as I enjoyed writing it!

For Dr. Ana Maria Belgado Naluz
Or simply, Ate Ana
Who left us much too soon

Thank you for giving me the gift of loving romance
novels. I will forever be grateful for this.
And to Gelo, her son and the person she loved
wholeheartedly. Your mom's love will never fade
or disappear, and we will never forget her
generosity and selflessness.

Chapter One

~~~~~~~~~~

London, England,
1st December 1853

No seven words could strike more terror into Lady Georgina
Abernathy's heart than those her new companion Miss Sophia
Warren was about to utter.

'Shall we go for a walk outside?'

Lost in her embroidery, Georgina was distracted by the dreadful suggestion, causing her to poke her finger with her needle.
'Ouch!'

Drat.

She quickly drew her finger into her mouth, thankful the
blood hadn't stained the expensive white silk handkerchief. She
scowled at Miss Warren.

'You cannot spend another day cooped up inside.' Miss Warren gestured to the window. 'It's an unusually warm winter
morning. Why would you object to going for a stroll outdoors?'

Truly, Georgina had no objections to most of the seven words
in that sentence. 'Shall we' implied that Miss Warren would
be with her, to which she did not take issue. Even the 'go for a
walk' part sounded like a good idea, if her sore bottom, which
had been seated for hours, had any say in the matter.

No, Georgina could only protest to one of those words. *Outside.*

She shuddered.

That earned her a stern look from the companion. 'Lady Georgina.'

Georgina placed her embroidery into her basket and splayed out on the settee in a most unladylike manner. 'Going outside requires that I put on my coat and my hat, as well as my gloves and boots.'

'Yes, and...?'

'But that also means I must leave this lovely warm sitting room and my tea.' She nodded to the tray next to her on the table. 'And step out through the door.'

'Yes, that is the general idea of outside.'

'And why would I want to do that?'

'Lady Georgina, since I arrived here at Harwicke House, all we've done is embroider, read, paint watercolours, drink tea, and occasionally sit in the gardens.' A wry smile played on Miss Warren's lips. 'You don't mean to stay indoors for the remainder of the year, do you?'

'I do.'

'Truly?'

'Yes.' Rising to her feet, she brushed her hands over her skirts. 'Miss Warren, when you assumed the role of my companion from Great-Aunt Leticia a few weeks ago, you probably expected a young debutante, not an unmarried lady of seven and twenty.'

'To be quite honest, I did not know what to expect, Lady Georgina.'

'In any case, as you will learn, I do not participate in society. At least, I haven't for three Seasons now.'

In her first Seasons she had attended every ball, gathering, and social event Leticia had deemed necessary. Under the watchful eye of her chaperone, she'd had no choice after all. But then Leticia's health had declined and while she did not rejoice in her chaperone's failing health, it had been an excellent excuse not to attend any social gatherings in the last three years. Besides, six failed Seasons seemed quite pathetic and she wasn't about to humiliate herself for a seventh.

'Here I am, in my tenth year since I came out. I think it is quite apparent that I will never find a husband.'

'That is simply not—'

'Oh, it's all right, Miss Warren, I have accepted this fact and rejoice in it.' She paused. 'My brother, the Duke of Harwicke, has pledged to take care of me for as long as I need.'

It had been after her last Season, when no gentleman had offered for her, that he had made the remark. Trevor was not being unkind, only pragmatic. Georgina was painfully shy, and too plain, and despite years of being on the so-called marriage mart, no man had come close to buying what she had to offer.

'Did you not wonder why my brother did not find me a chaperone? And why you were hired to be my companion instead?'

Miss Warren's mouth pressed tight. 'I did not think it my place to ask.'

'I am no longer a fresh young debutante with a reputation to protect—meaning I'm much too old for a chaperone. I have no other close relatives, and with my brother unmarried, there is no other lady of the house.'

'And propriety requires that another woman, such as a chaperone, be present when he is not around?'

'Exactly. I didn't want him to find another distant relative who would drag me to balls and society functions, so we compromised by hiring a companion for me.' Trevor had been against it, but she'd told him that eventually, once she was old and feeble, she would need one anyway, so why waste time when she could just have a companion now and be done with it.

'Surely you could still find a husband, if you searched hard enough.'

She snorted. 'The Ton, if they remember me at all, has already placed me on the shelf.'

'The shelf?'

'Oh, you know, *the* shelf.' She gesticulated with her hands, raising her arms high up. 'The spinster shelf, where all the other old, unmarried ladies of the ton gather dust. Frankly, I am relieved that I no longer have to go into society.'

'Ah, so it is not the outside you object to, but the people.'

'Precisely. I would find the outside quite tolerable, except for the pervasive presence of people.'

She shuddered again at the thought of bumping into acquaintances and having to exchange pleasantries with them, never mind actually making conversation. No one could ever speak their mind or be honest or even just excuse themselves when they grew tired of the interaction because it was impolite.

How everyone simply agreed that this was how society worked was beyond her. People were always such a drain on her mind and body—whenever she came back from any sort of event she often found herself exhausted for hours afterwards.

And when she thought of those events where crowds of people gathered…

No, she did not even want to think of that.

With her great-aunt indisposed, she no longer had to worry about *that*.

She also didn't have to be around *people* any more. And while she said a silent prayer to the heavens to keep Leticia in good health, she also added one of thanks—because now she stayed at home all she wanted and never had to see any member of the Ton for as long as she lived.

'So you do not plan to attend any balls, accept invitations to teas, musicals, or even take morning calls?'

'No, no, no and no,' she said decisively. 'I have packed up my ball gowns, left my dancing slippers to gather dust, and tossed out all my dance cards.'

'I see.' Slipping her hand into her pocket, Miss Warren retrieved an envelope from her reticule. 'I suppose that means you do not want to attend the planning meeting for this year's Christmas fundraiser for St Agnes's Orphanage for Girls?'

'I—' Georgina stopped short. 'When?'

'The day after tomorrow.' Her companion waved the envelope around. 'This was addressed to Miss Leticia Abernathy but, seeing as she is no longer your chaperone, Dawson thought to give it to me. The people at the orphanage probably hadn't been informed about Miss Abernathy's retirement. It's a wasted effort, though, seeing as you don't—'

'Of course we will attend—we always do,' Georgina exclaimed, snatching the envelope from Miss Warren's fingers.

'Is that so?' Miss Warren asked wryly. 'I thought you said you didn't venture into society?'

'This is not society,' said Georgina, holding the envelope to her chest.

Aside from her brother, there were only two other things she loved most in the world—St Agnes's Orphanage and Christmas, and this yearly fundraiser was a convergence of the two, which was why she made an exception to her no-socialisation rule for this particular event. Besides, many of the ladies who participated in the efforts preferred to plan the event and not necessarily do any of the work, or even mingle with the children. Why on earth they would do that, she never would understand, but it didn't matter to Georgina.

'And the people?'

'These are not just people, either. These are *children.*'

And how she adored the girls at St Agnes's. Children were such a joy to her—so refreshing and so honest. They spoke whatever was on their mind about anything that interested them, and with such varied conversation Georgina never found herself bored or impatient to leave. If there was one regret she had with regard to her spinsterhood, it was that she would never have her own children. But that was why she enjoyed visiting St Agnes's and did so regularly throughout the year.

'We must prepare for our visit,' Georgina declared as she crossed the room towards the door.

'Now? But the committee doesn't meet for another two days.'

Looking over her shoulder, Georgina said, 'Which means we have very little time.'

And so, two days later, Georgina and Miss Warren, with the help of the Harwicke House staff, loaded up the carriage with baskets of goodies for the children and the staff at St Agnes's.

Miss Warren peeped out of the window when the carriage stopped. 'That didn't take too long at all. Have we passed Hanover Square?'

'Yes. We're just at the end of Boyle Street.'

'Right in the middle of the busy commerce district?' the companion asked, astonished. 'I know there are a few orphanages around London, but most of those are in the East End or far in the outskirts of the city. How ever did St Agnes's manage to acquire a building in this neighbourhood?'

'It's quite unusual, I know,' Georgina began. The door opened, and as she took the footman's offered hand she continued. 'But according to Mrs Jameson—she's the matron here at St Agnes's—one of the orphanage's first benefactors was a wealthy merchant who offered to let the entire building to them for a very reasonable price.'

'Interesting...' When she alighted, Miss Warren glanced up. 'This is not what I expected.'

The carriage had stopped outside the doorstep of a four-storey building made of red brick and stone. On one side was a milliner's shop and on the other was a solicitor's office, while a bank occupied the building across from it. There was no sign outside proclaiming what it was, and it certainly did not look out of place on the busy commercial street.

'It was not what I expected either, when I first came to visit,' Georgina said. 'And I assure you, the children here are treated well. It's not very old—established only three years ago. There are twenty-seven girls living here and the oldest is about ten years old. They have tutors who help them learn to read and write, and one day, when the children are old enough, we hope to help them find a trade or learn skills to help them into adulthood.'

Georgina walked up to the door and knocked. Seconds ticked by, but no one answered.

'Do you think perhaps they are out?' Miss Warren asked.

'There's always someone here, and the children don't usually all leave at the same time.' She looked around them. 'Hmmm... there doesn't seem to be anyone else here yet.' Usually by this time carriages would be waiting in line to drop off the other ladies in the planning committee. 'Are we sure it's today?' She had glanced at the letter last night, but wondered if she'd read it wrongly.

'Yes, I'm quite certain, and the letter said ten o'clock in the morning,' Miss Warren said.

'Then why—?'

The door flew open, cutting Georgina off.

'I'm sorry, we— Lady Georgina!' The harried-looking woman on the other side curtseyed. 'What are you doing here, milady?'

'Mrs Jameson,' she greeted here. 'Miss Warren, this is Mrs Jameson, the matron of St Agnes's. Mrs Jameson, this is Miss Sophia Warren, my new companion, who has replaced Great-Aunt Leticia.'

Mrs Jameson wrung her hands together. 'Oh, dear, is your aunt…?'

'Great-Aunt Leticia has simply retired,' she said.

'I see. That must be why you did not receive the letters.'

Georgina frowned. 'We received one letter. I thought the planning committee was to meet today for the Christmas fundraiser?'

'Oh, milady, I sent out the *second* set of letters yesterday, but yours was addressed to Miss Abernathy. We have had to cancel the fundraiser.'

'Cancel?' Georgina exclaimed. 'Why ever would you cancel the fundraiser? It's the biggest event for St Agnes's, and raises enough money to cover the rent for the year.'

'I… Please come in and I'll explain.'

The matron ushered them inside into the foyer. Georgina could not help but notice how the house seemed unusually quiet. Usually as soon as she entered, children were running up and down the stairs or rushing about, not to mention laughing or shouting down the corridors.

'Would you like some tea, milady?'

Georgina searched Mrs Jameson's face. The usually pleasant woman had dark circles under her eyes and the lines on her forehead were etched deeper than the last time she had seen them. 'Please just tell us what happened, Mrs Jameson.'

The older woman sighed. 'I'm afraid there's no nice way to say it. We are losing our home.'

'What?' Georgina exclaimed. 'How? When? Why?'

Mrs Jameson's lower lip trembled. 'We received notice to vacate the premises the day the invitations for the planning meeting were sent out.'

'Vacate? But what about your patron?'

'Unfortunately, Mr Atkinson passed away a few weeks ago.' Mrs Jameson sniffed. 'I didn't even know he had died. His heirs have sold the building and now we are being evicted.'

'When?'

'On December the twenty-fifth.'

Miss Warren gasped. 'What cruel man would make orphans homeless on Christmas Day?'

Georgina had the same thought, though the words she would use to describe such a man were much more severe than 'cruel'— not to mention something she would never say in polite company. 'Who is the new owner? Do you have the eviction letter?'

'Yes, it's in my office. Come, I'll show you.'

They followed Mrs Jameson to her office, where she produced the letter. 'Here.'

Georgina took the letter and began to read it, her blood simmering with rage as she read its contents. '"Notice seeking possession...vacate premises... December the twenty-fifth..."' The edges of the letter crumpled under her fingers. '"Face legal action..."' Her gaze scanned up to the letterhead on top of the document. '"ES Smith Consolidated Trust"?' She chewed at her bottom lip. 'What is the "ES Smith Consolidated Trust"?'

'The name of the business who bought the building from Mr Atkinson's heirs,' Mrs Jameson supplied.

'Have you tried to speak with the heirs?' Georgina asked. 'Or with the owner of this company?'

'The solicitor who brought the letter said that Mr Smith— that's the new owner—was not interested in any counter offer unless it was for more than the amount he paid.'

'And how much is that?'

'Much more than we can afford.'

'And that is?' Miss Warren enquired.

When Mrs Jameson said the amount, Georgina gasped. 'He paid *that* much?'

The matron nodded. 'And see...there's not much we can do except pack our things and prepare—' The creaking of the door hinges interrupted her. 'Charlotte! Eliza! What are you doing here?'

Two children rushed inside, both of them running to Georgina. 'Lady Georgina! Lady Georgina,' the smaller of the two cried as she wrapped her arms around her legs. 'You're finally back in London.'

'Yes, Eliza, I'm so sorry I took so long. Great-Aunt Leticia needed more time to settle into her new home in Hampshire, then I had to wait for Miss Warren to join me—' She nodded up at the companion '—before I could come for a visit.'

'Lady Georgina, we have to leave St Agnes's,' said the taller one, Charlotte, her blue eyes sombre.

'Yes, Mrs Jameson told me.'

'Where will we go?' Eliza's eyes filled with tears. 'I don't want to leave at Christmas.'

As Georgina knelt down to their level to wrap her arms around both girls, her temper beginning to rise once more. 'Do not fret, girls. I shall take care of this. Mrs Jameson, Eliza, Charlotte—if you'll excuse us…' Rising, she straightened her shoulders. 'We must be on our way.'

'And where are we going, Lady Georgina?' Miss Warren asked, puzzled.

Georgina waved the eviction letter in the air. 'To the offices of the ES Smith Consolidated Trust.'

'I'm happy to report profits are up.'

No seven words made Elliot Smith happier than those just said by his recently hired man of business in London, Andrew Morgan.

Well, usually they did.

However, he'd heard it so many times that the effect on him had lessened over the years. Indeed, he had more money now than he knew what to do with, and would not be able to spend it all in ten lifetimes. His reputation for making spectacular returns on his investments had earned him the nickname 'The Midas of San Francisco'. Others said he had the luck of the devil.

Elliot scoffed silently. Only fools and dreamers sat around, hoping and waiting for their luck to turn. Everything he had now, he had earned with his own sweat and blood.

Having grown up dirt-poor, Elliot only had two assets: himself and time. He'd seen how his own wastrel of a father had squandered both, barely eking out a living, throwing away his hard-earned money on drink and women while Elliot and his mother nearly starved at home. When Ma died, when he was ten, he'd vowed to never waste a single second of his life. Sitting in that grubby hovel alone, next to his mother's lifeless body, his father nowhere to be found, he'd vowed that he would make something of himself.

Still, he did not discount the fact that he had a knack of being in the right place and time. If one could call such a thing 'luck', then he supposed his first stroke of luck had been his mother passing and his being forced to work, finding odd jobs in New York City's harbours, doing everything from selling papers to shining shoes just so he could eat. But it was at this time that Elliot had observed the ferries crossing the river, carrying dozens and dozens of passengers to and from their destinations. This had given him the idea to run his own service. And he'd begun to form a plan in his mind—specifically, a ten-year plan with one goal: get himself out of poverty.

So, he'd worked even harder, saved every penny he could, borrowed some, and purchased his first periauger when he was fifteen. He'd ferried people from Staten Island to Manhattan, and in a few short years had a fleet of ships plying New York's rivers.

Having seen success with his first ten-year plan, he'd created another one with a different goal: expand his business interests. It was then that his second stroke of luck had come, when gold was discovered in California. Elliot, however, had not rushed west to mine for the precious metal. No, he'd moved to San Francisco and invested in steamships to transport the gold back to the east coast. By focusing on transport, and monopolising the routes southward through Nicaragua, he had expanded his business empire and grown his fortune.

Perhaps some might say that his third turn of luck had been selling his steamship business for a king's ransom and moving to New York just before all the gold had dried up. However, it hadn't quite been *good* luck that had made him move back east, and then even further east across the Atlantic to London.

'Mr Smith?' Morgan repeated.

His voice was firm, but polite, in the way that only these posh English people could sound.

'Apologies, Morgan.' Elliot sat up straight behind his desk and drummed his fingers on the surface. 'You were saying the owner of that textile factory in Manchester is ready to sign the contract for the purchase?'

While he might have been lost in his thoughts, Elliot never missed any business-related chatter.

'Yes, Mr Smith.' Morgan slid a piece of paper across the table. 'Here are the final figures. Mr Davis is quite eager for the sale to proceed as soon as possible.'

Elliot quickly scanned the document, checking the final number at the bottom. From his calculations, after investing in newer looms, he'd be able to turn a profit in two years—three years at the most.

'All right.' He quickly signed on the line at the bottom. 'See that the payment is released.'

'Of course, Mr Smith.'

Though Morgan did not say it aloud, Elliot could tell from the man's tone and countenance that he did not believe the factory was a wise investment. Indeed, if one were merely looking at profits for the last five years, Davis Mills' numbers were abhorrent. They were bleeding money faster than a dinghy with holes. Elliot, however, had seen the potential in the business, as well as in the textiles industry in England. And with Davis eager to sell, he was getting it at a bargain.

Morgan's scepticism was rather refreshing at this point.

Back in San Francisco, everyone waited for Elliot to make his move before making theirs. After his success in the steamship trade, he'd invested in various businesses and real estate around the city, and everything he'd touched had indeed turned to gold, earning him the 'Midas' moniker. Word had spread around town and soon every businessman and investor watched his every move. Stocks would rise and fall based on his decisions, and the value of companies would skyrocket if he even expressed an interest in them.

Elliot had made more money than God, and continued to expand his empire in San Francisco. And, seeing as his previous ten-year plans had brought him great success, he'd created another one—only this one would cement his legacy. At that time he'd been a man thirty years of age, and there were things expected of him. He was not immortal, but there was one way he could live for ever and be remembered after he passed.

And so he'd set the goal for his next ten-year plan: marry a refined woman of quality who would elevate his status and give him a passel of bright young children to pass his legacy on to.

But, as he had learned, one could plan for any eventuality, but life could always drop an unexpected situation at his doorstep.

'If that is all, Mr Smith...'

Elliot rose, signalling an end to their meeting. 'Yes, that's all. If you could—'

'Mr Smith!' The door flew open and a flustered-looking young man of about twenty rushed inside. It was his assistant, Michael Grant. 'Apologies for the intrusion—'

'We were just finishing up.' Still, he crossed his arms over his chest and scowled, as Grant knew better than to interrupt his meetings. 'What is it?'

Grant swallowed. 'S-Sir, one of your house staff just arrived and asked to see you.' As he stepped out of the way John, one of his footmen, hurried inside. He looked even more harried than Grant.

'M-Mr S-Smith, I... I...' he stammered.

Elliot tapped his foot impatiently. 'Why are you here?'

'Er...' He took a deep breath. 'I came to tell you that the governess is quitting. Again.'

Ah, yes.

The unexpected situation.

Quite literally dropped at his doorstep five years ago on a foggy night, in the form of two little girls, aged four and eleven.

'And that is all?' he said, irritated. 'Why rush here like the sky is about to fall on our heads? Surely my sisters are not alone, fending for themselves in a ten-bedroom house in Mayfair?'

He employed a staff of nearly two dozen people at his newly purchased London home, all hand-picked by him, from the butler to the scullery maid.

'Er...no, sir. B-But there is the matter of the fire.'

He sprang from his chair, slamming his palms on the table. 'Fire?' Terror struck him straight in the chest. 'Where are Anne-Marie and Lily? Are they safe? Was the fire brigade called? Well, John? Speak!'

The footman turned even paler. 'I—I—I...'

'Breathe, man,' Morgan urged. 'Then speak.'

John took a great heaving breath before words spilled out of his mouth. 'Everything is under control. Your sisters are safe and the fire was limited to the drawing room. The staff was able to put it out. But Miss Jones is quitting—and not *quietly*, she says, unless you come and pay her this month's wages, plus severance.'

So the shrew wants money.

While Elliot had lots of money—he could certainly meet her demands without even blinking—that wasn't the point. When he'd hired Miss Jones as a governess, he'd had the most peculiar inkling about her. Her references were impeccable, and she was in demand, having just left the employ of a baronet whose children were now full-grown. However, something about her just hadn't felt quite right. But he'd been desperate because he'd already had three governesses quit, and they'd only been in England for six months. He'd hired Miss Jones anyway, because he was far too busy, but he should have trusted his instincts.

It was obvious Miss Jones was much too nosy and shrewd for her own good. It was likely she'd figured out why Elliot had left New York and was now in England, and was using that to her advantage.

She was blackmailing him, plain and simple, and threatening to ruin his and his sisters' reputations if she was not paid out.

Damn, if he didn't hate her right now, he would admire her audacity.

'Grant, grab my coat, my hat...' He let out a huff. 'And my cheque book. John, go back to the carriage and wait for me.'

The footman nodded and his assistant scurried off.

'Morgan?'

'I'll be on my way, Mr Smith,' the older man said. 'I'll see you in the morning.' Tipping his hat, he turned and left.

Elliot drummed his fingers on his arm as he waited for Grant to retrieve his things. Too anxious to sit, he faced the large window behind his chair, the grey London winter sky greeting him. There was something soothing about the scene outside, in some ways reminding him of foggy days in San Francisco. Ironically, it had been on a day like today that two little girls had appeared on his doorstep all those years ago.

Well, not so little any more.

Lily was now nine years old and Anne-Marie sixteen, practically a woman.

Still, he would never forget the sight of the two of them in threadbare clothing, shivering and clinging to each other at his doorstep. There'd also been a woman with them, who claimed to have known his father—in the most biblical sense—and said these two waifs were his half-sisters.

He hadn't seen nor heard from his father, Harold Smith, since he'd left New York for California. When his ferry business had begun to prosper, he'd spent a good deal of money trying to re-form his father—employing him on his ferries, paying off his debts, and even setting him up in a modest apartment in Queens. Yet his father had always turned to drinking and gambling, never showing up to work and running up more debts. Before he'd moved to San Francisco, he had given Harold a generous bank draft and told him that after this he would never receive a single cent from Elliot ever again.

Seeing as his father had conveniently died a year prior, and could not be there to prove her claims, Elliot hadn't been about to take this stranger's word for it. But then the two girls had looked up at him with the same green eyes he had inherited from Harold. He could not deny that they were related to him, so he'd had no choice but to welcome them into his home. The woman—their mother—had not been interested in staying, but she'd been very aware of Elliot's recent good fortune. She'd happily left with a fat roll of bills, leaving behind her daughters.

The sound of the door opening jolted him out of his thoughts.

Running his fingers through his hair, he spun around. 'Damn it, Grant, what took you so—?' He sucked in a breath. 'You're not Grant.'

No definitely not.

For one thing, the figure standing in the doorway was a woman.

'No, sir, I am not.'

Elliot fixed his gaze on this woman who had dared to enter his office without an appointment. She looked like any of the dozens of fashionable English women he'd seen shopping or having tea on Bond Street. The fabric of her white and red walking dress was fine silk, and the wool cloak around her shoulders was trimmed with mink. He couldn't tell what colour her hair was, because most of it was hidden under a large bonnet, though he spied a bit of blonde. Her face was nothing out of the ordinary, with round cheeks and the tip of her nose all pink from the chilly air. As he locked his gaze on hers, he found himself staring into large eyes the colour of bright copper pennies.

He cleared his throat. 'Can I help you, Miss…?'

'Lady Georgina Abernathy,' she said.

A lady.

Now he was intrigued. 'Lady Abernathy.'

'It's Lady Georgina,' she corrected. 'There is no Lady Abernathy.'

His interest was piqued further, and his mind began to form possibilities.

'So it is a courtesy title? From your father?' As part of his preparation for his move to England, he had read *Debrett's Peerage*.

'Yes. He was a duke.'

Now *that* caught his attention. Dukes were the highest ranking of all titles in England, save for royalty.

Her pink nose twitched. 'Are you Mr ES Smith?'

'Yes, I am.'

'The owner of ES Smith Consolidated Trust?'

'Yes, I am Elliot Smith and I own this company, as well as a few others.'

Her brows snapped together. 'You're American?'

'Yes. May I ask a question as well?'

'And what is that?'

'What are you doing here, Lady Georgina?'

'I…' She hesitated, then straightened her shoulders. 'I've come to ask you not to evict the residents at number fifty-five Boyle Street.'

'Boyle Street?' He rubbed at his chin. 'Ah, yes. I purchased that building from a Mr Andrews…no, Atkinson.'

And it had been a fine deal as well, as Atkinson had been eager to sell to stave off his creditors. Desperate sellers always offered the best bargains.

'But why would I need to evict the residents? Isn't it some shop or factory?'

Lady Georgina's mouth pursed. 'I'm afraid it is not, Mr Smith. Number fifty-five Boyle Street happens to be St Agnes's Orphanage for Girls.'

'An orphanage? In the middle of a busy commercial district?'

She let out an exasperated sigh. 'You bought it, didn't you? You didn't know it was an orphanage?'

'I did not.' He frowned. While he had instructed Morgan to clear the building, Atkinson definitely hadn't mentioned there were any occupants, nor that they were orphans.

Damn.

'Oh, now I see!' She clapped her hands together. 'There was a mix-up then? And you really aren't evicting the girls?'

'I didn't say that.'

She blinked. 'You mean to throw over two dozen orphaned girls onto the street?'

Elliot ignored the knot forming in his gut and erased the vision of shivering waifs out in the cold her words had conjured in his mind. He'd made many cutthroat decisions in business before, and this one would be no different.

But his next move would no doubt be the most ruthless one he would ever make.

'I could change my mind. I mean, *you* could change my mind.'

'Me?' Her delicate brows slashed downwards. 'And what is it I can do to change your mind?'

'Marry me.'

Her bright coppery eyes grew to the size of saucers. 'I—I b-beg your pardon?'

'You heard me. Marry me and I will rescind the eviction notice.'

'You can't be serious.'

He was deadly serious. After all, this was the very reason he'd come to England: to marry a refined, blue-blooded English lady.

To say that the two little girls had thrown his entire life into chaos would have been an understatement. The children had been practically feral, for one thing. They hadn't known how to behave in polite company and both had run wild, sending his household into disarray. From what little bits and pieces they'd told her, their mother was likely a whore and they'd lived in a bawdy house before they'd left for San Francisco. He'd immediately hired a nanny for them, but had known a paid staff member would not be enough to turn the girls into proper and civilised young women. It had been evident that the girls needed a strong feminine influence.

Then there was his ten-year plan to marry and have children he could pass his legacy on to. If news came out that he had two illegitimate sisters—and it would, because San Francisco was still a small town—no woman would want to marry him. Unless he sent his sisters away, which he would never do.

And so he'd decided to move back to New York, setting them up in a grand house on Fifth Avenue where he could simply pass the girls off as his legitimate sisters. He had determined to find a suitable wife with all the graces and refinement necessary to raise his sisters and ensure that they, too, would make good matches when they were of age.

Flush with cash from the sale of his steamship business, he'd bought and sold a few properties in and around the city, invested in some businesses, and after a few years had once again been reaping the benefits of his golden touch.

But Elliot had miscalculated this move.

He had mistakenly thought his newfound wealth would allow him to mingle with the Knickerbocker set, so he could find a suitable wife—preferably with the pedigree that could open the right doors for him and his sisters. New York's high society salons, however, had remained closed to those who were not one of them. Though the society matrons of New York had not known about the girls' illegitimacy, they also had not known about *him*—and that had been the problem. Except for business acquaintances, Elliot had no social connections in the city—at least none that mattered. To the elite of the Fifth Avenue, no matter how much money he made, how many properties he owned, or stocks he traded, he would never be good enough to marry one of their daughters.

After three years of attempting to infiltrate New York's upper crust, with no victory in sight, he'd been about to give up when he'd seen a story in the newspaper about a duke and duchess from England visiting New York. There was to be a grand celebration that would take place at the home of the Commodore and Mrs Baldwin, *the* foremost socialites in the city. Apparently the Duchess was a born-and-bred American—the former Miss Grace Hathaway from Rockaway, New York, daughter of Richard Hathaway, who owned hotels along the beaches in Queens. Elliot didn't know the girl, but he remembered Hathaway—a jovial old fellow who swore like a sailor and drank like one too, with the manners of a goat. Elliot couldn't believe that Hathaway would be invited to this celebration and not him, just because his daughter had married some fancy duke from England.

This news, however, had given him an idea for a new ten-year plan. If Miss Grace Hathaway of Rockaway could marry into English society and come back as a celebrated success, why couldn't he?

However, he'd been in London for more than six months now, and he had yet to meet any eligible ladies. It seemed the English elite were even more prejudiced than New York's. In fact, Lady Georgina was perhaps the closest he'd come even to speaking with anyone who had a potential to be his bride.

'Well, Lady Georgina? What is your answer?'

The entirety of her face had turned red. 'I am not a chattel to be exchanged or bargained for,' she blurted out. 'I will not sell myself to you. How dare you suggest something so utterly offensive?'

'When you say it that way, it does sound offensive...' He

paused. 'But what is marriage anyway? When you take it down to its barest bones, it's nothing but a contract between two parties from which both benefit. Not much different than let's say…a deed of sale. There's even property and money exchanged. In this case, if you become my wife, I will simply void the contract.'

And he would have his refined English bride, who would not only elevate his status, but that of his sisters. Once they came of age they, too, would marry well and provide him with nieces and nephews who could continue his legacy. Why, Lady Georgina wouldn't even have to bear him an heir. After the wedding they could live separately, like most married couples of the Ton.

'Y-You are insane, Mr Smith,' she spluttered.

'Why not? I'm very wealthy, you know, and would be generous to my wife. I could buy you jewels, gowns, houses, a yacht. I have several houses in America and I am negotiating to purchase a lovely estate in Surrey. Anything you want that I don't have, I can provide.'

It was just money after all.

Her face turned even redder and her hands curled into fists at her sides. 'I will not marry you. I will *never* marry you.'

Elliot ignored the small pang in his chest at her words. 'All right, then. I guess your orphans will have to find another home.'

'You're a fiendish, miserly…' She seemed to struggle to find the words to describe him. 'Scrooge!'

'A what?'

'Scrooge,' she repeated. Her eyes turned bright with fury. 'As in Ebenezer Scrooge! Ha! You even have the same initials—ES. I can't believe you would be so cruel as to toss orphans out of the only home they've ever known! And on Christmas Day too.'

'Christmas?' He looked at the calendar on the wall. 'Is it Christmas already?'

'It's December the first,' she informed him.

'Ah, so it's not Christmas yet.'

'But it is the season of Christmas,' she said. 'Does that not mean anything to you?'

If she had thought that would help her in pleading her case, she was, unfortunately, deeply mistaken.

Because, for him, Christmas wasn't a special day. It wasn't

even an ordinary day—at least not since he'd woken up that one Christmas morning and found his mother coughing, her body weak as a baby bird's. She'd been hiding her illness for some time and the cold weather had made it worse. They'd had no money for a doctor, so she'd died in their makeshift shack on the Lower East Side.

'Elliot, come here,' she had rasped. *'There is something I need you to do for me...'*

His mind blocked off that memory instantly.

As the years had gone on, Christmas had become just another day to him. He never celebrated, or decorated, and he certainly never gave or received presents. The closest he'd come to celebrating it had been in the last five years, if only to indulge Lily and Anne-Marie, watching them open presents on Christmas Eve. However, he let his staff deal with the festivities, and on Christmas Day itself he preferred to spend the day at the office, where he could actually get some work done as no one was around to disturb him.

Lady Georgina turned those pleading copper eyes on him. 'Can't you find it in your heart to allow the children to stay, Mr Smith? Their rent was paid to Mr Atkinson every month without delay.'

He'd seen the figures, of course, and had to bite his tongue to stop himself from laughing at the dismal amount they'd been paying. It had been barely enough to pay the taxes.

'You know my terms, Lady Georgina.'

Her eyes blazed once again. 'I told you, I will not—'

'Then we have no deal.' He crossed his arms over his chest in a firm, final motion.

She let out a small high-pitched sound as her lips pressed together. 'Good day to you, then, Mr Smith.'

'Good day, Lady Georgina.'

He didn't even wince when she slammed the door behind him. Instead, he turned back to the window and glanced out. Moments later, Lady Georgina marched out of his offices and into the magnificent carriage waiting on the street. He continued to watch the carriage as it rolled away, disappearing into the distance.

'Mr Smith?' Grant poked his head in. 'I heard voices and didn't want to interrupt.' He held up the coat and hat in his hands. 'The cheque book is in the front pocket, sir. Shall I cancel the rest of your meetings for the day?'

'No need.' Elliot blew out a breath and forced Lady Georgina out of his thoughts. 'This shan't take very long. I expect we'll be back within the hour.'

Chapter Two

4th December

'And there is truly nothing you can do about it, Trev?'

Trevor Abernathy, Duke of Harwicke, who also happened to be Georgina's brother, shook his head. 'I'm sorry, Georgie. As much as I want to help you save the orphanage, we simply cannot afford it.'

'You've looked into it? There's nothing we can sell to purchase the building? What if I go without new dresses for a year? Two years?'

'All of our lands are entailed, and therefore I cannot sell any of them.' Trevor smiled fondly at her. 'And I'm afraid it would cost more than two years' worth of dresses to purchase a building like that.'

Drat.

'How about your friends? Couldn't you pool your resources together and make an investment?'

'Yes, but that would take time. And, Georgie…' He took her hands into his. 'It's not really an investment—you do understand that?'

'Pfft.' The breath she blew out made a stray lock of wispy

hair fly off her forehead. 'I know.' She stared up at her brother's kind face. 'I appreciate you trying.'

And she also appreciated the fact that he was not condescending to her—never had over the years. Perhaps because since they had lost both their parents in a terrible carriage accident twelve years ago they'd understood that they only had each other from then on, and their relationship had grown stronger over the years. Truly, there was no one else in the world she adored more than Trevor.

'I shall continue to search for alternative lodgings for them,' he said. 'And you should perhaps reach out to the other patrons and patronesses to start a new fundraising effort? Even if I can find a new place for them, the landlord will still expect rent.'

'Of course.'

Unless the Good Lord dropped another generous donor into their laps, any location they secured for the children would have to be paid for. Raising funds would be a good start, but December the twenty-fifth was fast approaching and the orphanage could be shut down before Trevor secured anything for them.

'I've also enquired about this Mr Smith fellow, to see if I can find anything he would want in return for giving up the property. From what little I've heard, he's supposedly a very rich and shrewd businessman. He's called the Midas of something—everything he touches turns to gold. We would have to find something truly valuable to make him want to change his mind about the eviction.'

Georgina avoided Trevor's gaze and bit the inside of her cheek. After all, she already knew *one* thing Mr Smith wanted. *No. Never.*

She crossed her arms over her chest and pouted.

And how dared that boorish man even suggest such a thing?

'Are you all right, Georgie?' Trevor cocked his head to the side. 'You seem rather piqued all of a sudden.'

Georgina managed to smooth out her frown. 'I…yes, I was just thinking about that…er…the last bit of the banister in the main hall. It's still missing evergreen and holly. Mrs Harris didn't order enough, and now it's all lopsided.'

Trevor chuckled. 'You're still not finished? You've been decorating for three days now. Why, we must have more baubles, bits and bobs than Windsor Castle.'

After her encounter with Mr Smith, Georgina had been so fraught that she'd thrown herself into decorating Harwicke House for the festive season. Since she loved Christmas, she always dressed the house in yuletide finery, but this year she'd added more decorations, leaving not a single inch of space uncovered by fir branches, holly, ivy leaves and sparkly ornaments.

'I doubt that,' she said. 'But you know how much I love Christmas. Which makes it even more awful for the orphaned children.'

'I know, Georgie.' Standing up, he walked from behind his desk and placed a hand on her shoulder. 'We will do our best. If anything… I suppose we could place the girls in different orphanages.'

Her heart sank. That was what Mrs Jameson had said they would have to do if they didn't find a new home. It was something she dreaded, as she'd heard about the conditions in other orphanages around London. Many of them were not well kept and the children were squeezed into small spaces. And those were the better ones.

'Thank you, Trev.' Rising to her feet, she covered his hand and squeezed it. 'I should go and find Miss Warren.'

She left her brother's office and found her companion in the library, having a cup of tea.

'What did your brother say?' Miss Warren asked as soon as she entered.

Georgina sighed. 'What do you think?' She sank down on the settee next to Miss Warren. 'It's hopeless.' She relayed the conversation with her brother to her companion. 'Trevor tried his best to soften the blow, of course, but I do not think we will find a new home for the children by the twenty-fifth. We might not have any choice except to place them in different orphanages around the city and beyond.'

'I am so sorry.' Miss Warren placed a sympathetic hand on her shoulder. 'You tried your best.'

'I know, but it's not good enough!' She rose to her feet and paced across the Persian rug. 'There is still time…surely there must be something else I can do.'

'It seems to me you've run out of options. Was Mr Smith truly stone-hearted? Did he not even budge or offer to delay the eviction? At least until after the New Year?'

'Yes, he truly was an uncharitable, greedy scoundrel.'

Her temper flared once more, thinking of that lout. Did he think everything could be bought and sold, like goods at a market? And to think the moment she'd laid eyes on him she had thought him quite handsome, in a rugged sort of way. He was quite tall, and his shoulders were unfashionably bulky, even under his tailored shirt, and he seemingly spent too much time in the sun, judging from his swarthy complexion. His dark hair had stuck up at angles, as he'd raked his fingers through it, and those eyes…bright green, like jade…had been so stark against his tanned skin. She'd never seen anything quite like them before.

'And very rich too, from what I heard.'

Georgina stopped pacing and planted her hands on her waist. So, he had not been exaggerating when he'd said he was wealthy and could provide all those things for her when he proposed. But she wanted to know more.

'What *have* you heard, Miss Warren?'

'He's only been in London for a few months or so, but has already bought property and businesses all over England,' Miss Warren relayed. 'A man like that has to be sitting on a very large fortune indeed.'

'Well, Trevor did say they called him a…what did he say? Oh, a Midas of something. But why come to England, then, if he's already wealthy in America?'

'London seems to be teeming with these moneyed foreigners lately.'

'Lately?' Since Georgina hadn't participated much in society these last few years, she hadn't noticed.

'Yes. And many of them are obscenely wealthy, having made their money from industry and commerce back in America.'

'And what are they doing here? Are many of them doing business in England?'

Miss Warren's eyes narrowed. 'Actually, I've only encountered the wives of these rich businessmen. And their daughters. They travel all the way here, hoping to catch husbands.'

'These girls travel across the Atlantic for marriage?' Georgina chuckled. 'Is America bereft of eligible men?'

'Yes. At least, titled ones,' Miss Warren clarified. 'America has no royalty and aristocracy, after all. Apparently these young women arrive at our shores to marry titled lords.'

'Not much different from any woman in England,' Georgina said dryly.

'Yes, except for their very, *very* generous dowries. And many of them do succeed in attracting those lords who have been left in dire straits, due to their failing estates. These young women then return to America with their shiny new titles and elevated social status.'

To her irritation, Mr Smith's words about marriage being a contract surfaced in her mind.

'What's wrong?' Miss Warren asked. 'Is the idea of the exchange of a dowry so disagreeable to you? You yourself have one, do you not?'

'I do, but…' She sat down next to her companion. 'I just wonder why Mr Smith would ask me to—' She covered her mouth with her hands, muffling the audible gasp that had escaped her lips.

'Ask you to *what*?' Miss Warren's face was scrunched up. 'Lady Georgina…did something happen in that office that I should know about?'

'Well…' Georgina shifted in her seat uncomfortably.

The companion let out an outraged sound. 'I knew I should not have allowed you to go up there alone. Did he say or do something improper?'

'He wasn't improper! Or not in the way you think.'

'I can think of a great many things that could be interpreted as "improper". Tell me now or I shall be forced to tell your brother—'

'No! Please…' It wasn't that she was afraid of her brother, but it was difficult to describe how she felt about the whole fiasco. Embarrassed, perhaps?

'Lady Georgina…'

'All right.' She folded her hands in her lap. 'Mr Smith asked me to marry him in exchange for not evicting the children.'

'What?' Miss Warren's eyes widened. 'I... How...? I cannot even comprehend.' Her nose twitched. 'No one heard him, I hope?'

She shook her head.

Miss Warren's mouth puckered. 'I will never allow you to be alone anywhere from now on. I was foolish, staying in the carriage and allowing you to go in there by yourself.'

'You'd think you'd be happy that I have finally received an offer of marriage,' she said dryly.

'I thought you said he was a scoundrel?'

'He is, but...' Georgina could not explain it, but she attempted to. 'Despite the ridiculousness of his request, he sounded...well, sincere.'

And perhaps that was why she could not forget Mr Smith's proposal. She was insulted and shocked by his forwardness, but knew he'd been deadly serious about it. He'd acted and sounded as if he really, truly wanted to marry her.

'Sincere?' Miss Warren echoed.

'Yes.'

'Do you know why he would ask such a thing of you?'

'I don't—' She gasped. 'That's *it*!'

Miss Warren's eyebrows snapped together. 'What's it?'

'Why he wants—and how we can save the—' The ideas bounced around in her mind so fast she could barely form a coherent sentence.

'Lady Georgina? You look ready to faint. Are you all right?'

'Yes, I'm all right.' She inhaled a deep breath. 'And I know how I will save the orphanage.'

'How?'

Smirking, she crossed her arms over her chest. 'I will find Mr Smith a wife.'

'You will? Why?'

'It's quite apparent to me now—thanks to what you've told me about these American women—why he asked me in the first place. He wants a titled wife to elevate his own status. That's why he asked me to marry him.'

'I was speaking of the American *women*, and Mr Smith would not gain a title if he were to marry you.'

'Yes, but a titled wife would open so many doors for him,' she pointed out. Being a shrewd businessman, as Trevor had said he was earlier, such an association would be priceless for Mr Smith. 'He was very much interested in the fact that I was a duke's daughter. He knows that by marrying me he would be able to raise his position in society, both here and in America.'

'I suppose that makes sense...'

'Then you agree that I must go to Mr Smith and tell him that I will find him a bride, in exchange for his allowing the orphanage to remain.'

'Now, *that* I did not agree to,' Miss Warren retorted sharply. 'As I mentioned, I will never allow you to be in the company of a man by yourself—and certainly not Mr Smith.'

'Then you shall accompany me,' she said, rising to her feet. Sensing Miss Warren's protest, she pre-empted it with a plea. 'Won't you do this with me, Miss Warren? This is for a good cause. And your job is to be my companion, after all, so...accompany me. Think of those poor children.'

Miss Warren's stern expression softened. 'I suppose...'

'Excellent! Let us leave now, so we may catch Mr Smith in his office.'

To her surprise, Mr Smith's assistant ushered them into his office even without an appointment. Once again, those jade-green eyes pierced right through her the moment she stepped in.

'My lady,' he greeted her. 'I'm surprised to see you return.'

From his tone, Georgina didn't think he sounded surprised at all. 'My companion, Miss Warren,' she introduced with a quick nod. 'Thank you for seeing me today.'

'Of course.' He gestured towards the chairs in front of his desk. 'Please, have a seat.'

As soon as they'd both sat down, she spoke. 'Mr Smith, I've rethought your...er...proposal.'

'I see.' He threaded his fingers together and rested his chin on top of them. 'And you are accepting it?'

'No.' When his eyebrows lifted, she quickly added, 'I mean,

yes. Or no. Er...' She glanced at Miss Warren helplessly, who only shrugged, as if it say, *What do you expect me to do?*

'No and yes? You do realise those words are the opposite of each other?'

'Yes.' Georgina straightened her shoulders. 'What I am trying to say, Mr Smith, is that while I still decline your first proposal, I have a different one to make to you.'

'You do, do you?'

'Yes.' Trying to appear confident, she placed her hands on the table as she leaned forward. 'I know why you asked me to marry you. You want a proper English bride with the right background, preferably the daughter of a titled lord. Correct?'

Mr Smith's expression remained impassive, but she didn't miss the glint in his eyes. 'Go on.'

'And I suppose the reason you asked me, despite the fact that we had only just met, is that you've had no luck on your own?'

'Your powers of deduction are astounding,' he said dryly.

'So I have a counter proposal.' She folded her hands together in a similar manner to his. 'Or rather, a *business* proposal for you: I will help you find a bride, and in return you will rescind the eviction notice.'

'You believe your assistance has equal value to a prime piece of property?'

'You certainly believed *I* was when you made your first offer,' she pointed out. 'Surely one lady is no different from another? And wasn't it you who said marriage is nothing but a contract? In this case, I will act as your...er...'

'Agent?' he supplied. 'Middle man?'

'Matchmaker,' she said.

Mr Smith lifted an eyebrow at her sceptically. 'Tell me, Lady Georgina, what exactly do you bring to the bargaining table? London is full of eligible debutantes and unmarried misses searching for a match. If I, a wealthy man of considerable means, have yet to find a bride amongst the stable of eligible ladies, what makes you think you could?'

'Ah, but I have something you do not.'

'And that is?'

Scrounging up every bit of confidence, she said, 'The right

pedigree and connections. My brother is a duke, after all. Our family is invited to all the best balls and events in town, and we know everyone in London.'

'Everyone?'

'Why, yes. Everyone who is anyone.' She thought she had sounded quite convincing, so she continued, 'I can make the necessary introductions for you.'

'Introductions are one thing, but delivering an actual bride is quite different,' he said. 'I would need something solid if I am even to consider your proposal.'

Desperation crept into her chest. 'How about...an engagement by Christmas? To a lady from one of England's finest families?'

Miss Warren's eyes enlarged, as if sending her a warning. But the words were already out of her mouth, and Georgina could not take them back.

The corner of his mouth curled up into what appeared to be a smile. 'An engagement? In...' he looked at the calendar '...less than twenty days.'

'That's plenty of time. A quick courtship is not unheard of, after all, and once a woman begins accepting calls from you, that means she is already considering a proposal.'

'You said "an engagement by Christmas".'

'Not in the literal sense. I will do my best to lead the right lady to you, but it is up to you to propose, now, isn't it? It won't be my fault if you fail to ask the question. Surely you don't think I will be asking on your behalf?'

The look on his face told her that, yes, he did expect that.

She stifled the urge to roll her eyes. 'Allow me to explain to you how things work here in England, Mr Smith. A lady's father or guardian will not allow you even to begin courting her unless the lady already has an inkling to accept. Otherwise, if she continues to toy with numerous men, she will be branded a flirt. The best I can do—the best anyone can do—is advise you which ladies would be most...er...suited to your needs and open to accepting your proposal. Besides, you will need at least a full year's engagement before you can marry.'

She paused, trying to gauge his thoughts, but found his face was unreadable. She would have to do her best to persuade him to give her a chance.

'Of course, you could keep on with your current method of finding a wife, as that certainly seems to have brought you success.' She tapped a finger on her chin. 'Oh, wait—it hasn't, has it? Because otherwise you wouldn't have made that offer to me two days ago.'

He remained silent, though his nostrils flared. Finally, after what seemed like an eternity, he spoke. 'All right.' He huffed. 'I will propose to the most suitable woman you introduce to me by Christmas, and if she accepts I will rescind the eviction.'

She clapped her hands together. 'Excellent. I accept the terms.'

'Of course, you do know this means that your choice must be guaranteed to accept my proposal?'

Well, she hadn't quite thought of *that*.

'Of course.' She ignored the growing lump of stone in her stomach. It would be a Herculean task, but it wasn't as if she had any other way to save the orphanage. 'Should we have a contract drawn up?'

'No need.' Rising from his chair, he leaned over the desk and extended his hand. 'We shall seal our deal with a handshake. A fiancée by Christmas for me, and in exchange your orphans can stay in their home.'

Elation shot through her, and before she could even think she took his hand. 'We have a deal.'

As his ungloved fingers closed around hers, she couldn't help but notice how much larger his hand was compared to hers, nor how warm they felt even through her gloves. She wondered how they would feel if her fingers were bare too. The very thought sent a strange flutter behind her ribs. Lifting her head, she met his jade-green gaze, and warmth spread up her neck.

Miss Warren cleared her throat, and both of them released each other's hands.

'So,' Mr Smith began, sinking down into his seat. 'What is your exact plan, then?'

'Plan?' She gawked at him. 'Do I need a plan?'

'Yes. Every goal requires some sort of plan of action in order to achieve it. What are the steps in your plan and how will you execute them?'

Georgina swallowed a gulp. She honestly had not thought she would get this far—at least not far enough to require an entire plan from beginning to end.

'Well?' Mr Smith asked. 'You *do* have a plan, don't you?'

'Of course I do,' she said quickly. 'I just…left it at home.'

'You left it at home?'

'Yes.' Quickly, she stood up. 'Silly me—how could I do that? Miss Warren, we should head back to Harwicke House immediately, before…er…one of the maids throws it away whilst tidying up.'

Mr Smith rose as well. 'And when will I be made a party to this plan of yours, my lady?'

'I shall send you a note,' she said. 'As soon as possible.'

'I hope so.' He glanced at the calendar. 'After all, you only have nineteen days left.'

She let out a nervous laugh. 'Of course. Come now, Miss Warren. Good day, Mr Smith.'

Before he could even bid her goodbye, she rushed them out of the office and into the street, where they hurried into her carriage.

'What in the world were you thinking?' Miss Warren admonished.

Georgina wilted into the plush velvet seat. 'I'm afraid I was not.' But then again, she would do anything—almost anything—to save the orphanage.

'You do realise fulfilling your end of the bargain and finding him a bride requires the one thing you swore you would never do?'

Her head snapped towards the companion's. 'And what is that?'

'Venturing into society.'

'I— Oh…'

Drat.

'So, am I to assume we should unpack your ballgowns, dust off your dancing slippers, and perhaps acquire some new dance cards?'

Double drat.

While she hated to admit it, Miss Warren was right. To find Mr Smith a bride and save St Agnes's, she must re-join society. After all, how was she to make introductions and find these potential brides while sipping tea and doing embroidery at home? No, she would have to leave the comfort of her home and attend those dreadful balls and parties.

The very thought of it made dread pool in her stomach.

But she reminded herself this was for a good cause.

Think of the children.

'And what of this plan Mr Smith expects?'

'I haven't got to that yet,' she confessed. 'But I have an idea of where to begin.'

Chapter Three

5th December

Elliot had expected never to hear from Lady Georgina again. After all, her 'proposition' was absurd. Surely, if she had any sense, she would have stayed away. She was far too young and naive, now that he thought of it, and he never should have offered to marry her in the first place.

So he was very much astonished to receive a note the next day, unsigned, and written in a loopy, feminine handwriting.

Please come to Harwicke House for tea today at two o'clock.

And so that very afternoon he found himself on the steps of an elegant mansion at Mayfair's most fashionable address, Grosvenor Square. The two-storey villa itself—red brick, with white window frames and a gabled roof—was well-kept, and obviously belonged to someone very important.

Not that Elliot didn't already know that the Duke of Harwicke was a leading member of society. After all, he always did his due diligence when it came to both his business and personal life. One of the first things he'd done when he'd arrived in London had been to hire a private investigator to ferret out information on anyone he was to have dealings with. In the last twenty-four hours, he'd had his man gather every bit of available information on Trevor Abernathy.

Trevor Charles William Abernathy, aged twenty-nine, had received his title upon the untimely death of his parents twelve years ago, when he was only seventeen. His estates were well-maintained and profitable, he had made a number of wise investments over the last few years. While his assets paled in comparison to Elliot's, the Abernathys were still rich. No wonder Lady Georgina was not at all tempted by his wealth.

'May I help you, sir?' The stodgy-looking butler on the other side of the door asked as soon as it was opened.

'I'm Mr Elliot Smith. I'm here for—'

'Yes, come in.' The butler glanced around, as if he were checking for robbers outside—or perhaps for any prying eyes watching the house. 'She is waiting for you.'

Before he'd arrived here he had pictured in his mind what Lady Georgina's home would be like. He'd imagined elegant decor, antique furniture, plush carpeting and portraits on the wall sneering down at him, telling him he didn't belong here.

As he followed the butler inside, however, he was unprepared for the sight that assaulted him.

It seemed every square inch of the entrance hall had been covered in evergreen and ivy. Boughs of holly hung from the doorways, and red and green ribbons were wrapped around the fir-covered banister. Glass balls and bulbs sparkled from where they hung from the ceiling, tinkling as they clinked against each other. The smell of pine and sugar wafted into his nostrils. He suspected it came from the large tree he spied in the drawing room, just to his left—were those actual sweets and biscuits hanging from its branches?

'Dear God, man, what happened here?' he exclaimed. 'Did they bring in an entire forest?'

The butler merely sniffed. 'This way, if you please.'

He followed the butler through the richly decorated corridors of Harwicke House. He did not think it were possible, but the deeper he was drawn in, the more bits and baubles he saw, hung from the walls and springing forth from the ceiling and floors.

When they reached a door at the end of the corridor, the butler stepped inside first. 'Mr Smith is here,' he announced, then stepped aside to allow Elliot inside what appeared to be a sitting room.

Like the rest of the house, this room was decorated with all kinds of Christmas trinkets and knick-knacks. However, this time the garish display faded from his vision as something else caught his eye—Lady Georgina herself, who sat by the window.

Now that she was not wearing a hat, he could finally see what colour her hair was—light blonde, the colour of wheat. It was swept up in wispy waves around her head and threaded through with a blue ribbon that matched her day dress. He wondered how long it was and what it would look like undone.

'Thank you, Dawson. You may leave,' she said. 'Mr Elliot, welcome to Harwicke House.'

'Thank you for your invitation.'

'You remember my companion, Miss Warren?' she said, gesturing to the woman who sat in an armchair to her left.

'Miss Warren,' he greeted her.

Of course he had not expected to be alone with her, though he did think her much too young to have a companion. He'd thought companions usually accompanied doddering old women. Perhaps in England a chaperone and a companion were the same thing.

Miss Warren murmured a greeting in return, her suspicious gaze remaining on him for a few seconds before she bowed her head curtly.

'Would you like tea to be served now or later, after we speak?' Lady Georgina asked.

'If you don't mind, perhaps we could proceed with our business,' he replied.

'As you wish.' She motioned for him to sit on the chair across from her.

He spoke first. 'So, Lady Georgina, are you ready to tell me about your plan?'

'Ah, yes.' She cleared her throat and placed her hands on

her lap. 'My plan. The one I have thought up to help you find a suitable bride.'

'Exactly.'

He tried not to sound impatient, but he'd had a distinct feeling yesterday that she had no plan at all. Why, if he were to trust his instinct, he would guess she'd simply thought up her proposal just before she rushed over to his office, hoping to entice him not to evict the tenants at number fifty-five Boyle Street.

'So, my plan consists of you and myself—but not together, of course—g-going to several balls so that you can meet the right people.'

He paused, waiting for the next part. When a few awkward seconds passed without another peep from her, he said, 'That's it?'

'Er…yes.'

'But surely there must be more? You need several steps, at least, and a timeline…milestones you must achieve.' He curled his hands on the arms of the chair, stifling the urge to stand up and walk away. 'And you must also put in some contingencies in case of failure.'

She stared at him as if he had declared himself the King of England. 'Failure?'

'Yes.' He clicked his tongue. 'You don't actually have a plan, do you?'

'Of course I do,' she spluttered. 'I have just told you.'

'But not a real plan,' he countered.

She crossed her arms over her chest. 'Love cannot be planned.'

'I do not need love, Lady Georgina,' he stated firmly. 'I need a wife. If you cannot help me find one, then I will bid you goodbye.'

He stood up.

'No, please.' She sprang up from her seat, her hands grasping at his forearm. 'I do have a plan…it's just that…he's late.'

He froze at her touch. Much like it had yesterday, when they'd shaken hands, his body seized at the contact, and a curl of lust coiled inside him. He had brushed it off as a fluke—after all, it had been months since he'd been with a woman…not since New York. He'd been much too busy with the move to London, and dealing with his sisters, not to mention establishing his company here. Too busy to have time for dalliances. That had to be it. Because by most standards Lady Georgina was no stunning temptress.

Yet now, this close, he couldn't help but notice how velvety her skin seemed, and how the sun shining through the window highlighted the streaks of gold in her hair. He took in a deep breath, and he swore he could smell the light, powdery scent of her perfume.

'Apologies for my lateness.'

The new and very male voice caused them to jump apart. Lady Georgina's face turned crimson as she turned away. 'I… ah… Trev, you're finally home.'

'There was an accident outside my solicitor's office. Overturned cart. Took bloody for ever to clear the street so my carriage could get through.'

The man—whom Elliot guessed was His Grace the Duke of Harwicke himself—walked over to him.

Lady Georgina cleared her throat. 'Trev…er… Your Grace, may I present Mr Elliot Smith? Mr Smith, this is His Grace the Duke of Harwicke.'

'A pleasure to meet you, Mr Smith,' the Duke said.

He was fair-haired, like his sister, but that was the end of the resemblance between the siblings. Harwicke was nearly as tall as him, with broad shoulders, and he had a handsome face with strong, masculine features and sharp blue eyes. Blue eyes that, much to Elliot's frustration, were unreadable. While the Duke was putting on an affable demeanour, as if they were being introduced at a dinner party, Elliot could not help but feel that Harwicke was hiding his true feelings behind that facade.

He bowed his head. 'Likewise, Your Grace.'

'I'm not usually late to meetings,' he said. 'I see you've started without me.'

'You're to be part of this meeting?' Elliot asked, incredulous. 'Lady Georgina has told you everything?'

Did Harwicke know he'd proposed? From the nervous look he saw on the lady's face—because she, on the other hand, was very easy to read—he guessed not.

'Of course.' Harwicke walked over to his sister, ruffling her hair affectionately before sitting down next to her. 'She has told me she needs my assistance, so what is a brother to do but offer it?'

'This is the first part of my plan, Mr Smith,' she said. 'My brother will make you the necessary introductions to the right people in London. Fathers, brothers, guardians of potential brides…that sort of thing. I didn't mean to make it seem I was unprepared, but I was hoping to stall you before Trevor arrived and I could explain.'

'And you have agreed to this?' he asked the Duke.

'Well, my sister certainly can't make you introductions to these men. She is unmarried and still under my protection.'

'I see.' Elliot sat back down. 'And then what, Lady Georgina?'

'Once you become associated with us—with Trevor—then you'll be invited to various society events around town.'

'And you'll be there too?'

'Of course,' she said.

Elliot observed that the smile forming on her face did not reach her eyes, but he did not mention it. After all, her plan was solid for now. Having the Duke as an acquaintance would definitely get him into the right places.

'All right, that sounds like a logical plan.' He wouldn't say it was good but, as Lady Georgina had said yesterday, what did he have to lose?

'Excellent.' Harwicke patted his sister's arm, then stood up. 'Now, Mr Smith, would you mind joining me in my study for a moment?'

'But, Trev, Mrs Harris is preparing tea.'

'You and Miss Warren will enjoy it, then.' His blue eyes speared right through Elliot. 'Mr Smith and I need to speak alone.'

Not missing the Duke's serious tone, Elliot rose and followed him out of the sitting room to his study, just across the corridor.

Harwicke walked over to the liquor cabinet. 'Drink? I have whisky, sherry, port—'

'No, thank you, I don't drink.' He occasionally had a glass

of wine with dinner, but nothing stronger—not after he'd seen how it affected his father.

The Duke's eyebrows shot up, but he said nothing as he poured some brown liquid from a decanter into a glass. 'Let me get straight to the point.'

'That's how I like it myself,' said Elliot.

'As I mentioned, Georgina is unmarried and under my protection.' The edge in his tone could have cut through a rock. 'Ever since our parents died, it's just been her and I. She is my sister and my only remaining flesh and blood. You may not understand why, but I will do anything for her.' He took a sip of his drink. 'But I will also do anything to protect her. I am only agreeing to this because of her—I don't care about your reasons. And while I know Georgie may never marry, that does not mean that I will risk her reputation.'

Never marry? What in God's name was Harwicke talking about? Any man would be lucky to marry Lady Georgina.

Except him, which she had made abundantly clear that first day she'd barged into his office.

'Do we understand each other?' asked the Duke.

'Of course,' he said.

'Good.' Harwicke downed the rest of his drink. 'Meet me tonight at Brooks' for dinner. Eight o'clock sharp. You do know where that is?'

'Yes.'

Brooks' was one of the most exclusive gentlemen's clubs in London—of course Elliot knew where it was. If Harwicke could get him in there, even for just a meal, then the Duke truly was influential.

'I'll see you there,' he said in a dismissive tone, then turned his back on him.

Elliot guessed that was the signal for him to show himself out, and so he did. Thankfully, he managed to follow the trail of fir branches and crystal baubles and found his way out of that festooned madhouse.

As he climbed into his carriage, Harwicke's words rang in his head.

'You may not understand why, but I will do anything for her.'
He scoffed to himself. If only Harwicke knew.

'Home,' he said to his footman.

The trip back to his house took only a few minutes, as it was only a small number of streets away, on Upper Brook Street. As soon as he entered, the lingering traces of smoke invaded his nostrils. Elliot glanced left at the door to the drawing room.

'We're doing our best to air it, Mr Smith,' said his butler, Fletcher. 'Mrs Jenkins, the housekeeper from next door, has recommended we place bowls of vinegar all over the room to absorb the smell.'

'Then the entire house will smell of vinegar and not smoke.' His eyes slid heavenwards. 'All right…do what you must.'

He was just glad no one had been hurt in the fire. When he'd arrived home two days ago, to deal with the situation, Miss Jones had been in a fiery mood. Lily had clung to him the moment he'd stepped through the door, but Anne-Marie had stood there, defiant, as Miss Jones had lashed out.

'Your sisters are the worst charges I've ever had!' Miss Jones had screamed at him. 'And if you do not give me what I demand, everyone will know what devil spawn they are.'

Elliot had done his best to control his temper. 'What happened here?'

'They tried to set me on fire!' the governess had raged.

'Is that true, Anne-Marie?' he had asked. 'You could have hurt Miss Jones and razed the entire house to the ground.'

'She's a liar!' His sister had shot back. 'She knocked that candle over by accident.'

'Because you attempted to assault me.'

Anne-Marie had bared her teeth. 'You had grabbed my sister and twisted her arm until she screamed in pain!'

Cold fury had risen in him. 'Lily?' The child had not answered, but instead had tightened her grip on him. 'Girls, please go up to your rooms.'

'But she—'

'Now.'

Once both girls had left, Elliot had focused that splintering rage on the governess. 'Listen to me, you insignificant flea. I will pay you your wages until the end of the month and nothing more. And if you dare say anything about my sisters to anyone, or attempt to ruin them, I will make it my life's mission to thwart your every move and prospect. I will find every family, every position you apply to, and make it worth their while not to hire you. You will never find a job in this city higher than scrubbing floors or washing dishes in a public house. Am I making myself clear?'

The way the blood had drained from the old hag's face had been almost satisfying enough to make him forget his problems.

Sighing now, he looked up towards the stairs, making his way to the schoolroom, where Lily sat at one of the tables, writing something down as the new tutor, Mrs Howard, kept a keen eye on her.

'Very good, Lilian,' Mrs Howard said. 'Your penmanship has vastly improved.'

'Hello,' he called to Lily.

The little girl looked up from her writing, her face lighting up. 'Elliot!' she screamed as she pushed away from the desk and jumped off her chair.

'Oomph!' he exclaimed as a tiny bundle of red curls and lace jumped into his arms.

'You're home early!' she said.

'I am.'

'Are you home so we can go somewhere? Maybe you can take Anne-Marie and I skating on the Serpentine.'

'Anne-Marie and *me*,' Miss Howard corrected.

'That's what I said,' Lily said with a small huff. 'So, are you taking us?'

'Perhaps—but not today. It is already dark out, and the skating is finished.'

'Oh…' Her tiny lips pursed. 'Another time, then?'

'We'll see.' He kissed her forehead. 'In the meantime, please do pay attention to Mrs Howard's lessons. She's making sure you grow up to be a proper lady.'

Her little nose wrinkled. 'All right.' She beamed up at him and then bounded back to her chair to resume her lesson.

Elliot watched for a few more seconds, then left the room, closing the door behind him and leaning against it with a heavy sigh.

Now the easy part was done. Glancing down the corridor, he stared towards his other sister's rooms.

Perhaps it was unfair to compare Lily and Anne-Marie. Lily had been so young, after all, when she'd come to live with Elliot. Still, he recalled Anne-Marie as a quiet, sweet young thing, and it seemed only recently that she'd grown a rebellious streak.

Trudging down the corridor, he stopped outside her room and knocked. 'Anne-Marie? Anne-Marie, are you in there?'

No answer.

'Young lady,' he said in a sterner voice, 'I would like to speak with you.'

He hadn't seen her in three days—not since he had sent them up to their rooms so he could deal with Miss Jones.

'Anne-Marie, open this door now!'

He heard some rustling from inside before the door opened. Anne-Marie's pretty face was drawn into a scowl. With the same curly red hair and green eyes, she was an older, ganglier version of her younger sister.

'What do you want?' She crossed her arms over her chest.

So much for that sweet young thing.

'Mrs Murphy has told me you haven't eaten since yesterday.'

'I'm not hungry.'

'Surely that's not true,' he said. 'You must eat. And you must leave your room for lessons.'

Her pretty face scrunched up. 'Which ones? Those futile dancing lessons or the pointless lectures on social graces?'

'They are not pointless,' he said through gritted teeth. 'Those lessons will help you later in life. And I've paid for the best tutors in London to come here and teach you girls so that you may become elegant young ladies when you enter society.'

'That's all you care about, isn't it? Your money? Why don't you just stop wasting it on me?'

'Young lady, how—?'

Blam! The door slammed shut.

'I hate this damned place,' came the muffled sob from the other side.

Elliot blew out a breath and knocked his head against the wooden door. Could he really blame Anne-Marie for being angry with him? For the past five years he'd dragged them from one coast of the United States to another, and then all the way across the Atlantic to a strange place. Anne-Marie in particular had been furious when he'd announced the move to London, as she was finally making friends in New York.

He straightened his shoulders. 'I'll send a tray up and you won't leave this room until you've eaten every last bit of food,' he said in a determined tone before he walked away.

Elliot raked his fingers through his hair. How could one slip of a girl thwart his plans? He was halfway through this ten-year plan and he was nowhere near achieving his goals, nor had he even met any of the milestones he had set.

But perhaps his luck had turned—not that he believed in such a thing. He'd been in the right place at the right time, after all, when he'd decided to purchase number fifty-five Boyle Street and a certain flaxen-haired lady had barged into his office. If Lady Georgina's plan worked, then before the year ended he would have a blue-blooded bride who would solve all his problems.

A knot of anticipation formed in his chest at the thought of Lady Georgina. He wasn't quite sure why. Perhaps he'd seen something different in her this time. How he had thought her ordinary that first time she'd burst into his office, he didn't know.

In any case, he had to set his sights elsewhere. Since Lady Georgina would never marry him, she would have to be the key to the success of his ten-year plan.

7th December

Just as Harwicke had promised, he dined with Elliot that evening at Brooks'. The Duke made the introductions to other members they encountered as they made their way to the dining room, though they dined alone. The other members watched him curiously, but said nothing out of politeness. After dinner they had port and cigars, while watching some members play cards, and then they left.

The next two evenings were spent at Brooks' too, though they were joined by more of Harwicke's acquaintances for dinner and they lingered on much longer each time. Elliot allowed Harwicke to lead the conversation, and he was quite surprised when some of the men asked him questions. In fact, when he started speaking about investments and such, they listened with rapt attention.

'Is it true you are called the Midas of San Francisco?' asked Lord Kensington, whom Harwicke had said was a schoolmate from Eton, during the third evening they were at the club.

'Midas?' echoed Mr James Galwick, another of their schoolmates.

'Yes. I heard Smith here made more money than God in the gold mines,' Kensington added. 'Did you strike a particularly rich vein?'

Elliot grinned. 'No, I'm afraid I've never entered the gold mining business.'

'And why not?' Galwick asked. 'I heard of one claim that resulted in nearly twenty thousand dollars' worth of gold in one week.'

'Ah, yes, the Weber's Creek claim.' That had happened the year before he'd arrived, but it remained the talk of the town for years. 'Unfortunately, for every Weber's Creek claim dozens of others turned out to be worthless. The risk was much too high for me, and I didn't know the first thing about mining. I did, however, spend ten years building my ferry company.'

And he told them about how he'd invested in building the shipping lines from west to east.

'What great luck. And very perceptive of you,' Kensington remarked. 'Perhaps I should have gone to California and sold... I don't know...perhaps picks and shovels.'

All the men laughed—even Harwicke.

While Elliot was certainly having a grand time—it had been much too long since he had done anything except read reports in the evenings before going to bed—his patience was running thin. He'd been running around with Harwicke for three evenings, but he'd only met gentlemen.

Still, he didn't say anything to the Duke, and they continued with their merriment. By the time they made their way out of Brooks' the sky was streaked with the pinks and purples of dawn. Elliot cursed himself as he hadn't noticed the time. It was also a reminder that another day had passed.

'I'll see you tonight,' Harwicke said as they awaited their carriages. 'We'll be—'

'When will you introduce me to some potential brides?' Elliot asked, frustrated. 'We've been wasting time here, while the deadline grows closer.'

Harwicke lifted an elegant blond eyebrow. 'I was beginning to like you, and then you had to bring up that damned agreement with my sister.' He sighed. 'This is but a first step, as Georgina explained to you.'

Elliot ignored the way his heart jumped at the sound of her name.

'Normally, these connections take weeks to foster. But because of this deadline of yours I've had to make these introductions quickly.'

'And these gentlemen…do they have daughters? Perhaps sisters I can marry?'

The corner of Harwicke's mouth twitched at the mention of sisters. 'No, but they have wives.'

'And?'

'As you will quickly learn, when it comes to matters of society it is the wives who matter. With your wealth, some impoverished gentleman with a languishing estate will definitely want you for a son-in-law, but ultimately it's the mamas you must win over. I've learned over the past few nights that I do not need to choose my words with you, so I shall be blunt: any lady you marry will be stepping down from her station, so you must convince the mothers that you will be a worthy enough match that they can overcome your background.'

'I see.'

The Duke's words made sense. Men, after all, were in charge

of the money, while the women were in charge of the home and the children.

'If you had allowed me to finish my earlier sentence,' said the Duke, 'I was about to tell you that tonight we will be at the opera.'

'Opera? I hate the opera,' he said. 'A waste of a perfectly good evening.'

'But that's where you'll be seen by the wives of the Ton,' Harwicke explained. 'You'll sit in my box, with myself and Georgina.'

His heart quickened again at the mention of her name. It seemed so long since he had seen her. Last night, he'd come to Harwicke House to pick up the Duke, as his carriage was being repaired. He hadn't even seen a glimpse of her, though he had spied her companion walking across the hall, which had meant Lady Georgina was home.

'She'll be there? At the opera?' he asked.

'Naturally,' said Harwicke. 'You'll have a grand time with her, I'll bet. She hates the opera, too—hasn't joined me in years. But she'll go because she needs to. Being acquainted with me will help you, but Georgina, being a duke's sister, will open doors for you, and with her approval, you will be allowed access.'

'But she isn't a society matron. She's not married, I mean.'

'True, but she is still one of them. As the daughter of a duke, she still outranks many of the women of the Ton—even the married ones. And, though she's approaching spinsterhood, her reputation has remained un-besmirched all this time.'

That last sentence certainly sounded like a warning to El-liot's ears. 'Why is it that you think your sister a spinster? She cannot be that old. Surely she's had many proposals over the years? Why has she not chosen anyone?'

'My sister is seven and twenty, which I personally do not believe makes her a spinster, but unfortunately that's what so-ciety believes. And as for your last question—that's her busi-ness. My sister is sheltered, but she knows her own mind. I will do whatever it takes to make her happy, and I have promised I will support her whether she marries or not. Now, I'll see you tonight—seven o'clock,' the Duke said as he got into his carriage.

As Elliot waited for his own carriage, Harwicke's words about Lady Georgina rang in his head. How could she have remained unmarried all this time? Perhaps she was a shrew—she's certainly acted like one when she called him a... What was it? A Scrooge or whatever the hell it was?

But still he couldn't help but admire her bravado, entering his office all by herself like some avenging angel, though she'd looked more like a cherub with her cheeks and nose all pink from the chilly air. He wondered what it would be like to warm those cold cheeks and those lips. She had looked so damn lovely in the sitting room, her hair and her lush curves on display in her casual morning gown, instead of bundled up in her coat and outdoor finery. He wondered how soft those wisps of blonde hair would feel in his hands, or how they would look splayed on the pillow—

He huffed, pushing down the surge of lust that had made his cock twitch and his heart race once more.

He shook his head. He could not let his thoughts go astray, and certainly not in her direction. Lady Georgina had struck a bargain with him and she was there to help him as a means to an end. He'd best remember that, no matter what certain parts of his body might think.

Chapter Four

'Do you like the opera, Lady Georgina?' Miss Warren asked.

'Not particularly,' Georgina replied, whipping her fan faster to circulate the air around her. They had arrived minutes ago in the Abernathys' private box and sat down in the two front seats. 'The air in here is stifling. Why are there so many people here tonight? I don't recall it ever being this crowded.'

Ever since she could remember, large groups of people in one place had frayed her nerves. She had got used to it in her earlier Seasons, since her come-out, but it seemed that ever since she'd withdrawn from society it had become worse.

Miss Warren placed a calming hand on her shoulder. 'Breathe, Lady Georgina. That's it…open your mouth…inhale…'

Georgina took two big gulps of air. 'Th-thank you.'

'See? It's not so bad, being out and about, is it?'

'I suppose not. At least I'm not expected to speak to anyone, like at Lady Chisholm's tea party.'

'It wasn't that terrible, was it?' Miss Warren asked.

'I nearly passed out in the necessary,' she reminded her.

Her companion rolled her eyes. 'You ran there because the Countess of Allenvale asked what you thought of the weather.'

'Exactly.' She snatched Miss Warren's fan, opened it, and fanned herself with it as well as her own.

Ah, much better.

Perhaps it was just the stale air inside that set her nerves on edge.

'You've been doing splendidly, dear,' Miss Warren said. 'I'm so proud of you.'

To be honest, Georgina was rather proud of herself too. She had managed not one, but two social events in the last three days, after all. Aside from the nearly disastrous tea, she'd called upon an old friend, Cordelia Wentworth, now Viscountess Gilliam, who'd used to live near their estate in Northamptonshire.

Actually, Georgina wasn't quite sure if the woman she'd met *had* been her friend, as she could only vaguely recall playing with her a few times when they were little. However, during their short call, the Viscountess had regaled her with stories from their childhood, to which Georgina had nodded and smiled, though she couldn't remember any of them. The call had ended with Cordelia promising to return her call, which of course had sent her into a state of dread, because etiquette deemed that after *that* call Georgina would have to pay her a call and so on, with the cycle never ending until one of them died.

Georgina seriously hoped she would be the first to go, because the thought of attending Cordelia's funeral with all those mourners around them made her want to hide in a closet.

'While I still do not approve of this bargain you have struck with Mr Smith,' Miss Warren began, 'I am glad it is compelling you to come out. And you do look lovely tonight, dear.'

Georgina scratched at the lacy edges of her cream-coloured satin opera gown. 'I'd forgotten I had this dress made three years ago. I should have asked the modiste to remove the lace. And perhaps raise the décolletage another inch or two.'

She felt rather exposed, and now she wished she'd worn a larger necklace to cover her chest, which threatened to spill over the edge. Sadly, she had filled out these last years, and the dress now hugged her more generous body. When they'd arrived at the opera house she had stared enviously at all the beautiful, slim ladies walking about, not worried about having to limit their breathing to keep their modesty.

Miss Warren cleared her throat. 'Lady Georgina...' She nodded behind them.

'What is—? Oh.'

Her brother had entered the box, but he was not alone. Mr Smith came in after Trevor, his bulky frame seemingly filling the confined space. Georgina's dress seemed to lace itself tighter, and she wished she had a third hand to fan herself with. She'd seen him twice now—thrice, really, if she counted that time she'd peeped through the window when he'd come the other night to fetch Trevor—but never in formal attire. His swarthy complexion against the white of his cravat and shirt was a startling contrast, and the near-perfect fit of his coat on his large shoulders made him appear even more imposing.

'Georgie... Miss Warren.' Trevor's voice, thankfully, interrupted her thoughts.

'Good evening, Your Grace.' Miss Warren stood up and curtseyed.

'Apologies. I couldn't escort you here. But it was probably fortunate as I found Mr Smith wandering outside and was able to guide him here.'

'My lady... Miss Warren.' Mr Smith greeted them, his jade-green eyes lingering on her.

For the past few days she'd been wondering what it was about them that she found so unique. Now she realised that it wasn't just the colour—no, there was a keen sense of alertness in them, perhaps even a hunger that she'd never seen in anyone before. He had the look of a predator, ready to consume anything he deemed prey.

Trevor indicated for him to take the seat behind her companion—which was unfortunate, because from where Georgina sat she could catch him from the corner of her eye.

'What's playing tonight?' Mr Smith asked.

'*The Marriage of Figaro*,' Miss Warren replied.

Georgina stifled a laugh as she spied Mr Smith wince. Mercifully, the lights were turned down, indicating that the performance was about to start, and everyone settled into their seats.

While she was no fan of going to the opera, Georgina actually adored opera music. It had been years since she'd come here to watch a performance. How she loved the elaborate scenes, the dramatic singers and the sound of the orchestra blaring into the audience! If there was a way for her to enjoy music without leaving her home, she would truly be in heaven.

Tonight, however, she couldn't help but be distracted by the presence of the person sitting just at the edge of her vision. The temptation to turn her head and watch Mr Smith was strong, but she managed to resist it until the lights were turned on again for the interval.

'That was lovely,' Miss Warren said. 'Mozart is truly a genius.'

'Yes, he is. But now the real work begins,' Trevor said. 'I spoke briefly with the Earl of Rutherford when I saw him in the lobby earlier this evening. He's invited us all to their box for champagne during the interval.'

Ugh. Georgina winced inwardly. This was why she didn't come to the opera. All that socialising just ruined the experience.

'Must we?'

'Lord and Lady Rutherford are hosting their annual ball tomorrow,' Trevor reminded her. 'We've already accepted their invitation.'

She blinked. 'We have?'

'Yes. And once we have become reacquainted with Lady Rutherford, I will ask her to extend the invitation to Mr Smith, as there will be many eligible ladies there.'

'Oh. Of course.' Good Lord, was she truly about to subject herself to the torture of conversing with near strangers?

Think of the girls at St Agnes's.

This would be a small price to pay to keep them in their home.

'Shall we head over to them, then?'

Seeing as she had no choice, she followed Trevor out of their box and down the crowded corridors to a box a few doors down.

'Your Grace,' the Earl of Rutherford greeted Trevor. 'Welcome.'

'Your Grace.' Lady Rutherford curtseyed. 'How wonderful

to see you. I was so delighted when my husband told me he had invited you and your party to join us.'

She nodded to a footman in the corner, standing next to a table with champagne flutes and an ice bucket. The footman quickly filled several glasses.

'And Lady Georgina, is that you? You look lovely tonight. That lace on your gown is so elegant. French, I think?'

'Lady Rutherford,' Georgina said with an acknowledging nod.

Trevor sent her a meaningful look, likely meant to remind her that she had to respond to the Countess's compliments. However, she had a difficult time finding something nice to say because she was nearly blinded by the obscene amount of diamond jewellery around Lady Rutherford's neck and wrists, not to mention the heavy tiara on her head that looked as if it might snap her neck.

She attempted to compliment her gown, which was actually the colour of what could only be approximated to a baby's vomit.

'Your gown…it's an interesting shade of green.'

'Thank you. The brocade is Italian.'

It reminded Georgina of the wallpaper in one of the guest rooms at Harwicke House.

The Countess snapped her fan open and flapped it against her chest. 'Why, it's been a while since I've seen you last. And where is your Great-Aunt Leticia?' She lowered her tone. 'She's not…passed on, has she?'

'No, but she's been ill for a few years. She recently decided to return to Hampshire and enjoy the peace and quiet.' She gestured to Miss Warren. 'Miss Warren has replaced her.'

'Ah…' The Countess closed her fan and slapped it on her palm. 'That is why we have not seen much of you these days, is it? Such a devoted niece you are…caring for her all this time.'

'Er…yes.'

Thank you, Lady Rutherford.

The Countess had now given her a plausible excuse for her absence in society.

'Lord Rutherford… Lady Rutherford,' Trevor interrupted. 'May I introduce you to my guest for this evening? Mr Elliot Smith of New York City.'

The Earl and Countess turned to acknowledge Mr Smith. 'Welcome to London,' the Earl said.

'Thank you, my lord…my lady.' He bowed his head.

'We also have a guest,' the Earl said, gesturing to the young man behind him. 'Your Grace, this is Viscount Bellamy. Bellamy, this is His Grace the Duke of Harwicke, his sister Lady Georgina Abernathy, Mr Elliot Smith and Miss Sophia Warren.'

'Lovely to meet you,' Bellamy said.

Taller than herself, the Viscount was slim and fair-haired, with light blue eyes. As his gaze passed over her, Georgina could not help but feel it linger slightly, and the corner of his mouth curled up with the tiniest smile. She guessed him to be perhaps her age, maybe a year or two younger, and like many of his peers, he was dressed and groomed fashionably.

The Earl tutted impatiently at the footman, who had just finished filling the glasses and was now scrambling to bring the tray. 'And what brings you to London, Mr Smith?' he asked.

'Business,' Mr Smith replied.

'Now, now, Smith,' Trevor said with a short laugh as he took a glass of champagne from the tray the footman offered. 'We are here to enjoy ourselves. Don't get him started on business—he won't stop. There are other more enjoyable things we can speak of. Such as your ball tomorrow, Rutherford. Georgina and I are looking forward to it.'

'We are? Er… I mean, yes, we are,' Georgina said, taking a glass from the footman. Glancing over at Mr Smith, she managed not to down the entire flute by thinking of the girls at St Agnes's once more.

'How go the preparations?' Miss Warren asked smoothly. 'You must be very busy.'

'Very,' the Countess said in a dramatic tone. 'But I'm quite proud of how it's turning out. This year, we are doing a yuletide-themed ball.'

'Yuletide-themed ball?'

Georgina and—much to her consternation—Mr Smith spoke at the same time.

'Why, yes.' The Countess clapped her hands together. 'The Duchess of Haverston threw such a ball last year. It was the most lavish and splendid event I'd ever seen, and ever since then I've wanted to do one of my own. This year, the entire ballroom at Rutherford Hall will be decorated with Christmas trees—'

'And a lot of them,' the Earl interrupted with a laugh. 'What a strange tradition, isn't it? We didn't have that when I was young… In fact it didn't become all the rage until ten years ago, when the Queen herself started putting up these trees inside the palace and decorating them. I was told it was a tradition from the Prince Regent's side of the family.'

'If it's good enough for the Queen, then it's good enough for us. There will still be the usual merriment and dancing, of course,' the Countess added.

'Sounds splendid,' Trevor said. 'Lady Rutherford, I believe my friend from America has never been to a proper English ball. Wouldn't it be a privilege to be the first to show him how we throw a ball on this side of the pond?'

'I…' Lady Rutherford hesitated, but when her husband sent her a warning look, she smiled and said, 'Of course, we would love to have you, Mr Smith. If you are not too occupied with business.'

It was evident that Lady Rutherford was hoping he would decline, but Mr Smith raised his flute to her and said, 'Thank you, my lady, I accept.'

'And I will see you all there,' said Bellamy, raising his near-empty champagne glass. 'And perhaps you can save space on your dance card for me, Lady Georgina.'

She was tempted to tell him that, sadly, there would be no competition for the very empty spaces on her card, but instead said, 'Of course. Er…if you'll excuse me? I must refresh myself.'

Handing her half-empty flute to the footman, she exited the box and made her way to the necessary, holding her breath as she waded through the throng of people. If it wasn't for her urgent need, she would just leave, but she braved the crush.

After finishing her business, she quickly left—but had forgotten where the Rutherford box was located. Had she turned left or right when she'd left it?

Drat.

The crowds in the corridor seemed to grow, enclosing her, making her vision swim.

Sometimes the strain of being surrounded by too many people, or barraged by the presence of others, gave her these spells. It made it hard to breathe, as if a heavy weight was pressed on her, and all her energy would drain away.

Breathe, Georgina.

Somehow, she managed to remember the way back to their own box, and she reached the door just before her nerves completely unravelled. Hurrying inside, she let out a loud, cleansing sigh.

'I thought you'd head back to the Rutherford box.'

Her heart leapt into her throat at the sound of the familiar voice. 'I thought you'd still be there, Mr Smith.'

'The conversation turned boring,' he said. 'I— Are you all right?'

'Yes, I'm perfectly fine, Mr Smith.'

'You look pale, and you're sweating like you've run a race.'

'Isn't it impolite to remark on a woman's appearance?'

'Not if she looks ready to fall down.'

Clicking his tongue, he strode over to her, placing a hand on her gloved elbow to guide her to her seat. To her surprise, he planted himself on the seat next to hers, instead of retreating to his own.

'Here.' He offered her his handkerchief.

'Th-thank you.' She patted it on her brow. 'The crowds...'

'Yes, it seems all of the Ton is here tonight,' he remarked. 'But you look like you've gone through a harrowing experience. Would you like me to fetch you some water?'

'Do not bother yourself,' she said. 'I am fine.'

'Did anything happen?'

'No, but...' How was she to explain to him? 'There's just not enough air in places like this. It's suffocating. They should have built more windows.'

'True...but then again I don't think that would be very good for the acoustics. But still, you seem—'

'I'm looking forward to tomorrow's ball,' she interrupted, hoping to steer him away from further questions about her current state. 'I don't think I've ever attended a Christmas-themed event. I love Christmas.'

He stared at her as if a second head had grown out from her shoulders. 'Why?'

'Why not? I love how everything looks festive, and it feels as if people are nicer to each other. Giving gifts, sharing meals, contributing to charity and whatnot.'

He harrumphed. 'I truly do not see what is so special about it. It used to be just another day in the calendar and now there are celebrations and expectations around it. And think of all these decorations and baubles that must be tossed into the rubbish after the season is done—it seems incredibly wasteful to me.'

That, she couldn't argue with, and guilt crept into her as she thought of what she'd spent on decorations for Harwicke House and what the staff did with them every year once Christmas was done.

'But what about sharing with the less fortunate? And giving to charity?'

'I happen to contribute to several charities all year round.'

His tone did not sound arrogant, or boastful, just matter-of-fact.

'And not just once a year when "the spirit of the season" expects it.'

'Ah, so it is not giving you are against.' She smiled wryly at him. 'And I thought you were as miserly as Scrooge.'

His lips pressed together. 'Who exactly is this Scrooge character you keep comparing me to?'

'He's from a book. *A Christmas Carol* by Charles Dickens. The lead character is Ebenezer Scrooge.'

'Ah, ES.'

Embarrassment warmed her cheeks at this reminder of their first encounter at his office. 'You should read it sometime, Mr Smith,' she told him. 'It might be enlightening.'

He leaned closer. 'Do you think that, since we will likely be in each other's company more in the next few days, that perhaps you may call me Elliot?'

That bold question so took her by surprise that she did not respond right away. Then: 'I beg your pardon?'

'I would still call you Lady Georgina, of course. But I give you permission to use my first name. Is that not done here?'

'I d-do not think so.' At that moment she couldn't recall what was deemed appropriate as she was much too distracted by the luminous jade-green eyes and the handsome face that was now mere inches from hers.

'You don't? Well, in any case, do feel free to use it at any time.'

'I—'

He pulled back before she could say anything further, then stood up—which was fortunate because Trevor and Miss Warren entered the box at that very moment.

'Georgie, there you are,' Trevor said. 'You had me worried. We were waiting for you in the Rutherfords' box.'

'I got lost,' she said. 'So I just made my way back here.'

'And so did Mr Smith,' Miss Warren said. 'How—' The lights began to dim, interrupting her. Sending Georgina a knowing look, she sat down beside her.

As the orchestra began to play Georgina allowed herself to sneak one very quick look at Mr Smith.

Elliot, she corrected herself. The name had sounded strange to her own ears, but she supposed it didn't hurt to refer to him by his first name in her mind. After all, he did spend an inordinate amount of time there.

Not that she could help that. After all, she needed to think about him—or rather, think about finding him a bride to save her orphanage. And, despite what he'd said about giving to charity, she reminded herself that he would still evict the children if she did not succeed.

And he hated Christmas.

That still made him a Scrooge, in her opinion.

*9th December,
Lady Rutherford's ball*

'My, my, it seems Lady Rutherford has truly been imbued with the Christmas spirit,' Miss Warren remarked as they entered the ballroom at Rutherford Hall. 'I wonder if there are any trees left in the forests?'

Georgina laughed. 'You're jesting, of course. I only count thirteen—no, fourteen Christmas trees in here.'

'You must be in heaven,' the companion remarked.

'Oh, yes.'

The Rutherford ballroom showcased a true Christmas scene. Aside from the scattered trees, fir garlands had been strung across the ceiling and sparkly crystal ornaments that mimicked icicles hung from them. The magnificent chandelier was decorated with baubles and trinkets, while swathes of white fabric were strewn across the floor to mimic snow. Meanwhile, roaming footmen offered guests Christmas treats—sweetmeats, merengues, candies, mini-plum puddings and chocolate creams.

Georgina had to stop herself from taking more than one of each. Thankfully, her maid had found her something to wear that didn't need to be let out. The green satin gown wasn't new, but it was good enough for tonight. And as she'd been coming downstairs earlier tonight, one of the holly berry twigs had fallen from its perch on the balustrade. Instead of replacing it, she'd instead stuck it in her hair, to add a more festive look to her outfit.

'Is Mr Smith here?' Miss Warren enquired.

'I don't know.'

Georgina craned her neck, trying to find him, but didn't see him. She wasn't sure if he would be coming with her brother, though Trevor had said that he would travel in his own carriage, as he was going to Brooks' for dinner first.

'He will probably hate this ballroom,' she said with a chuckle. She could already imagine him scowling at all the 'waste' and 'frippery'.

'And why is that?'

'Because he hates Christmas, apparently. Thinks it's much too wasteful and unnecessary.'

'And how do you happen to know that?'

Georgina avoided her companion's suspicious gaze. 'Perhaps it's time I begin fulfilling my end of the bargain with him by finding him a potential wife. I will start tonight.'

'How exactly do you plan to do that?'

'I may be out of practice, but my social graces have not completely left me.' After all, she'd had six Seasons under the watchful eye of her Great-Aunt Leticia, who had taught her all the proper manners and conversation topics when meeting acquaintances. 'And so—' she swallowed audibly '—I will mingle and socialise.'

'I see...'

'And as I go I will make a list of potential brides.' She opened her reticule and retrieved a small card. 'I will write them down here, then present them to him.'

Miss Warren peered at the card in her hand. 'Is that your dance card?'

'Yes. I won't be using it for dancing anyway.' Straightening her shoulders, Georgina inhaled a large gust of air. 'Come, Miss Warren, we must begin at once.'

If only so she could finish sooner.

'You look as if you're about to go into battle,' her companion remarked. 'It's just conversation.'

Georgina sighed. 'Exactly...' But she would do it, if only to save the orphanage.

And so she roamed the ballroom, reacquainting herself with the women of the Ton, though she approached her subjects thoughtfully. She avoided most of the women her age, because after all, they would be of no use to her as they were already married and only had children who were a few years old. She sought out the older matrons whom she spied protectively shielding young women of marriageable age like mother hens. Thankfully, many of them remembered her, though a few raised their eyebrows at her unmarried state.

'Good heavens, I am exhausted,' Georgina declared eventually.

They had been speaking with Lady Mary Hammersmith about the latest trends in hats when Georgina had decided she'd had enough and excused herself.

'It's only been an hour,' Miss Warren pointed out.

'Feels like it's been days...' Her body felt sapped of all strength. 'But our efforts weren't for naught. I have collected a few names of possible brides.' She waved the card triumphantly at Miss Warren. 'And I—'

'Lady Georgina, here you are.'

'Lord Bellamy,' she greeted as the Viscount approached them. 'What a surprise.'

'I told you I would be here.' His gaze went to the card in her hand. 'Ah—I see your dance card is filled.'

'What—? Oh.' She quickly hid it behind her. 'N-Not at all. I mean, I'm all finished.'

Bellamy's face lit up. 'Ah, then perhaps I might have the next dance?'

Georgina glanced at Miss Warren helplessly. 'Er…'

'I'm afraid she's already promised me this next one,' came a voice from behind.

She didn't need to turn around, as she immediately recognised the low drawl, but she did anyway. Mr Smith—*Elliot*, she reminded herself—once again looked impressive in formal wear, and that curious flutter in her chest returned.

'Ah, Mr Smith,' Lord Bellamy said. 'How are you enjoying your first English ball? Is it just as you imagined?'

Elliot glanced around the room. 'Yes…exactly as I imagined.'

Georgina had to bite the inside of her cheek to stop herself from giggling as he looked less than enthused.

'As I mentioned, I would like to claim my dance now, Lady Georgina?'

'I will wait for the next one, then,' Lord Bellamy said. 'I shall be ready whenever you are, my lady.'

Elliot offered his arm, which she took, and led her to the dance floor, where the waltz was announced. Georgina thanked the heavens as it was one of the dances she remembered, and would require very little from her except to follow her partner's lead.

'*Is* it exactly as you imagined?' she asked in a teasing tone as she placed her hand on his shoulder.

For a moment she could have sworn the muscles under her palm jumped, but the movement had been so fleeting she wasn't sure if she'd imagined it.

'Why, yes. It's just as extravagant and excessive as I pictured it. Maybe even more.'

She chuckled. 'Why am I not surprised to hear you say that?'

'What did Bellamy want?' His hand landed on her waist.

'He—' The unfamiliar grip of his fingers on hers made all the air in her lungs disappear. It had been a long time since her last waltz—were partners really supposed to stand this close? 'Just a dance—as he said. Oh, that reminds me… I have made a list of potential wives for you.'

'You have?' The music began and he led them around the dance floor. 'Who are they?'

'Well…' The card was tucked between her fingers on his shoulder, so she shifted her hand to read it. 'To preface: you gave me no other requirement for your bride except that she has to be the daughter of a peer.'

'Correct.'

'All right, then. There are eight women on my list…'

'I'll take any one of them—whoever you think wants to marry as soon as possible.'

'I b-beg your pardon?' She would have stumbled had he not pulled her closer to him. 'I haven't even asked on your behalf— they do not even know you are interested. You can't just pick a name from a list and be married on the morrow.' She clicked her tongue at him impatiently. 'That's not how things work, Elliot.'

Those muscles jumped again at her use of his name, and the strangest look passed over his face, though it was gone in a moment and that serious mask slipped back on.

'Then tell me, how *does* it work?'

'First you will be introduced to them—which I can do tonight. Then you must meet them once more, and then you can call on them. After that, you may ask permission from her parents to court her.'

'That seems a rather drawn-out process.'

'If you want a quality bride, then you must go through it.' She blew out a breath.

He let out a resigned sigh. 'All right. Which of the eight women do you think would be the most amenable to marrying me? Your top three choices.'

She squinted at the card. 'My first choice would be Lady Amanda Garret, daughter of the Earl of Hastings. This is her third Season, and I hear her father is eager to curtail her spending on the new gowns and jewellery she and her mother buy each year. Lady Hastings has lamented that her husband is complaining of the last bill from their modiste.'

'Excellent. Who else?'

'Lady Lavinia Wright, the Marquess of Arundel's daughter,' she said. 'Her sister, Lady Genevieve, is said to be the most beautiful debutante of this year, so she's overshadowed poor Lady Lavinia.'

Which was a crime, in her opinion, as she thought Lady Lavinia was lovely.

'The Duke of Waldemere wants to court Genevieve, but her father refuses to allow the younger sister to marry before the older. Thus, the mother wants Lady Lavinia married off.'

'Acceptable. And the third?'

'The Honourable Miss Penelope Philipps. Her father is a viscount, the only son of the Earl of Halifax. Supposedly, he is awaiting the Earl's death, so he can take over the estate and open up the coffers. He's always been put on a very limited allowance.'

'Sounds like Miss Penelope would be the best candidate.' He paused. 'But your frown tells me you do not approve.'

'I just find it distasteful…waiting for a parent to die,' she said. Though distasteful was perhaps too mild a word.

'Because you lost your own parents at a young age and so suddenly?'

Her head snapped up to meet his jade-green gaze. 'How did you know that?'

'I have my ways. Now, perhaps it's time for you to make those introductions.'

'What—? Oh!' She hadn't noticed that the dance had ended. 'Of course.'

They bowed to each other, and he led her away from the dance floor. Lady Amanda had been dancing with Lord Dorset, so Georgina steered Mr Smith towards her mother, Lady Hastings, and they reached the Countess at the same time.

'Lady Hastings,' she greeted the Countess. 'And Lady Amanda—did you enjoy the dance?'

'Oh, yes. Lord Dorset is an excellent dancer.' She nodded to the older man, whose arm she clung to.

'We were also dancing—oh, allow me to introduce you to my brother the Duke's very good friend from America.' She quickly introduced Elliot.

'An American,' Lady Hastings said, the sneer in her tone evident. 'How many more of you are coming over to our shores?'

Georgina winced, but before she could say anything Elliot spoke. 'With the advancements in steamship mechanics, a great many more, I imagine. Good evening to you, ladies…my lord.'

Placing a hand on her elbow, he guided her away from the trio.

'Wait…wait!' She stopped, forcing him to halt. 'We weren't finished. You did not even get a chance to speak with Amanda.'

'Oh, I think we were very much finished,' he said. 'From the look of disdain on Lady Hastings' face, it's clear she will never accept me for a son-in-law, and Lady Amanda seems to be already enamoured of Lord Dorset, and he of her.'

She hadn't even noticed that.

'Who's next? Where is Lady Lavinia?'

'I last saw her there, by the lemonade table. The one in the blue dress. The two women beside her are her mother and her sister.'

Crossing the crowded room, they made their way to the Marchioness and her two daughters. After a pretence of fetching some lemonade, she quickly introduced Elliot to them.

'How is New York these days?' Lady Arundel enquired. 'I travelled there a few years ago with one of my very good friends—Jane, the Countess of Landsdowne. She grew up in New York, and moved here when she married the Earl. I found New York to be delightfully exciting.'

'New York is still exciting—perhaps even more so, my lady,' Elliot answered smoothly. 'Lady Lavinia, have you ever been?'

'No,' she said. 'I'm afraid not. I never go anywhere,' she added with a sigh.

'She was still but a child then, and I had to leave her here,' Lady Arundel said.

'But perhaps one day I might,' Lady Lavinia added. 'I mean, perhaps my mother will take me.'

'Mayhap, if the Countess visits her childhood home again,' the Marchioness said.

'I think you will enjoy it.' Elliot flashed her a charming smile—something Georgina had never seen before—which made the young lady blush.

'I think I might,' she replied.

A short stab of unknown emotion pierced Georgina's chest. Ignoring it, she turned to Lady Genevieve. 'How about you, Lady Genevieve? Would you like to visit America?'

Her brows snapped together. 'I do not think so. I am rather fond of England. If I ever do travel, it will perhaps be for my honeymoon, and I should like to go to Paris or the north of Italy.'

As Elliot and the ladies continued their conversation, Georgina felt as if she were fading into the background. Which was, she told herself, exactly what she wanted, so she didn't have to make further conversation. But the problem was that she couldn't leave either. No, she was trapped there, watching as Elliot and Lady Lavinia chatted amiably. Frankly, she was surprised that he could be so charming when he wanted to. And that unknown emotion seemed to bury itself deeper as she continued to watch them.

'I nearly forgot.' Lady Arundel slapped her fan on her palm. 'We will be attending the Earl and Countess of Landsdowne's musicale tomorrow, at their home. I'm sure I could persuade Jane to extend you an invitation, seeing as you're her countryman.' She turned to Georgina. 'Of course you and your brother the Duke have probably already received an invitation. So, what do you think, Mr Smith?'

'If you think it won't be an imposition…'

'Not at all. It is already a large gathering, and there is always room for more.'

'I should like to come, then.' Elliot glanced at Lady Lavinia. 'And you will be there as well, my lady?'

'I never miss it,' she replied with an expectant smile. 'And now there's more reason for me to attend.'

The stab in Georgina's chest turned into a flickering hot sensation.

'Oh, dear, I've been away from my chaperone for far too long,' she exclaimed. 'She must be worried. If you'll excuse me, I must go and find her.'

The other ladies nodded, and she turned on her heel. Despite being faced with the crowd of people, she managed to push herself through the throng.

Georgina rubbed her fist on her chest. Good Lord, what was happening? Her heart raced, her breath came in coarse pants, and the burning sensation in her chest would not go away. And when she thought of Elliot's smile directed at Lady Lavinia it worsened. It was like one of her 'spells', but it manifested a physical pain within.

'Lady Georgina!'

Surprise at hearing Elliot's voice—as if she'd conjured him up just by merely thinking of him—made her halt.

He quickly caught up to her and obstructed her path.

'What's the matter?' He searched her face. 'Why did you leave all of a sudden?'

'I... I told you... Miss Warren is probably looking for me.'

'You're acting strange again,' he said. 'Though this time your face is red instead of pale. Are you ill?'

'No!' Heavens, she wished she could escape this crowd. And him. 'It's so stuffy in here...with all the people around.'

'I see.' Gently, he took her by the arm and led her away. 'Come.'

'Where are you taking me?'

'To your brother.' He nodded ahead, to where Trevor and Miss Warren stood, just off to the side of the dance floor. 'Your Grace,' he said when they reached them. 'I think your sister is ill.'

'I'm fine,' she insisted, now annoyed with Elliot. 'Mr Smith is exaggerating.'

Trevor frowned. 'Perhaps all this pine is making her sick.'

'Never,' she insisted. 'I am not sick.'

'I will have the carriage brought round,' Trevor said, concern on his face. 'And you can go home.'

Home?

Oh, the thought of leaving this place and going back to her own rooms, where she could be alone, made her nearly weep with relief. She pressed a hand over her forehead.

'Perhaps I am feeling faint...'

'I should retire for the evening as well,' Elliot said.

'Of course. Miss Warren, would you mind watching over Georgina while Mr Smith and I bid goodbye to our hosts?'

Miss Warren hooked her arm through Georgina's. 'I shall take care of her, Your Grace.'

As Trevor and Elliot hurried off in search of the Earl and Countess, Miss Warren led her out of the ballroom and towards the front door. Georgina took a quick glance at Elliot's retreating back as he quickly disappeared into the crowd.

While she was thankful that she was finally going home, she couldn't help but feel disappointed that her time with him had been cut short. That dance between them had actually been pleasant. More than pleasant. She'd never felt so at ease in a man's arms.

'Hurry along, Lady Georgina,' Miss Warren urged as their carriage arrived.

Putting Elliot out of her mind, she climbed into the coach and closed her eyes, feeling the silence and darkness like a soothing blanket around her.

Chapter Five

10th December

It was just Elliot's luck that, as well as Lady Lavinia, the Honourable Miss Penelope Philipps was also in attendance at the Landsdownes' musicale the very next day. He was introduced to her by their hostess Jane, the Countess of Landsdowne, who had taken an immediate liking to Elliot because she too was a New Yorker. Her father had founded one of the largest banks in New York City and, much like him, she'd been shut out of society there because of her humble beginnings.

'Are you finding London to your liking, Mr Smith?' Miss Philipps asked as she accepted the lemonade offered to her by a passing footman.

'Indeed, I find myself settling in quite nicely,' Elliot replied, waving the footman away. 'Have you lived here all your life?'

'I have,' she said. 'But while I mostly spent my childhood here, summers were spent at Colworth Hill—that's my grandfather the Earl's seat in Devonshire—where we would…'

Elliot's mind drifted off as he pretended to listen to Miss Philipps wax lyrical about idyllic summer days at her grandfather's estate. All he could think about was Lady Georgina and the fact that he hadn't yet seen her tonight. Harwicke had said last night that both he and his sister would be in attendance, but perhaps she had been taken ill.

Guilt turned his stomach to stone. Had he been asking too much of her these past days? First it was the opera, then last night's ball... She was likely exhausted from attending two evening events in a row. The fact that he did not know her current condition was driving him to distraction.

But there was nothing out of the ordinary about his concern for her. After all, they had a bargain, and if she were unwell then she would not be able to fulfil her end. He needed her for the doors that she would open for him. Of course, he did not require her tonight, as he had already met Miss Philipps on his own.

Where the devil was she?

Harwicke was nowhere to be found either, so perhaps they'd had some trouble on the way here. It wasn't unusual for carriages to break down... Or perhaps they'd had to attend to a family matter.

'Mr Smith?' Miss Philipps' voice broke into his thoughts.

'Yes?'

'I was asking if you've been anywhere outside London.'

'No, I haven't.'

'You should take a trip to the countryside, then.' She batted her eyes at him. 'There's nothing like it...especially in the spring.'

'I will have to take your word for it. Perhaps—'

He stopped short as he saw a flash of blonde hair at the edge of his vision. Sure enough, it was Lady Georgina. And, once again, he found himself unable to tear his gaze from her.

That gown she'd worn at the opera had been indecently snug, pushing her full breasts up for anyone's perusal. He had shifted in his seat several times during the performance lest anyone— Harwicke especially—catch him embarrassing himself, like a young man seeing a woman for the first time. Last night's gown had been much more modest. But holding her close and feeling her hands on him had been torture of the sweetest kind for that entire three-and-a-half-minute dance.

Tonight was no different as she was once again a vision of loveliness in a violet gown that showed off her shoulders and creamy skin, as well as a modest amount of décolletage. Her blonde hair was swept up in a simple hairstyle, away from her face and pink cheeks, the chandelier above lighting the gold strands in them like a halo. She didn't seem ill, thank goodness, though her face was full of apprehension as she quickly perused the room.

'Miss Philipps,' he began, 'if you would excuse me, I think I see my friend, the Duke of Harwicke. I must give him my thanks, for if it wasn't for his intervention I would not have received an invitation to this soiree.'

'Of course, Mr Smith. The programme should begin soon. Perhaps I could save a seat for you?'

'Yes, I would very much like that.'

Nodding at her, he turned and walked in the direction of Lady Georgina, who was, as usual, accompanied by her companion, though Harwicke was nowhere in sight.

'Lady Georgina… Miss Warren,' he greeted them.

Her head snapped up to meet him, her copper-brown eyes widening. 'Mr Smith,' she replied. 'How lovely to see you here. I'm glad the Countess extended an invitation to you tonight. Trevor sends his apologies. He's taken to his bed with an illness.'

'Nothing too serious, I hope?'

She shook her head. 'Just a run-of-the-mill cold. His constitution has never agreed with the cold weather.'

'And you? I hope you are all right after last night?'

'Yes, I'm fine.' She let out what sounded like a forced laugh. 'Nothing a good night's sleep couldn't cure. Unlike my brother, I adore the winter weather.'

'Excellent. When I didn't see you here, I was beginning to think you were reneging on our deal.'

'Never!' Her tone was light-hearted. 'In fact, I have it on good authority that not only is Lady Lavinia here tonight, but Miss Penelope Philipps as well. I could introduce you to her, if you like.'

'There is no need as our hostess has already made the introductions.'

'Is that so?'

'Yes.'

'And how do you find her?'

'She is as you described her.'

Eager, that was for sure. He had not missed Miss Penelope Philipps' interest in him either, from the way her eyes roamed all over him—including his three-carat diamond tie pin and matching cufflinks.

'Excellent, then. There are many more unmarried young ladies here, and I can enquire about them. Or perhaps I could invite Miss Philipps and Lady Lavinia, plus a few more ladies and some gentlemen, for tea at Harwicke House tomorrow? After you meet them for a second time you may call upon them at home.'

'Do you know any gentlemen who would come?' he asked. 'Since your brother is currently indisposed?'

'Hmm…' She tapped her finger on her chin. 'You're right… Oh, wait! I know at least one gentleman I could invite. Lord Bellamy.'

That name left a sour taste in his mouth. He had not missed the young fop eyeing Lady Georgina's *assets* that night at the opera. His eyes had lingered on her chest much too long, and Elliot had had to stop himself from pulling them out from their sockets. When he'd seen him approach her last night, during the ball, he'd sprung into action to obstruct him, lest he molest her with his eyes again. He would be damned if he would let that lech near her again any time soon.

'What do you think, Mr Smith? Shall I approach them tonight?'

'Perhaps it would be a more efficient use of your time to find at least two more candidates before you invite anyone to your home.'

'True. I will have to find more candidates—'

'Excuse me…forgive me for the intrusion…but are you Mr Elliot Smith?' An older man in a black and white uniform asked the question as he approached them.

'Yes, I am. Mr…?'

'Bourne, sir. The butler.'

'And what can I do for you, Bourne?'

'Your footman, John, is waiting outside and wishes to speak to you. He claims it's urgent.'

'John?'

For a moment, a sense of foreboding washed over Elliot, as he thought of the last time John had come to him for an urgent matter. But surely it couldn't be bad news from the household again, because the footman had accompanied his carriage here and now waited with it outside. Perhaps there was a problem with the carriage or his coachman. 'Bourne, I believe the programme is about to start. Do you think you could ask John to come in and explain?'

'Of course, Mr Smith. Why don't you wait in the hall and I shall bring him in? All the guests we expected have arrived, so I shall be closing the doors shortly.'

'Thank you, Bourne.'

'What do you think is the matter?' Lady Georgina asked.

He shrugged. 'Something with the carriage, I presume.'

But then again how urgent could it be that John would interrupt his evening? He could always take a hansom cab if the carriage had broken down.

'Lady Georgina, Miss Warren, why don't you take your seats and I shall deal with this?'

'Let us stay here and wait for you,' she said.

'I—'

She placed a hand on his arm. 'Please. Then we can all sit together, even if it's at the back.'

It was difficult to say no to those sweet brown eyes. 'If you wish.'

They followed Bourne out to the hall, where he left them to go outside. When Bourne returned, however, he was alone.

'Mr Smith, he insists that you come outside to see to your carriage.'

'My carriage?'

Why the devil would he need to see the carriage? If it was broken, it wasn't as if he could fix it.

Irritated, he stormed out through the door. 'John, what is the matter?'

The footman paled as soon as he saw Elliot. 'Mr Smith, sir, we have...er...a delicate situation.'

'What is it? And why are you whispering?'

John swallowed, making his Adam's apple bob up and down.

'Please, Mr Smith. You must see for yourself.' He nodded to his carriage. 'I-In there, sir.'

He grabbed the handle and yanked the door open—and a bundle of black fabric tumbled into his arms.

'Whee!'

Though the voice coming from the bundle was muffled, he immediately recognised it.

'Anne-Marie!' he whispered as he righted the bundle and pulled off the dark cloak covering his sister's face. 'What in the name of all things holy are you doing here?' His nose picked up a suspiciously familiar scent, so he leaned closer and sniffed. 'Have you been drinking?'

Anne-Marie smiled dreamily up at him. She opened her mouth to speak, but only a belch came out. 'Whoops! 'Scuse me!'

'How the—? What the—? Why—?' The fury building in his chest tied his tongue in knots. 'John—explain.'

'She—she says she followed us here, Mr Smith,' the footman began. 'I saw her walking in the street and put her up inside the carriage.'

'Why didn't you take her home?'

Anne-Marie let out the most godawful wail. Elliot was pretty sure it would leave his ears ringing for days. He covered her mouth in an attempt to muffle her.

'That's why, sir,' John said. 'She wouldn't stop screaming when we tried to drive away. The coachman—'

'Elliot, let go of her. The poor thing can't breathe.'

He froze—not just because of the feminine voice that had spoken his name, but because of who had said it. He immediately withdrew his hand. Anne-Marie, thankfully, stopped screaming.

'What are you doing here?' In his haste, he had forgotten about Lady Georgina, but here she was, along with her companion, standing right behind him. Had she been there the entire time?

'You left us in the hall.' She sounded rather miffed, or perhaps like a mother scolding a child. 'What is happening here? Are you all right, dear girl?'

Anne-Marie, for the first time in her life, looked stunned as she stared at Lady Georgina, her mouth hanging open.

'She's fine…just a little…er…sick.'

'Smells as if she's drunk,' Miss Warren said, her tone laced with acidity. 'Do you often keep intoxicated young girls in your carriage, Mr Smith?'

'She's my sister,' he snapped at the companion.

'Half-sister,' Anne-Marie slurred. 'My father was also his father, but my mother was a dock—'

'Enough, Anne-Marie!'

Shame pooled in his gut. This was not how he'd wanted Lady Georgina to meet his sister. Damn it, he hadn't wanted them to meet *at all*. Surely now Lady Georgina would be utterly scandalised and would never want to associate with him again, even if it meant losing the orphanage.

'Are you feeling ill, dear girl?' Lady Georgina said as she pushed past him and placed a hand on Anne-Marie's forehead. 'You're pale and chilled.'

'I don't feel so good…' she murmured. 'The floor won't stop spinning.'

When she swayed to one side, Lady Georgina caught her and propped her against her shoulder.

'There, there…' She patted Anne-Marie on the shoulder. 'What happened?'

'I got into Cook's special cabinet and saw the bottle…drank most of it…felt good.'

'And then what?'

'I hate it here,' she sniffed. 'I wanted to tell him how much.' She sent Elliot a seething look. 'I saw the invitation on his desk and so I walked here.' She moaned as her eyes rolled. 'I don't think that was a good plan.'

'No, I'm afraid not, dear girl. You're shivering, and now you're turning an alarming shade of green. Why don't we take you back home? Wouldn't it be nice to have a hot cup of tea and a thick, soft blanket?'

'Uh-huh…'

Lady Georgina nodded at the carriage. 'Mr Smith—the door, if you please.'

Unsure what else to do, Elliot opened the carriage door for them.

'There you go.' She assisted Anne-Marie up the step. 'Now—'

'No!' Anne-Marie moaned when Lady Georgina released her. She grabbed her arm. 'Don't leave me, please!'

'You must go home,' she said. 'And I must stay here.'

'Don't leave me alone,' she cried. 'In that big old house. With no one but my silly little sister.'

'Anne-Marie,' Elliot began, 'Lady Georgina cannot go home with us.'

'Please! Please come home with me.'

'I…' Lady Georgina looked at him helplessly, and then to Miss Warren. 'Perhaps—'

'Do not even think about it,' Miss Warren warned, her voice steely. 'You cannot go with an unmarried man to his home in the middle of the night!'

'It's not the middle of the night,' she said. 'It's barely eight o'clock.'

'And what if someone sees you? Or notices that both of you are missing?'

'Everyone is seated inside at the musicale,' she reasoned. 'No one will see us. And no one knows Mr Smith so they will not note his absence. Lady Landsdowne didn't even see us arrive—she will just assume we are ill, like Trevor. We will ride in the carriage, deliver the girl to her home, and be back here in no time. Or we could just go home. Please, Miss Warren, if you come along no one will think anything of it.'

Miss Warren pursed her lips, as if contemplating her request. 'Do not make me regret this, Lady Georgina.'

'I won't. Now, Mr Smith, does that sound like a good plan? May we ride with you?'

Elliot could only stare at her, a million thoughts in his head. Once again Lady Georgina had robbed him of his ability to think straight. But he had to consider Anne-Marie's reputation. If anyone were to find her out here, three sheets to the wind, she would be ruined even before she came out.

'Yes, please. Go right ahead.'

They all settled in the carriage, Elliot on one side and the ladies across from him, Anne-Marie in between them, clinging to Lady Georgina like a vine on a trellis. The absurdity of this whole situation slowly dawned on him, and he couldn't blame the companion for the glares she shot him every chance she could. Lady Georgina was risking a lot, being here. If anyone saw them she would take the brunt of any scandal.

But should all go well, and no one would ever know she was with him. Once they arrived at his home he would take Anne-Marie inside and then have his coachman deliver them back to Harwicke House.

His plan, however, was thwarted by Anne-Marie, who began to wail drunkenly once more as soon as Elliot tried to take her into the house when they arrived.

'I want Lady Georgina to take me in and tuck me under some soft blankets with tea,' she said, and pouted.

'For God's sake, Anne-Marie.' He raked his fingers through his hair. 'She's a lady, not a maid. She can't undress you and put you to bed.'

'You promised!' Anne-Marie cried to Lady Georgina. 'You promised tea...and blankets.' She hiccupped.

'I... I suppose...' Lady Georgina's voice drifted off as she stroked Anne-Marie's hair. 'A few minutes...'

Miss Warren sent Elliot a murderous look. 'Do not even think it! The Duke will sack me if he finds out.'

'Well, maybe he doesn't have to find out?' Lady Georgina said. 'Five minutes. We will be in and out. Won't we, Anne-Marie?'

'Five minutes...' she echoed. 'Please, Miss Warren? I want you to come too. You're so nice and pretty... I wish I had a friend like you.'

Miss Warren let out a strangled sound. 'I— Fine. Five minutes.'

They quickly bundled up Anne-Marie and hurried into the house, rushing past a startled Fletcher.

'Do not let anyone upstairs,' Elliot barked.

The butler could only nod.

Once the three of them had led Anne-Marie up the stairs, Elliot thought his troubles were over. However, the sound of small feet running across the carpeted floor made him groan inwardly.

'Elliot! What—? Anne-Marie!' Lily stood barefoot at the

top of the stairs, red curly hair all wild, green eyes wide as she watched them. 'Who are you?'

'I'm...er...a friend,' Lady Georgina said as she prised Anne-Marie's hands from the banister. 'We're friends. Ah... Come now, dear girl, just allow me to help you. That's it...one step at a time.'

'I like your gown,' Lily called.

'Lily, go back to bed,' Elliot ordered.

Lily, however, did not budge. 'Are you a lady? Elliot keeps talking about bringing a lady home to live with us.'

The most delicate blush appeared on Lady Georgina's cheeks. 'I'm afraid not, poppet.'

Lily's mouth pursed. 'What's a poppet?'

By this time they had reached the top of the stairs, so with her free hand Lady Georgina brushed back a lock of wild red hair from Lily's face and tucked it behind her ear. 'Why, you are a poppet.'

'I'm not a poppet. I'm a Lily,' she said. 'But... I suppose you could call me poppet.'

Elliot sighed. 'Go to bed, please, Lily.'

'But why?'

'Because it's bedtime and I said so—that's why.'

'You're being mean.' Lily crossed her arms over her chest. 'Why can't I come with you?'

'We're just putting your sister to bed,' Lady Georgina said. 'We aren't going anywhere fun.'

'We never do anyway,' Lily retorted. 'Elliot, you said we could go skating on the Serpentine.'

'It's not cold enough yet, poppet,' Lady Georgina said. 'Winter has only just begun. And the ice isn't quite hard enough to go skating on.'

'Oh. Then why didn't you say so, Elliot?'

He could not stop himself from grinning at the exasperated expression on Lily's face. 'I'm sorry, Lily.'

'Ahem...' Miss Warren cocked her head to one side.

Lady Georgina clicked her tongue. 'Er... Lily, is it? Why don't you help us get Anne-Marie ready for bed.'

'What happened to her, anyway?' She sniffed. 'And why does she smell odd?'

'Your brother will explain later.' She offered her hand to the little girl. 'Well? Are you coming?'

'Yes!' she replied, taking Lady Georgina's hand.

Elliot led them to Anne-Marie's door. 'This is her room.'

Lily opened the door and let Lady Georgina and Anne-Marie inside. When he attempted to enter, Miss Warren blocked him.

'I think we can take it from here.'

'But—'

'Please.' She raised a palm. 'I'm already risking a lot, allowing Lady Georgina to be here. Your sister is safe with us. Just allow us to help her into bed so that we may leave as soon as possible.'

'All right...' He relented, then stepped back.

As soon as the door closed he leaned against the wall and closed his eyes. What a mess this whole situation was. And what kind of brother was he? Allowing Anne-Marie not only to become intoxicated but to escape the house and wander the streets of London?

A terrible one.

He scrubbed his hand down his face. What was he to do? He'd come here so that he could do what was best for the girls, but no matter how hard he tried he couldn't do anything right.

I just want what's best for them.

'Mr Smith?' Miss Warren called.

His eyes opened and he stood up straight. 'Miss Warren? Is she all right?'

'We have changed her into her nightrail and put her to bed. She has brought up her dinner, but aside from that your sister is fine. Nothing that some water, rest and food won't cure.'

And didn't he know it? He'd often come home to see his father in a drunken state. 'I assure you, Miss Warren, this is not a common occurrence in the house. I'm going to have everyone responsible for this sacked.'

She raised a dark brow. 'If you are seeking the source of this misbehaviour, perhaps you should look a little closer.'

'I beg your pardon? Are you implying—?'

Lady Georgina's sudden appearance in the doorway made him close his mouth.

'She's asleep,' she whispered as she quietly closed the door behind her. 'They both are. Lily's curled up beside her.'

'Thank you...both of you,' he said.

'You are very welcome,' Lady Georgina said. 'I'm sorry your evening was spoiled and you were unable to spend more time with Lady Lavinia and Miss Philipps.'

'Who?' He shook his head. 'Oh, yes. But your evening was spoiled as well, thanks to my sister's impetuousness. I should be the one to apologise.'

'I didn't know you had sisters,' she said quietly. 'I—'

'I believe it is time we leave,' Miss Warren declared.

'Of course.' He bowed his head. 'I shall not impose on you any longer.'

'Do not worry. I will find more eligible ladies of the Ton,' Lady Georgina said. 'With Trevor sick, we won't be able to attend any functions tomorrow, but I will shortly arrange that tea we spoke of. I will send you the details.'

Miss Warren took her elbow. 'Come along, Lady Georgina. Mr Smith, we will see ourselves out.'

He didn't bother to protest, but he continued to watch Lady Georgina as she walked away. It was such a strange sensation, seeing her inside his home. It was like the merging of two different worlds.

Once he heard their footsteps fading, he cracked open the door to Anne-Marie's room open and poked his head inside.

His heart lurched at the image that greeted him. Anne-Marie and Lily were facing each other under the covers, their arms over the sheets as they held hands.

The first few years after the girls had come to him, they'd refused to be separated, even while sleeping. He would often come home after a long day at work to see both girls curled up in the same bed, clinging to each other.

The lump in his throat grew, and he quietly backed away and closed the door.

This plan had to work.

For them.

Chapter Six

11th December

Georgina loved nothing more than a quiet afternoon of reading by the fire on chilly days. Today was especially nippy as she settled down on one of the well-worn wingback chairs in the library with a brand-new novel. This truly was heaven for her.

Except that she'd re-read the same page for the last half-hour and hadn't understood a single word of it.

'Oh, bother!' She placed the book on her lap and rested her forehead on her palm.

'What is the matter, Lady Georgina?' Miss Warren paused from her mending to glance up at her. 'Is the novel not to your liking?'

'It's not that.'

'Do you have a headache?'

'No, I'm fine.'

She picked up the book once more. Unfortunately, the words refused to make sense.

It was all Elliot's fault.

The events of last night repeated in her head, making it difficult to focus on anything else. Recalling parts of it made her laugh—like the absurdity of the three of them trying to abscond with one young lady without being discovered. Other parts of it made her sad—like Anne-Marie saying how much she hated London or how Lily had seemed such a lonely child, from the bits and pieces Georgina had picked up from their conversation while she'd helped them dress Anne-Marie for bed. And as for the rest of it... She could not quite describe the emotions elicited in her when Elliot had shown such obvious love and concern for his sisters.

I didn't even know he had sisters.

He hadn't said a word about them this entire time. Granted, they had only known each other a few days, and he did not owe her anything. Still, it would have been nice to know about them. Questions fired in her mind: where were their parents? Why were they in his care? Why had he dragged them all the way to London if Anne-Marie hated it here?

'You are still thinking about them, aren't you?' Miss Warren said.

'And you are still angry about last night,' said Georgina.

'Yes.'

'But nothing happened.'

Miss Warren sighed and put her mending down. 'Yes. But still, it could have been a disaster—someone could have seen us, and then we would be having a very different conversation at this moment—if we would even *be* conversing, as I'm quite sure your brother would have sent me away by now.'

'But nothing *did* happen,' Georgina said. 'So we should not worry about what *could* have happened.'

'I assume you are still determined to help Mr Smith find a bride by Christmas?'

'Yes.'

The reminder of their bargain sparked a different thought in her. When she had first hatched this scheme to find him a bride, she'd thought he had a very selfish motive, which was to elevate his own status and gain a foothold in society. But now that she'd met his sisters... Perhaps she was not entirely correct.

'Miss Warren, do you suppose that El— Mr Smith wants a wife because—?'

A knock interrupted her, and Dawson appeared in the doorway. 'I beg your pardon, Lady Georgina, but you have callers.'

'Callers?'

Miss Warren's nose twitched. 'Tell them to return tomorrow, during Lady Georgina's calling hours.'

'I do not have calling hours.' At least, she couldn't remember the hours Great-Aunt Leticia had set when she had still been receiving. 'Who are they, Dawson?'

'Mr Elliot Smith, with Miss Anne-Marie Smith and Miss Lilian Smith,' he said.

Elliot and the girls were here?

'Send them in, Dawson, without delay.' She shot to her feet. 'No, wait... Bring them to the parlour instead, and have Cook prepare afternoon tea.'

'Yes, my lady.'

'Are you truly going to entertain them?' Miss Warren asked as the butler disappeared through the doorway.

'Why not? Is it not proper that we welcome guests?'

'Your brother is still abed with a cold, and Mr Smith has not left his card or even asked the Duke for permission to call on you. This is all very improper.'

The idea of Elliot calling on her as if he were courting her sounded absurd—yet it sent a zing of excitement all the way to bottoms of her feet.

'Nonsense. He is my brother's friend and has been here before, and therefore he is welcome in this house. It is also past the middle of the day, my brother is present in the house—as are you, and Mr Smith's sisters, not to mention a house full of servants. There is nothing improper about this.'

'You sent no invitation to them,' her companion reminded her.

'Who would know that? And I did promise Anne-Marie a hot cup of tea—which, in my opinion, is a good enough invitation. Now, let us see to our guests, shall we?'

If Miss Warren protested further Georgina didn't hear it, because she hurried out of the library, practically skipping all the way to the parlour. Before she entered, she paused and took a deep breath, trying to control her excitement.

'Good afternoon,' she greeted them.

'Good afternoon, my lady.' Elliot nodded to the girls. 'Allow me to introduce you to my sisters, Anne-Marie and Lily.'

She found it odd that he would introduce them so formally, but then again, they had never been properly introduced, and her presence in their home last night was to remain a secret.

'Hello, Anne-Marie... Lily.' She smiled at them. 'Welcome to Harwicke House.'

Anne-Marie acknowledged her with a bow of her head but said nothing, her expression taut with tension. Lily, on the other hand, flashed her a bright grin.

Elliot bowed his head. 'Thank you for agreeing to see us, my lady.'

'Of course. Now— But wait...why are you still wearing your coats? Dawson should have taken them.'

He shook his head. 'There is no need. We aren't staying long.'

'Not staying long? But Cook is preparing afternoon tea. We have cucumber sandwiches, petits-fours, scones, trifle and teacakes. Doesn't that sound lovely?'

The two girls looked at each other, excitement brimming on their faces, but they remained silent as Elliot spoke again.

'Thank you, but we must decline. We are here because Anne-Marie would like to apologise for her behaviour last night.'

'Is that so?' No wonder the poor thing looked as if she was off to the gallows. She turned to Lily. 'And why are *you* here, poppet?'

Lily's smile grew wider. 'I'm here because Elliot said if I promised to forget what I saw last night, I could come.'

Georgina could barely stop the laugh bubbling in her chest. 'Ah, I see you've stooped to the bribery of children, Mr Smith.'

The corner of his mouth pulled up. 'Only when necessary, my lady. Now, Anne-Marie, is there something you would like to say?'

The girl stepped forward. 'Lady Georgina, Miss Warren, please accept my apology for my behaviour last night. It was unladylike and I will never do it again.'

Georgina strode over to her and took her hand. 'I will accept your apology—'

'Good,' Elliot interjected.

'But only if you stay for tea.'

Jade-green eyes so much like Elliot's widened. 'Really?'

'Yes. Well, Mr Smith?'

He crossed his arms over his chest. 'She's supposed to go straight back home after this, because she is being punished for her actions, not rewarded for them.'

Unable to help herself, she repeated his words back to him. 'You know my terms, Mr Smith.'

He snorted—although it sounded as if he was trying to stop himself from chuckling. 'All right. But we are staying for half an hour, not a second more.'

The two girls exchanged delighted looks.

'Come, let's sit down,' she said. 'Tea will be served at any moment now.'

'Just so you know,' Elliot began as they made themselves comfortable in the parlour, 'I didn't force Anne-Marie to come here to apologise.'

'You didn't?'

Anne-Marie smiled weakly at her. 'I felt terrible about what happened, and I asked Elliot if I could write an apology letter.' She took a spot on the empty settee and patted the space next to her, indicating to her sister to sit there. 'But he said I should do it in person.'

'She's scared of you,' Lily said.

'Lily!' Anne-Marie whispered, her face turning red.

'I don't know why she would be scared of you,' the youngest Smith said as she fiddled with the lace hem of her dress. 'Elliot said she was sick and you helped her. Why would that scare her?'

Ah, so that was his explanation. 'She...er...ripped my favourite dress while I helped her,' Georgina offered.

Lily cocked her head to the side. 'Elliot said it was your glove.'

'That too,' she said smoothly. 'Anyhow, Anne-Marie, I'm glad to see you are feeling better this morning.'

'Thank you, Lady Georgina, I am,' she replied sombrely. 'I had a headache, but the housekeeper gave me some powder that helped ease the throbbing.'

'Are you a real lady?' Lily interjected.

'Lily, you can't ask questions like that,' Elliot said with an apologetic look. 'I'm sorry—you don't have to answer that.'

'No, not at all,' Georgina said with a chuckle. She found children's questions so honest and refreshing—they were asked with curiosity and not malice. 'To answer your question, poppet, yes. My father was a duke and so I am, indeed, a lady.'

'Can I be a lady too?'

'If you marry a lord. Would you like to be one?'

She cocked her head to one side and wrinkled her nose. 'Maybe… I don't know if I want to get married. I don't like boys. All they want to do is play with sticks and throw mud at my dress.' She stuck out her tongue. 'Except Elliot. I like him very much. Do you like him?'

It took all of Georgina's willpower not to glance over at him as heat crept up her cheeks. Mercifully, Dawson entered at the precise moment, a silver tea service in his hands while a maid carried a tiered tea stand heaped with food.

Lily's eyes lit up. 'Is that all for us?'

'Yes!' Georgina chuckled. 'And there's more, so please help yourselves.'

'Tea in the Abernathy household tends to be an elaborate affair,' Miss Warren said as Dawson and the maid began to serve them. 'I'm surprised we have any appetite for dinner at all.'

'It's a tradition,' Georgina said. 'My mother loved afternoon tea, and she and I would have all these treats until we…' Her voice faded as a lump formed in her throat at this reminder that her mother was no longer here. 'I…' Though she attempted to dislodge it, it remained there, and an awkward silence crept into the air.

'Lady Georgina, your Christmas decorations are quite…er… interesting,' Elliot said, though he seemed to struggle with finding the right adjective. 'They look to be made of the highest quality materials.'

Her head swivelled towards him. She was surprised he would even notice the decor, or say anything nice about it, given how much he hated Christmas.

'Everything looks beautiful,' Anne-Marie remarked. 'Is the entire house decorated?'

'From the roof to the cellar—and I did most of it myself.'

Elliot took a sip of his tea. 'You did an excellent job.'

Now that, at least, sounded like a true compliment.

'Thank you.'

'Do you decorate your home for Christmas?' Miss Warren asked.

'Only for Christmas Eve and Christmas Day. Then it all gets packed away as soon as we go to bed,' Anne-Marie said, taking a sip of her tea. 'But we have gifts, and a feast, with roast goose and all the trimmings.'

'And cake!' Lily added, her eyes growing large as saucers as the maid placed a generous portion of trifle on her plate. 'But none as nice as this.'

Georgina sneaked a glance at Elliot. 'And I thought you were a Scrooge.'

'Oh, Elliot doesn't celebrate with us.' Anne-Marie sniffed at a scone before taking a bite. 'He's at the office all day, and we don't see him until the next morning.'

'But why not?' Georgina asked.

'I'm always working.' He waved away the plate the maid was about to put in front of him. 'It's the only time I can get anything done.'

She tsked. 'I take back what I said, then.'

Anne-Marie snorted. 'Oh, I see.' Her eyes darted to Elliot. 'Yes, definitely a Scrooge.'

Georgina, Lily and even Miss Warren all looked at each other with knowing smiles.

'Am I the only person to have never read this novel?' He grumbled as he fiddled with his teacup.

'Oh, hello, there…good afternoon,' came a booming voice from the doorway. It was Trevor, up and about, and though he was fully dressed, his hair remained dishevelled and the stubble on his chin indicated he hadn't shaved. 'No, don't get up,' he said. 'And please don't let me interrupt.'

'Trev, you're supposed to be in bed.' Georgina rose to her feet and strode over to him. 'Are you still feverish?'

He waved her hand away as she attempted to touch his forehead. 'No, no, I am fine, Georgina.'

'That wasn't what you said last night,' she said wryly. 'You said you were on your deathbed.'

'I did not.'

'And you promised me I could have Odin when you passed.'

'I know you are definitely lying, because not even on my deathbed would I give you my best stallion.' He turned to the other occupants of the parlout. 'Pardon me for my rudeness, ladies,' he said to Anne-Marie and Lily. 'Trevor Abernathy, Duke of Harwicke, at your service.' He waved his hand with a flourish as he bowed. 'And who might you lovely ladies be?'

Anne-Marie blushed and Lily giggled.

'These are my sisters, Miss Anne-Marie Smith and Miss Lilian Smith.' Elliot gestured for them to stand. 'Girls…?'

'Delighted to make your acquaintance,' Anne-Marie said as she executed a clumsy, though serviceable curtsey. 'Your Grace.'

'I thought his name was Trevor?' Lily said in a loud whisper.

'It is…but you're supposed to say "Your Grace" to a duke, you ninny,' Anne-Marie admonished. 'Don't you remember anything from those lessons?'

'I'm sorry.' Lily hung her head low.

'It's quite all right. Since I am the first duke you've met, you are hereby granted a pardon,' Trevor said. 'I didn't know you had sisters, Elliot. Why have you never mentioned them?' He scratched his chin. 'And, by the way, what brings you here this afternoon?'

Panic rose in Georgina as she met Miss Warren's gaze. 'Er… Mr Smith told me about his sisters last night, during the musicale, and so of course I had to invite them to tea. Can you believe they've never had a proper English afternoon tea?'

'Ah, yes…' Striding over to the table, he plucked a cucumber sandwich from the tray and popped it in his mouth. 'And you've never had afternoon tea until you've had it in the Abernathy household.'

'Do you want to join us?' Georgina asked. 'I can have Dawson bring a chair from the library.'

'No need. I think I shall head back upstairs for a nap and eat at dinner.' Still, he leaned down to contemplate the tiered tray of goodies. 'But I heard voices, and my valet said we had guests, so I had to investigate for myself. Oh—' Standing up straight, he whirled to face Elliot. 'I'm glad you're here, actually.'

'Why?'

'I meant to tell you last night. Georgina and I will be heading up to Foxbury Hill, my estate in Northamptonshire, in a few days. We mean to stay until the eighteenth.'

'Oh, dear, is it that soon?' She hadn't even noticed. Usually she'd be brimming with excitement in the days leading up to their stay at Foxbury Hill.

'Northamptonshire? What for?' Elliot asked.

'It's where we celebrate our First Christmas.'

'First Christmas...?' he echoed.

'Another Abernathy tradition,' Georgina explained. 'And perhaps my favourite one.'

'Papa abhorred town during Christmas, while Mama hated being away from the social whirl during the festivities. So they compromised—First Christmas mid-December in Northamptonshire and Second Christmas on the twenty-fifth in London.'

'Ah, I see.' Elliot folded his hands on his lap. 'I suppose I'll be on my own, then.'

Georgina's stomach dropped. With her away in Northamptonshire, how was she to continue with her work on finding him a bride. 'Trev, perhaps we can...' she swallowed '...postpone First Christmas?'

'Nonsense.' He waved a hand at her. 'I was going to invite you, Elliot.'

'You were?' Georgina and Elliot said at the same time.

'Yes. And, Georgie, you should invite your potential candidates as well.'

'Candidates for what?' Anne-Marie eyed them suspiciously.

Georgina sent her brother a warning look, then said, 'Er... best friends. Yes, I'm looking to find some very good, very best friends.'

Lily's jaw dropped open. 'You must be very popular if people are vying to be your best friends. Can I help you find some friends?'

'Er...yes, poppet. Whatever you want.'

'And we can celebrate your First Christmas with you?'

'Of course you can.'

Anne-Marie let out a small squeal. 'We are leaving London!' She grasped the edge of the table. 'I can't believe it.'

Lily let out a whoop. 'Hooray!'

'Girls, girls!' Elliot exclaimed as he raked his fingers through his hair. 'The Duke has not invited you—he has invited me.'

'Well, of course they are invited,' Trevor said. 'You can't leave them alone in London while you go gallivanting off to Northamptonshire. Elliot, bring as many of your staff as you need—including nannies, tutors and governesses...'

'We don't have a governess any more,' Lily said. 'Anne-Marie set her on fire.'

'I beg your pardon?' Trevor said, looking taken aback.

Elliot let out a strangled cry. 'No, you girls will be staying in London.'

'But Lady Georgina said we could,' Lily whined.

'You *always* do this,' Anne-Marie seethed at Elliot.

'I am your brother and what I say goes,' he retorted. 'Now, girls, please compose yourselves.'

Georgina deftly manoeuvred herself between them. 'Anne-Marie, Lily, have you ever seen a winter garden before? No?' She glanced at her companion. 'Perhaps Miss Warren can show you. If you don't mind, Miss Warren?'

'Of course, my lady.' Rising to her feet, Miss Warren urged both girls to do the same, then deftly shepherded them out of the parlour.

'We have the room to host all of you,' Trevor assured him. 'I—ah—' He inhaled a breath, then covered his mouth. *'Achoo!'*

'I knew you were still sick,' Georgina admonished. Taking his arm, she hauled him towards the door. 'Go back to your room and rest.'

'But—'

'Go.' She pushed him out and then shut the door behind him. Brushing her hands together, she turned back to Elliot. 'It truly is no trouble to have your sisters come with us.'

'That is very kind of you, but—'

'They don't know, do they? That you are looking for a wife?' His expression darkened, like the sudden arrival of dark clouds on a sunny day. 'I would rather they not know my personal business. They are children.'

'Anne-Marie is what—? Sixteen? Seventeen? She is not a child any more.'

'Still, they are my responsibility.' He raked his hand into his hair once again, making tufts of dark hair jut out in every direction.

Georgina's fingers itched to put them back into place. Or perhaps to run through them as his had earlier.

'I understand—which is why you cannot just leave them in London. Please, do not fret about it. We have plenty of rooms and there will be many staff who can assist you and keep them company. *I* will keep them company.'

'And how are you supposed to do that when you are finding me a bride?'

She ignored the way her stomach turned to stone. 'My work shall be done before that,' she said. 'I will call on Lady Lavinia, Miss Philipps and their mothers tomorrow and extend our invitation for the party. Once they arrive in Northamptonshire, there will be every opportunity for you to get acquainted with them and woo them. I can't possibly do all the work, now, can I?'

'Hmm, I suppose…'

'I am but a shepherdess, leading the lambs to the—'

'Slaughter?' he finished.

She grinned at him. 'I was going to say fold.'

It was then that Elliot did something that took her by surprise—he smiled at her. A one hundred percent completely genuine smile that reached his eyes. Her heart fluttered madly in her chest.

'I haven't said thank you, by the way,' he said, the smile fading.

'For what?'

'For last night. And just now…with the girls. I don't think I've seen them as happy as they have been in the past half-hour in a long time.'

How she ached for those poor children.

'You may thank me by allowing the girls to come to Foxbury

Hill. They will be very much welcome and very much wanted there.' She grasped his forearm. 'Please, Elliot?'

He blinked at her, his eyes darting down to where she touched him.

Realising what a presumptuous move it had been, she quickly released him. 'Apologies…' Her emotions had got the better of her and she hadn't realised she'd grabbed him. 'And for using your name—'

'No, it's all right. I did give you leave to use it if we were alone.'

And they were, as he'd pointed out, quite alone—a fact that made her heart skip a beat. 'Of course you have the courtesy to do the same.' It was only fair, after all.

He made a noncommittal sound. Then: 'Now, about your invitation…'

'Yes?'

'I accept,' he relented. 'We will travel to Northamptonshire.'

She clapped her hands together. 'Excellent. Come, let's tell them together.'

As expected, Anne-Marie and Lily shrieked in excitement when Georgina told them that they were to come to Foxbury Hill with them.

'Is this real, Elliot?' Anne-Marie asked. 'You won't change your mind?'

He huffed. 'Yes, you and Lily are coming with me to Northamptonshire.'

'Whoopee!' Lily launched herself at Georgina, wrapping her arms around her legs. 'We get two Christmases this year! Thank you, Lady Georgina.'

She patted her on the head. 'You're welcome.' Grinning, she glanced back to Elliot, who had the strangest expression on his face. 'You shan't regret this,' she assured him.

'I hope not…'

Chapter Seven

14th December

Though the process of calling on people had always been more painful than walking over hot coals for Georgina, she somehow managed to do it twice in one day. Her efforts, however, had proved fruitful, because both Lady Arundel and the Viscountess had accepted her invitation with much delight. She had known they would accept because she had mentioned the one thing that that would pique the interest of any mother with daughters of a marriageable age—the fact that there would be unmarried gentlemen present as well.

Of course that meant she also had to invite other gentlemen to Foxbury Hill, but those who would pose no threat to Elliot's prospects. Thankfully Trevor had taken care of that. He'd invited the Duke of Waldemere, as he and Lady Lavinia's sister Genevieve were practically courting, and Mr James Galwick, whom he assured her had no intention of finding a wife.

And so there would be an even number of unmarried ladies and gentlemen, if she included herself, which should satisfy the marriage-minded mamas.

Having arrived at Foxbury Hill very late in the afternoon, Georgina had refreshed herself with a short nap. She had travelled with only her lady's maid and Miss Warren, as Trevor had business to attend to in London and would not be leaving town until the next day. All their guests would be arriving today, so now she felt rested she set off to check the preparations for the festivities.

Initially, the staff at Foxbury Hill had only begun preparing for Georgina and Trevor to come, as they did every year, but thankfully Dawson had been able to send word to them about the extra guests.

Georgina went down to the kitchens and met Mrs Galloway, the housekeeper, and Mrs Laramie, the cook, to ensure everything was ready.

'The decorations are lovely, by the way, Mrs Galloway,' she said. 'They are every year, but they are particularly delightful this time around.'

Even the outside of the house was decorated, with wreaths made of fir and ribbon, and when she'd entered the hall, she'd been greeted by not one, but two Christmas trees, bedecked with all sorts of decorations.

The housekeeper chuckled, the wrinkles on her weathered face deepening. 'I would never disappoint you, Lady Georgina. Dawson sent word that Harwicke House was especially festive this year, and so of course we said we must ensure Foxbury Hill is just as splendid—if not more. After all, this is where you spend First Christmas.'

'The roast turkey will be perfect this year too,' Mrs Laramie said, rubbing her hands together. 'I've perfected a new special sauce to baste it with. And I shall be preparing all your and His Grace's favourite dishes.' Her eyes practically gleamed with anticipation. 'As well as desserts.'

'Mrs Laramie looks more excited than you were as a young child while opening your presents on Christmas Day,' Mrs Galloway commented.

'It's been so long since we've entertained,' the cook said. 'I am just happy for the opportunity to use my talents, my lady. Thank you for this.'

'You're very welcome—and I'm very eager to taste the fruits of your talents. Now, I must see to our guests.'

Georgina left the two servants and headed back upstairs. But then she remembered she'd forgotten to ask Mrs Galloway what time they would serve dinner tonight, since the guests would be arriving at different intervals.

Turning back, she retraced her steps towards the kitchens, but stopped when she overheard her name being spoken aloud.

'Lady Georgina does look different, doesn't she?' said Mrs Galloway.

'Yes, she seems happier,' the cook replied. 'Maybe it's because that pinch-faced aunt of hers is finally gone.'

Mrs Galloway laughed. 'Miss Leticia was an excellent chaperone—perhaps too excellent.' She sighed. 'It's too bad that Lady Georgina is now on her way to spinsterhood.'

Georgina winced. While her unmarried status was a fact in her in her mind, hearing about it from others still stung.

'Or is she?' Mrs Galloway said.

'Of course she is… Wait, what have you heard?'

The housekeeper chuckled. 'That the guests we are having are mostly unmarried ladies *and* gentlemen.'

The cook gasped. 'Do you think His Grace means to find a bride?'

'Perhaps. Or is Lady Georgina on the hunt herself?'

Georgina had to bite the back of her hand to stop laughing. Gossip really was quite funny in that way. When people added their own interpretations to the most innocuous news, it tended to spiral in a completely different direction from where it had begun.

'Whatever the reason, I'm glad to finally have some life and excitement here. It makes me miss the old days with the Duke and Duchess.'

Me too, Georgina thought, pressing her fist to her chest as if that would ease the sudden heartache there.

'His Grace sometimes has parties,' Mrs Galloway said.

'With his "gentleman" friends.' The cook made a disgusted sound. 'Those lot don't appreciate my cooking—not when they spend their days here carousing. But now we will have quality people—ladies and true gentlemen.'

'It will be nice to fill the rooms of Foxbury Hill with guests once again.'

'Perhaps His Grace will find a bride and we will once again hear laughter in these corridors...'

Deciding she had eavesdropped enough, Georgina crept away from the two women and made her way back upstairs. The servants were still putting some finishing touches to the decorations, so she decided to check on their progress. Dawson told her they were in the library, and she headed there, arriving just in time to supervise the footmen and the maids.

'That's it,' she told the footman perched up on a ladder, hanging holly boughs over the windows. 'Just a little more to the right...a little more...there. Perfect. Thank you, Andrew.'

'Lady Georgina! Lady Georgina! We're here!'

She whirled around to the sound of a voice.

'Lily! Anne-Marie!' The two girls rushed towards her, stepping into her open arms. 'I'm so glad to see you.'

In truth, though they had spent only a short time together, she had grown fond of the two girls and had missed them in the last two days.

'Thank you so much for inviting us.' Anne-Marie's jade-green eyes sparkled with joy—such a contrast from the first time they had met. 'This truly is the most excitement I've had in months.'

'It was my pleasure. Are you tired? Have you eaten? Would you like some tea?'

'No, we aren't tired. We're too excited to nap,' Lily said. 'So we've decided to go exploring.'

'Foxbury Hill is perfect for that. I'll show you my favourite places.'

The little girl looked up at her expectantly. 'Now?'

'I'm afraid not, poppet. I'm a bit busy.' She nodded at the servants.

'Can we help?' Lily eyed the box of tinsel and Christmas ornaments on the table beside her.

'If you like.' She signalled to the maid waiting in the corner. 'Flora, could you show Miss Lily where those should go?'

'Yes, my lady.'

For the next half-hour or so the three of them, along with the servants, put the finishing touches to the house. Lily in particular seemed to enjoy the task given to her—spreading tinsel—while Anne-Marie assisted Georgina in directing the footmen on hanging more fir garlands.

'Lady Georgina, may I ask a question?' Anne-Marie said.

'Of course, dear girl, what is it?'

'Am I truly not allowed to join in the festivities here at Foxbury Hill?' Her lips turned out in a pout. 'I'm sixteen years old. Why can't I eat at the table instead of having my dinner upstairs with Lily?'

How Georgina wished she could trade places with Anne-Marie. What she wouldn't do for some solitary meals for the next few days.

'I'm so sorry, but that's just how things are done here in England. Until you are out in society you must stay with the other children. Lady Arundel's youngest daughter, Lady Hannah, will be here. She's about fourteen, I believe. Perhaps the two of you can keep each other company?'

'Stupid rules,' Anne-Marie grumbled. 'I can't wait until I'm out. Then I can do what I want.'

Georgina let out a chuckle. 'You should enjoy this time, because soon you'll have even more rules and restrictions placed upon you. Unlike if you had been born a boy, like Trevor.'

'Your brother seems nice,' Anne-Marie sniffed. 'Not like mine. I bet your brother has never made you do things you didn't want—like move you away from your home twice in less than five years.'

'Twice?' Georgina asked, shocked.

'Three times,' said Lily, who had appeared between them. 'We moved three times.'

'No, ninny. The first time doesn't count. That was when Ma brought us—' She closed her mouth.

'Why did you move twice in five years?' asked Georgina. 'Where were you before you were in New York?'

'We lived in San Francisco, then New York, then here,' Anne-Marie said. 'We barely stayed long enough in one place to settle in. I was finally starting to make friends in New York and then *he* had to bring us *here*.'

Ah, so that was why Anne-Marie was so angry with Elliot. But Georgina could hardly blame the girl—change was difficult, and such big changes in so short a time would be even more so.

'I don't think I'll be out any time soon,' Anne-Marie said. 'Elliot says we must wait for the right time. When we have the right connections. So that I may have a proper society debut and no one will turn us away, like back in New York.'

Turn them away?

It was at that moment that Georgina realised her earlier suspicions had been correct.

She drew in a sharp breath.

Elliot didn't want an aristocratic wife for himself. He was doing it for his sisters. He was sacrificing his own needs—maybe even the chance of finding love—just so they could have better prospects.

A lump grew in her throat and her eyes misted.

'My lady?' Andrew said, interrupting her thoughts. 'We are finished.'

Taking a deep, cleansing breath, Georgina took a step back to examine their handiwork. 'Excellent work—thank you everyone.' As the servants began to clear up the boxes, ladders and tools, and took their leave, she turned to the two girls. 'And thank you both. I could not have done it without you.'

'Anne-Marie, Lily—there you are.'

Georgina's heart sprang up at the sound of the familiar baritone. 'Mr Smith,' she greeted him as he entered the library. 'Did you rest well?'

He bowed his head. 'I did, thank you, my lady. However, I went to the girls' room and didn't find them abed. Aren't you two tired?'

'I'm too excited to nap,' Lily declared, then gestured around them. 'Look, we helped Lady Georgina decorate.'

'I see.' He glanced around. 'Once again, you have outdone yourself, my lady.'

It did not escape her notice that Elliot did not comment on the decorations directly—declaring that he thought they were nice or he liked them. It was as if any mention of Christmas would make him spontaneously combust.

'Thank you, Mr Smith. But what do you think of the trees? And the boughs? The tinsel?'

'I helped with the tinsel!' Lily said excitedly.

'Ah, yes...' He looked around, examining the silvery bits of paper. 'Excellent choice of placement. Even distribution. And...'

'And?' Georgina asked, hopeful that he would find one actually nice thing to say.

'And...' He tapped a finger on his chin, then strode towards her, stopping when he was right beside her. 'I commend your managerial skills on picking the right person for the job.' He winked at Lily.

'I'll get you to say something nice about my decorations one day,' she said, placing her hands on her hips.

'I like *all* of the decorations,' Lily said. 'The trees, the ornaments, the—' She frowned. 'What's that?'

'What's what, poppet?'

Lily pointed above her head. 'That?'

Georgina glanced up and saw a bunch of green twigs with white berries wrapped together in a bright red ribbon. 'Why, that's—'

'Mistletoe,' Anne-Marie finished, gasping as she covered her mouth, her eyes darting from Georgina to Elliot.

'What's wrong?' Elliot asked. 'Anne-Marie, are you ill?'

She shook her head, then burst out, 'You have to kiss her!'

Georgina's cheeks burned as if someone had set them on fire. 'I... It's a silly tradition.'

Elliot cleared his throat. 'Yes, just a silly old wives' tale.'

'But you have to,' Lily squealed. 'Or you'll have bad luck!'

'There's no such thing as luck,' he retorted.

'What about all those strokes of good luck you've had, Elliot?' Anne-Marie asked. 'What if you lose your golden touch and all your money disappears?'

Lily's head bobbed up and down in agreement.

It took all Georgina's willpower to glance at Elliot without melting into a pile of shame. 'We don't have to—'

'I suppose the girls are not wrong,' he said. 'And it's just a kiss under the mistletoe.'

True. But there was one thing he didn't know.

It would be her first—and maybe only—kiss.

Elliot's mesmerising light green gaze fixed on her. 'My lady? What do you say?'

She squared her shoulders. 'Well, we can't send you to the poorhouse, now, can we?' She turned so that her cheek faced him. 'If you please, Mr Smith.'

Though she kept her gaze straight ahead, she could still see him from the corner of her eye, and her heart thumped madly in her chest as his head descended towards her. His lips were curiously soft on her cheek, though they lingered much longer than she'd thought they would. Also, his mouth was much closer to hers than she'd expected—the corner of it even touched her own. And this close she could smell the spicy scent of his cologne, which sent the most curious tingling sensation straight to her belly.

Lily clapped as soon as he pulled away. 'Hooray! No bad luck for you, Elliot.'

'Thank you.'

'Who has bad luck?'

Georgina sprang away from Elliot at the sound of a stranger's voice.

'Who—? Lady Arundel,' she greeted the older woman. 'And Lady Lavinia.' She felt that hot stab in her chest once more at the sight of Lady Lavinia. Today she looked absolutely radiant in her yellow travel gown, not a hair or thread out of place. 'Welcome to Foxbury Hill.'

'Lady Georgina!' Lady Arundel exclaimed as she strode over to her and took her hands in hers. 'Once again, thank you for your invitation. My girls and I are delighted to be here.'

'Where are Lady Genevieve and Lady Hannah?' she asked, referring to Lady Arundel's other daughters.

'Upstairs, resting in their rooms,' the Marchioness said. 'But I wanted to come and see you to thank you before going up to ours.'

'As did I,' said Lady Lavinia.

'And I see Mr Smith is already here,' Lady Arundel added.

'Good afternoon,' he greeted them with a respectful bow.

'Lady Arundel, Lady Lavinia—may I present my sisters?' He quickly made the introductions.

'How delightful they are,' Lady Arundel said. 'Are they not, Lavinia?'

'Yes,' she said. 'Anne-Marie, your dress is lovely. And Lily, you look very nice as well.'

'My…this place…' Lady Arundel's head swivelled. 'These decorations are even better than those at Harwicke House. By the way—thank you very much for giving me that catalogue of Christmas decorations, Lady Georgina. I didn't even know they were sold in such a way.'

'I only recently found out myself,' Georgina said. 'Hopefully they have not run out.'

'I helped decorate,' Lily announced. 'I did the tinsel.'

Lady Lavinia bent down to her level. 'You did a very good job. The tinsel is very beautiful.'

'Want to see?' Lily held out her hand and Lady Lavinia took it. 'Let's start over here.'

'Mr Smith would probably like to take a closer look too,' Georgina suggested.

'I would?' He frowned.

She nodded meaningfully towards Lady Lavinia. 'Yes.'

'Of course.' He took Lily's other hand into his. 'Why don't you show us, Lily?'

As Lily led Lady Lavinia and Elliot over to the fireplace, Georgina quietly moved away from the charmingly domestic scene. She turned quickly, lest the stabbing pain in her chest bury itself deeper, her steps hastening as she drew further away.

Truly, she would be happy for Elliot and the girls if he ended up marrying Lady Lavinia. She was the daughter of a marquess, her sister would soon be wed to a duke, and the Wrights were pillars of society. Elliot wouldn't be able to find a better match.

Except for you, maybe, a voice inside her said.

She clicked her tongue at that voice. In ranking and social connections perhaps she was a step above Lady Lavinia. But the truth was Georgina would make the worst chaperone and patroness for the girls. Sadly, Anne-Marie and Lily already had two marks against them—they were common-born and American. But someone like Lady Lavinia, who was experienced in manoeuvring through the waters of the Ton and avoiding the pitfalls, would help them successfully navigate the Season and increase their chances of a good match.

Unfortunately, that was not a something a reclusive spinster like Georgina could do for them.

Her hand crept up to her cheek, remembering their kiss under the mistletoe. His lips had seemingly left their brand there, the heat of them still lingering on her skin. How she wished they had been alone, with no audience. Then she could—

She stopped those thoughts before they could further grow and taunt her.

No, they would be better off with Lady Lavinia, or even Miss Philipps. And now more than ever Georgina knew she had to help Elliot make a match—not just so he wouldn't evict the girls at St Agnes's, but also to secure his sisters' futures.

She would do that, no matter how she might feel about him.

Chapter Eight

15th December

'That is the most amusing story I've ever heard,' Lady Lavinia remarked. 'Your journey on a steamship sounds exciting and not at all tedious, Mr Smith.'

'Not as amusing at the tale he told me during luncheon,' Miss Philipps said, batting her eyelashes at him.

'Won't you please tell me as well?' Lady Lavinia pleaded.

'Perhaps he can do it after dinner,' Lady Arundel said. 'So he may enjoy his pheasant. He's hardly taken a bite with all the questions we've been peppering him with.'

It was their second day at Foxbury Hill and all the guests had arrived—including Harwicke, who had been detained by some business in London. The day had been filled with amusements around the estate—a brisk walk in the gardens after breakfast, a hearty, leisurely luncheon, and then carriage rides. Before dinner, Elliot and the other male guests—Thomas Carlisle, Duke of Waldemere, the Marquess of Arundel and the Viscount— had played billiards, while the ladies had gathered in the sitting room for their own leisure activities. But now that they were complete, and their host had arrived, everyone was finally able to sit down to a formal dinner.

'It has been a delightful meal so far,' Elliot remarked.

'Yes,' Lady Lavinia agreed.

'Truly, the cook here is talented,' added Miss Philipps, flashing him a smile.

Though he didn't believe in luck, the events of the last fortnight were perhaps starting to change Elliot's mind. After all, he was in the company of not one, but two ladies of marriageable age and impeccable breeding.

Well, three, if he were to count *everyone* at dinner. But the third lady in question had already made it clear that she was not interested in marriage.

Not to him anyway.

'As I was saying, Lady Georgina, Foxbury Hill looks splendid,' said Lord Bellamy. 'Why, I don't think we have half as many decorations at my father's estate in Somerset.'

'Thank you, Lord Bellamy,' Georgina replied. 'But it was mostly the servants who did it all.'

Once again she looked incredibly lovely, in a blue satin gown trimmed with black lace, her hair pulled away from her beautiful face and allowed to cascade in waves down the back of her head.

'Ah, but surely it was your idea.' Lord Bellamy raised a glass to her and winked, which made her cheeks turn pink.

Elliot turned back to his plate and stabbed his pheasant with a knife, not caring if the poor bird was already dead and stuffed.

He's not even supposed to be here.

Bellamy had arrived earlier today with Harwicke, much to Elliot's confusion and consternation. The Duke had explained that Mr Galwick was unable to come, due to having broken his leg that morning. Not wanting to have an imbalance of gentlemen and ladies, he had invited Bellamy, who had happily accepted.

At first Elliot had been annoyed, because he did not want competition, but apparently he needn't have worried. Since he had arrived, Bellamy had not left Georgina's side. She didn't seem to discourage his attentions, either.

He sneaked another glance at them, seething as Georgina smiled at something Bellamy had said. What could she possibly see in that dandy? Sure, he was titled, but he was only the third son of an earl. Bellamy wasn't even that wealthy—at least not from what his private investigator had gathered. If she married him she would be comfortable, but extravagances like adorning an entire house with decorations every Christmas would not be feasible.

Elliot's resources, on the other hand, would allow her to decorate an estate ten times the size of Foxbury Hill for the entire year—for the rest of her life, if that was what she wanted.

'Ah, dessert is here,' Harwicke announced.

The footmen removed the used dishes and placed a new plate in front of each guests with the evening's first dessert—a steamed pudding with raspberry cream. Everyone *oohed* and *aahed*, just as they had with every dish, and dug in heartily.

As the dinner continued, Elliot found it increasingly difficult to focus on his conversation with Lady Lavinia and Miss Philipps. He sneaked glances at Georgina and Lord Bellamy. The latter was plying her with compliments and amusing stories, and the former was seemingly open to his attentions. She did not seem to notice the others at the table and did not attempt to make conversation with anyone aside from the man beside her.

'That was a splendid meal,' Harwicke declared as he polished off his cheese, the last of the courses. 'Please convey my compliments to Mrs Laramie,' he said to the butler. 'And now we have more amusements in the parlour, as well as port for the gentlemen and sherry for the ladies.'

All the guests rose from their seats and followed the Duke to the parlour. As he'd promised, there were more refreshments for the guests, as well as sweet treats if the elaborate dinner had not satisfied them. There was also a card table, a pianoforte and even a chess set, as well as other board games for them to use.

The guests helped themselves to port and sherry and settled in. No one seemed inclined for any of the games, so they sat around the pianoforte while Miss Philipps entertained them. To Elliot's annoyance, Bellamy once again cornered Georgina at one end of the settee, so that only he would be able to converse with her.

'Do you play, Mr Smith?' Lord Arundel asked, and gestured to the chess set.

'Not very well,' he confessed.

He had no time or patience to learn more than the basics of the game.

'I love it,' he said. 'I would play for hours if I could.'

'And he does,' Lady Arundel said, bemused. 'He's very good at it.'

'Papa has a wall full of the trophies that he has won at tournaments to prove it,' Lady Lavinia added.

'Then perhaps you could teach me some strategy, my lord? I would be honoured to learn from a master.'

A little flattery wouldn't hurt. After all, Lord Arundel might very well be his future father-in-law.

Lord Arundel sat behind the white pieces. 'I would be happy to teach you.' He gestured to the seat across from him. 'Let us begin.'

At first Elliot thought he would just play along and let his opponent win and be done with it. However, the Marquess seemed to take his role as mentor seriously, explaining Elliot's every move and why it was the wrong one. But at least it was taking Elliot's mind off Georgina and Bellamy, as they continued their conversation in their own cosy little corner of the room.

'Ah, see—I told you not to put your knight there.' Lord Arundel grabbed his queen and placed it next to the black king piece. 'Checkmate.'

'Congratulations, my lord.'

And thank goodness this game is over.

'I am only sorry that I was an unworthy opponent.'

The Marquess looked at him knowingly. 'Do not fret. You have other admirable qualities, Mr Smith.'

Elliot hoped this was some sort of stamp of approval. 'Thank you, my lord.' He stood up and glanced around the room. 'And now—'

He stopped short, and the most curious feeling washed over him. Something did not feel right.

Georgina was gone. As was Bellamy.

His stomach turned to stone. Where the devil were they? He glanced over at Harwicke, who was laughing at some story the Viscount was telling, without a care in the world, and meanwhile his sister had disappeared with a man.

Biting his lip, Elliot stifled the urge to ask if anyone had seen the couple. He didn't want to bring attention to their disappearance as it would put Georgina's reputation in peril. And people loved gossip. If anyone found out he and his sisters were here they, too, might be affected by any scandal that happened in Foxbury Hill.

'If you'll excuse me? I must refresh myself.' He nodded to the Marquess and Marchioness and discreetly left the library.

Dread and fury swirled inside him, but he could not allow his emotions to overcome him. He would find the couple and break them up before anyone discovered them. Perhaps he could persuade Bellamy to leave immediately, and he'd never have to see the smarmy fop ever again.

If I were a scoundrel, like Bellamy, where would I bring a young woman to take advantage of her?

Foxbury Hill was enormous, but surely they wouldn't be so daring as to sneak upstairs. So he began to search all the rooms downstairs, going into them one by one. When he entered what appeared to be a music room, he spied a familiar figure clad in a blue gown sitting by a harp. However, she was alone.

'Who's there?' Georgina called out. 'I heard you come in.'

Elliot stepped inside. 'It's me.'

'Oh.' Relief struck her face. 'What are you doing here?'

He paused, thinking of a good excuse. 'I got lost on my way to the necessary. This place is enormous.'

'Ah, yes, that can happen.'

'And you?'

Where was Bellamy? He glanced over to the windows. Was he hiding behind the drapes like some coward? They certainly were thick and voluminous enough that he could hide there without being detected.

'I was just feeling…overwhelmed.'

Drawing closer to her side, Elliot examined her face. Like that night at the opera, her face was once again pale, and a sheen of perspiration had collected on her brow. Her breaths came in short, shallow pants.

'What's wrong? Did he do something to you?'

'He?'

'Bellamy.'

She frowned. 'What would he do to me? He retired earlier tonight, complaining of stomach pains.'

So that's where he is.

'I didn't notice that he'd left. Are you feeling ill as well? Did you perhaps eat what has made Bellamy sick?'

'Oh, no.' She shook her head, sending waves of blonde hair shimmering under the glow of the chandelier. 'Like I said, I was feeling overwhelmed by today's activities. And sometimes, when it is too much, I get these…spells.'

Once again, guilt crept into him. This was time she usually spent alone with Trevor—for their First Christmas, she had said. It was because of him that they now had to share their home with all these near strangers.

Sighing, he retrieved an object from his pocket. 'Here,' he said, handing her the flask.

Her nose wrinkled delicately. 'I don't think liquor will help.'

'It's just water,' he clarified.

'You take water with you in a flask everywhere you go?'

'Why not? It's quite refreshing.'

Well, the truth was he'd only begun carrying it after the Rutherford ball, when he'd seen her so ill after dancing with him. He was afraid he'd over-exerted her, and he wanted to be prepared in case it happened again. That, apparently, had been good forethought on his part.

Though hesitant, she took it anyway, unscrewed the top, then took a sip. 'Thank you. That is very refreshing.'

'You're welcome.' He took the flask back and replaced the cap.

'And I'm sorry.'

'Sorry? For what?'

'Well, I promised you that I would watch over Anne-Marie and Lily, and yet I hardly saw them today.'

'Ah, I see.'

Elliot wasn't sure why, but finding them with her yesterday, decorating the house, had been disconcerting. He had meant it when he'd told her that he hadn't seen them as happy as they were when they were with her. However, seeing them laughing and joking together had sent an emotion straight to his heart that had caused a disquiet in him he'd never experienced before.

Perhaps it was best not to encourage his sisters to pursue a friendship with Georgina. Soon he would be married to Lady Lavinia, or Miss Philipps, so it would be best if the girls spent time with them instead of Georgina. Lady Lavinia seemed to be friendly with them, especially with Anne-Marie, and he'd seen them conversing during breakfast.

'I'm sure the girls are fine,' he said.

'They seem to be enjoying themselves. They are quite excited to share our First Christmas.'

His chest tightened at this reminder of why they were here. Frankly, after being exposed to Georgina's abundance of decorations, he'd grown mostly numb to the thought of Christmas.

'At least they will be able to celebrate with you, for once.' She grinned at him. 'And you'll be forced to sit down and celebrate with them on our First Christmas Day.'

Her tone was clearly meant to be light-hearted, but his mood still darkened—just as it did any time he was reminded of Christmas Day.

'*Elliot, come here,*' Ma had rasped. '*There is something I need you to do for me...*'

Pushing those thoughts away, he cleared his throat. 'We've been gone for far too long. We should return to the others before anyone finds—'

The sound of the doorknob turning made them both freeze. *Too late.*

The hinges creaked loudly as the door began to open. Panic crossed Georgina's face, and Elliot knew he had to take action before they were discovered.

Without a single thought, he pulled her up, then dragged her behind the first thing he saw that could conceal them—the thick brocade drapes covering one side of the room. The very same ones he had suspected Bellamy to be hiding behind. He quickly drew them aside and pressed her against the window, covering her with his body.

'Don't move...don't make a sound.'

He felt the nod of her head against his chest.

A feminine giggle came from the other side of the curtain.

'Shh...my love. Someone might hear us.'

'They are all in the parlour, Tommy. No one's going to hear.'

The female voice sounded like Lady Genevieve, and 'Tommy' could only be Thomas, the Duke of Waldemere.

'Now, kiss me,' Lady Genevieve urged.

'My pleasure...'

Elliot groaned inwardly as the unmistakable sounds of ardent kissing filtered through what he had now discovered were definitely *not* thick drapes.

'Oh, Tommy...there,' Lady Genevieve moaned. 'Touch me. There.'

Lady Georgina stiffened in his arms and their tiny hiding space suddenly shrank further. She attempted to move. But, fearing they would be discovered, he pressed against her to keep her still. Unfortunately, that meant all her luscious curves were now tucked against his body.

Damn it to hell.

'Genevieve, my love, please... I need you.' There was a rustling of skirts. 'Let me touch you...'

'Yes, it's been so long, Tommy. I— Oh, yes. That's it. Touch me. Your fingers...'

'Have you missed this?'

Lady Genevieve gasped.

'Or how about when I do this?'

'Oh! Oh! Yes, Tommy.'

Elliot quickly considered the ramifications of opening the curtains before Lady Genevieve and Waldemere progressed any further. On one hand, if they revealed themselves to the amorous couple now they wouldn't be subjected to these aural displays of affection. On the other, Georgina's reputation was still at stake, while Lady Genevieve's would be saved because Waldemere would surely marry her anyway if they were discovered.

He decided to remain, hoping 'Tommy's' fingers were skilful enough to quickly bring this torture to an end.

'Eeep...' Lady Georgina pressed her face against his chest to muffle herself.

'What was that?' Waldemere exclaimed.

'Bloody hell!' Genevieve cursed. 'Probably a mouse.'

'Or a squeaky hinge.' Waldemere sighed. 'I'm sorry, my love. Did you…?'

'No.' She sounded disappointed. 'You should return to the parlour and I'll go to my rooms. I think Mother and Father were fooled by my excuse that I was feeling ill, like Lord Bellamy, but if Hannah were to tell them I didn't go to bed right away…'

'Of course, my love. Come, let me help you right yourself.'

There was more rustling of clothing, followed by the sound of the door opening and then latching closed.

Elliot exhaled, the tension seeping out of his body. 'Are you all right?' He looked down to check on Georgina, but to his surprise she was staring right up at him, her copper-brown eyes luminous even in the scant moonlight from outside.

'Georgina, we should—'

He stopped as her hands slid up his chest, her palms resting on his shoulders. She took in a breath, making her breasts rise up and strain over her décolletage.

He couldn't.

He mustn't.

'Georgina, this isn't—'

'Elliot…' she breathed, and his name was like a reverent prayer on his lips.

She tilted her head to one side, angling it so that their lips would line up if he just lowered his mouth.

'We can't—'

'Please…'

Her unnamed request rang in his ears, and he had no choice but to grant her wish.

Just one quick kiss.

Leaning down, he let his mouth find hers as his hand cradled the back of her head. He told himself to be quick and pull away, but instead he increased the pressure of his mouth, moving it over hers until she pressed her body against his. Instantly his cock stiffened and he pinned her against the window, his hips brushing against her belly.

Her arms drew around his neck and she opened her mouth to him. His instinct was to invade her, but he held back, instead brushing his tongue inside her mouth, coaxing hers to join him in an erotic dance. Her tongue darted out hesitantly, but soon she was tasting him as eagerly as he was her.

She sighed against him, arching her body up as if they might possibly get closer. He broke the kiss so he could move down to her jaw and throat. Her pulse throbbed frantically when his mouth reached that sweet spot behind her ears, and she let out a moan when he licked at the delicate skin. His other hand, which had been resting against her waist, slid upwards to cup her breast through her clothes. He expected her to panic, or push him away, but instead she raked her fingers up the nape of his neck and gripped his hair.

He inhaled sharply, his hardened cock throbbing as she continued to undulate against him. Feeling bold, he caressed the tops of her breasts, then delved under her neckline.

She whimpered and whispered his name. He bent his head lower, raining kisses down her neck until his mouth was inches from his hand. Manoeuvring his fingers, he eased down the bodice of her gown, revealing one generous breast. He bit his lip to keep from groaning at the sight of the creamy globe topped with a delicate dusky-pink nipple which hardened at its contact with cool air.

She was so beautiful, so lushly feminine, and if he died now, having just tasted her, he would be happy. But thankfully he didn't expire on the spot, so he leaned down to take the nipple into his mouth.

'Elliot!' She clung to him, her fingers nearly ripping the hair from his nape. But he could only suckle her and lavish her nipple with his attention. She tasted so sweet…the skin of her breast so tender…

'Ah, there it is.'

They both stiffened, and Elliot pulled his mouth away from her breast.

'Thank goodness.' It was Lady Genevieve again. 'I thought I'd lost it.' She giggled. 'Next time, please be more careful, Tommy.'

'I'm sorry, my love,' the Duke said. 'I'm glad you have found your earring.'

'And I'm glad you saw that it was gone before we parted. If Papa found out...'

'Then maybe he'd let us marry before your sister does.'

'Patience, Tommy... I think the answer to our problem is already here. Lavinia may soon be wed.'

The mention of Lady Lavinia cooled Elliot's heated body, and he felt Georgina draw away from him.

'Come, let us go before anyone sees us.'

As soon as he heard the door close he let out the breath he'd been holding. 'Georgina, I'm so—'

'Do not apologise.' She turned away from him as she adjusted her bodice. 'I... I practically begged you...' Her face turned scarlet. 'I don't... This isn't... I've never...'

'Was that your first kiss?'

'No.'

An unreasonable stab of jealousy cut into his chest. 'And who gave you the first?'

'Y-you. Under the mistletoe.'

Damn.

He was a bastard. A scoundrel. No better than Bellamy, whom he had accused of doing exactly what Elliot had now done to Georgina.

'If there's someone who should apologise, it is me.'

The air around them was much too stifling, so he drew back the curtains. The rush of cool air helped, but still his body hummed with lingering desire.

'I should not have allowed it to continue. We should forget it happened.'

'Forget?' She wrapped her arms around herself. 'Why?'

'Well, for one thing your brother would kill me.' Harwicke had warned him off that first day they'd met. 'And—'

'And you want to marry Lady Lavinia or Miss Philipps.'

And you don't want to marry me.

When he didn't answer, she continued. 'Both of them are good prospects. You have done well. I think they are keen on you. While I—' She bit her lip.

'While you what?'

'N-nothing. You should not let anything impede you in your

pursuing them…seeing as they are exactly what you want. Proper English brides.'

He swallowed the growing lump in his throat. 'Yes.'

'And I, too, will get what I wish for.'

That damned building and her orphans. If he had known that number fifty-five Boyle Street would cause so much chaos in his life, he never would have bought it in the first place.

'Perhaps…perhaps you are right.' She still refused to look him in the eyes, and she stared out of the window into the cold winter night. 'We should forget this happened.'

'Agreed.' His entire chest felt as if it had been captured in a vice.

'You should leave first,' she said. 'And I will head up to my rooms. Trevor will think I'm having one of my spells, and assume I left without taking my leave.'

'A practical plan.'

He was barely two steps out of the music room when he wanted to go back to her…tell her that he did not want to forget what had just happened. And that he wanted to continue kissing her and perhaps more.

But she was right.

What he wanted was within his reach. He suspected that if he asked Lord Arundel or the Viscount for permission to court either of their daughters they would grant it to him, which would all but guarantee an engagement and then marriage. His ten-year plan would come to fruition.

Anything else—including Georgina—would simply take him off course, which he could not afford to happen.

So he would have to do whatever it took to forget that kiss, and eventually forget Georgina—hopefully before she made any further mark on his soul.

Georgina pressed her forehead against the glass of the window-pane, as if that would chill the heat that still lingered in her body. But despite the abrupt end to their passionate encounter, the fire it had ignited in her remained.

She'd been curious about kissing, of course, and perhaps a long time ago had even been interested in experiencing it for herself. She had read novels about it, and had heard other debutantes and recently married acquaintances whisper about their encounters with eager gentlemen and amorous husbands. But over the years, as she'd drawn away from society and resigned herself to spinsterhood, the interest had faded.

But now she could not stop thinking about it.

Or rather, *him*.

She blew out a breath. Elliot was right. They should forget it had ever happened. The words had hurt when he'd first uttered them—how could she forget such a wonderful thing? For once in her life she didn't feel like a stranger in her own skin. His touch had been like magic, making her soul sing and her toes curl. She wasn't Lady Georgina, spinster and on the shelf. She was just herself—Georgina.

And for once in her life she'd felt *wanted*.

Unfortunately, he had wants bigger than her—bigger than him, even. He wanted a wife who would be a patroness and advocate for his sisters, providing guidance and counsel—not someone who broke out in hives at the mere thought of going to a ball, or who would panic in the crush of a busy ballroom. Under her care, Anne-Marie and Lily would never flourish or see success during their Seasons.

She wasn't sure how long she had stood there, but knew she had to leave soon. So she quietly crept out of the music room and back to her own chambers.

Once her maid had arrived, and she'd finished undressing, she slipped under the covers and closed her eyes. Tomorrow she would have to face them all again, which would be a challenge, but she would find a way to do it. She would forget about what had happened and pretend everything was as it had been before that kiss. Thankfully tomorrow was First Christmas Eve. There would be many activities to keep her occupied, and she would be surrounded by people for the entire day, all the way until midnight.

She groaned aloud and pulled the covers over her head.

These last two days of constant activity and socialising had taken their toll on her. But perhaps she'd only have to endure it for another two days. By the time they were all headed back to London, Elliot might very well be on his way to proposing to either Lady Lavinia or Miss Philipps, and she would save St Agnes's.

And that, she reminded herself, was what really mattered. The real reason she had concocted this mad plan to find Mr Elliot Smith a bride in the first place.

Chapter Nine

16th December,
First Christmas Eve

The following day, Georgina crept into the breakfast room early, hoping no one would be around. Usually on First Christmas Eve she would be the first to wake, as she loved walking around the house in those quiet hours by herself, admiring all the decorations. This was also the day she and Trevor, as per their household tradition, shared gifts with all the staff, the tenants and children from the village. It was the one time a year she managed to tolerate being around people and speaking with them without having one of her spells in the middle of the day.

With their guests around, though, she and Trevor had decided to let them do as they pleased during the day, while they continued with their tradition. Tonight, however, there would be more games and amusements, and the girls of course would be allowed to join them and open their presents at midnight. That meant she would at least have some peace and quiet to herself this morning.

Or at least that was what she thought until she entered the dining room.

'I can't believe you're doing this again,' Anne-Marie said, her voice shaking with anger. 'You promised we could stay until the eighteenth.'

'I *said* we could come to Northamptonshire,' Elliot retorted. 'I never gave you a date when we must return.'

'It's not fair,' Lily whinged. 'We will miss First Christmas Day if we leave in the morning.'

Georgina gasped. 'Wait…you're leaving in the morning?'

Three sets of eyes turned towards her. A small thrill raced up the back of her knees when Elliot's jade-green eyes landed on her, though he quickly averted them.

'Good morning,' Elliot murmured. 'I didn't realise you would be up so early.'

She strode into the room, hands on her hips. 'Did I hear that correctly? Do you truly mean to leave on the morrow?'

'That's what he said,' Lily cried, flinging herself at Georgina and burying her face in her skirts.

She smoothed a hand down the girl's back. 'But why?'

'I have business to attend to—an emergency that requires my presence,' he said, though he did not meet her gaze. 'Sometimes these things happen and I cannot do anything about them.'

She couldn't believe he would leave so suddenly. Was he doing this because of what had happened between them last night? Was being in her presence now so abhorrent that he could not stand being in the same house as her?

Lily moaned. 'But what about First Christmas…?'

'What about it?' Elliot shrugged. 'You still get to open your gifts tonight at midnight. And may I remind you that I bought both of you a second set of presents to open here.'

Anne-Marie let out a frustrated sound. 'Who cares about presents? I hate you so much!' With that she stomped off, Lily following her.

Elliot's jaw ticked and his hands curled into fists at his sides, but he remained silent as a rock.

'You can't mean to leave right away,' she said, once they were alone.

'We aren't. We are leaving in the morning. They can still enjoy whatever you have planned for today. Now, if you'll excuse me, my lady, I must inform my staff of our change of plans.'

Georgina's heart sank as she watched him leave without another word, without looking her in the eyes.

'My lady', he had called her.

Not Georgina, as he had done last night.

How could he be so cruel as to just leave and take the girls away? And besides, what about Lady Lavinia and Miss Philipps? How could he possibly leave now that he had spent all this time and effort in getting acquainted with them. It would all be for naught and he would end up without a wife.

Unless, of course, he already had an understanding with one of them…

She sank down on the nearest chair, her knees weakening. Her stomach was tied into knots and her chest clenched up tight. Pressing her palm against her chest, she attempted to ease the ache, but to no avail.

Perhaps he didn't need to stay any longer. Perhaps he had what he wanted and now he could go back to London and to his business, doing whatever it was he did—making money, turning everything he touched into gold, maybe finding more properties with orphans he could evict.

Glaring back at the doorway, she decided she would no longer care about what Mr Elliot Smith did. But she *did* care for those poor girls, whose lives were upturned with his every whim.

Rising to her feet, she set her shoulders with a determined shrug and marched up to their rooms.

'Anne-Marie? Lily?' she said as she knocked on their door. 'It's Lady Georgina. May I come in?'

'Yes,' came Lily's answer.

'Hello, girls.' She closed the door behind her. 'I'm so sorry you have to leave so soon.'

Anne-Marie pursed her lips and crossed her arms over her chest. 'I knew he would do something like this. I was finally enjoying myself and now he has to ruin everything.' She plopped herself on the bed. 'I hate him so much.'

'Must we go?' Lily asked. 'Can't we stay here and Elliot can leave for London by himself? We can ride back with you.'

'I wish that were possible, poppet.' She stroked her hair, tucking a stray curl behind her ear. 'But Elliot is your guardian and so you must stay with him.'

'Lady Lavinia said she would take me into the village for shopping tomorrow,' Anne-Marie said.

Georgina's ears pricked up. 'Oh? What else did Lady Lavinia say?'

'That there's a lovely little shop that sells the most precious little trinkets, like buttons and ribbons and scarves.' She pouted. 'And we were to have tea in one of the tea shops.'

'That does sound fun.'

'It does—did. Lady Lavinia is the only person who treats me like I am an adult.' Anne-Marie harrumphed. 'She came to see me yesterday, you know, while you were all in the sitting room. We had a lovely conversation in the library.'

Georgina's mouth went dry, but she managed to croak out, 'About…?'

'Oh, you know…the usual. Gossip…our favourite activities. And she asked about Elliot too.'

'I see.'

Perhaps Lady Lavinia wanted to know more about her potential suitor—which was clever, she had to admit.

'What did you tell her?'

'The truth,' Anne-Marie said. 'That Elliot is very rich and devoted to his business and nothing else. You are right, Lady Georgina. He truly is a Scrooge.'

'He hates Christmas. He's truly never celebrated it with us.'

'Never?'

'Never,' Lily said. 'I think… I think it makes him sad.'

'Sad? Why do you say that?' asked Georgina.

'I don't know. But whenever he leaves for his office on Christmas Day I see his face and he looks sad.'

Why would Elliot—or anyone—be sad on Christmas Day?

'Who cares?' Anne-Marie reclined dramatically on the bed. 'I wish we could stay here. And never leave.'

'Me too,' Lily added, lying down beside her sister.

Georgina couldn't help but feel sorry for the girls. And, while there was nothing more she could learn about Lady Lavinia and

Elliot, perhaps it would be best if she used the girls' remaining time here to cheer them up.

'Girls, I'm so sorry you must leave tomorrow, but we still have today.' Placing her hands on her hips, she hovered over them. 'Come, now, get up.'

Lily raised her head. 'Why? Where are we going?'

'Well, do you know what the best part of Christmas is?'

'Christmas pudding?' the little girl answered.

Georgina chuckled. 'No, no.' Taking their hands, she pulled them upright. 'Sharing and giving gifts, of course.'

'Giving gifts?' Lily said. 'But we're too little to give gifts. We receive them.'

'Not today—and not when you're with me,' she stated. 'Let's go.'

She led the two girls downstairs to the parlour, where Trevor and Miss Warren were already waiting for her.

'There you are, Georgie,' said her brother. 'I was beginning to think you'd forgotten.'

'Never.' She brought Anne-Marie and Lily forward. 'And I have brought some helpers.'

'Hello, girls,' Trevor greeted them. 'Are you ready to assist us?'

'With what?' Lily asked.

Trevor gestured to the pile of wrapped gifts behind him. 'With distributing gifts to our staff. It's a First Christmas Eve tradition at Foxbury Hill.'

'You give them all presents?' Anne-Marie asked.

'Of course.'

Lily cocked her head to one side. 'Why?'

'It's tradition. Our mother and father used to do this with us when we were children. And besides, everyone deserves presents,' Trevor said. 'Now, they will be here any minute, so we must be ready. Are you both willing to help?'

The two girls looked at each other and said in unison, 'Yes.'

Soon, as Trevor had said, the servants arrived in the parlour. There were refreshments for them, like hot apple cider, tea and biscuits, that the kitchen had prepared. Since Trevor and Georgina spent the real Christmas Day in London, this had become the time to give their gifts to their staff at Foxbury Hill. As they came in, Trevor or Georgina would hand a wrapped gift to either Lily or Anne-Marie and ask them to give it to the recipient, then offer them treats. As Foxbury Hill had many servants, it took the entire morning to distribute the pile of gifts.

'That was fun,' Lily said. 'I feel like St Nicholas.'

'Who?' Miss Warren asked.

'It's from a poem,' Anne-Marie said. '*A Visit from St Nicholas*. Our butler back in New York read it to us one Christmas.'

'And who, pray tell, is this St Nicholas?' Trevor enquired.

'He's the man who gives all the boys and girls presents at Christmas,' Lily explained. 'He rides on a sleigh pulled by reindeer.'

'What?' Trevor exclaimed. 'Reindeer?'

'Uh-huh.' Lily's head bobbed up and down. 'Flying reindeer.'

'Why must they fly?'

'So they can land the sleigh on roofs and get into people's houses down their chimney,' Lily said matter-of-factly.

'It's a silly poem,' Anne-Marie said rolling her eyes. 'It's just about some guy who gives gifts to children.'

'Intriguing,' Georgina said. 'Well, my dear Saints Nicholas, I'm afraid your job isn't done yet.'

'It's not?' Lily glanced around. 'But all the presents are gone.'

'The presents for the servants *here*,' she clarified. 'But now we must go to see the tenants and take gifts to them, as well as the children in the village.'

'We are going to the village?' Anne-Marie's eyes gleamed.

'Yes,' Trevor said. 'Now, I'm afraid I don't have a sleigh, or flying reindeer, but I hope a horse and carriage will do.'

Both girls squealed in excitement.

And so they took Anne-Marie and Lily with them around the estate to deliver hampers of food and treats to the tenants. Afterwards, they went into the village to distribute the biscuits and sweetmeats Mrs Laramie had made especially for the children who lived there. As a reward for being their helpers, Trevor took the girls into the trinket shop and purchased a small gift for each of them, then they had luncheon at the tea shop before heading back to Foxbury Hill.

While Georgina was drained from all the day's interactions, as she always was, she had still enjoyed herself. How she'd loved handing out presents and seeing people's faces light up with joy. Truly, it was enough to make her forget her troubles—at least until the carriage passed through the gates of the driveway going up to the main house.

'Is that Elliot?' Trevor pointed out of the window. 'And Lady Lavinia?'

Georgina peeped out to look where his finger directed her gaze, and her heart sank. It was indeed Elliot and Lady Lavinia, out together for a walk in the front gardens, her arm tucked into his.

Trevor's gaze flickered over to the girls, who sat across from them with Miss Warren, dozing on each other's shoulders.

'It seems as if you've accomplished what you set out to do,' he told Georgina. 'Which I thought was an impossible task.'

'He's not engaged yet.'

And she wasn't quite sure how she felt about that statement.

He covered her hand with his. 'You must give yourself more credit, Georgie. And perhaps we must plan a different Christmas celebration this year…at St Agnes's?'

A small flicker of happiness lit up in her chest. 'I would like that.'

The carriage deposited them at the front door and Georgina woke the girls, instructing them to nap for the rest of the afternoon, because after all tonight they would be staying up late to join in the festivities.

The two of them of course shrieked in excitement and raced up to their rooms.

Later that evening, after she herself had taken a long, refreshing nap, Georgina prepared for the night's activities. After taking a bath, she'd had her maid assist her in styling her hair into loose waves around her head, and had changed into a new red and pink satin and velvet gown.

When the modiste had suggested it, Georgina had at first thought the colours much too bold, but now she realised they suited her quite well. The scooped neckline showed off a modest amount of skin, and the pink lace that went around the edges and tapered down to a V at the waist added a delicate touch. The underskirt was a light pink satin that draped around the front, while the overskirt was a rich red velvet.

She had, however, asked the modiste to make one design change. Instead of silk roses for the trimming on the shoulders, she had asked for holly leaves and berries, to add a more festive feel. There was also a matching holly hairpin, which her maid had tucked just behind her ear.

Satisfied with her attire, she thanked her maid and joined the others in the drawing room for drinks before dinner. Almost everyone was there, though Miss Warren had decided not to join in tonight's festivities. She was weary from their day in the village, so had stayed in her rooms.

As soon as Georgina entered, her eyes were immediately drawn to Elliot. How could they not be? His large, imposing presence overpowered everyone else in a room. Tonight, he was chatting with Lady Lavinia, Lady Arundel and Anne-Marie as they sipped on hot apple cider. Her traitorous little heart stuttered at seeing him looking so handsome in his finery.

'Lady Georgina!' Lily greeted her as she seemingly popped up from nowhere. 'You look so pretty.'

'And you look adorable, poppet.'

Lily was dressed in a green satin dress and her hair was tied with matching bows.

'I'm so glad you invited us.' She gestured around them. 'I've never had a Christmas Eve with so many people…at least people who aren't servants.'

Once again her heart went out to Lily. What a dreary existence it must be, never to have had a festive Christmas. Why would Elliot be so cruel as to leave them alone on Christmas Day? Was he truly so obsessed with making money that he could not even stop working over Christmas?

'Lady Georgina, how ravishing you look,' Lord Bellamy said as he sidled up to her.

'Thank you, Lord Bellamy. I am glad to see you up and about. How are you feeling?'

'Healthy as a horse,' he said. 'I think I overindulged myself last night, but it was nothing a good night's sleep couldn't cure.'

'I'm glad to hear that.'

'There you are,' Trevor said as he came up to them. 'Seems like everyone is here. Shall we begin?'

She nodded in agreement and took his arm. Her brother signalled to Dawson, who announced that dinner was ready, and everyone made their way to the dining room.

Though the main Christmas meal of roast turkey would be served for tomorrow's dinner, Mrs Laramie had prepared a delicious feast of roast beef and potatoes, fried sole, stuffing, herbed parsnips and slices of decadent cake.

Georgina was glad that the seating was informal, and sat down next to Lily, who was delighted to be at the dinner table. Anne-Marie, on the other hand, opted to sit near the adults.

'What's this?' Lily asked, waving the brightly wrapped package on her empty plate.

'It's a Christmas cracker,' Georgina explained. 'Here.' She picked hers up and opened it. 'See? There are treats inside.'

Her eyes grew wide and she took her own cracker and opened it. 'I love Christmas so much.'

Georgina chuckled. 'Me too.'

After dinner, they all went to the parlour, where more food, drink and amusements were set up. A few of the guests opted to play cards, including Elliot, who partnered Lady Lavinia for a game of whist.

Georgina did her best to steer clear of them, opting to play snapdragon with Lily and Lady Hannah at the other end of the parlour. Once in a while, though, she would inadvertently glance towards the card table and catch Elliot smiling at Lady Lavinia, or see her laughing and patting his arm.

'Ow!' She withdrew her hand from the fiery bowl of raisins. She had been so distracted by Elliot and Lady Lavinia that she had not seen the flame flicker towards her fingers.

'You lose!' Lily laughed. 'Lady Georgina, you must be more careful.'

She sucked her finger into her mouth, trying to soothe the pain. As she glanced back towards the card table her gaze collided with jade-green eyes. Elliot was staring at her, with the most discomfiting expression on his face. For some reason it made heat crawl up into her cheeks, and she quickly turned away.

After more games, and more food and drink, it was nearly midnight and time for presents. Georgina had prepared small gifts for all the guests, and she and Trevor distributed them.

'I'm afraid I didn't get you anything, Lady Georgina,' Bellamy confessed as she handed him the present that had been intended for Mr Galwick. 'Your brother's invitation came at short notice.'

'Do not worry, my lord, I understand. Besides, it would not be proper for you to give me a gift, even if it is Christmas.'

'I suppose not… But there is still time, as this is not really Christmas, is it?'

It was as real as actual Christmas to her, but she kept those thoughts to herself.

'Perhaps, with your permission, we could have a conversation in the sitting room tomorrow?' Bellamy went on. 'With your chaperone present.'

'Miss Warren? Why would you need her there?'

He frowned. 'Because when gentlemen call upon ladies they must have chaperones present?'

'Call—?' She clamped her mouth tightly, lest her jaw fall to the floor.

'Lady Georgina,' he began, his expression softening, 'how fortuitous that His Grace invited me here.'

The most curious desire to flee sprang into Georgina's mind. 'Er…it was because Mr Galwick broke his leg in a riding accident…'

'Oh, no! I mean, poor chap.' He clicked his tongue. 'But since we met at the opera I've been meaning to ask you if—'

'Georgina!' Lily collided into her legs, nearly knocking her aside.

'*Oomph!*' She managed to steady herself. 'What is it, Lily?'

'You got me a present.' She pointed to the large box by the Christmas tree.

'I did, poppet.'

'What is it?'

'Why don't we find out?' she asked, taking her hand. 'Please excuse us, Lord Bellamy.'

Relief washed over her as she allowed Lily to drag her towards the tree. Did Bellamy truly want to call on her? As if he was—she swallowed audibly—*courting* her? She could not believe it. She hardly knew him. They'd never even got the chance to dance at the ball. Why would he seek her out?

'It's a doll!' Lily exclaimed as she ripped the package open. 'Thank you, Lady Georgina.'

'You're very welcome.'

Thankfully she had enough time before they left London to do some shopping, so she'd been able to get presents for the girls. Aside from the doll for Lily, she'd bought Anne-Marie a gold necklace. She'd also bought Elliot a jade tie pin, though she had labelled the gift as being from Trevor, as she had with all the men's gifts, while she labelled the women's with her own name. Glancing over at him, she saw him holding the small gift box in his hand, but he did not open it.

In all the excitement over the presents, Bellamy did not manage to approach her again. Just as she was sneaking off to go to her room she glanced back towards Elliot, who was walking towards Lady Lavinia with two cups of tea in his hands.

'Look, you're standing under the mistletoe!' Lady Arundel exclaimed when Elliot reached her daughter's side.

Georgina's stomach was tied into knots as that stabbing ache in her chest returned. Turning away, she quickly fled from the parlour. By the time she reached her rooms her breath was coming in short, shallow pants, and the tightening in her chest was refusing to ease.

Ringing the bell for her maid, she ripped the holly hairpin from behind her ear and threw off her gloves. She tried not to think about Elliot and Lady Lavinia kissing under the mistletoe, but it was of no use. Her mind conjured up the image, torturing her with it. What a beautiful couple they made…him so handsome and her so lovely.

'Lady Georgina, are you ready for bed?' her maid asked.

She hummed and nodded wordlessly, and the maid helped her undress and put on her nightrail. Perhaps it was a good thing he was leaving in the morning. She wouldn't have to think about him again…maybe never even see him again.

17th December

Sleep escaped Georgina. She tossed and turned for a good hour before her lids became heavy. Unfortunately, just as she was at the edge of sleep, a noise in the distance—the neighing of a horse and the rumble of carriage wheels—shook her awake. She cursed at the sound, then closed her eyes, trying to catch the drowsiness once more, and eventually she began to drift off…

'Lady Georgina?'

The small voice followed by the creaking of her bedroom door made her eyes open.

'What—?'

She blinked away the blurriness from her vision. Only a tiny stub was left of her candle, but it was enough for her to see the small head with wild overgrown curls peeping in through the door.

'Lily? Is that you?'

The head nodded.

'What's wrong, poppet?' She waved her over. 'Can't you sleep?'

The girl rushed over and stood by her bed.

'Did you have a nightmare?'

Bright red curls shook as she replied in the negative. 'No…'

'What's the matter, then?'

Her light green eyes darted left and right, as if she was afraid someone was listening to them. 'It's Anne-Marie.'

'Is she feeling sick? Did she have a bad dream?' When Lily didn't answer, Georgina sat up, and urged her to climb into bed to sit on her lap. 'Tell me, poppet. Please. You won't get into trouble, I promise.'

'I promised I wouldn't tell Elliot, but…' Lily's lower lip trembled. 'She's gone. Anne-Marie.'

'Gone?' Georgina's voice rose, but when she saw Lily's eyes widen she calmed herself before saying, 'Tell me what happened.'

'We were already in bed, and I was almost asleep. Then Anne-Marie woke me.' Her eyes filled with tears. 'She—she said she loved me, but she had to leave. She said that once she was away from Elliot she would write to me and find a way for us to be together again.'

'Where was she going?'

'Scotland, she said. She was going with a friend.'

Scotland?

And who was this friend?

Panic began to set in, but Georgina knew she could not go into hysterics now. 'What else did she say?'

'I—I...' Fat tears rolled down Lily's cheeks. 'I don't know...'

'Shh...shh, it's all right, poppet.' She hugged Lily close and smoothed a hand down her back. 'Have you told anyone else? One of your servants?'

Lily hiccupped and shook her head. 'Everyone else is still downstairs in the parlour. What are we going to do?'

Taking a deep breath, Georgina gathered her thoughts. There was only one thing to do.

'I will tell Elliot. And don't you worry. He will bring her back.'

'Really?'

'Yes.'

If there was anyone who could do it, it was him. Still, time was of the essence...

'Stay here, poppet, and try to sleep. Anne-Marie will be back before you know it.'

After tucking her under the covers, Georgina rushed to her closet and pulled out one of her looser day gowns. She quickly removed her nightrail and put it on, though she didn't bother with her corset and petticoats. The dress pinched and pulled in the most uncomfortable places without her undergarments, but it would have to do for now. She put on her slippers, then grabbed a cloak before leaving her room, wrapping it around herself as she ran down the corridor.

The party was likely to go on until morning, so she would ask one of the footmen to discreetly ask Elliot to come out. As she reached the staircase she was so busy piecing together in her mind what she would say to him that she did not notice the figure heading up the stairs—and promptly bumped into it.

'Oh!' She stumbled, but strong hands caught her by the waist and she found herself pressed up against a long, hard body.

'Georgina?'

Elliot's warm baritone caressed her skin like velvet.

'Elliot…' she said breathlessly as the scent of his cologne tickled her nose.

'What are you doing—and why in God's name are you dressed like that?'

The arm around her waist tightened, and she didn't know if that was the reason she couldn't breathe, or if it was because she was so close to him.

'Are you going on a midnight tryst?' he snarled. 'With Bellamy?'

She blinked, the spell breaking. 'I beg your pardon?' Placing her hands on his chest, she pushed as hard as she could, but his grip was like steel. 'Elliot, let go of me!'

'Not until you tell me where you're going.'

'I was coming to find *you*!'

His face slackened, as did his arm. 'What?'

'Anne-Marie's gone,' she blurted out. 'She's left.'

The dark expression returned to his face. 'Explain.'

She told him what had happened, and what Lily had said.

'Scotland? Why in God's name would she be going to Scotland? If she wanted to book a passage back to America, she should have gone back to London.'

Just as she had suspected, he had no idea what going to Scotland meant. She had to tell him, and there was no delicate and quick way to do it.

'Elliot, here in England, when someone goes to Scotland in the middle of the night, it usually means they are headed to Gretna Green.'

'And? Am I supposed to know where that is?'

'Gretna Green is a place where couples can have a blacksmith's wedding—a hasty wedding.'

'Hasty wedding?'

'Yes. To escape parents and guardians who might be against the marriage.'

The way his expression shifted from confusion to bewilderment and finally to understanding would have been comical, had it not been for the grave situation at hand.

'Goddammit.' He raked his fingers through his hair. 'I don't even know...how...? Who?'

'I don't know either, Elliot, but you must go after her.'

'Damned right I'll go after her,' he muttered. 'Where are the stables?'

She grabbed his arm. 'Come. I will—'

'I am not taking you with me,' he thundered. 'Just tell me where—'

'It's faster this way, and you won't get lost,' she said. 'Now, let's hurry. You may still be able to catch them. I don't think they left more than half an hour ago.'

If her suspicions were correct, the noise of a horse and carriage that had jolted her awake had been Anne-Marie and her 'friend' leaving.

They made their way out of the house through the entrance to the gardens and set off for the stables. Georgina shivered and drew her cloak around her, thankful she'd thought to bring it.

When they reached the stables, Elliot hurried to the first stall and retrieved the saddle. 'Now, which way is Scotland?'

Georgina slapped her hand on her forehead. 'Of course. You don't know which way to go.'

'Do I look like I know where Scotland is? But I will figure it out. It's north, right?'

'I was merely making a statement.' She took a deep breath. 'I can show you the way. The fastest road going north leads to Derbyshire, where my grandfather's estate is located. I visit him every year.'

She didn't want Anne-Marie to feel alone once they caught up with her. While she knew Elliot would never hurt his sister, Anne-Marie was young, and likely frightened. Georgina wanted to be there to soothe her.

'No.' He whirled around. 'You cannot come with me.'

'Elliot, be reasonable. With each passing second they are getting farther and farther away. And if you get lost, you'll never find them.'

'I won't get lost because you will tell me which way to go.'

She crossed her arms over her chest. 'I won't unless I am with you. If we leave right this moment, we may be able to catch up with them and be back before sunrise.'

He muttered a curse under his breath that she heard clearly. 'Well?' she asked.

'One horse cannot take both of us—three of us when we retrieve my sister—and you are not dressed to ride side-saddle.'

'I wasn't suggesting we ride the horses. Now, take this horse's reins and come with me.' She led him to where the carriages were kept. 'We can use the phaeton.' She nodded to the small open carriage at the end of the row. 'It's smaller and lighter. We'll be able to catch up with them in this, and although it will be a tight fit, we will have room for all three of us when we return.'

He blew out a breath, but said nothing as he began to secure the horse to the phaeton. Once he'd finished, he helped her onto the carriage and sat down beside her, reins in hand. With a click of his tongue and a soft flick of the reins the horse pulled them out of the carriage house and down the path leading towards the main road.

'Which way?' he asked.

'Left,' she said. 'Then keep going until the fork.'

Elliot snapped the reins and the horse broke into a gallop. Georgina, caught unawares, let out a shout and grabbed for the nearest thing she could—his arm.

She sent him a dirty look. 'You did that on purpose.'

He didn't say anything, just snorted.

Settling back into the seat, she adjusted her cloak and pulled the hood tight around her head. The brisk pace of the phaeton blew the chilly air straight at them and she shivered again.

When they reached the fork, he asked her which way to go.

'Keep to this road for about another ten miles, and then I'll tell you,' she said, which earned her another grumble.

Oh, she wasn't about to reveal everything to him right away—lest he suddenly decide to turn around and take her back to Foxbury Hill.

Elliot slowed their pace, perhaps to conserve the horse's energy. 'How did you know Anne-Marie had run away?'

'Lily came to me, poor thing.' She told him all that had happened, including how she'd heard the horses and carriage.

His eyebrows slashed downwards. 'Why would she come to you and not me?'

'I don't know. I think perhaps Anne-Marie made her promise not to tell you, so she came to me instead. Or perhaps she was scared of you.'

'Preposterous. I would never hurt either of them.'

'I know that...but she's young.' The air was now positively freezing, despite their slower pace, and she wrapped her cloak tighter around her. 'I'm just glad I was able to find you in time. I was going to send a footman to fetch you...'

'I was the last to head upstairs. Everyone had gone to bed, thank goodness.'

'Even Lady Lavinia?'

That had come out before she'd been able to stop herself. Had he kissed her under the mistletoe? Had he liked it?

'Yes, she went to bed not much later than you, actually.' He stiffened. 'Thank you for coming to find me right away. And... apologies for what I insinuated about you and Bellamy.'

She had forgotten about that, with all the worry over Anne-Marie. 'I'm sure it was a surprise, seeing me in my cloak. But why would you even think I was going off on some tryst?'

It was bizarre and preposterous.

Elliot remained silent, his eyes gazing straight ahead at the road.

'It's not as if we are courting.'

'Not *yet*, you mean.'

Her head swivelled towards him. 'How did you...? Did he...?'

'I overheard him talking to your brother before he went upstairs.' A muscle ticked in his jaw. 'He said you have agreed to take his call in the morning.'

She didn't recall saying yes, but she hadn't said no, either.

'Would you accept his proposal?'

'He hasn't even asked to court me. It's just a call.'

'But that's where it begins, right?'

'I suppose…'

'Well? Would you marry him?'

'I don't know,' she said.

'Why not?'

'I just—' She gasped. 'Elliot!' She pointed a finger upwards. 'Look!'

'What in the world—?'

A single fat snowflake fluttered down, landing on Elliot's hand. A second one followed it, and then a third, and soon more descended from the dark sky.

'Does it usually snow at this time of the year?'

'Sometimes,' she says. 'We've had a few snowy First Christmases.'

He cursed again. 'We can't go back now.'

'I know. But this might slow them down too,' she reminded him.

With a determined grunt he said, 'Hold on tight, Georgina.'

As soon as she'd grabbed onto his arm he snapped the reins and the horse picked up its pace.

The snow continued to fall at alarming speeds, coming straight at them at an almost horizontal angle. Georgina shielded her face by burying it against Elliot's arm. Despite the protection of her cloak, she was still freezing, and she could only imagine how he was feeling.

His body shivered, giving her an answer.

Heavens, he must be miserable.

Without a second thought she slipped her arms around him, pressing her body against his to share her heat.

He stiffened. 'Georgina, this isn't—'

'Shh…it's all right. No one is around to see us, and you're shivering so hard I can hear your teeth rattle.' She moved her cloak aside, so she could wrap it around him and protect him from the snow. 'See? This is much better.'

She settled against him, the spicy scent of his cologne and the feel of his torso against her sending the most deliciously warm tingles straight down to her belly.

He answered only with a grunt.

Her thoughts went back to their encounter in the music room.

She'd been trying not to remember it, as it only left her with a lingering heat in her body she could never seem to get rid of. In her decision to remain a spinster she had never considered the fact that she would never know what it was like to lie with a man. It had never seemed important. But now that she'd had a taste of it, it was difficult to ignore. It had barely been two days since that night, and she could not forget it.

What would it be like to be with a man?

No, not just any man. Elliot.

His shoulders—no, his entire body, seemed so much larger this close to hers. How she wanted to slip her hands under his coat and his shirt, to feel his naked skin. The very thought of it warmed her cheeks and sent heat pooling in her belly, enough to ward off some of the chill.

Heavens, she needed to stop her thoughts now, before she did something foolish. She moved her torso away from him, though she kept her arms wrapped around his middle.

The snow did not relent, and the air was now bitingly cold. Her cloak was soaking wet and could no longer protect them. They had been driving for about half an hour in the blizzard when Elliot slowed down.

'The horse is tiring and there is still no sign of any other carriage on the road.'

'Wait!' She squinted her eyes. 'I think I see something.'

'Is it their carriage?'

'No…' But there was a very faint light up the road. 'If I recall, that should be a coaching inn. The Steed and the Sword. Let's stop and catch our breath…maybe they'll have a fresh horse for us.'

Elliot snapped the reins once again and pushed the horse towards the inn.

'We need a new horse,' he barked at the sleepy stableboy who greeted them when they arrived.

'Sorry, sir.' The boy scratched at his head. 'We ain't got no more 'orses.'

'What do you mean? This is a coaching inn. You're supposed to have them ready.'

'Been busy, we 'ave,' the boy retorted. 'An' with this snow comin' down we probably don' expect any more until mornin'.'

'Oh, dear.' Georgina wrung her hands together. 'What are we to do, then?'

'Better go inside the tavern,' the boy suggested. 'Let yer horse 'bate for an hour or two and ye can be on yer way.'

She looked at him. 'Elliot…?'

The expression on his face was inscrutable. 'We don't have much of a choice. I'll not kill the poor creature.' He handed the reins over to the boy. 'Come, perhaps we can have something warm to drink inside.'

Chapter Ten

As soon as they'd approached the tavern Elliot placed his arm around Georgina and held her close. 'Do not leave my side and do not speak.'

She nodded.

He breathed an inner sigh of relief. Finally she had found some sense in her head to obey him. But then again, from the look of the tavern, he wasn't surprised.

The stench of ale, boiled cabbage and unwashed bodies assaulted Elliot's nose as they entered. It was nearly empty, save for a few men scattered here and there, musing over their pints of ale or conversing loudly. However, all manner of activity ceased the moment he and Georgina appeared, and all eyes went to them. The men grinned and jeered as they passed by.

Elliot would bet all the occupants here would not be able to fill a whole head of teeth between them.

Hurrying her along, he sat them down in a far corner, next to the fire. 'Do you have anything to warm us up?' he asked the barmaid who approached them.

'This ain't a tea shop, love,' she sneered, glancing over at Georgina. 'We got ale.'

'Two pints,' he said, then waved her away. 'Are you all right, Georgina?'

'J-Just cold,' she said. 'But I think I can feel my toes now.'

He smiled, then eased the cloak off her shoulders. 'It's warm in here, and the ale should help.' He shrugged off his own coat, which was now soaked through, and placed it on the empty chair next to him.

The barmaid came back with their pints, and he thanked her as he gave her a few coins. 'Have a sip,' he told Georgina.

She wrinkled her nose at the drink, but took a sip anyway. 'That is vile.' Her face scrunched up and she pushed the pint away. 'I think I'll let the fire warm me up.'

He, too, took a sip. 'I agree with your assessment.' He sighed. 'This is all my fault.'

'It's not,' she said.

'Yes, it is.' Remorse coursed through him, followed by fear. 'I just want to know that she's all right and not hurt.'

'Me too,' Georgina said. 'But this isn't your fault.'

'Anne-Marie has expressed her unhappiness in so many ways and yet I have ignored it. She hates me.'

'She does not.'

'She has said it several times now. I'm quite certain she does.'

'She does not mean it,' she assured him, taking his hand and pressing lightly.

'I just want what's best for them. So they...' He couldn't bring himself to say it aloud. 'I want them to have something better than I had.'

Could Anne-Marie not see that? He was doing all this so they would never know what it was like to live in a home with dirty floors or go to bed hungry. He'd moved them all the way here to give them the best chance in life?

Silence hung between him and Georgina, and he could not bring himself to look at her, for fear that he might drown in her copper-brown eyes. Instead, he allowed himself to revel in the warmth of her soft palm.

''Scuse me, sir.' A burly man with a scruffy beard approached them. 'My stable hand Willy says ye're sittin' down for a rest before continuin' yer journey?'

Alarm bells rang in Elliot's head. 'And who are you?'

'Beggin' yer pardon, sir, I'm the owner of this establishment. Joseph Brown, at yer service.'

'And why are you enquiring about our business, Mr Brown?'

'Well, sir.' He nodded towards the window. 'That snow's comin' down hard and not lettin' up. From my experience, I don't think it'll stop until mornin'.'

Elliot cursed silently. 'I assume you didn't come here just to tell me your assessment of the weather?'

'Well, sir. You and your...' he glanced at Georgina '...wife seem tired. Why don't ye take a room upstairs? I run a clean establishment 'ere, and our linens 'ave just been laundered. A couple o' travellers took two rooms right before ye came in. I got one left. And if ye don't take it, I'm sure the next person who comes through that door will.'

Elliot contemplated the man's words. While he admired the man's business acumen in offering them a room, sharing a room—and a bed—with Georgina was the last thing he should be doing. Her embrace in the phaeton had nearly undone him. He would have driven off the road had he been a lesser man. Being alone in a bed with her would be pure torture.

On the other hand, the weariness on Georgina's face was evident, no matter how much she tried to hide it, and her dress was damp and no closer to drying. She might catch a cold.

'Sweetheart?' he said to his 'wife'. 'Would you like to lie down and rest for a while?'

She shook her head. 'We cannot. We need to catch up with—' Her eyes darted towards the innkeeper and she clamped them shut. 'There's no time to rest. We must hurry to our...next destination.'

'Ye won't be travellin' far in this weather,' said the innkeeper. 'Next coaching inn's about fifty miles. Besides, yer little phaeton, fast at it might be, will never hold up in those winds.'

'He's right, sweetheart.' His mind made up, Elliot said, 'Prepare the room, Mr Brown. And make sure there is a warm fire before we head upstairs.'

'Aye, sir.' He leaned forward. 'I notice ye have no luggage... I can have me girl lend yer *wife* a nightrail. For an extra fee, of course.'

Elliot did not miss the meaning in his words. 'And I suppose this "extra fee" includes your silence?'

'Aye.' The innkeeper grinned at him, showing three missing teeth. 'I am but yer discreet servant.'

'All right. Just add it to my bill.'

'Elliot, we can't stay here,' Georgina said as soon as they were alone. 'What about Anne-Marie?'

'I know. But we can't leave either. I only hope this storm has slowed her down too.' He didn't want to think of his sister in some coaching inn like this. 'We will set off as soon as it stops.'

A few minutes later Joseph Brown came back to show them upstairs to their room. Elliot supposed it was serviceable, and not as dirty as other inns he'd stayed at, despite the musty smell. He'd noticed that everything in England tended to be old, and it had been a challenge finding his home in Mayfair because not many of those grand old mansions had modern fittings. But, despite its shabbiness, this room was warm.

'Elliot, there is only one bed,' Georgina said.

That had not escaped him. 'I won't be sleeping.' Glancing around, he found a chair in the corner and pulled it towards the fire. 'I'll sleep. You can—'

He stopped short, his mouth going dry as he watched her remove her cloak and place it by the fire.

'Elliot?' She cocked her head at him. 'What's the matter?'

He opened his mouth but, embarrassingly, nothing came out. As he'd suspected, her dress was indeed soaked through—and quite transparent. She must not have bothered with undergarments in her haste, because he could clearly see the outline of her nipples against the wet fabric, and the darker shadow between her legs where the dress was pulled tight.

His cock immediately went hard.

'Elliot?' she repeated.

'Nothing.' He shifted around so he faced away from her, concealing his erection. 'I'm going to keep watch in case the snow slows down. You should get some rest. We will ride hard tomorrow.'

A poor choice of words, he realised, as it conjured the most erotic of images, which only tortured his poor cock further.

She didn't say anything, but his ears could hear the rustle of clothing as she began to undress. Eyes sliding heavenwards, he prayed to the Lord, promising that if he escaped this situation without embarrassing himself he would give away half his fortune tomorrow.

Elliot counted to sixty before glancing over his shoulder. Mercifully, Georgina was tucked under the bedcovers, staring up at the ceiling. He turned back and shifted in the chair, though his erection showed no signs of abating. Resigned to his fate, he leaned back and closed his eyes, trying to catch a few minutes of sleep.

'Elliot?' Georgina called.

'Yes?'

'You can't possibly be comfortable in that chair.'

No, he wasn't.

'There is enough space here in the bed.'

'No, thank you,' he bit back. 'I am perfectly fine here.'

He heard her sit up. 'No, you are not. I can see you. You won't be able to get any rest, and then you'll be too tired to drive.'

'I will be fine.'

'No, you won't. Why don't you just lie down beside me? Stay above the covers and I shall stay under.'

He sighed. 'If I do, will you go to sleep?'

'Yes.'

If she was asleep, then perhaps there would be no harm in that.

He glanced down at his lap, imploring his cock to behave. Standing up, he adjusted his trousers and headed towards the bed, where Georgina was, as promised, under the covers and facing away from him.

Heaving a sigh, he lay down beside her. His clothes were still damp. He should have asked Joseph Brown for some dry clothes as well, but he doubted he would have found anything that would fit Elliot. Besides, he would probably have charged him an exorbitant amount for a nightshirt.

He didn't dare remove any of his damp clothes, but he did untuck his shirt from his trousers and pull back the sleeves.

'Elliot?'

'What?'

'I can't sleep.' She turned to face him.

Georgina looked like an angel, lying on her side, waves of hair around her sweet face. Her coppery brown eyes were like molten pools, and as he'd suspected he was drowning in them. He could barely stop himself from touching her face. How he longed to feel her smooth skin underneath his palm...

'You must try.' He closed his eyes, which was the only thing he could do right now to block her from his sight.

'You can't sleep either.'

'Not if you keep talking to me,' he snapped.

Regret filled him as he heard her sharp intake of breath.

'Georgina...' He opened his eyes. 'What's the matter? You must be exhausted. I practically had to carry you up the stairs.'

'I know. I am tired. But my mind...it just won't rest.'

'Try not to worry about Anne-Marie.' That was his job, after all. 'There is nothing we can do at this moment.'

'It's not that.' Her teeth chewed down on her lower lip. 'You asked me a question in the carriage...'

'About what?'

'Bellamy.'

He tamped down the murderous urge that name drove in him. 'What about him?'

The smallest line appeared between her eyebrows. 'Don't you remember? You asked me if I would marry him.'

He did recall that conversation. Very much so.

'Why did you ask me that, Elliot?'

Because he very much wanted to know if she would marry Bellamy.

Would you accept his *proposal?*

Would you marry him?

And then there was the last question in his mind—one he didn't dare say aloud.

And why the hell not me?

'I don't know,' he lied.

'Do you want to know the answer?'

Not particularly.

'Will you go to sleep if I say yes?'

The corner of her mouth lifted. 'I do not think I would accept,' she said. 'I've been out in society for ten years now, and I have never received a single proposal in all this time.'

'Not one?'

Were the men of England blind?

She shook her head. 'I'm not exactly a desirable bride. In the beginning I was much too shy to attract anything more than fortune-hunters after my dowry. Trevor immediately dispatched them, before they even had a chance to court me.'

'Good.' He would do the same for his sisters.

'I went to balls, and other events, but I could hardly speak to anyone. My tongue would just tie up in knots and I would get the urge to flee. Then I would think that everyone in the room knew I was having these thoughts, which would only make me more anxious. And then I started having these spells.' She avoided his gaze. 'You've seen them.'

'Yes.' At the ball, and just before that unforgettable encounter in the music room.

'They just got worse and worse over the years. Sometimes I wouldn't be able to leave my bed for a whole day. Socialising with a large group of people leaves me drained, and large crowds send me into a panic. My chest seizes up so tight I can hardly breathe. My stomach churns like I'm at sea, and I even broke out in hives once. So when my previous chaperone became weak, and unable to accompany me to all those events, I simply stopped going. I hadn't been to any event in three years, and I'd stopped experiencing any of those things.'

'Until I came along.'

She sneaked a glance at him. 'Yes. But see... I've grown accustomed to my solitary life. After you find your bride I will return to my reclusive ways. It's the only way I can have peace.'

Once again guilt began to eat at him. He had been causing her physical pain and discomfort. Perhaps he should release her from their bargain and allow the orphans to stay. It was only money, after all.

'I could never be the perfect society wife,' she added. 'I could never go to events with my husband or entertain guests at his estate. Trevor has pledged to care for me, no matter what happens, so I have no need of a husband ever.'

'So you plan to be unmarried for the rest of your life?'

'Yes.'

The tightening in his chest eased. It wasn't that she didn't want to marry him. She just didn't want to be married.

'Which is why I wanted to ask you something. A favour.'

'What is it?' He was already going to give her the orphanage, but he knew he wouldn't say no to anything else she might ask.

She didn't answer right away, and her eyes avoided him again. As he waited for her to speak, he searched her face for any clue as to what she might want from him. Her cheeks had grown scarlet and she was worrying at her bottom lip.

'Georgina…?'

'Will you make love to me?'

His heart—no, his entire body seized. 'I beg your pardon?'

'You heard me.' Though it should have been impossible, her face turned even redder. 'I want you to make love to me.'

His mouth went dry and he could only stare at her. 'This is ridiculous,' he finally said, when speech returned to his tongue. 'Think of what you are asking of me.'

'I have. I've thought about it for most of the ride here, and then when we sat down, right up until this moment. Elliot, I want this.'

'You don't know what you're asking.' He made a motion to turn away, but her hands quickly darted out of the covers to grab at his shirt. 'Georgina, let go.'

'No.' Her fingers tightened. 'Not until you consider my request.'

'I have. And the answer is still no.'

'Why not?'

Was she insane? 'You are a lady. I will not ruin you.'

'But you would make love to another lady?' Her voice was choked.

'That's different. She would be my wife in that case.' Gently, he took her hand and prised it from his shirt. 'I cannot do this to you.'

'But I'm asking you. Just give me this one time. I just want

to know... I want to feel like I did in the music room. I want...
I just want to feel wanted.'

'Oh, sweetheart...'

This was a dangerous game they were playing, and he had
to stop it now before it was too late. If he ever made love to her,
there was no way on God's green earth it could only be for one
time.

'We cannot.'

But he wasn't sure if he was convincing her or himself.

'We should not.'

Her wrist was so delicate underneath his palms...the skin
so soft.

'We can,' she whispered. 'No one will know.'

'I would know, sweetheart.' His chest tightened once again,
his control barely hanging by a thread. He should leave her here
now, wait out the storm downstairs.

'Then I will never make love to anyone.'

That statement stunned him, as if he'd been hit on the head
with rocks.

'Georgina, don't say that.'

'It's true.'

'You will want someone else someday.' The very words left
a bitter taste in his mouth.

Her chin jutted up, those coppery brown eyes spearing into
him. 'It is you or no one else.'

Lord Almighty, of all the things she could have said in this
moment, she just had to say that...

God, he muttered to himself, before his mouth captured hers.

Finally.

Georgina sighed as Elliot's mouth devoured her like a hungry man in search of his next meal. His fingers threaded into
her hair as he pulled her closer to him.

This was it...it was truly happening.

How she'd longed for this, for him, and now he was going to
make love to her.

His tongue licked at the seam of her lips and she opened eagerly for him. His hot tongue delved right into her mouth, seek-

ing hers, while his hand threw the blankets away. It had grown hot under the covers, so the chill of the room was welcome. His hand landed on her thigh, grabbing at the fabric to raise it.

She froze.

He paused, but his lips remained barely an inch from hers. 'Do you know what's going to happen, sweetheart?'

'N-not quite,' she confessed. 'Great-Aunt Leticia promised me she would tell me before my wedding night, and since there was none...'

'She never told you?'

She shook her head and turned away from him, hiding her face against his neck.

'Do not hide, sweetheart.'

He placed his finger on her chin and tilted her head to face him. His eyes glowed bright in the light of the fire, and the most curious, delicious warmth filled her chest.

'There is nothing shameful about what happens between a man and woman. It's pleasurable for both, though you may experience some pain.'

She had overheard married women and some of the maids at home speaking of the sexual act, but she'd only been able to piece together some of the mechanics of it. 'I've heard there may be pain...down there.'

'Do you want to hear the rest of it? So you are not surprised?'

Her ears burned at the thought that he would school her on such matters. How she wished she knew more—at least enough so he did not have to teach her.

'What's wrong, sweetheart?' Concern marred his face. 'Why are you frowning?'

'It's nothing.'

'Please tell me. I do not want to do this if you are unsure.'

'I'm sure,' she said quickly, cupping his cheek, feeling the bristle underneath her fingertips. 'I'm just scared that you'll be disappointed in me. I don't know anything, and you'll have to teach me. It will be boring for you.'

He let out a soft chuckle. 'Bored is the last thing I'll feel, or disappointment.' Leaning down, he kissed her again, cradling her face with one hand. 'You please me just by being here. It will be nearly impossible for me not to feel pleasure. But I will do what it takes to make sure you feel good too.'

'I… I want to feel good. I want you to make me feel good.'

His eyes blazed. 'I will. Do you remember the music room?'

How could she ever forget? 'Yes…'

'When I touched you? And kissed you?'

'Y-yes.' Just the memory of it sent the most furious blush across her skin.

'May I do it again?'

'Please,' she said. 'I want to feel you.'

His hand cupped a breast through the nightrail. When his thumb found her nipple it hardened and poked against the rough fabric. Bending down, he placed his mouth over the nub as he continued to massage her flesh. At first, she couldn't feel his mouth, but when his tongue lapped at her, and the spot under his mouth became wet, the friction of his tongue against the fabric sent gooseflesh rising down her arms. He teased her with the flat of his tongue, further moistening the fabric. When he sucked, a jolt of pleasure made the place between her legs throb.

She gasped, and dug her hand into his hair. When she scraped her nails into his scalp, he moaned and canted his hips against her side. He removed his hand from her breast and back to her thigh. She let out the most embarrassing sigh of disappointment when his mouth released her nipple.

'What else do you remember from the music room? Did you hear Lady Genevieve? When she was crying out?'

'A little bit.' The curtains and his body had blocked out most of the sound.

'Do you know what the Duke was doing?'

'T-Touching her?'

'Do you know where?'

She had an idea, but she didn't want to say it, so she just nodded. 'Down…there?'

'Hmm-hmm. May I touch you there?'

She closed her eyes and nodded, her throat dry.

He pulled up the fabric, his fingers skimming along her thigh. It felt like for ever, and the anticipation growing within her was too much. Finally, his hand moved to the inside, all the way up. Her hips jumped the moment his fingers landed on the soft mound between her legs.

'Does this feel good?' His fingertips moved over the downy hair.

'Oh, yes. More, please.'

'Only if you open your eyes and look at me.'

Mortification flooded her. 'I cannot.'

'Yes, you can, sweetheart.' His mouth was on her temple for a gentle kiss. 'I promise this part doesn't hurt.'

Slowly, she opened her eyes. The expression on his face was a mix of wonder and contentment, yet she still felt the burning of her cheeks.

'That's it. Thank you. Just look at me. Unless you want to see what I'm doing—?'

'No.' She couldn't possibly look down there. 'Just... I will look at you.'

The corners of his mouth drew up into a sensuous smile. 'Good. Now, relax your body. Don't tense up.' He parted the mat of hair and sought out her nether lips. She gasped the moment his fingers slid against her most secret part. 'You're starting to get slick,' he said. 'The wetness will help with the pain.'

'H-How?'

'Ah, I'm getting ahead of myself.' His other hand fumbled with something at his waist and he shimmied his hips, then he took her hand and put it between them.

She gasped when the palm of her hand grasped something firm under the fabric of his shirt. 'That's your—?'

'Cock. Can you say it?'

'N-No, thank you.'

He stifled a laugh. 'Maybe later. Touch it,' he said. 'Grasp it.'

The bulge was warm under her palm, but she did not dare do as he asked. 'Will I hurt you?'

'No, just as long as you don't do it too hard—oh!' He groaned when her fingers clutched at the hardness.

She immediately let go, as if she'd touched a hot pan. 'Sorry.'

'N-No, no.' He took her hand and replaced it. 'It was good. Much better than I had imagined.'

'Oh.' She gripped the length again. It was much thicker and longer than she'd anticipated. 'Wait—you have imagined this?'

'Oh, yes, sweetheart.' He moaned when her grip tightened. 'Too many times.'

It was fascinating, feeling the hardness under the fabric. 'What do we do next?'

'Let me tell you what's going to happen…'

His fingers began to stroke her, and she found herself getting even slicker. Slowly, he pushed at her, the tip of his finger entering her. She froze once more.

'It's all right. It's going to feel good. My cock will go inside you. Right. Here.' He inched his finger into her.

Georgina couldn't find the words to describe the sensations in her body at that moment. She already felt terribly full of his finger. How was his…? How would he fit in there?

He pulled back, then pushed into her again, and repeated the motion. 'It will feel like this, but more. Does it feel good now?'

'Y-Yes.'

'I can tell. See how you clasp at my finger, sweetheart?' He continued his gentle ministrations at her entrance. 'You'll do that for me again, around my cock. It will feel wonderful for me.'

'Oh, yes…' she moaned.

The heat was too much, and his words were blisteringly embarrassing, but she wanted him to keep going.

'That's it. Move your hips just like that.'

She hadn't even realised that she was, indeed, thrusting her hips up to meet his hand.

'How do you feel?'

'Just…so hot.'

He paused and adjusted his hand. 'There is one more place I will touch you, and you will feel even better. Do you trust me?'

'Yes, Elliot,' she panted.

His thumb brushed at the top of her mound, and her hips shot off the mattress. 'Elliot!'

His hands and fingers worked at her like magic, spreading heady pleasure all over her. She couldn't think, and her chest seemed to squeeze out every last bit of air from her. She hadn't even realised, either, that she'd grasped his length and was stroking it in the same rhythm as his fingers worked her.

The sensations made her mindless, and her body exploded in pleasure. He captured her scream with his mouth, his tongue thrusting into hers savagely.

She sank down, every bone in her body like liquid, unable to hold her up. Her eyes fluttered open as feeling finally returned to her limbs.

'How do you feel?' he murmured against her temple.

'I… Tired. But at the same time…not.'

Though her body felt sated, she knew there was more. And she wanted all of it.

'Good.' He brushed the hair from her sweat-dampened brow. 'Do you want to rest?'

'No. But, Elliot…?'

'Hmm?'

'How…how will you fit?'

It seemed impossible, with his girth, and she had already felt full with just his finger.

'That's what I meant when I said the wetness will help. And when you experience pleasure, like you did just now, your body produces even more of that slickness which will help ease me in.'

'I think I understand.'

'It hurts for many women, especially during their first time, because often the man does not prepare them in this way.'

'So it won't hurt any more? When you—?'

'It still might. You're very tight, Georgina. But that's because you have never experienced this before. I promise you, your body will accommodate me. I will do my best to ensure you are comfortable, but I cannot predict what will happen. You must promise to tell me if it's too much and we will stop.'

Lord, she didn't want him to stop.

'And you will feel pleasure too?'

'Yes. When I—' He frowned. 'There is something else. You do know this is how children are conceived?'

'Y-Yes.' She swallowed hard.

When she'd asked him to make love to her, she hadn't considered the possibility.

'There is something I must do to stop from getting you with child,' he said. 'At the last moment, I will pull out and spill my seed outside your body. That should prevent you from conceiving.'

'I… All right.' She didn't quite understand, but she trusted him.

He nuzzled at her cheek. 'You are so incredibly beautiful, Georgina.'

Normally she would not believe that, but in his arms she did feel beautiful.

'Let me look at you?' he said.

Her heart thumped in her chest. 'M-Must you?'

'I don't have to, but I want to. And this is really better without clothes.'

'Y-You as well? You'll be naked?'

'Yes, that's the general idea.'

The room felt much too bright with the fire blazing. The thought of him looking at her, and her at him, was too much for her mind to sort through. She now understood why couples did this in the dark.

'Be brave for me, sweetheart. Looking at you will give me pleasure. You don't have to look at me if you think it will frighten you.'

'N-No, I'm not frightened.' She took a deep breath and relaxed. 'All right.'

'Thank you.' He kissed her again, then proceeded to lift the nightrail over her head and toss it aside. 'So lovely you are, Georgina.' His hand slid up from her hip, over the soft mound of her belly and cupped a breast. 'So gorgeous.'

'You do not think I am…that my body is much too well-endowed?'

'Too well-endowed? Never.' His hands—rough and callused—squeezed a breast gently and thumbed a nipple into hardness. 'There's so much of you to enjoy. More for me to hold and touch and kiss.' He bent his head to lick at her nipple. 'Delectable. I could feast on you all day.'

'Oh…' That tension had begun to build in her body once more. 'Elliot…'

To her annoyance, he released her.

'One moment, sweetheart.' He moved away from her and off the bed, towering over her. Grabbing the hem of his shirt, he pulled it over his head and tossed it aside.

Georgina could not tear her eyes away from him. He was so…solid and powerful. His shoulders were wide, the muscles making him look bulky. His arms were like small tree trunks, and his large chest was covered with a mat of dark hair.

'I was always tall for my age, but then I spent ten years rowing passengers across New York's rivers, and before that I carried cargo from the ships,' he explained. 'Do you find my body displeasing?'

She shook her head. 'N-No, not at all. Just…overwhelming.'

The buttons of his trousers had already been unbuttoned and the waist shoved down to his thighs. He pushed them further down, revealing the jutting column between his legs.

Georgina swallowed hard, and quickly averted her eyes.

'I promise to be gentle.' The mattress dipped as he joined her again. 'And you must promise to let me know if it is too much. Please do not bear the pain for my sake.'

She could only nod.

He stretched his body along the length of hers. Seeking her mouth, he melded their lips together, then covered her body.

The weight of him was pleasant, though she suspected he was not putting all of it on her—after all, his great big body would crush her. He nudged her legs open and settled between them. A hand reached down to her sex, his fingers once again stroking her sensitive flesh. When she was panting, and clawing at the mattress, he spread her open and something blunt pressed at her.

She sucked in a breath as the invasion seemed to split her open. Though she winced at the pain, she felt herself open up to him as he applied pressure gently. She stretched and accommodated him, and despite the slight burning she could feel small shocks of pleasure down the base of her spine. It seemed to take for ever and he filled her until she couldn't take any more.

'I'm sorry, sweetheart, that this has to hurt. You must relax… it will ease the pain.'

That task seemed impossible, but she let out a breath and

forced her muscles to obey. Just as he'd said, the pain began to ebb away and her inner muscles loosened. Reaching up, she dug her fingers into his shoulders, fascinated by the powerful contours shaped by years of rowing under the sun. When she moved her fingers, those muscles jumped under her fingers. Fascinated, she trailed them down his arms.

He moaned aloud, his body tensing. 'I must move...or else.'

'Please...'

Slowly, he began to move. There was more burning, but after a few thrusts it all but disappeared, replaced by frissons of excitement. He drew back, then pushed forward, again and again, and Georgina found herself shamelessly pushing up to meet his thrusts, as if her hips had a life of their own. With each upward movement that knot at the base of her spine tightened, waiting to snap.

He paused, then his hand slipped between them, spreading her further and caressing the bud there, making her squirm and moan louder. Then he began moving again, building the rhythm slowly, gradually, until she could feel herself completely open to him. His breath hitched, then he reached under her knees to pull them up. It changed the angle of his hips in just the right way so that her body began to shudder, the pressure building, ready to burst.

'Elliot!'

He pumped into her, riding out her pleasure until it washed over her. She heard him groan, then quickly pull out of her. A guttural moan ripped from his throat just before she felt a splash of wetness on her belly. With a rough grunt, he rolled over and collapsed beside her.

Georgina closed her eyes, her muscles refusing to move. She felt the mattress rise as his weight lifted. A few moments later, it dipped, indicating he was back. She opened one eye.

He held a washcloth in his hand. 'I need to clean you up.'

She nodded, and he used the cloth to wipe the sticky substance from her belly. He moved lower and pressed the fabric gently between her legs. She stifled the urge to wince, though he must have seen the discomfort on her face as he quickly withdrew the cloth.

'I'll place it by the basin in case you need it.'

She watched his naked back as he walked over to the wash-stand, admiring how the muscles moved and the light from the fire played across his golden skin.

When he came back to the bed, she turned on her side to look out of the window. 'The snow hasn't relented,' she observed.

He sidled up behind her, then nuzzled at her neck as his arms wrapped tight around her. 'Sleep. There is nothing we can do now but wait until morning. We will set off as soon as possible.'

And so she closed her eyes and let sleep take over.

Chapter Eleven

17th December

Elliot wasn't sure how long he'd slept, but it couldn't have been more than an hour or two. He did not feel as refreshed as he did after a complete night's sleep and he was more tired than usual. Of course, that probably had something to do with the woman in his arms.

He did not allow himself any regrets. What was done was done. And if Georgina was truly set against marrying, then he did not feel guilty that he was robbing her future husband of her maidenhood. No, it was a gift that she had given freely, one that he would treasure.

Still he wanted her. His cock was now rock-hard and rubbed against the smooth flesh of her buttocks.

'Are you awake?' she asked sleepily.

'Yes. But you can keep sleeping.'

She rubbed her body against him. 'Elliot... I want...'

'Sweetheart.' He gently laid a hand on her hips. 'Stop. We cannot.'

'Why not?'

'You are still sore. I do not want to hurt you again.'

'You won't.'

'Yes, I will.' He sighed. 'But we can do other things that won't hurt you.'

She flipped around to face him. 'Other things?'

'Oh, yes.' Anticipation swirled in his gut. 'Would you like me to show you?'

'Yes, please.'

He pushed her down so she lay flat on her back. 'Just lie there…' He kissed her again on her swollen lips, then trailed his mouth lower, over her neck and breasts, stopping to kiss each nipple. Then he moved lower still, until he was between her lovely thighs.

'Elliot? Are you—? Oh!'

He buried his face into her mound, spreading her thighs so he could access her sweetness. He licked at her flesh, swirling his tongue, tasting her and licking at her. He traced his tongue up and down her seam, stopping at the top to lick at her bud, to tease her until her body was shaking with need. He lost himself between her thighs, forgetting everything outside this room.

His cock rubbed painfully against the rough sheets, so he reached down and circled his palm around the shaft. He continued to pleasure her with his tongue, thrusting into her with the tip until she was panting and moaning. When her body began to shudder with her climax he increased the pressure and speed of his hand. Pumping furiously, he let himself go, the shocks of pleasure from his orgasm nearly blinding him. His body sagged into the mattress, aching deliciously from the release.

'The snow has stopped.'

'What?' The after-effects of his orgasm made it difficult to think.

'The snow.' She nodded at the window. 'It's stopped.'

'Why—?' Oh. Anne-Marie. 'We must make haste.'

His body protested as he heaved himself off her, but as the cloud of lust left him his mind began to think rationally. Anne-Marie was still out there, with God knew who, doing God knew what, and they had to catch up to her.

Elliot retrieved his clothes, which were thankfully dry, and began to put them on.

'Do you need my help?' he asked as Georgina struggled with her dress.

'No.' But when she got it over her torso, she frowned.

'What's wrong?'

'It's unfair how women's clothes are so numerous and restrictive.' She glanced over at him. 'I never realised men wore so little compared to us. All you need are your undergarments, your shirt, trousers and coats.'

'You're not wearing undergarments.' The very thought of her naked underneath her dress made his cock twitch, but he ignored it. 'And you seem to be fine.'

Her mouth puckered. 'Without the proper undergarments, this dress hardly fits at all. See how the torso and hips are too small?'

All he could see was how her luscious curves strained against the fabric. The tops of her breasts nearly spilled over the neckline of her dress and her nipples poked through the fabric. The skirt, on the other hand, hugged those full, womanly hips that had cradled him last night.

'It's awful.'

He agreed. He wanted to peel it off and—

Damn it, he had to stop lusting after her and follow after Anne-Marie.

Once they'd finished dressing, he led her towards the door. 'I shall see to the carriage. Try and see if that damned innkeeper will make us something warm to drink, and perhaps give us a loaf of bread to take with us.'

'Of course.'

'Hopefully, Anne-Marie and her "friend" were also forced to stop during the blizzard and we can catch up to them.' He opened the door and gestured for her to leave first. 'We must find—'

'Anne-Marie!' Georgina exclaimed.

'Yes, we must find her.'

'No!' She grabbed him by the lapel and pulled him out of the room. 'Anne-Marie.' She gestured to her right, down the corridor.

'Yes, of course. I—' He stopped short, finally understanding her meaning.

Anne-Marie. His sister. Standing outside one of the doors down the corridor.

Her green eyes were wide, shock on her face.

'Anne-Marie.' He didn't dare move. She looked like a frightened deer, and he was afraid she would bolt at any moment. 'Are you—? *Oomph!*'

His sister hurled herself at him, and he was caught so off guard that he could only wrap his arms around her as her body began to shake.

'There, there...' he soothed. 'I'm here.' Great heaving sobs racked her shoulders, and he held on to her tighter.

Georgina nodded back to their room. 'Elliot, should we maybe...?'

Gently, he guided Anne-Marie backwards until they crossed the threshold. As Georgina closed the door behind them, he sat Anne-Marie down on the bed. Still, she clung to him, as if her life depended on it, and her tears soaked the shoulders of his shirt.

Rage began to boil in him as all the things that blackguard might have done to her began to fill his imagination. 'I'll kill him,' he whispered. 'Then chop him into pieces so no one will ever find him.'

Anne-Marie stiffened in his arms. 'Who?'

'Whoever did this to you.'

She raised her head. 'Did what to me?'

Now he was confused. 'Whoever seduced you and convinced you to elope to Scotland.'

'How did you—? Wait...seduced me?' Anne-Marie wiped the tears from her cheeks. 'What do you mean?' Glancing around, she cocked her head at Georgina. 'And what is Lady Georgina doing here?'

Georgina's face turned crimson, but she seemingly managed to compose herself as she sat down next to Anne-Marie.

'We came after you. Lily came to me and told me what had happened.'

'And what did she say?'

'That you'd left with a friend for Scotland.'

Anne-Marie let out what sounded like a half-hiccup, half laugh. 'I had. Lady Lavinia.'

'Lady Lavinia?' Elliot released her. 'What do you mean, Lady Lavinia?'

'It was her idea.'

Elliot raked a hand through his hair. 'I don't understand... You can't get married to her.'

Anne-Marie blew out a breath. 'I wasn't intending to. She is getting married—but to someone else.'

Georgina cleared her throat. 'Perhaps you should start from the beginning, dear girl.'

'Yes.'

Elliot crossed his arms over his chest. He definitely wanted to hear this.

'L-Lady Lavinia...she...' Anne-Marie swallowed hard. 'I thought she was my friend. She was so nice to me the entire time at Foxbury Hill. She...she let me complain about Elliot, and I told her how much I hated it here, and that you won't let me do anything fun.' Her lips pursed. 'Then she said that she was planning to run away, after the party. A friend was helping her and I could come along. We could stay with her friend and I could find a job and have Lily come join us.'

Georgina gasped. 'And then what happened?'

'I agreed, and she told me to be ready at one o'clock. Her friend came in a carriage.'

'And who is this "friend"?'

'I don't know him, but I think... I mean, at first he acted friendly to her. Then the snow storm came and we had to stop here. He rented two rooms, but instead of sharing one with Lady Lavinia, I ended up alone.'

Her lower lip trembled as hesitation crossed her face.

'It's all right, Anne-Marie.' Georgina placed a hand over hers. 'You can tell us. We won't be angry.'

'Th-this morning I caught them trying to leave without me. When I confronted her, Lady Lavinia called me a s-stupid girl. She said I was naive for believing she would take me with her to Gretna Green. And then they left.'

'They just left you here? Alone?'

'Y-Yes...' She sniffed. 'I was so scared. I just stayed in my room and...and then I heard your voice, Elliot.' She looked at him, her face so innocent and vulnerable. 'I've never been happier to see you.'

And he had never been more relieved in his entire life.

'I don't understand why she would do that,' Anne-Marie cried. 'She was so nice to me. Why would she just leave me here?'

Georgina murmured, 'Perhaps they meant to use you as a distraction.'

'How?' Anne-Marie asked.

'I think… I wonder if Lady Lavinia's lover is someone known to her family? Perhaps someone entirely unsuitable for her—which is why they had to resort to eloping. If she'd disappeared by herself, her parents would immediately have known it was this suitor and chased them all the way to Gretna Green—'

'Ah…' Elliot interrupted. 'But two missing girls would throw the household into chaos and confusion. And, knowing Anne-Marie, I would have suspected you two would attempt to return to London.'

'Or perhaps that we'd been abducted from our beds?' Anne-Marie offered.

'Either way, I would never have thought to follow you north to Scotland.'

Elliot had to admit it was a cunning plan. But he was just happy that Anne-Marie was safe. Still, even though there was no secret lover, something bad *might* have happened to his sister. His fists curled at his sides as he thought of the danger Lady Lavinia had put his sister in, leaving her here alone to fend for herself. The very thought of it enraged him.

'Elliot?' Georgina's soothing voice interrupted his thoughts. 'Why don't you get the horse ready and we can be on our way?'

'Right… Stay here.'

Rising to his feet, he marched out of the room and made his way to the stables. Knowing Anne-Marie was safe had made the tension from his body seep away. Of course now his thoughts were occupied with something else entirely.

Georgina.

They had to marry now—there was no question about it. For one thing, he no longer had any immediate prospect of his own, seeing as the one lady he had invested his time in had absconded to Gretna Green with her lover.

There was not much more time left as Christmas Day was only eight days away.

And, of course, there was the fact that he had ruined her.

Damn it all to hell.

'Morning, sir,' Willy the stable boy greeted him. 'What can I do fer ye?'

'Have our phaeton made ready at once.' He flipped a coin towards the boy and then left.

Heading back into the inn, he stopped at the bottom of the stairs to gather his thoughts. He would go up there and tell Georgina they had to get married. He should not have allowed her to come with him in the first place. Even if they hadn't slept together, someone would surely see them when they arrived back at Foxbury Hill. Harwicke would demand he marry her anyway, so he would at least gain some favour from the furious Duke by offering marriage himself first.

Yes, that was the only solution here.

Georgina would surely see reason in this matter.

Squaring his shoulders, he climbed up the rickety stairs and entered their room. Georgina was alone, however, as she sat by the fire, staring into the flames.

'Where is Anne-Marie?'

Startled, she swung her head back towards him. 'She went back to her room to gather her things.'

'Is she...all right?' he asked.

Standing up, she faced him. 'She is.'

He swallowed. 'Did...anything happen to her?'

'No, nothing bad.' She adjusted her cloak around her shoulders. 'I believe everything happened just as she said. She spent the night alone.'

He blew out a breath. 'Thank God.' He raked his fingers through his hair. 'I never suspected Lady Lavinia...'

God, if she wasn't a woman—

'Neither did I,' Georgina answered in a quiet voice. 'She seemed so nice. And so very interested in the girls too.'

Yes, and now he knew why.

'We must go back. The phaeton should be ready soon.'

'Yes, we must. And I have an idea.'

'An idea?'

'For how we can avoid a scandal.'

Ah, yes. This was the time to talk to her about marriage.

'About that—'

'You cannot afford a scandal, after all.' She wrung her hands together. 'There is still Miss Philipps.'

'Who?'

'Miss Penelope Philipps.'

'Yes, and what about her?'

'If it came out that you and I were…and Anne-Marie had been gone the entire night…there would be a scandal. Miss Philipps would never agree to marry you. Nor would any lady from the Ton.'

He could only stare at her, dumbfounded. She was thinking of *his* marriage prospects. And probably her precious orphanage too. How could he forget that was the reason she'd even deigned to help him in the first place?

'I have a plan.' Her delicate brows drew together in thought. 'It's quite early, and we should be able to return to Foxbury Hill in less than an hour. Everyone will still be asleep, and most of the staff won't be coming in until later as they have the morning off. When we arrive, instruct your coachman to get your carriage ready and keep Anne-Marie in it. Did you bring any other staff to Foxbury with you?'

'Just my valet,' he said. 'He should be waiting for me to ring for him as soon as I wake.'

'Leave a note for him and instruct him to tell Trevor that you and the girls were called away before dawn. Tell him if anyone asks, he must say he saw you off. He can pack up all your things and then he can ride home with our servants tomorrow.'

'And Lily?'

'She should still be in my room. I shall wake her and send her to you.'

'And you? What will you do?'

'I will sneak back into my room and go back to sleep,' she said. 'See? My plan makes perfect sense.'

'Yes, it appears that it does...'

And if they were to pull it off successfully, there would be no need to marry her.

'Elliot? Georgina?' Anne-Marie whispered as she poked her head through the door.

Georgina strode over to her and placed an arm around her. 'Feeling better, dear girl?'

She nodded and embraced her. 'Thank you.'

'I will settle our bill and see you out front.' Elliot told them. Without another word, he left the room.

After paying the practically extortionate bill Joseph Brown had handed him, Elliot retrieved the phaeton and drove it around to the front of the inn, where Georgina and Anne-Marie waited. It was a tight fit, but all three of them managed to squeeze themselves into the small carriage.

As he took the reins, he could not help but glance down. Beside him, Anne-Marie sat in the middle, her head on Georgina's shoulder as she smoothed a hand over his sister's head.

His heart lurched at the sight, and for the first time in his life he felt like a failure. This was what the girls needed—a feminine hand to guide them and a shoulder to cry on. That miserable shrew who had birthed them had never shown them any care or affection, and both his sisters were crying out for some tenderness from a mother figure.

His eyes were drawn towards Georgina's lovely face, and when those coppery brown eyes met his own, they seemed startled.

Tearing his gaze away, he snapped the reins.

Elliot drove as fast as the horse and the roads would allow them, and soon Foxbury Hill was within sight. He manoeuvred the phaeton back into the carriage house, then dropped down to untether the horse as Georgina and Anne-Marie alighted. He guided the horse back to the stables, then returned to the carriage house.

'Lady Georgina has returned to the house,' Anne-Marie informed him. 'She said I should stay here and that you would take care of everything.'

'Yes.'

So she'd left. Without even saying goodbye.

Perhaps it was better this way. All she'd wanted was one night with him. He had been a fool to think there could be anything more between them. Georgina should not have to be saddled with a husband like him, nor be responsible for the well-being of two young women—illegitimate at that.

No, she deserved someone better, who would not hurt her because of his demands that his sisters be embraced by society.

Besides, if she did marry him he would get all the benefits and she would receive nothing in return. He could not offer her the affection and love she deserved. He could not even celebrate the one time of the year that made her happy. The loss he had suffered on that day was something that had left an indelible mark on him. And he could not go through that again.

'Elliot, come here,' Ma had rasped. *'There is something I need you to do for me...'*

'What is it?' Elliot would have done anything for her.

'When your pa comes home...tell him I waited as long as I could.' Her eyes had gone bright, like a candle before it burned out. *'I love you, my Harold.'*

It was on that day Elliot had sworn he would never rely on anyone, and that he would use the only assets he had: himself and time. He'd plotted out his life for the next ten years, and the ten after that, growing wealthier than he'd ever imagined. And if he just followed his current ten-year plan, he would achieve the success he'd craved his entire life.

'Elliot...' Anne-Marie's voice cut into his thought. 'I'm so very sorry for all the trouble I've caused.' Tears once again welled in her eyes. 'I was so scared when I realised I was alone, and I thought—'

He embraced her again as she began to cry. 'Don't worry. It's all right. You know I wouldn't have stopped until I'd found you.'

She nodded.

For now, he would have to forget his own desires and steer himself back onto the path he'd set out to follow. There was no other way now—only forward.

Chapter Twelve

17th December,
First Christmas Day

Georgina heaved a sigh of relief as soon as she entered her room. Her heart had beat madly the entire time as she'd sneaked into the house, fearing she would be caught by a servant or—God forbid—one of the guests. But, just as she'd predicted, everyone was still abed, exhausted from the previous night's merriment, and she'd made it to her room undetected.

'Lady Georgina?' came Lily's voice from the bed. 'Is that you?'

'Yes, poppet.' She ran over to her. 'I'm here.'

She sat up and blinked at her with sleepy eyes. 'Did you find Anne-Marie?'

'We did. And thank you for coming to me last night and telling me about her.' She kissed the top of her head. 'Now, poppet, you must do something for me.'

'What is it?'

'You must keep this a secret between us.'

'Like when you and Miss Warren came to the house?'

'Exactly.' She smiled down at her. 'Elliot will give you an extra-special gift if you do.'

It seems she, too, was not beyond bribing children.

'What's that?'

'He'll tell you when you see him. Which reminds me—you must go to him now.' She tugged the child gently from the bed. 'Go straight to his rooms and wait for him.'

She let out a yawn. 'All right...'

After she'd led Lily out of her room, Georgina changed out of her cloak and dress, hid them under her bed, then changed back into her nightrail before slipping under the covers. As the rush of excitement left her body, and left alone with only her thoughts, she could not help but think of the events of the night before.

Oh, Lord, she had taken a lover.

Not just any lover.

Elliot.

And now she understood what all the fuss was about.

Her hand went to her neck, where the bristles from Elliot's cheek had left their brand. Actually, his whiskers had left marks all over her, even between her thighs, when he—

Heat rushed over her as she recalled the delightful things he'd done with his mouth that morning. Everything about it had been wonderful, and there had been nothing shameful about it. At least, she didn't feel any shame about the things they'd done. Elliot had been considerate and kind throughout, and the pleasure had been unlike anything she'd ever felt. More than that, the fact that she had given him the same kind of ecstasy made her feel empowered. Hearing his cries of pleasure, feeling the way he'd gripped her with those rough hands, as if he couldn't get enough...

She turned to her side, hugging a cool pillow to her heated body. Now she had felt passion and pleasure, and it would have to be enough to last her for the rest of her life. It couldn't happen again, and certainly she wouldn't seek Elliot out—not if he were to marry someone else.

The very thought of him making love to another woman sent a searing pain into her chest—an emotion she recognised as jealousy.

How awful it was.

Perhaps once he'd announced his engagement and the orphanage had been saved, she would be able to think of those pleasant memories without evoking that mad, searing emotion that burrowed into her. For now, she would have to put those memories aside before they drove her mad.

Georgina could have sworn she had only momentarily closed her eyes before opening them again. However, the chill in the air indicated that the heat in her room had dissipated and no one had come in to stoke the fire.

Groggily, she got up and rang for her maid.

After performing her morning ablutions and dressing in a brand-new blue silk day gown, she headed downstairs to the dining room. Her maid had informed her that it was already noon and lunch would soon be served.

Before she entered the dining room she took a deep breath and smoothed her hand down her skirts. Would the other guests suspect anything when they saw her? Would they know she had spent the night with a lover and she was no longer a virgin?

Just go in, she told herself. *You cannot stay out here for ever.*

Scrounging up her courage, she took one step inside the dining room—the very *empty* dining room.

'Trevor?' The room wasn't completely unoccupied. Her brother was at the head of the table, enjoying his morning tea.

'There you are, Georgina.' He put his teacup down, rose from his seat and walked over to her. 'Miss Warren said you were sleeping like the dead when she peeped into your room.'

'She—she did? When?'

'Oh, I don't know…an hour ago?'

Thank heavens.

Had the companion peeped in earlier in the morning, she would have discovered Lily there and Georgina gone.

'I was much too fatigued by yesterday's activities.'

Of course she didn't mention all the activities—including those that had made her muscles sore and that place between her thighs ache.

'Um…where is everyone?'

'You missed all the excitement this morning, I'm afraid. The Marquess of Arundel and the rest of his family had some sort of family emergency. I think a cousin died.'

'You think?'

'I could not elicit the exact story as it was pure chaos and the Marchioness seemed inconsolable...poor thing wouldn't stop bawling.' He tsked. 'They were half packed by the time I came downstairs, and the daughters had already left in the first carriage.'

Georgina harrumphed to herself. It seemed she was not the only one who had thought of the plan to leave before anyone noticed the disappearance of one girl.

'Oh, that's too bad. We must send our sympathies.' *Sympathies for having a foul and malicious daughter, anyway.* 'And the others?'

'Well, you know that Elliot had already planned to return to London today, so I assume they left at first light.'

'Er...of course.'

'And, seeing as Arundel and his family had left, Waldemere declared that he wished to support them in their time of need and followed them. The Viscount and his family have decided to leave for London as well, and are packing up as we speak. I think with the lack of eligible gentlemen they decided staying wasn't worth it. Miss Philipps looked quite disappointed when Elliot remained by Lady Lavinia's side for the entirety of last night.'

Well, perhaps she will be pleased when Elliot calls upon her after she returns to London.

'Ah, I see...'

'And as for our last remaining guest—I am afraid I have bad news.'

'Last guest?'

'Bellamy.'

'Oh. Of course.' She'd forgotten all about him. 'What's the bad news?'

'He's taken ill once more, and the doctor says it's much more serious this time. He's advised Bellamy to stay abed for a few days. So he'll remain here for now, and we may not see him before we leave for London tomorrow.'

'How...terrible.'

Georgina nearly fell to her knees in thanks to the heavens.

'So it's just us for today.' A bright smile spread across her brother's face. 'Happy First Christmas, Georgie.'

She gave him her cheek as he bent down to kiss it. 'Happy First Christmas, Trev.'

They spent their First Christmas as they usually did—next to a warm fire in the library. Trevor read quietly in a corner, while Georgina was tucked under a soft blanket, embroidering a cushion and drinking tea. They had the roast turkey feast Mrs Laramie had prepared, and instructed her to serve the second bird and the extra dishes she had prepared to the servants. There was still so much leftover food, the kitchen staff had to pack everything up and send it to some of their less fortunate neighbours in the village.

The day's activities and the chance to finally be free of the presence of guests had given Georgina a chance to feel energised. However, throughout the day her mind still wandered to Elliot. Try as she might, she could not stop herself from thinking about what had happened between them—but more than that, it gnawed at her that she didn't know what he was doing and how he was feeling right now.

He'd looked incredibly relieved when they'd found Anne-Marie, but had been quiet during the entire ride back to Foxbury Hill. Did he blame himself for her running away? Would he try to mend things with his sister? Was Anne-Marie still feeling the shock of being left behind in a strange place?

Perhaps she would never know the answers. She would have to resign herself to that.

18th December

The following day they left Foxbury Hill, as planned, and set off for London.

'Welcome back, Your Grace...my lady.' Dawson greeted them as soon as they crossed the threshold of Harwicke House.

'Thank you, Dawson.' Trevor handed him his hat. 'How is everything? Nothing exciting happening, I presume?'

The normally stoic butler's face turned ashen. 'I...uh...' He cleared his throat. 'Nothing at all, my lord.'

Georgina noticed Miss Warren had sent Dawson a pointed look, but said nothing.

'I'm exhausted,' Georgina said. 'I think I shall lie down for a nap.'

Heading upstairs to her rooms, she changed out of her travel clothes, freshened up after the journey, then lay in bed. She had barely settled when Miss Warren burst into her room.

'What—? Miss Warren, are you all right?'

Her companion's face was crimson, and her nostrils flared as her breaths came in short bursts. She held a newspaper in her hand and waved it around.

'Dawson has tried to hide this from your brother.'

'Hide what?'

'This morning's *London Daily Herald*.' Miss Warren dropped the paper on the bed. 'Read it.'

Picking up the paper, which appeared to have been opened to the society gossip column, Georgina began to read:

We are delighted to reward our most loyal readers with news that is exclusive only to our paper, but we believe will be the talk of the town by tomorrow.

We have it on great authority that a certain 'Lady G', whom we have not seen in society for nearly three years now, has not mysteriously disappeared. No, it seems that the lady in question has not hidden herself away in shame after six failed Seasons, but rather has been enjoying the rewards of what she may believe is anonymity after hiding from society.

What rewards? Well, it seems the reserved, shy violet we knew has blossomed into a rose—one in full bloom and open for pollination. 'Lady G', who is said to have been carrying on a flirtation with a certain 'Lord B', was discovered by a sharp-eyed witness leaving a coaching inn in the company of another man yesterday morning. This

*particular inn is said to be near this vixen's family estate,
well situated for a quick getaway.*

*Were the lovers off on an adventure or was this a one-
night tryst? We do not know, readers, but we will let you
decide.*

Georgina's stomach dropped and she felt the blood drain from
her face. 'I… There are no names…'

'Don't be daft, Lady Georgina,' Miss Warren snapped. 'Of
course there are no names. Otherwise the paper would face hun-
dreds of lawsuits a year. But they add enough detail for readers to figure out who it is. What other "Lady G" could they be
referring to with six failed Seasons, who hasn't been seen in
society in three years. And vixen—a female fox—is a clue to
*Fox*bury Hill.'

'This Lady G could be any number of women,' she retorted.
'There's…there's… Lady Grace Ashton.'

'Lady Grace is seventy-two years old. I very much doubt she'd
be conducting a tryst at a coaching inn.' Miss Warren covered
her face. 'This is my fault. I should have been there to keep an
eye on you. I knew I should not have taken the night off—'

'It's not your fault,' Georgina blurted out. 'Please.' She patted
her hand on top of the mattress. 'Have a seat and I will explain.'

Crossing her arms over her chest, Miss Warren sank down
at the foot of the bed. 'First tell me who is the man that article
is referring to? Is it Mr Smith?'

'H-How did you know?'

'I guessed as much.' Miss Warren sighed. 'I am not blind,
you know. I've seen the way he looks at you.'

'L-Looks at me?'

Her companion scowled. 'Never you mind. Now, please continue.'

'All right.'

And so Georgina told her everything that had happened—at
least the part about Anne-Marie running away and their finding her at the inn.

'So, you see, we weren't having a tryst of any sort at that inn.

And whoever saw us leave is lying—we weren't alone. Anne-Marie was clearly with us.'

Miss Warren's lips pressed together tight. 'It doesn't matter. You were still seen away from your home at an ungodly hour in the morning with a strange man and no chaperone in sight.' She sighed. 'But at least nothing happened between you and Mr Smith, did it?'

Georgina did not want to lie, but she couldn't bring herself to admit the truth either. However, her hesitation only confirmed her guilt.

'That vile blackguard!' Miss Warren shot to her feet, her hands curled into fists at her sides. 'How could he take advantage of an innocent girl? And one who was risking her reputation to save his sister at that!'

'Please, Miss Warren, calm down. It's not like that. And I am almost thirty years old—hardly a girl.'

'That's not the point.'

'Yes, it is. I asked him to make love to me.' Her cheeks burned, but she had to make Miss Warren understand. 'I just… I told him that I will never marry and so I wanted to…'

Her companion held up a hand. 'Please, spare me the details.'

Oh, thank heavens.

Georgina wasn't sure she'd survive the awkwardness of telling Miss Warren *everything*.

'But answer me honestly. Did he force you in any way? Coax you into doing things you did not want? Did he hurt you?'

'He didn't strike me, if that's what you're asking.' Elliot would never do that to any woman. She'd seen the care he displayed with his sisters. 'And, no, there was no force. If anything, I was the one who convinced him—'

'You may stop right there.'

'You think I am disgusting,' she accused. 'And that what I have done is shameful.'

That was what Great-Aunt Leticia would have thought if she'd been there last night. She had always called relations between a man and an unmarried woman wicked.

Miss Warren's expression fell. 'What? Oh, no.' Gently, she took Georgina's hand. 'Darling girl, I was just scared that he'd forced you into this.' She swallowed hard. 'Men are known to do that.'

He's not like other men, Georgina wanted to say.

'There was no force and it was my idea. We agreed it would only be that one time.'

'And what if you conceive?'

'I won't,' she said. 'He made sure of that.'

The relief on her companion's face was evident. 'Even so, your reputation is now in tatters. You will be a pariah by the end of the week.'

'So? It's not as if I'm searching for a husband. If anything, now I won't even have to worry about being invited to balls.'

Miss Warren clicked her tongue. 'Have you no sense? This doesn't just affect *you*. Think of your brother. The Duke will be affected by this, as will your family name. Do you think he will be able to find a wife of good quality with such a scandal staining the Abernathy name? He'll only be able to marry title-hunters. His children, too, will suffer. Many doors will be closed to them, thanks to your actions.'

Georgina wrung her hands in her lap. She hadn't thought of that. 'M-Maybe Trevor won't find out. It's just one newspaper...'

Miss Warren let out an indignant sound. 'I'm afraid once a rock starts rolling down a hill it cannot be stopped.'

19th December

And Georgina found out exactly what that meant the very next day, as her maid shook her awake. The maid told her that Trevor had ordered her to get Georgina up and dressed, and to tell her that she was to come to see him as soon as she was finished.

Sweat grew on her palms as she made her way downstairs, in her heart hoping against hope that this was not about the looming scandal.

Dread immediately filled her when she walked into his study and counted five open newspapers on his desk.

'Trev, I can explain—'

'Can you?' her brother thundered.

She flinched. In all her life, he'd never raised his voice at her.

'It was Elliot, wasn't it?'

Dropping down into the nearest chair, she nodded.

'Why?'

'I was trying to help him.'

She recounted the entire episode for him. When she'd finished, he did not seem convinced or mollified.

'Do not even try to lie to me and say that nothing happened,' Trevor said, not missing a beat.

How did he know?

As if answering her question, he said, 'I know you very well, Georgina. Your face gives you away. You'd be a very poor poker player.'

The glib joke gave her hope that he wasn't entirely furious with her. That he didn't hate her.

'I'm sorry for the trouble I—I've c-caused you. I just wanted to help.'

'I know, Georgie.' Circling his desk, he came to her and took her hands in his. 'But what are we to do now?'

She shrugged. 'Nothing. We don't have to do anything, nor dignify those gossip rags by making it appear that we care.'

'I do not care,' he said. 'But what am I to do with you? What if you are with child?'

'There's no possibility of that.'

His mouth twitched. 'If you are saying what I think you are saying, I'm sorry to inform you that is not a guaranteed method of preventing conception.'

'But we won't know for a while, will we? And by then he may be married to someone else.'

Jealousy once again reared its ugly head as she thought of Elliot with another woman.

'True. And of course we will find a way to deal with it. But there is something I would like to know.' He placed her hands back on her lap. 'Georgie, the reason I guessed that it was Elliot, and that the story was true, is because I could see the attraction between you. I saw it in him, especially, from the beginning. But I soon started to see the signs from you as well.'

'Y-You did?'

Oh, heavens, how mortifying.

'I warned him off at first, because I know… I know you aren't keen on marriage.'

'It's not that I'm not keen, Trev. No one has ever asked me or even courted me.'

'You truly think that is the reason?'

'I…' Her brother's words made her pause. 'What do you mean?'

'Ah, I will let you think on that. But tell me, if Smith wanted you, and you wanted him, why not agree to marry? Why this farce with finding him a bride? Did you think I would disapprove because he is not a peer? Do you not trust that I would consider your happiness above all?'

The hurt on his face plucked at her chest. 'Oh, no! Dear heavens, Trevor.' She stood up to embrace him. 'Of course I trust you and love you. You've been nothing but supportive and kind since…since…'

His arms came around her. 'Since Mama and Papa died.'

She did not want to think of that right now. 'He did ask me, Trev. To marry him.'

'And you said no? After what he did?'

'What *we* did,' she corrected. 'And, no. He asked me when we first met.'

His hands dropped down to his sides. 'Explain.'

She dropped back down to the chair. 'He said he would rescind the eviction notice on the orphanage if I married him. He wants a titled wife—not for him, but for his sisters. New York society shunned them, you see, which is why he brought them here. A wife with the right name and connections could open so many doors for Anne-Marie and Lily.'

'Ah, I see. And when we couldn't find a way to save St Agnes's, you offered your services as a procurer.'

'Matchmaker,' she corrected. 'And I truly did try to find him a bride in earnest. I didn't mean for…for all this to happen.'

'I know, Georgie. You were trying to help. You've always been kind-hearted.' Her brother tsked. 'But I'm afraid no good deed goes unpunished. And now you must bear the consequences.'

'And what are those consequences?'

'For now, there are two: weather the scandal or mitigate it with a quick engagement.'

The unease swirling inside her settled deep in her belly. 'I can't... I don't want to.'

'I won't force you, Georgie,' he said. 'Legally, I cannot. And you know that no matter what I will support you.'

'Then there is no need for all this fuss,' she said. 'It's not as if I'm some debutante on the marriage mart.'

'Yes, but there are other consequences.'

Oh, yes. Those that Miss Warren had mentioned. Trevor would never show it, but he would resent her once he decided to seek a bride, or when it was his children's turn to join society. Would she really have to choose between Anne-Marie and Lily and her future nieces and nephews?

'I must leave you for now, Georgie,' he said.

'Wh-where are you going?'

'To see Elliot. Since he has not come to see me, I assume he hasn't seen these newspapers yet and probably has no inkling of what has happened.'

Hope sparked in her. 'If that's the case then perhaps we do not have to tell him anything.'

'Of course we do. And also, do you not think it strange that his name isn't mentioned in any of the articles?'

'Is it not?'

'No. And I think he might be interested in finding out why.'

Georgina bit her lip. 'Maybe whoever saw us didn't know who he was.'

'Possible...but very improbable.' He kissed her temple. 'Now, stay here. Do not leave the house. I have told Dawson to turn away anyone who comes to the door.'

She remained in his study even after he'd left, stunned, her limbs refusing to move. How could this have gone so wrong? Who could possibly have seen them at the inn? No one who might know her or Elliot, that was for sure, based on the kind of clientele there.

Would Trevor force Elliot to marry her now?

A different sort of emotion coursed through her. Like when

she was having one of her spells, she felt like fleeing. Her stomach churned at the thought of marriage. To be with one person for ever, until they—

She shut down her mind, unwilling to venture further. Besides, what could she do now but wait?

Chapter Thirteen

19th December

'Mr Smith, there is someone here to see you.'

Elliot did not look up from the contracts he was reading at his desk. 'Do they have an appointment, Grant?'

'N-No, sir,' his assistant stammered.

'Then send them away.'

'Yes, Mr Smith.'

With an impatient grunt, Elliot turned his attention back to the contracts. Which was, frankly, a futile effort as he'd spent the last fifteen minutes trying to decipher the same sentence. The words individually made sense, and he could read them forwards and backwards. But his mind refused to make sense of them because it was currently preoccupied with one thing.

One person.

Georgina.

He closed his eyes, allowing himself to think of her. Just for this moment. Just for a minute. Which was a mistake, because once he began he could not stop thinking of her. Had he imagined it all? It seemed that way at times. As if she'd been a fevered dream. But the smell and taste and feel of her imprinted on his mind felt real, and no matter how much he told himself to forget her, he simply could not.

He'd questioned his every move and decision since leaving Northamptonshire. He should not have left Georgina. Should not have taken her with him to chase after Anne-Marie. Or even gone to Foxbury Hill in the first place. Perhaps he shouldn't have proposed to Georgina, or even bought that damned building.

This continued on and on, until his thoughts spiralled out of control and he had to shake himself to stop.

At the very least, his sisters were safe at home. And Anne-Marie didn't seem as angry as she usually was—at least she hadn't for the last two days. She was quiet, and there was no longer that simmering rage he'd used to feel from her.

'Mr Smith?'

'What is it now, Grant?' he asked, irritated.

'He—that is, His Lordship—insists on seeing you.'

His head snapped up. 'His Lordship?'

'Yes, sir. The Marquess of Arundel.'

Why the devil would he come here?

Elliot blew out a breath as he glanced back at the contracts. It was not as if he was getting any work done anyway. 'Send him in.'

He sympathised with the Marquess. After all, he too knew the panic and horror of having a girl under his care disappear in the middle of the night. Perhaps Arundel was here to ask for his assistance in locating Lavinia, or maybe even an insight into what she might have been thinking, running away. He wasn't sure if he had any advice for the Marquess, but he would do his best to help.

'The Marquess of Arundel,' Grant announced, and then stepped aside to let him through.

'Good morning, Mr Smith,' Arundel greeted him.

'Good morning. Please have a seat, my lord.'

Elliot observed the Marquess as he approached his desk. For a man whose daughter had eloped with a lover two days ago, he did not look distraught. In fact, if he hadn't known better, Elliot would have said he looked rather pleased with himself.

'What can I do for you, my lord?' he asked.

Arundel retrieved some newspapers he had tucked under his arm and dropped them on his desk. When the Marquess remained silent, Elliot picked them up and began to read.

At first he was confused as to why the Marquess had brought him these gossip columns. But then, as he read through the second one, it became apparent what—or who—they were about. They were dragging Georgina's name through the mud, calling her all sorts of names and making insinuations, all for the sake of selling papers.

Elliot gritted his teeth, trying to tamp down his anger. He would not show any emotion in front of the Marquess—at least not until he'd figured out why he was here.

'I assume you did not come here so that we might discuss the latest gossip, my lord?'

'You're welcome,' the Marquess said with a smug smile.

'I beg your pardon?'

'I said, "you're welcome."'

'For what?'

'For not having your name dragged into this scandal.'

It took a moment before the words sank in and Elliot comprehended him. 'You...you have spread these vicious rumours?' His hands curled into tight fists at his sides.

'You and I both know they aren't rumours.'

'And how would you know that?'

'I have my ways.' Arundel threaded his fingers together.

'You can leave, or you can tell me.'

The Marquess paused, planting his chin on his linked hands. 'I suppose you'll find out anyway... Lavinia saw you when she returned to the inn.'

That she-devil.

'Oh? Did your dearest daughter grow a conscience and decide to return for the innocent girl she dragged into this scheme of hers?'

The Marquess's face turned scarlet. 'Your sister is safe, as I heard it. No harm done. My daughter, on the other hand—'

'Oh, yes, please do enlighten me on the "harm" Lady Lavinia has suffered in all this.'

'Foolish girl,' he spat. 'I told her…warned her that fool was a worthless rake and fortune-hunter.'

'Who is he?'

'Some third son of a baronet—who cares who he is?' Arundel waved a hand dismissively. 'The bastard changed his mind about eloping with Lavinia once they were on the way. He turned the coach around and dropped her back at the inn—where they saw you and our dear "Lady G" as you were leaving. Thankfully, Lavinia found her way safely back to London the very same evening. I barely had time to write that anonymous letter to the *Herald* so they could print it in the following day's morning edition.'

'And now you are here to ask for my forgiveness, are you?'

He might have considered forgiving Lady Lavinia had she come back because she'd felt remorse about leaving Anne-Marie alone.

'Forgiveness?' The Marquess laughed. 'How about you show me some gratitude for excluding your name from the story?'

That fact still boggled him. 'And why would you do that?'

'Why do you think?'

'Stop wasting my time and tell me.'

The Marquess tsked. 'You know, Mr Smith, when we played that game of chess I could read your every move even before you made it. Don't feel bad—it's an amateur mistake. Masters of the game plan everything from the beginning—which pieces to move where, and which to sacrifice in order to win. And when things do not go their way, they adapt.'

'I'm tiring of this,' Elliot said. 'Get to the point.'

'When my foolish daughter came crawling back, after she'd been spurned by her lover, she told us of an unfortunate consequence of her actions.'

'Ah, she is—?'

'Yes.'

'Congratulations on being a grandfather.'

'And that is why I left your name out of the papers.'

'What—?' Elliot snapped his mouth shut as he grasped the true reason the Marquess was here. 'So you wish me to marry your daughter and claim the child as my own.'

'You are a very rich man.' A gleam appeared in the Marquess's eyes. 'Rich enough that I can overlook your low birth. You see, as a man with only daughters I have to be smart about how to use them to my advantage. After all, you can only play the cards life has dealt you.'

Something about the comment struck Elliot straight in the gut.

'Genevieve is already going to marry a duke—Waldemere is all but in the bag. Now I need to secure my financial future and collect another powerful son-in-law.'

'Collect? Like your chess trophies?'

He laughed. 'Yes. But after Lavinia's actions… That damned fool would have cost me both you *and* Waldemere if she had gone through with it. The Duke, of course, would never marry Genevieve if Lavinia's failed elopement and her current condition became public. But, as I said, when an opponent makes a move you did not anticipate, you must adapt.'

Elliot remained silent as he gathered his thoughts and herded his emotions.

'So, Mr Smith,' the Marquess said, smiling craftily. 'Shall I accept your proposal on Lavinia's behalf? Or perhaps tomorrow's edition of the *London Daily Herald* will publish the name of "Lady G's" lover: "Mr S", the man with the famed golden touch? I daresay if they do you might very well find it difficult to procure a wife from Mayfair or Belgravia…unless perhaps you scour the kitchens for a scullery maid.'

Elliot calmly placed his palms on top of his desk and stood up. 'Allow me to clarify the situation at hand. You thought you would sacrifice a pawn—Lady Georgina—not only to shield your daughter from scandal, but also to blackmail me into marrying her?'

The Marquess did not reply, though Elliot saw the slightest tic at the corner of his mouth. Unfortunately for the Marquess, while Elliot may not be a good chess player, he knew people and could see when they were caught off guard. And from the look on the Marquess's face, he was very much caught off guard by Elliot's cool demeanour.

'Well, my lord?'

'Y-You owe m-me for not exposing your name. Think of your sisters—'

'Enough!' He slammed his fists on the table. 'You are a vile man, with an equally abhorrent daughter who put my sister in danger.' Fury rushed into his veins. 'I will never marry Lavinia, and I don't care what you say. But if I hear anyone even whisper my name or those of my sisters in connection with any scandal, I will place your head on a spike and parade it up and down Upper Brook Street.'

The Marquess spluttered. 'You dare threaten *me*? A *marquess*?'

'You doubt me? Or perhaps you would prefer ruin and shame?'

As he did with all his business prospects, he had already had his private investigator compile a file on Arundel.

'My lord, it isn't quite true that you only have daughters, is it? Hmm?' He tapped a finger on his chin. 'What about those strapping young boys hidden away in that cottage in Devonshire? They live with their mother, right? A "Mrs" Vanessa Howard.'

Arundel's face drained of colour. 'H-How did you—?'

'I, too, have my ways.' He folded his arms over his chest. 'Will you see yourself out? Or should I have you tossed out?'

The Marquess rose from the chair. 'You think you could do better than my daughter?' He harrumphed. 'I am a marquess. A common tradesman like you will never be as good as me, even if you marry the Queen!'

Elliot didn't flinch when the door slammed.

Good riddance.

Still shaking with anger, he unclenched his fists and his jaw. Though not a man of violence, Elliot had never been more tempted to hurt another person than he had this day. He imagined putting his hands around Arundel's skinny neck would feel immensely enjoyable.

But he had more important things to think about.

Such as Georgina and her ruined reputation—which was, of course, his fault.

He had to go to her…make sure she was all right. He would also go to Harwicke and explain everything, and then ask for his permission to marry Georgina. It was the only way to save her from complete ruin.

'Grant!' He shouted. 'My coat and hat—now!'

He marched towards the door and yanked it open to step out-side—and promptly collided with the person who was about to step in.

'Oomph!'

Elliot stepped back, steadying himself, as the Duke of Har-wicke bounced back from their crash. There was something comical about the surprised expression on the Duke's face, and Elliot nearly laughed—except the Duke's superior reflexes had him springing forward, his fist slamming straight into Elliot's cheek.

Elliot's head snapped back as pain exploded in his face. For a man who had likely never worked at any manual job, Harwicke had a mean right hook. Covering his face with his hands, he peered at Harwicke through his fingers. The Duke was hunched over, his breathing shallow, face scrunched up.

If that punch hadn't told him clearly enough, it was evident that Harwicke had already read the papers and guessed Elliot was the unknown lover.

'I had to do it.' Harwicke shook his hand and winced. It gave Elliot a modicum of comfort, knowing he had caused the Duke some pain.

'I wouldn't have expected anything less.'

He soothed his cheek with his finger. That would definitely bruise, but at least nothing was broken.

'You do not deny anything that has been said in the papers?'

Elliot stepped aside to let him in. 'Let's speak in private.'

He had hoped to see Georgina, but he supposed he should deal with the Duke first.

'Listen here, Smith—'

'I will marry her,' he interrupted.

'You damned *better* marry her. But it's not me you have to convince.'

'Convince? What are you talking about? She must marry me. She has no choice.'

'She will always have a choice as long as I am around,' Trevor said firmly. 'I won't force her, if that's what you are thinking. Besides, why do you care? Your name was never mentioned.'

'And I know exactly why. You should have seat, Harwicke. We need to talk.'

'All right.' The Duke glanced around the office. 'Damn it, don't you have anything to drink around here?'

'I have tea, coffee and water,' Elliot offered.

'No whisky or cognac?'

His eyes slid upwards. 'One moment.'

'Where are you going?'

'Someone in this damned office must have a bottle of something stronger.' Elliot poked his head out through the door. 'Grant! Find me something to drink.'

'Drink?' Grant scratched his head. 'Like…tea?'

'No, a *drink*. Pilfer it from one of those damned accountants who think they can hide their midday tipples from me.'

'Yes, sir!'

Elliot returned to his desk and sat down, indicating that Harwicke do the same. Moments later Grant reappeared, a flask in his hand.

'Give it to His Grace.'

Harwicke accepted it, opened the top and took a sip, wincing as he swallowed. 'Now, what do you know of those damned rags knowing about you and Georgina?'

'It was Arundel.'

And Elliot explained the entire situation to Harwicke, including how the Marquess had tried to blackmail him into claiming Lady Lavinia's child as his own.

'Bastard!' Harwicke spat. 'If only I'd arrived a minute sooner, I would have smashed his nose in.'

'Lucky for me, then…' Elliot groaned as the pain in his cheek throbbed.

'I still would have punched you in any case.' The Duke scowled. 'I warned you to stay away from her.'

What could he say to the man? He would not tell him that his sister had requested to be deflowered. In any case, he was the more experienced of the two of them, so he should have known better.

'I have no defence to that, but I seek to make it right and re-store her honour.'

'I have told you that you will have to convince her to marry you.'

'She still does not want to marry me? After all this?'

Elliot had to admit that stung something fierce.

The Duke scowled. 'She does not want to marry at all—never had any interest in it.'

'Because of her spells?'

'You know about those?' Harwicke appeared taken aback.

'I've seen it happen and she has told me. She doesn't think she'd make a good society wife for me because she can't stand being in crowds and entertaining people.'

'Yes, but I think there may be more.'

Elliot leaned forward. 'More?'

'I suspect, anyway…' Harwicke shook his head. 'We lost our parents at a very young age, you see. She was only fourteen. They were a love match, and we had grown up with love and affection…' He cleared his throat. 'I think losing them not only destroyed her confidence, but her belief in love.'

Elliot could understand that feeling. He knew love never lasted.

'You must find a way to convince her,' said the Duke.

'I don't know how you think I can do that.'

Georgina had made herself very clear about not wanting mar-riage to anyone, and he would never do anything that might hurt her.

'It's not that I don't want to marry her…'

'Ah, so that's not in question, then?'

'Of course not. Who wouldn't want to marry Georgina? She's kind, thoughtful—and my sisters already love her. Lily won't stop talking about her.'

The Duke seemed pleased by what he'd said. 'I see.'

'But if she's damned set on not marrying, then I can't change her mind.' He paused. 'And I don't think I can give her what she wants.'

'Do not be too sure of that. What if she is with child?'

'I made sure—'

'You and I both know that method is not always effective.'

Damn. The Duke was right. He was a damned idiot for sleeping with her.

'What would you do if she still refused me then?' Elliot asked.

Still, the thought of her pregnant… Christ, she would look so lovely…her belly large and full.

Nine months from now he could be holding his son or his daughter.

His legacy.

'I will do whatever I need to to help her,' said Harwicke. 'Send her away to the Continent to have the child and find a couple to adopt it.'

The very thought of his own flesh and blood being raised by strangers sent Elliot into a rage.

'Are you finished with that?' He nodded at the flask.

'I was after the first sip. *Blech.*'

'Good. We're leaving for Harwicke House—now.'

Being required to stay inside and not answer any calls was usually not difficult for Georgina. In fact, if Trevor ordered her never to leave the house again, she would normally be in heaven.

But today Harwicke House, the sitting room, and the very chair she sat upon seemed like a prison.

Glancing up from her book, she saw that Trevor had now been gone for at least an hour.

'Watching the clock will not make it go faster,' Miss Warren remarked.

'I know. I just…' She'd been on tenterhooks since Trevor had left. 'I don't even know why I'm so anxious.'

Placing her book down, she stood up and began to pace across the carpet.

'It's not as if I can do anything.'

Elliot would not agree to marry her—not when he wanted a wife who could bring his sisters into society. And she certainly wouldn't marry him.

'You do realise that if certain consequences arise nine months from now, you will have to marry?'

Her hand immediately went to her belly, then quickly dropped.

'No, it won't happen.' She continued before Miss Warren could protest. 'And if it did then…then I will go to the Continent and have my child there.'

Of course with the news of her indiscretion all over London, she doubted that her sudden disappearance would go unnoticed.

'Georgina, I'm back.'

She started at the sound of Trevor's voice. 'What did you—?' She froze on the spot.

Trevor was, indeed, back—but he was not alone. Elliot stood beside him.

A jolt of shock coursed through her as his jade-green gaze collided with hers. 'Good morning, Lady Georgina,' he greeted her. 'Your Grace, may I speak to your sister alone?'

'Trev, no—'

'Of course. Miss Warren? If you please?'

'Is that wise, Your Grace?' her companion asked.

Trevor's jaw hardened. 'Miss Warren, do not make me ask you twice.'

'Yes, Your Grace.' She shot Georgina a knowing look, but turned and followed Trevor out through the door.

An awkward silence hung between them until he finally spoke. 'It was Lady Lavinia.'

'I beg your pardon?'

What was he talking about?

'She was the one who saw us at the inn. You and me.'

'She—she saw us? What was she doing there? I thought she was on her way to Scotland with her lover.'

'It's a long story.' He made his way to the settee. 'Why don't you sit down and I'll tell it to you?'

Curious—and confused at the same time—she did as he asked.

Elliot sat down beside her and began to explain what had happened from the beginning and including Arundel's visit.

'And so I told the Marquess to leave.'

Georgina could only stare at him as her mind processed the events he had recounted. 'I can't believe she did that…and he tried to blackmail you.' Lady Lavinia truly was vicious, and it seemed she had inherited it from her scheming father. 'I'm sorry.'

'It's quite all right. He'll be dealt with.'

The coldness in his eyes made her shiver.

'But you see, now we must marry.'

She shot up and away from him as if she'd sat on a pin. 'There is no need for us to marry.'

'There is every need for us to marry,' he replied. 'Your reputation is ruined.'

'But yours is not.' If there was one thing she was grateful for in this situation it was that. 'Miss Philipps—'

'To hell with Miss Philipps!' He stood up. 'I don't want to marry her. I want to marry you.'

'Why? I would be the worst choice.'

'That's not true.'

'It is,' she insisted. 'Anyone else would be better than me, and—'

'You need a husband.'

'I beg your pardon?' She had to stop herself from chuckling. 'I do not.'

'Yes, you do. It's the only way to save your reputation. The scandal will not just affect you, but your entire family. Think of your brother.'

'He is a duke— What are you doing?' Elliot had reached out towards her. 'El—' The touch of his palm on her cheek made her gasp. 'Elliot…'

Heavens, his rough hands felt wonderful on her skin. Her knees shook and she had to brace herself on the closest thing she could reach—which was his chest.

'Weren't we good together, Georgina?'

He leaned down, bringing his mouth so close to her ear that she could feel his breath.

'It could be like that every night.'

'Huh…?'

What was he saying? She couldn't quite think…not when his lips were inches from her.

'I would make a good husband to you.'

Frustration grew in her, from wanting to feel his mouth on her bare skin, but he didn't move an inch.

'Elliot…this isn't fair.'

'What's not fair? I am merely reminding you of what was, and telling you what could be.'

She sighed.

'How about I show you how serious I am?' He drew away from her.

'How?'

Jade-green eyes stared down at her. 'I will rescind the eviction notice.'

'You mean, if I marry you?'

'Even if you do not. I had already decided to anyway…before the scandal broke.'

'Truly? When?'

'The night at the inn—before you offered yourself to me.'

She searched his face, looking for deceit or any indication that he was lying. But she found none.

'You would do that?'

'Yes. For you.'

Her heart leapt into her throat, and she could only stare at him,

'There is no downside to your marrying me,' he said. 'Only positives. Your reputation will be saved. And if we were to have a child…'

She couldn't argue with him. He was right.

'But there will be a downside for you.' Whirling away from him, she wrapped her arms around herself and began to pace. 'I know… I know why you want to marry a lady. It's not to raise your own standing, is it? It's for your sisters. You want someone who can help them gain a foothold in society once they are out. I'm sorry, Elliot, but I cannot be that wife. I cannot be the kind of wife who can guide your sisters so they will make successful matches. I am a liability, not an asset. I cannot be what you need me to be.'

'You're speaking of your spells?'

'Y-Yes.'

'They do not matter—not any more.'

'Why not?'

'Because of something Arundel told me.'

'Arundel…?'

He raked his fingers through his hair. 'They are illegitimate.'

That made her halt her pacing. 'What?'

'Anne-Marie and Lily. They are illegitimate. My father never married their mother. She was a dockside whore who dropped them off at my doorstep one night and then disappeared.'

Those poor girls.

She pressed a hand to her chest. 'Why are you telling me this?'

'Because you should know. Those girls… I just want what's best for both of them. And for them to have a fighting chance in this world.' When his voice hitched, he paused to clear his throat. 'In this world, we can only play the cards we are dealt. I want to give them the best chance, since life has not been kind to them. Arundel said something similar about his daughters, and it got me thinking… I do not want to be like him.'

'You are nothing like that scoundrel.' She clicked her tongue. 'Life may not have been kind to them, but it has dealt them *you*, Elliot.' Her soft hand covered his. 'You give yourself too little credit. Even if you weren't wealthy, they would still have a fighting chance as long as you are on their side. They do not need anyone else.'

And certainly not me.

'And I don't need a wife to open the Ton's doors for them. Anne-Marie and Lily will choose to be whatever they want to be.'

'Exactly. You don't need a wife.'

'No, but I *want* one. I want you.'

Catching her hands, he lifted them to his face and kissed her palms. The shock of the contact made her shiver.

'If you marry me, you will never have to attend any ball, tea party, opera—'

'I actually like the opera.'

He smiled against her hand. 'Noted. But if you were my wife, you would never have to take calls from anyone you don't like, or throw dinner parties. You don't even have to lift a finger. You can stay at home embroidering, drinking tea, or doing whatever the hell you want. You'll never be troubled with your spells again.'

She sighed, feeling her defences slowly breaking down. 'This truly isn't fair.'

'What's not fair? Me offering you the world and everything you want? All I ask is that you take my name and have my children.'

Her breath hitched at the idea of having children.

And with Elliot.

'So, what do you say, Georgina?' He got down on one knee. 'Will you marry me?'

She was about to answer, then paused. 'Wait… Before I answer that, there is something I must know.'

'What is it, sweetheart?'

'Did you kiss Lady Lavinia under the mistletoe?'

'You want me to answer that *now*?' He gestured to himself. 'As I am on my knees, asking you to be my wife?'

'Yes.'

He blew out a breath. 'No, I did not. When Lady Arundel pointed out that we were under it, I simply pretended not to hear her and moved away. There. Does that make you happy?'

'Immensely.' She gazed into his jade-green eyes, revelling in them. 'Then, yes, I will marry you.'

Elliot got up and wrapped his arms around her, then melded his mouth to hers. Her heart nearly burst from her chest and she sighed into his mouth. She'd missed this…missed the press of his body along hers and the scent of his cologne. How different they were—small and large, soft and hard. Her hands moved up, so she could rake her fingers into the soft hair at his nape, but disappointment filled her when he pulled away, ending the kiss early.

'Elliot?'

'We cannot…not here.' Stepping back, he smoothed his hands down his front. 'Come, let's tell your brother the happy news.'

'I—yes, of course.'

Georgina knew she should be happy. St Agnes's was saved, and she would have everything she could ever want.

But a part of her still felt unsure about her decision. It felt like…falling. As if the world had been pulled out from under her, sending her stomach swooping. She couldn't understand it. She was about to get all she wanted.

But then, it could all be taken away from her.

'So she said yes?' Trevor said, as soon as Elliot opened the door.

'She did indeed.'

Her brother looked relieved. 'I'm glad.' He placed a hand on her arm and kissed her on the cheek. 'I am very happy for you, Georgie.'

'Thank you, Trev.'

'Congratulations, Lady Georgina.'

Miss Warren, who had apparently waited outside the door with her brother, smiled. Her companion seemed genuinely pleased.

'Thank you, Miss Warren.'

'We still have to deal with the ramifications of the scandal,' she replied.

'I have a solution to that,' Elliot announced.

Trevor cocked his head. 'You do?'

'Yes. Arundel gave me the idea, actually. See, I happen to know the editors of three out of the five newspapers that printed that gossip.'

'What do you mean "know" them?'

'I was looking to buy them. But I never make a purchase without doing my due diligence, so I have a private investigator who specialises in finding information for me. No one can keep anything hidden for long. Each of those owners has something to hide, and I'm sure they could be persuaded to come to our side.'

'B-But what about the freedom of the press?' Georgina said. 'You can't possibly blackmail them into printing something that isn't true.'

'I won't. I'm going to ask them to print a different piece of gossip—saying that you were with me that night. They will run the story we give them, which is that we were in love, but afraid that your brother and society wouldn't approve, so we tried to escape. Then we changed our minds and came back, and I did the right thing by seeking your brother's approval. After our version of the story has spread we will announce our engagement, and everyone will assume that was the truth all along.'

'That sounds plausible,' Miss Warren agreed.

'Quite brilliant, actually,' Trevor said. 'Not quite the truth, but not a complete lie.'

'Those three newspapers will print nothing but flattering pieces about our love story,' Elliot said. 'And the others will follow suit. The Ton will eat up the gossip and forget about our one indiscretion.'

'Because they will be too busy sneering down their noses at your supposed "love match",' Miss Warren said. 'Society will think it unfashionable. They would have respected you more if it was simply an arrangement.'

'Georgina?' Elliot asked. 'What do you think?'

All eyes turned to her as she considered the plan. 'I don't particularly care what the Ton think of us.'

Elliot beamed at her.

'So, shall we celebrate?' Trevor asked. 'Champagne, maybe? Or coffee for you, Elliot?'

'I don't mind a sip of champagne—especially on the right occasion.' Elliot smiled at her.

And although Georgina smiled back at him, that swooping feeling in her belly returned...as if she truly was falling into something unknown.

Chapter Fourteen

20th December

'Are you certain the Serpentine is not yet frozen solid enough for skating?' Lily asked.

'I'm afraid so, poppet,' Georgina said.

'How do you know?'

'Because usually, once the ice is ready, the chestnut sellers will set up over there.' She pointed to the banks of the pond.

'And how do the chestnut sellers know?'

Georgina laughed. 'How many questions do you ask a day?'

'Much more than this,' Anne-Marie interjected.

'Enough questions,' Elliot declared. When Lily made a face, he added, 'For at least the next ten minutes, so we can enjoy our walk in the park.'

Anne-Marie shivered. 'It's lovely out here, but I don't understand why we are walking in Hyde Park in the middle of a cold day. Why, there isn't anyone else here but us.'

Elliot caught Georgina's gaze. 'Exactly.'

When they'd been deciding where to go to break the news of their engagement, Georgina had suggested they take the girls shopping on Bond Street, or perhaps somewhere lively like Leicester Square. But Elliot knew those places would set off one of her spells, which was unacceptable, so they'd settled on a walk through Hyde Park.

She had seemed nervous about telling the girls, because she didn't know how they would react to her marrying Elliot. He, of course, had assured her many times that the girls would be ecstatic, but had relented and promised not to tell them until the following day. Once the girls were informed today, they would set their plan into motion. The three newspapers Elliot had 'convinced' to print their version of the rumours would publish their columns tomorrow. Then, he and Georgina would announce their engagement the day after.

Elliot hadn't expected that he would feel nervous about telling the girls. It was a strange emotion…to be so unsure of himself and a decision he'd made. While he had assured Georgina that Anne-Marie and Lily would be happy at the news, there was a small kernel of doubt in him. Despite all the years he'd spent with his sisters, it occurred to him that he didn't truly know them. What if they didn't want him to marry at all? Or—worse—what if they didn't care?

His hand came up to the breast pocket of his coat, feeling the small, rectangular object hidden away inside. Last night when he'd come home, he hadn't been able to sleep, so he'd thought a book might help him relax. Everything inside the house he'd purchased had been included with the sale, even the library books. So he had browsed the shelves, looking for something to read. As he'd approached one of the shelves, the very first book that had caught his eye had been a small, leather-bound book at the very end. The spine was thin, which meant it wouldn't be too long or boring, which would be perfect. When he had peered closer and read the title, he'd nearly laughed aloud: *A Christmas Carol* by Charles Dickens.

He had picked up the book and, sure enough, he had finished it in one sitting. And now he had some *thoughts*. Perhaps he would have time to share them later with Georgina—for he wanted to see her reaction when he told her he had read it—but for now, the tome was a comforting weight against his breast.

'What are we doing here, anyway?' Anne-Marie said, interrupting his thoughts. 'Not that I mind seeing you again, Lady Georgina.' She smiled warmly at her, then mouthed a *Thank you*.

'Yes, about that...' Elliot stopped in the middle of a path and turned to them. 'Girls, there is something I must—we must tell you.' Sidling over to Georgina, he slid his hand into hers. 'I have proposed to Lady Georgina and she has accepted.'

The two girls' eyes widened and their mouths formed into perfect Os.

'Yay!' Lily let out a scream that rang through the empty park, then threw herself at Georgina. 'You're to be our sister!'

'Elliot... I...' Anne-Marie's gaze bounced from Georgina's to his. 'This is probably the only good decision you've ever made.' She embraced Georgina. 'I'm so happy.'

A lump formed in his throat as he saw Georgina's eyes water as she attempted to compose herself and received more hugs from the girls.

'When will you get married?' Anne-Marie grabbed at her hand excitedly. 'And will we go back to New York afterwards?'

'What colour dress will I wear?' Lily tugged at her skirt. 'Can I wear pink, please? Can I hold your flowers?'

'I—I don't know,' she stammered. 'I mean, we haven't discussed anything about the wedding or what will happen after it yet.'

'We can discuss that another time.'

It was true they hadn't ironed out the details, but he remembered that Georgina had said that their engagement period would be for at least a year.

Damned if he was going to wait that long to have her again.

Clearing his throat, he said, 'It's getting much colder than I anticipated. How about we go to the new shop that has just opened by my office? I've heard they specialise in serving hot chocolate.'

Both girls heartily agreed, though he could see Georgina hesitate, perhaps thinking of the crowds that would surely be around the busy commercial district.

So he added, 'Maybe we don't have to go there. We can go home.'

'But I want hot chocolate,' Lily said.

Georgina tucked back a stray hair from Lily's cheek. 'Then you shall have it, poppet.'

'Are you sure, Georgina?'

'Of course. Do not worry about me, Elliot,' she assured him. 'I will be fine.'

They all returned to their respective carriages and drove towards the chocolate shop. When they reached it, it was already crowded, as Elliot had predicted. He could see the people inside standing shoulder to shoulder as they queued up to the counter, bumping into others who were already squeezed in at the tables, trying to enjoy their drinks.

'Oh, my, I don't think we will even be able to get in.' The apprehension on Georgina's face was already apparent. 'Maybe we should just…go home.'

Elliot thought for a moment. 'Actually, I think we may be able to persuade the proprietor to allow us to bring the chocolate to my office. Wouldn't that be better instead?'

'But I want to see the inside. I'm small and won't take up too much space,' Lily whined. 'They have all sorts of chocolates on display too. Can we look at the chocolates? Please, Lady Georgina?'

Georgina stammered. 'I…er…'

'Maybe Miss Warren can accompany you?' Elliot suggested. 'I think Lady Georgina may have been chilled by our walk. Why don't I take her to my office—it's only two doors down—and the three of you can look at the chocolates? Maybe even purchase a few treats for us? Just tell the owner to send the bill to my office.'

Lily waved her hands in excitement. 'Oh, Miss Warren, could you, please?'

'I suppose that should be all right.' The companion sent Elliot a look, as if sending him a warning. 'We will not be too long.'

'Of course. You know the way to the office, correct? Then I shall see you there.'

Taking Georgina's hand, he tucked it into his arm and began to walk towards his building. He ignored the gapes and stares from his employees, concentrating only on Georgina. While she didn't seem to be having one of her spells, she certainly looked as if she was close.

'How are you feeling?' he asked when they were alone in his office.

She took a big gulp of air. 'I am fine now. Thank you.' She clicked her tongue. 'I really thought… I thought I would be all right. Lily wanted so badly to…and I couldn't…'

'Don't be upset, sweetheart. And do not worry about pleasing Lily if it is a detriment to you.'

'She's a child and I am the adult.'

'Exactly.' Drawing her into his arms, he kissed her temple. 'She's a child—you do not have to cater to her whims. I am not marrying you because I want you to spoil them. I meant it when I said that, as my wife, you will never be forced to do anything that would cause you pain.'

'Elliot…' She breathed a sigh, then lifted her face up to meet his, coppery eyes all large and luminous. 'I…'

Something shifted in the air, and her eyes darkened. Before he knew it, she'd lunged at him, pressing her mouth to his.

Though initially surprised, he quickly recovered and returned her ardent kisses. The hunger that had been stalking at the edges of his mind pounced, taking over his body and demanding to be sated. Wrapping his arms around her, he pressed her close, revelling in the delicious curves and dips of her body, which would soon be his.

She deepened the kiss, her pert little tongue demanding entrance to his. He obliged, opening his mouth so their tongues could dance together. His body was on fire and his cock twitched, hardening as her hips brushed against him.

'Georgina…' he murmured between kisses. 'I want you.'

'Me too,' she confessed. 'I haven't stopped thinking about that night.'

'I wish we had time.' His hand reached up to cup her breast through the layers of her clothing. 'I want to make slow love to you again.'

'We have some time.'

Wait… Was she suggesting…? 'Are you sure? I can't be slow. Or gentle.'

'I don't need slow or gentle,' she urged. 'Just you.'

Christ.

He backed her up until they reached his desk, which thankfully was clear of any papers or other items. Lifting her up, he placed her on top. 'You must be quiet. Can you do that?'

Coppery eyes wide, she nodded.

Spreading her legs, he lifted her skirts as high up as he could and reached between them. He found the seams of her drawers then pushed his fingers between them. She was damp, but not quite ready for him yet. Finding that nub at the crest of her womanhood, he gave it soft, gentle strokes. When she began to moan and undulate her hips, he increased the pressure and rhythm, bringing her to a quick orgasm that left her shuddering in his arms.

'Elliot,' she moaned. 'Please, I need you.'

He did not need any further instruction or invitation, and he unbuttoned his falls and grabbed his already hard cock. Manoeuvring himself between her legs, he pressed the tip at her entrance, then slowly began to push into her.

Georgina threw her head back, then moaned. 'Yes…please. It doesn't hurt at all. Oh!'

He thrust all the way inside her. 'You feel incredible, Georgina.'

Her arms tightened around him. 'Make me feel good again, Elliot.'

Gritting his teeth, he reached under her and cupped her bottom, then began to thrust into her. She let out a soft cry, then pressed her mouth to his shoulder to stop herself from making any more noise.

Elliot drove into her like a madman, as if his life depended on it. He did not want to be interrupted, so he had to quickly bring her to another orgasm. Pushing harder, he changed the angle of his hips. He must have done something right, because she was panting and biting at his shoulder. Soon she was shaking once more, and her body squeezed him, milking him, so that it took all his might not to spill into her right then and there.

He tried to withdraw. 'We must stop now… I can't…'

'No.' When he made a motion to withdraw she grabbed at his shoulders. 'Not again. Just…don't leave me.'

'Georgina, we're not married yet. I must.'

'No! Please. Stay.'

Unable to deny her anything, he continued to thrust into her, her tightness sending shocks of pleasure down his spine. He put his hand over her mouth to muffle her cries and she closed her eyes tight as her body clasped around him. In that moment his entire world was Georgina, and she was the world.

'Christ, Georgina…you're so…' He groaned as she pulsed around him.

At that second, he realised that he would do anything to keep her happy, to make sure she never suffered a day in her life. He would crawl over broken glass if that was what she wanted. Because…

'I lo—'

'Elliot!'

Georgina buried her face in his neck as her orgasm made her body shake violently, and her tightness clasping around him triggered his own. He almost went blind as pleasure burst from the knot at the base of his back, spreading over his body.

When his breathing had returned to normal and his muscles had relaxed, he withdrew from her. His heart still pounded in his chest, though, at what he'd so nearly said to her.

'Elliot?' she panted. 'What's wrong?'

He cleared his mind of all those thoughts.

'Nothing. Nothing at all.' Using the sleeve of his shirt, he wiped the sweat from his brow. 'Miss Warren and the girls could arrive at any moment.'

'Of course.'

She hopped down from the table and smoothed her skirts down, then proceeded to fix her coiffure. Elliot too, righted himself and his clothes.

'Do you think anyone will know…what we did here?'

Georgina's face was flushed, and her skin had taken on the most beautiful glow. Miss Warren would definitely figure out that something had happened.

'No, sweetheart.'

'Thank heavens.' She blew out a breath. 'I'm sorry… I don't know what got—'

'Shh…' He silenced her with a quick kiss. 'There is nothing wrong with what we did.'

'But it's broad daylight and we are in your office.'

'And? If you think our activities will be limited to the bedroom at night, then perhaps you should find a different husband.'

Her cheeks turned the most delightful shade of crimson.

'I may not be able to wait a whole year to marry you,' he said. 'I will convince Harwicke to let us marry next month.'

'Next *month*?'

'Yes. Don't you want to be married soon?'

Besides, with what happened just now, they might not have a choice.

'I do, but… I was thinking a Christmas wedding would be lovely.'

Irritation pricked him at the mention of that damned word. 'I—'

'Elliot we're here!' Lily announced as she burst through the door, waving the packages she had in her hands.

'Girls!' Georgina hurried over to them. 'What did you buy?'

'About half the shop,' Miss Warren said wryly. 'Apologies, Mr Smith. I wasn't sure if it was appropriate for me to chastise them for buying so much.'

'Not at all,' he said. 'Do not worry. I don't think they could buy enough chocolate to bankrupt me.'

'How was the shop?' Georgina asked.

'Wonderful! They had all sorts of chocolates, truffles and…'

Georgina listened patiently as Lily recounted her time at the chocolate shop, with Anne-Marie interrupting every now and then with anecdotes of her own.

For a moment, doubt entered his mind. In the throes of passion, he had nearly said the words he'd sworn he would never utter to a woman. He'd felt as if the words had been stuck in his throat, waiting for the right moment to be uttered. He had guarded himself well, though, until his own pleasure had nearly had him undone.

He could never say those words.

Love.

No, their marriage would be one of mutual respect, admiration and lust for each other. Harwicke had said that Georgina no longer believed in love. And he knew all too well the pitfalls of love, as he'd learned from watching his mother die while she called for the man she loved.

You're doing the right thing, he told himself.

The girls clearly loved Georgina already, and she them. They would grow under her care and example, and perhaps Anne-Marie's rebellious, churlish nature would be quelled. He, too, would have everything he wanted, including the fulfilment of his latest ten-year plan. And in a few short years, Georgina would bear him a passel of children, so that his legacy would live on.

That was all that mattered, and he would make damned sure nothing would stop him from marrying Georgina.

Georgina, Miss Warren and the girls stayed for another hour, but then unfortunately, they had to leave as Grant came and announced that his next appointment was in fifteen minutes. Georgina said something about taking the girls with her to visit St Agnes's the following day as they were leaving, which he agreed to.

After seeing them off, Elliot returned to his office to await his next meeting.

'Mr Charles Garret Brimsley III,' Grant announced. 'Of Brimsley & Company.'

A young fair-haired man who was perhaps a few years younger than him entered, dressed fashionably in what Elliot guessed was an ensemble from one of Savile Row's finest tailors.

'Elliot Smith,' he greeted him, and offered his hand. 'Nice to meet you, Mr Brimsley.'

The man took the hand he offered. 'Thank you for seeing me, Mr Smith.'

'Ah, you're American too,' Elliot deduced from his nasal accent.

'Chicago,' Brimsley said.

'Nice to see another American on these shores.' He gestured for Charles to sit on the chair across from him.

'Indeed... I've only been here three months, and I'm starting to get tired of these stiff Londoners.' He laughed, his voice booming over the room.

'Yes, I know, they can be tiring. But London is a place of opportunities.'

'Indeed—which is why I'm here. I'm hoping to establish an office here. We specialise in real estate and railroad.'

'I see...'

A bit too late for that.

Unfortunately for Brimsley and his company, the English railway boom had gone bust a few years ago. The market had become much too saturated and shares in railroads had lost their value. Only the large companies were now building lines, and although Elliot predicted a small surge in interest in the railway once more in a year or two, it would likely not be as big as it had been in the beginning. If Brimsley was only entering the business now, then it was much too late.

Of course, Elliot kept that assessment to himself.

'So, what can I do for you, Mr Brimsley?'

'Well...uh...' Brimsley scratched at his collar. 'I find myself in a bit of a bind, Mr Smith.'

'What bind?'

'You see, my father and grandfather sent me to London so that I may establish an office here.'

'A clever move on their part.' Elliot knew he would have established his own office here in half the time it had taken him if he'd had someone he could trust, like a son or grandson. 'How fortunate they are to have you.'

'Indeed. They are very shrewd. My grandfather, Charles Senior, made his fortune trading fur in the Great Lakes region.'

'Congratulations to him.' Elliot tapped his foot impatiently. 'So, how can I get you out of your "bind"?'

'Yes, about that... I was supposed to acquire a building—one they had already pre-approved for me to purchase. I told them I had made an offer and they wired the money to me.'

'So, should I give you congratulations on your business deal as well?'

'No. I mean... You see...' He cleared his throat and shifted in his seat. 'Unfortunately, I found myself distracted.' He laughed. 'You understand, right? London's offerings are so much more sophisticated than those back in America. Anyway, in my distraction, someone else bought the building we intended to turn into our headquarters. That building is number fifty-five Boyle Street.'

Ah. It finally made sense why Brimsley was here.

Elliot shook his head mentally, feeling pity for Charles the II for having raised such a wastrel of a son. Of course, it did not surprise him at all. Charles the III likely had had everything handed to him on a silver platter, and prioritised his own gratification over work. He couldn't even be trusted to purchase one building—one whose owners had been eager to sell.

'I'm told you are the new owner of number fifty-five Boyle Street.'

'I am,' said Elliot. 'And what can I do for you?'

'I would like to purchase it. Please.'

Brimsley flashed him a charming smile, which Elliot guessed he used to disarm people, so he could get what he wanted. Unfortunately for him, Elliot did not care for smiles from empty-headed fools.

'It is not for sale.'

Besides, he was about to send word to the matron of St Agnes's about the cancellation of the eviction notice.

'Anything is for sale,' said Brimsley. 'Name your price.'

What a complete idiot Brimsley was. No businessman began a negotiation with 'name your price'. It was a guaranteed way to lose.

'Why did you not purchase it right away if you received the funds and arrived three months ago?'

He himself had only discovered the building was for sale at the end of November.

'I told you… I was distracted,' he replied, impatient.

'By what?'

'Does it matter?' he snarled. 'You have something I want and I have the money to purchase it. We were given a valuation of the building, and I'm willing to pay you ten percent over the asking price.' He retrieved a folder from his document case and handed it to Elliot. 'Here.'

Curious, he took the folder, opened it and began to read. It took all his might not to burst out laughing. Elliot had bought it for about half the market price because Atkinson had been so eager to be rid of this father's assets and to pay off his debts. That meant Brimsley was actually offering him *sixty* percent over what he'd paid.

'That's the starting figure for our negotiations, of course,' he said. 'How much do you want?'

Elliot closed the folder. 'You seem terribly eager. Why not purchase another building in the same area? You'll get far more value if you find a location a few streets down.'

'No, I must have this one.' Retrieving a handkerchief from his pocket, he wiped the perspiration from his brow. 'It must be number fifty-five Boyle Street.'

'But why—?' Realisation struck him. 'You've already told your father and grandfather that you have bought it, haven't you?'

His eyes bulged, then he blew out a resigned breath. 'Yes. And I have also…spent the money they sent me.'

Elliot clicked his tongue.

What a damned fool.

'Where will you get your funds to purchase the building, then?'

'I—I have my sources.'

'A bank?'

Brimsley's silence told him no. There were, of course, many enterprising businessmen everywhere, who loaned money at usurious rates.

Elliot leaned back in his chair and rested his chin on his clasped fingers. On one hand, he would love to teach this idiot a lesson and allow him to face the consequences of his actions. But on the other, making over fifty percent profit was much too tempting. Besides, Brimsley would find his comeuppance one way or another—his 'sources' were likely charging so much interest that the repayments would soar so high he would not be able to pay them. And when that happened, they would extract payment through whatever means necessary.

Of course there was the question of the orphanage—but that could easily be solved. With the money from the sale Elliot could purchase a bigger and even better home for the orphans—perhaps somewhere outside London, so Georgina would not have to deal with the crowds here.

Yes, that was what he would do. And as a wedding present to Georgina, he would not charge a single penny in rent.

'All right, Mr Brimsley, we have a deal.' He held out his hand.

'I… Of course.' He took the offered hand and shook it.

Elliot did not miss the way Brimsley's nose had turned up at the thought of shaking his hand; he was not the least bit surprised. Coming from two generations of wealth, the Brimsleys were likely the kind of family who would have shut Elliot and his sisters out of society. The very idea of taking his money was an added sweetener to this already favourable deal.

'I'll have my solicitors draw up the papers,' Elliot said. 'You can look them over and sign them, and we can finish the deal by tomorrow.'

'By the way, there is one clause I must add.'

'And what is that.'

'I must take ownership now.'

'Right now? Are you mad?'

'My father and grandfather arrive in six days. I must take ownership before then.'

'But the contracts and the funds will take a few days,' Elliot reasoned. 'And then we must wait for the deed to be transferred.'

'I don't care. I must show them a complete, functioning business office in six days.' He eyed Elliot, his nose turning up once again. 'Make it happen or the deal is off.'

Elliot considered his options. As long as there were no changes to the contracts they could be finalised in a day or two. Since they had already settled on the amount, the banks could begin to release the funds as well.

There was, of course, the question of the orphans at St Agnes's…

He snorted. How difficult could it be to move two dozen girls?

He could hire people to help them, and he could afford to buy them brand-new furniture, bedding, even personal belongings. They could leave number fifty-five Boyle Street today, with only the clothes on their backs, and Elliot would ensure they would want for nothing.

'All right, Brimsley. As long as you don't cry foul on the terms we have already discussed, you can take possession in… five days.'

Yes, from his estimates, that should be enough time.

'Wonderful.' The relief on the other man's face was palpable, as if he'd just got a stay of execution. 'Just send everything to my house. I shall leave the address with your assistant.'

'A pleasure doing business with you, Mr Brimsley.'

'Likewise.'

He escorted Brimsley out of his office and as soon as he was gone turned to his assistant. 'Send word to Mr Morgan. I need him here, now.'

'Yes, sir.'

Elliot returned to his desk, then sank back into his chair, thoroughly pleased with himself.

What a glorious way to end the year.

When he'd moved to London six months ago and nothing had gone his way—the Ton refusing him entry into their hallowed halls, Anne-Marie continuously being difficult—he'd thought he would never progress on achieving the goals of his ten-year plan. Now, he had a wonderful fiancée, his sisters were happy, and he had just closed the easiest and most profitable deal of his life.

Perhaps, just this once, he would believe in luck.

Chapter Fifteen

21st December

'We cannot thank you enough, my lady,' Mrs Jameson said. 'It is because of you the girls will be able to stay in their home.'

Before they'd left his office yesterday, Georgina had asked Elliot if she could take the girls to the orphanage for a visit, and he had agreed. She'd decided that although she could not show them the more crowded and exciting sights of London, she would do her best to take them to places where she was comfortable. After all these months in England the girls had never gone farther than Hyde Park, where they would go for their daily morning walks with their governess or tutor.

So this morning she and Miss Warren had picked them up in her carriage. However, she had not arrived empty-handed. She'd had the footmen pack up one of the smaller Christmas trees at Harwicke House and brought it with her, along with several gifts for the girls and Elliot. The girls had shrieked in excitement as soon as they'd seen it. Georgina instructed their butler and housekeeper on how to put it up, and then she and the girls had driven to Boyle Street together.

'There is no need to thank me, Mrs Jameson.' Georgina patted her hand. 'First of all, it was a misunderstanding. Mr Smith had no idea he had bought an orphanage! Can you imagine his shock upon his discovery?'

That wasn't a complete lie, of course, as Elliot had said he wasn't aware there were people living in the building he had bought. However, she didn't want anyone to think he was the kind of man who would deliberately toss orphans out on the street during Christmas.

'He must have been beside himself…' Mrs Jameson tutted.

Thinking of his initial reaction—which had been to try to bribe her into marriage—Georgina nearly choked, trying not to laugh. 'That's one way to put it… But all is right in the world again. We needn't worry—at least not for the foreseeable future.'

'Still, I am glad you could make Mr Smith see the error of his ways. Why, it must be the spirit of Christmas working its magic.'

'Er…indeed.'

'Lady Georgina!' Lily waved at her from the top of the stairs, where she stood with five or six girls around her age, including Charlotte and Eliza.

'Look at me!'

'Look at what—? Lily, no!'

The little girl had climbed on the banister and was sliding all the way down, much to the delight of the other girls.

'Hooray, Lily!' Charlotte cried.

'So brave!' Eliza screamed.

Georgina's heart leapt into her throat as she sprang towards the stairs, catching Lily just in time before she reached the bottom. Setting her down, she said, 'Lilian Smith, don't you ever scare me like that again.'

'But it was fun!' Her jade-green eyes sparkled. 'None of my governesses ever allowed me to do this.'

'Oh, dear…is she all right?' Mrs Jameson asked. 'And did you say her name was Smith?'

'Er…yes.' She had introduced Lily and Anne-Marie to Mrs Jameson earlier, but had not mentioned the connection to St Agnes's new landlord.

'As in Mr Elliot Smith?' Mrs Jameson said.

'Elliot is my brother,' Lily stated. 'And he's marrying Lady Georgina. She's going to be my sister.'

That was another thing she hadn't mentioned to Mrs Jameson, as she'd been afraid the matron would make the connection between the cancellation of the eviction notice and her engagement.

'I see.' A knowing smile spread across the matron's face. 'Perhaps it's not the Christmas spirit that has inspired Mr Smith's generosity. But rather *love*?'

Georgina's heart seized at the word. 'Er...um...' It was difficult to breathe, as if her corset was laced too tight. 'Excuse me. I must...head to the necessary.'

She turned on her heel and hurried away from them, down the long narrow corridor that led to a sitting room at the end. Once she was inside, she closed the door and leaned against it, closing her eyes as she took deep, calming breaths.

Perhaps she was having one of her spells. But no, it couldn't be. She never had them here at St Agnes's. The anxiousness felt similar, but worse in some ways, as if she wanted to burst out of her own skin.

Could it be what Mrs Jameson had said?

It was a preposterous notion. The love match was a story they'd concocted to save her reputation. It was no more real than...than the St Nicholas that Lily had spoken of, who gave away toys to children.

No, Elliot couldn't possibly love her.

Her breathing returned to normal, and with a determined shrug of her shoulders she marched out. When she reached the main hall, Mrs Jameson was nowhere to be found.

'Girls, where did Mrs Jameson go?'

'Someone knocked on the door,' Eliza said. 'And she went to answer it.'

'I see.' Georgina headed towards the front door, arriving just in time to see the matron close it. 'Apologies for running off. I was— Mrs Jameson? Is something the matter?'

Mrs Jameson was shaking her head, her face utterly distraught.

Concerned, she hurried over to the matron's side. 'Who was at the door? Did they upset you?'

'Mr Morgan.' The matron lifted her head to meet Georgina's eyes. 'Mr Smith's man of business.'

'What did he want?'

'H-He…' She swallowed. 'He came to reiterate the terms of the eviction.'

'What?' Georgina asked, incredulous. 'There must be some mistake.'

'I—I'm afraid not, my lady.' She handed her a piece of paper. 'We must vacate in four days' time.'

'Four days—on Christmas Day?'

Snatching the paper from her, she read it, her heart sinking with every word.

No, it couldn't be true. There had to be some mistake.

Perhaps Elliot had forgotten to tell his man of business that he was rescinding the eviction. Whatever the reason, she would get to the bottom of this.

'I shall speak to Mr Smith and clear up this misunderstanding.' Hopefully she sounded cheerful enough that the matron would not worry. 'Could you let Miss Warren know I have had to leave for a short while?' Last time she'd seen her companion, she and Anne-Marie had been on a tour upstairs. 'I will be back soon.'

'Certainly, my lady.'

Georgina's stomach was tied up in knots for the entire carriage ride to Elliot's office. She could not believe he would go back on his word, despite the evidence written in his own hand. The letter was dated today, which meant he had given the order to send it sometime between yesterday and this morning.

Her worry shifted into anger when she realised the suspicious timing of the eviction. The gossip columns were set to print the story of their supposed love match today, which would pave the way for the engagement announcement tomorrow.

Indignation rose in her. Did he think he could betray her now that it was impossible to break their engagement without ruining her reputation?

By the time she had alighted from her carriage in front of his office building she was brimming with rage. She ignored Mr Grant's greeting and burst into Elliot's office.

'Georgina?' He looked up from the papers he was signing. 'Sweetheart, what are you—?'

'Do not "sweetheart" me.' Marching over to the side of his desk, she tossed the eviction notice in front of him and crossed her arms over her chest. 'Tell me this is a mistake.'

A twinge plucked at her chest. *Lord, please let it be a mistake.*

He picked up the eviction notice and scanned through it. 'Where did you get this?'

'I was at the orphanage, with the girls, when Mr Morgan came to deliver it.'

'You weren't supposed to see this,' he said, his voice calm.

'Ah, so it is true?' Fury swirled inside her. 'You're breaking your promise to me now because it's much too late to stop the newspapers and I have no choice but to marry you.'

He sprang to his feet. 'Too late? What in God's name are you talking about?'

'Oh, you very well know what I'm talking about,' she shot back. 'The gossip columns about our lo—our postponed elopement will come out today and we are announcing the engagement tomorrow. Now that it's all done, you have decided to proceed with the eviction because you have already got what you wanted!'

His expression fell. 'No, that's not it. That's not it at all.'

'Is that so? This eviction is a joke, then? A mistake? You're not really tossing over two dozen orphaned girls into the street?'

'I—' He snapped his mouth shut. 'It is not a mistake.'

The confirmation of his actions made her heart sink and turned her stomach to ice. 'H-How could you?' Her throat felt raw...as if she'd swallowed nails.

'Morgan should not have come... He must not have known you were going to be there. I wanted to tell you...' He raked his fingers through his hair. 'Someone has made me an offer on the building—a very good one—but they asked that the premises be vacated quickly.'

'By Christmas.'

'What?'

'Christmas Day,' she reiterated. 'That's when the girls have to leave.'

Frowning, he glanced at the calendar. 'I had no idea...'

'Of course you didn't,' she spat. 'Why would you?'

He harrumphed. 'If you'd just let me finish—'

'Go ahead. I'm not stopping you.'

'As I said, I'm selling the building for an enormous profit. With the money I'm making on the sale I've arranged to purchase a house in Camden. Twenty-two rooms, two gardens, and a stable with two carriages and horses. The owners have accepted my offer and the girls can move in on the twenty-fifth.' His shoulders sank. 'Did you really think I was so heartless as to leave them homeless, knowing how much they mean to you?'

'I—' Her throat tightened and she stiffened under his scrutinising gaze. 'Y-You still cannot ask them to leave on Christmas Day. Go away from the only home they've known. It's cruel.'

He huffed. 'What does it matter what day they move? They're children—it's not as if they'll know the difference. It's just another day.'

'Just another—' she spluttered, brimming with indignation. 'You really are a Scrooge. You planned this eviction and this move so you don't have to celebrate Christmas, I bet.'

Anger rippled along her spine, and the dam that had held her emotions broke.

'Is this what it's going to be like, Elliot? For the rest of our lives will you find ways to completely avoid Christmas? Will you hide away in your office every December the twenty-fifth, while the girls and I—and our children—celebrate Christmas on our own?'

'Now, wait a damned minute here.' He took a step towards her, towering over her. 'How in God's name did we even arrive at this conversation? What does Christmas have to do with anything?'

'I just don't understand, Elliot. Why don't you celebrate Christmas? You act as if it were the worst thing in the world.'

Her questions were met with stone-cold silence, but she continued.

'Anne-Marie and Lily have noticed. You provide the girls with every material thing they want, but not what they need—you to understand them and listen to them. To treat them as something more than an extension of yourself or a way to right the wrongs that fate has set upon you. Why won't you open yourself up?'

'That's rich, coming from you,' he sneered.

'I beg your pardon?' she asked, taken aback.

'You come in here, accusing me of these terrible things without even asking me for an explanation.' Bitterness sharpened his voice as he continued. 'Why do you assume the worst after everything that's happened between us? Have I not proved myself worthy of you?'

A slash of guilt struck her in the chest. 'Elliot—'

'And now what? You want to end the engagement? You're walking away from me because you cannot get your way? Can there be no discussion, no compromise?'

'I didn't—'

'Or did you just want a reason not to marry me? What are you truly scared of, Georgina?'

'Wh-what do you mean?'

Her back hit something solid—the wall behind her. When had he backed her into a corner? She'd been so blind with rage she hadn't even noticed.

'Why have you been hiding yourself away all these years? Why haven't *you* opened yourself up to the possibility that you could find someone to share your life with?'

Anxiety built in her chest, making it difficult to breathe. 'I… I told you…my spells… I'm not making them up.'

'I know that. But at some point perhaps you've begun to use them to hide behind the fact that you're afraid.'

'Afraid of what?'

His eyes burned with an emotion that stole her breath.

'Of meeting someone who loves you deeply and passionately with all his heart. Someone who would do anything for you and give you the world.'

'I… I…'

The anxiety erupted into full-blown panic and Georgina felt the walls and Elliot closing in on her. So she did the only thing she could—she fled.

Ducking away from Elliot, she raced out of his office, nearly tripping as she took the stairs all the way to the ground floor. Her carriage was waiting outside, and she didn't even bother to wait for the footman to open the door as she grabbed the handle herself and hurried inside.

Tears burned at her throat and she clawed at her chest, wanting to rip off her clothes so she could breathe.

'Lady Georgina?' came the voice of the footman. 'Where would you like to go?'

'Home,' she called out. 'Take me home.'

The moment the carriage lurched forward Georgina burst into tears.

Heavens, this was a mess.

She buried her face in her hands. Was he right? Had she come here accusing him and thinking badly of him because she wanted a reason not to marry him? Her spells felt so real to her, and there were truly times when she physically could not breathe. But perhaps…perhaps they were rooted in something else. A fear of some kind.

'We've arrived, my lady.'

Using the sleeves of her dress, she wiped her face, and then she composed herself, took a deep breath and stepped out of the carriage. 'Could you please go back to St Agnes's and fetch Miss Warren a-and the girls?'

'Of course, my lady.'

Nodding her thanks, she dashed into the house, hoping to reach her room before anyone saw her.

Unfortunately for her, she ran smack into the one person she didn't want to see right now.

'Georgie?' Trevor exclaimed, grabbing her arms to steady her. 'Have you been crying? What's wrong?'

'I—n-nothing,' she stammered.

'It's not nothing.' His voice was soothing. 'Tell me. I'm your brother.'

She promptly burst into tears. 'Oh, Trev…'

Georgina wasn't quite sure what happened, but somehow she started babbling about the eviction and Elliot and their broken engagement. At some point Trevor gently guided her into the parlour, closed the door and led her to the settee.

'I've made a mess of things,' she said, blowing into the handkerchief he offered. 'I was wrong, wasn't I? Not to trust him?' She sighed. 'I don't even know why.'

Trevor's gaze pinned her to the spot. 'Are you sure you don't know why?'

'I swear, I don't.'

He placed an arm around her and she laid her head on his chest. 'Georgie…you were so young when we lost them.'

'Who?'

'Mama and Papa.'

The heart stopped. 'Trev, I don't want to talk—'

'But perhaps we should. The days and months after they died I was too busy with the estate and all the arrangements. I never had the time to talk with you and ensure you were all right.'

'You were busy with far more important things. I was—I *am* fine. But why are you bringing this up now?'

'Why do you think? Georgie, have you ever thought that perhaps…perhaps you shy away from others? From forming attachments because you are afraid? Afraid of the pain of losing someone you love?'

She shook her head. 'N-No, that's not true. My spells—'

'Is it not true?' He kissed the top of her head. 'Have a think. And do not despair. I do not think Elliot will allow you to break the engagement that easily.'

Oh, heavens, she had just run out on him. 'I'm not so sure…'

'Do not discount yourself. I believe he will come to you.'

She sat there, staring at the wall, for what seemed like a lifetime after Trevor left. When she finally shook herself out of her trance, her mind began to whirl with possibilities? Was Trevor correct? Was she hiding herself because she didn't want to be hurt by love?

And what was she to do now?

Chapter Sixteen

24th December

Whenever Elliot faced a problem he could not overcome, he did the one thing that he did know how to do—he worked. He worked on the issue until it was solved, never relenting or giving up. Of course, the current problem he faced could not be solved, even with all the skills he'd learned over the years. So, without any obvious solution, he decided just to *work*.

And that was what he'd been doing for the past two days. He was at the office from sunrise all the way to midnight, going home only to refresh himself and change his clothes. The exhaustion allowed him to sleep peacefully for a few hours, then he awoke and returned to the office once more. Keeping himself busy was the only way he could stop himself from going mad.

I shouldn't have told her those things.

He should never have accused her of not trusting him or claimed her spells were a manifestation of her fears.

And he certainly should never have confessed his love for her.

While he hadn't actually said the words, he'd all but admitted it, and it had sent her running from him.

'Mr Smith, will that be all?'

'What?' Bleary-eyed, he looked up at Grant, who stood in front of his desk. 'Will what be all?'

'Uh…for today, sir? It's five o'clock.'

'Is it?'

Grant hesitated, as if Elliot would deny his claim. 'Y-Yes…'

'I see. Go home, then, and have a good evening.'

'Thank you, sir. And…uh… Happy Christmas Eve…'

What?

Before he could say another word, Grant hurried out.

Blinking away the blurriness from his vision, Elliot looked at the calendar. It was, indeed, the twenty-fourth of December.

Grunting, he turned back to his papers and continued to work.

25th December

There was an unfamiliar ache in Elliot's neck when he woke. When he opened his eyes it was light outside, and he was sitting in his chair, face resting on his desk.

He had fallen asleep at the office.

Rising to his feet, Elliot stretched his arms over his head. Perhaps it was time to go home. The banks and other businesses were closed anyway, and his deal with Brimsley had been signed and stamped, with the money now sitting in the ES Smith Consolidated Trust's bank accounts. And as far as he knew the Camden house was now in his name, and Morgan had hired people to help the occupants of number fifty-five Boyle Street pack up their things so they could move.

His stomach growled unhappily. Usually when he was in the middle of business negotiations the drive to succeed made him forget all his needs, including sustenance. But now his body clamoured for food…perhaps some coddled eggs, toast and a big pile of bacon.

His stomach clenched and his mouth watered at the thought.

Mind made up, he retrieved his coat and hat and sent for his carriage.

As soon as he arrived at the house, he asked Fletcher, 'Is breakfast ready?'

'Sir?' The surprise on the butler's face was apparent. 'You're having breakfast now?'

'Yes,' he snapped. 'Now, call the girls so that we may eat. I'm famished.'

It had been two—no, three days now since he had seen Anne-Marie and Lily, so surely they would be glad he was home, and maybe even overjoyed that he was actually here for Christmas.

'I shall wait for them in the parlour.'

After leaving his hat and coat with Fletcher, Elliot headed to the room on his right. To his surprise, there was a Christmas tree there, with presents underneath. Upon closer inspection he saw the loopy, feminine handwriting on the tags, indicating who they were from. He picked up one gift with his name on it—a small, rectangular object wrapped in pretty green paper. He turned over the tag to read it.

To Elliot,
May you honour Christmas in your heart and keep it all
year. Live in the past, present and future.
Yours always,
Georgina

A dull ache formed in his chest. How he missed her so. Perhaps it was time he went to her, so they could make things right between them. Surely whatever had broken between them could be mended?

'Sir!' came Fletcher's urgent call.

He whirled around to face the butler. 'What is it?'

'S-Sir.' Fletcher's face paled. 'Miss Anne-Marie and Miss Lily…they are gone.'

'What?' He had to stop himself from leaping at the butler and grabbing him by the lapels. 'What do you mean, gone?'

'They are not in their rooms.'

Alarm bells rang in his head, but he remained cool. 'Then check the other rooms,' he said, irritated. 'Check all the rooms.'

'Yes, sir.'

Minutes ticked by as he waited for Fletcher to return. Perhaps the girls were playing a joke on them. Or they were hiding in a closet or in the attic. Hell, there were rooms inside this house he'd never been in—perhaps they'd found some hidden chamber and were accidentally locked inside.

'Where are they?' he barked at Fletcher as soon as he returned.

'They are not in any of the rooms in the house, sir.'

'Are you certain?'

'Yes, sir. The maids are checking every room and closet once more, but they said they hadn't seen the young misses since last night.'

'How could this have happened?' Worry, fear and dread swirled in his chest. 'Where could they have gone?'

'I don't know, sir. According to Mrs Murphy, after the girls opened presents at midnight, they went up to Miss Anne-Marie's rooms and haven't come out since.'

They must have sneaked out.

'Have my carriage ready at once,' he ordered.

As the butler scurried away he calmed himself, tamping down the panic rising in him. Where would Anne-Marie and Lily go? And why would they have left? Were they angry that he hadn't seen them in three days? He often didn't see them for longer than that, especially when he was closing a deal.

He wondered if the girls had got wind of his quarrel with Georgina.

Yes, that had to be it. And they had to have gone to her.

'Sir, the carriage is outside,' Fletcher said, Elliot's hat and coat in his hand.

'Thank you, Fletcher.'

Rushing outside, he barked at his driver to take him to Harwicke House. 'And be quick about it!'

He could barely stay still as the carriage began to move. The ride seemed to take for ever, and when they stopped he nearly leapt out.

Just as his feet landed on the ground, he heard someone call his name.

'Elliot?'

Slowly, he raised his head. Georgina stood just outside her

door, staring at him, mouth agape. She looked so lovely, standing there in the morning sun, it made his heart clench.

'What are you doing here?' she asked as he approached.

'I...' He'd forgotten, just for a moment. 'The girls. Are they here? With you?'

'Anne-Marie and Lily? No, of course not.' She frowned. 'Why would they be?'

'I— Never mind.' When he made a move to turn away, she reached out to grab at his arm.

'Elliot, what's the matter? Where are the girls?' Her tone was firm as her grip tightened. 'Tell me, please.'

'They are gone. I think they ran away.'

'They ran away?' she echoed. 'How? Why?'

'I'm not sure.' He released the breath he was holding. 'I think they're angry with me. I haven't seen them in three days.' He thrust his fingers into his hair.

'Why not?' she asked in a quiet voice.

Why do you think?

'I've been busy. In any case, I shall go and look for them—'

'Where? I mean, where would you start? London is a colossal city. They could be anywhere.'

'Don't you think I know that?' he barked, then instantly regretted it. 'My apologies. I'm—'

'I know, you're frightened for them.' She smoothed her hand over his arm. 'But you cannot just run around London hoping to find them. You must think clearly. Where could they have gone?'

'I don't know.' He thought for a moment. 'If I had to guess... perhaps they might try to book a passage to America?'

'Hmmm... How? Do they have funds? Do you give them pin money?'

'No, all the bills for everything they may need or want get sent directly to me.'

Anne-Marie was still far too young to have an allowance of any sort.

'All right.' She chewed at her lip. 'Without any money, they wouldn't be able to hire a hansom cab. Which means they are on foot. How long have they been missing?'

'Since midnight, maybe. Fletcher said they opened their presents, then went to bed. When I came back from the office this morning they were already gone.'

'They don't really have anywhere to go. They haven't been to many places except Hyde Park.'

'And here,' Elliot supplied.

'Which is why you thought to come here.'

'Yes. Christ.' He raked his fingers through his hair. 'I just want them to be safe.'

'I do, too.'

To his shock and surprise, Georgina reached up to smooth the sides of his hair, her soft fingers brushing the outside of his ear. He suddenly became aware of how close she was, and his stomach knotted itself with the yearning he felt for her.

'There is one other place they know in London.'

'And where is that?'

'St Agnes's. I took them there.'

Realisation struck him. So they'd likely know about the eviction, perhaps overhearing talk of it while they were there. And since Elliot hadn't explained to them what had happened...

'I must go there now.'

She did not release him. 'I am coming with you.'

'No, you are not.' He attempted to shake off her grip, but she clung to him like a python. 'Release me, Georgina.'

'I am coming with you, one way or another.' A determined look set on her face. 'I need to know if those girls are safe. Please, Elliot, take me with you.'

'Where is your carriage?'

'It will take for ever to get it ready.' She nodded at his carriage. 'We can take yours. It makes more sense.'

'You can't ride with me in a closed carriage. Where is Miss Warren?'

'She has the next few days off,' she said. 'Please, we are wasting time.'

'Georgina...' he warned. However, she still refused to release him, so he let out a resigned breath. 'All right, let's go.'

He led her to his carriage and settled in across from her. The entire ride to Boyle Street was silent, and Georgina stared out of the window, wringing her hands on her lap. Had it been four days since he'd last seen her? She had run so fast from him he hadn't even had time to think.

It had occurred to him that that might have been the last time he would see her. He should not have pushed her so hard. Would it really have been so terrible to cancel his agreement with Brimsley? Or perhaps he should not have even entertained his offer at all. What had he been thinking? It was only money, after all, and he already had lots of it.

'We're here,' Georgina announced.

Alighting from the carriage, he helped her down and they bolted towards the front door of St Agnes's. He knocked furiously, not stopping until it was opened.

'Can I help you sir?' The woman's tone conveyed her annoyance. 'And what—? Lady Georgina?'

'Mrs Jameson,' Georgina began, 'are Lily and Anne-Marie here?'

'Why, yes— What do you think you're doing?' she cried when Elliot pushed himself inside.

He ignored the woman's shouts of indignation and began to call for his sisters. 'Anne-Marie! Lily!' he called. 'I know you are here! Come down right this minute.'

'I'm sorry, Mrs Jameson,' Georgina said. 'He thought they'd run away and he has been worried sick.'

'Girls!' he bellowed. 'Come here—Anne-Marie! Lily!'

The heaviness in his chest disappeared at the sight of his sisters as they stood at the top of the stairs.

'I'm so glad to see you both.'

He broke into a run towards the stairs and began to climb them, but just before he reached the top, he found himself blocked as an army of little girls began to pour down the steps. They surrounded him, their faces drawn into scowls as they stared up at him in challenge.

'What is going on?'

'We're not coming home with you,' Anne-Marie declared.

'We're staying here,' Lily said, nodding in agreement.

'Girls, you cannot stay here,' he said. 'You belong with me, at home. And these very lovely little ladies will soon be at their wonderful new home. I am sure they will enjoy themselves there. Why, there are even ponies for them to play with.' He glanced down at the child by his left leg, the smallest of the bunch. 'Wouldn't you like that?' he asked.

The girl only bared her teeth and growled.

Elliot blew out a breath. 'All right, what do you want?'

'We want you to make up with Lady Georgina,' Anne-Marie said.

'I want her to be my sister,' Lily wailed.

Elliot too, wished for that, with all his heart. 'I'm sorry, girls, but that's not up to me.'

'Can't you do something—? Lady Georgina?' Anne-Marie exclaimed.

Lily gasped. 'You're here.'

'Yes, I was very worried about you.' Georgina stood at the bottom of the stairs. 'Girls,' she said to the swarm surrounding Elliot, 'would you please let Mr Smith through? I think he and I need to speak alone.'

Smiling, she held out her hand towards him.

The children parted like the Red Sea, and so Elliot, like Moses, followed the trail downwards. He reached out and took Georgina's hand and allowed her to lead him away into the nearest room.

Closing the door behind her, she motioned for him to sit on the large settee by the fireplace. He did, and she joined him.

'I'm sorry—'

'Forgive me—'

They both stopped, and Elliot was sure the shock on his face mirrored hers.

'Georgina,' he began again. 'Forgive me. I should not have entertained that offer. I... I justified it because of the money, and because I wanted to teach someone a lesson. I made you a promise, and I broke it. Please forgive me.'

She blew out a breath. 'Elliot, I said some things to you that day that I regret so much. You're right, there should have been a discussion, a compromise of some sort, before I decided to run out on you. I was just scared—'

'Because I love you.' A lightness filled his chest as he said it aloud. He didn't care if she heard it or if it scared her. She *had* to know.

Her breath hitched audibly and tears welled up in her eyes. 'You were right. I was afraid. Afraid of the pain I felt when I lost Mama and Papa. They loved each other so much. I don't… I never thought I would ever have something like that. And even if I did, I knew it wouldn't last. I told myself I didn't want to feel it and have it taken away. I never wanted to feel…' She swallowed, and then she spoke in barely a whisper. 'I don't know what I would do if I lost you too.'

'Georgina.' Unable to help himself, he gathered her into his arms. 'Don't cry.'

'B-But I lost you anyway,' she sobbed. 'I ran away from you. And now you—'

'I am here,' he soothed. 'And I love you.'

'I…' Pulling away from him, she lifted her face to his. 'I love you too.'

Cradling her face in his hand, he leaned down to kiss her. A warm glow wrapped around him and his heart seemed to expand to twice its size and burst out of his chest. Her mouth was soft, and as sweet as he'd remembered, maybe even more. He couldn't get enough of her—but he would have to stop now before he went too far.

'Sweetheart…' he breathed. 'Will you marry me?'

'I haven't said I wouldn't,' she replied, smiling against his mouth. 'Will *you* marry me?'

'A thousand—no, a million—times over.'

'I just need the one.' She pulled away from him. 'I… I love you just the way you are. You are set in your ways, and I understand, as I am in mine. And if you can learn to accept me as I am, then I can accept you too.'

'What do you mean?'

'I know you don't seem to like Christmas, so if you'd prefer not to celebrate—'

He pressed a finger to her lips to stop her. 'Oh, no, sweetheart. Please don't… I don't.' He sucked in a breath. 'It's not that I hate Christmas, it's just…'

He closed his eyes, trying to forget the memory. But perhaps it was time for him to let go.

'My ma died on Christmas Day.'

She gasped. 'Elliot, I'm sorry.'

'It's all right.' He gathered his hands into his. 'The day never held any pleasant memories for me, even before that. We were too poor to celebrate. But that Christmas Day she died, crying out for my good-for-nothing father, was the day I decided I was going to make something of myself. I worked myself to the bone, accumulating wealth and power, trying to fill that hole she had left inside me. I came up with my ten-year plans so I wouldn't notice how real life was passing me by as I pursued my goals. I didn't stop—I couldn't stop. Because I was afraid when I did I would realise that having all the money in the world didn't matter. That *I* didn't matter.'

'But you do, Elliot.' Smiling up at him, she smoothed his hair back. 'You matter to Anne-Marie and Lily. You matter to me.'

'And you matter to me. All of you. I don't care about my ten-year plan any more. I want to slow down, enjoy my life with you and the girls...and our children.'

With an excited cry, she sprang at him, wrapping her arms around his neck as she crushed her lips to his. He toppled back and she landed on top of him, her curvy, soft body pressed against his. He groaned as her hips made contact with his lap and—

'Are you done kissing?' came Lily's faint voice from behind the door.

'And are you engaged again?' Anne-Marie added.

'We never stopped being engaged,' Elliot called out.

'May we come in now?' Lily asked.

They looked at each other and Georgina giggled. 'One moment!' She moved off him and then sat down on one side of the settee, arranging her skirts. 'All right, come in!'

Anne-Marie and Lily bounded inside, their faces bright with excitement.

'Have you truly made up?' Anne-Marie asked.

'Yes,' Elliot confirmed. 'We have. Can we go home now?'

'But we want to spend Christmas here,' Lily whined. 'And help the girls with packing for their move to Camden.'

'What if I told you they don't have to move to Camden?' Elliot said. 'And they can stay here.'

'Elliot?' Georgina stared at him, slack-jawed. 'Are you sure?'

'Yes. I will cancel the sale to Brimsley.'

Young Charles the III would have to face the consequences of his actions when the senior Brimsleys arrived—which, he supposed, was still a way for the fool to learn his lesson, even if Elliot did not profit from it.

'And the girls do not have to move out.'

'Hooray!' Lily raised a fist in the air.

'But what about the house in Camden?' Georgina asked. 'Won't it be a waste to have all that space?'

'I suppose… But it's still the perfect place for a new orphanage. Perhaps that could be a project for you?'

'Me?'

'Yes. I was planning not to charge St Agnes's rent on the place anyway, as my wedding gift to you. But now I'm thinking I should give you the deed instead and you can establish a second orphanage.' He'd noticed she had no trouble being around crowds of children, so it would be perfect for her. 'Would you like that?'

The smile on her face practically lit up the room. 'Yes, I would.'

'Can we still stay here?' Lily asked. 'And have our Christmas dinner here tonight with all the girls?'

'I think that would be lovely,' Georgina said. 'What do you say, Elliot?'

'I think I am outvoted,' he said with a resigned sigh. 'All right.'

And so the four of them stayed for the entire day, playing games, singing carols and eating Christmas pudding. Georgina and Trevor had already planned to spend Christmas at the orphanage anyway, so the Duke arrived later that day. He looked overjoyed to see that Georgina and Elliot had made up.

Trevor did not come empty-handed. He had brought two roast

turkeys for dinner. And Elliot had sent word to his own staff, who'd brought over the feast they had prepared.

They all sat in the orphanage's massive dining room as Elliot and Trevor carved the turkeys, and after dinner all the girls went upstairs to their rooms to continue with their merrymaking. Now Trevor had gone home, but Georgina had decided to stay for another hour or two.

She and Elliot sneaked back into the parlour so they could be alone.

'Happy Christmas,' Georgina said to Elliot as she laid her head on his shoulder and he put his arm around her. 'Your first. First time celebrating it, anyway.'

'And not the last.'

Georgina snapped her fingers. 'Oh, that reminds me—I have a gift for you. It's under the tree I had brought to your house.'

'I know. I saw it.'

She grinned slyly at him. 'I think you'll like it.'

'I think I will.' He already had a suspicion about what it was. 'But I'm afraid I've already read *A Christmas Carol*.'

'You have?'

Reaching into his coat, he retrieved the book from his pocket. He wasn't sure why he'd carried it around all this time, but now he realised it was the only way he could keep her close to his heart.

'Well, I had to—especially since all three of you had accused me of being a Scrooge.' He tickled Georgina's nose, sending her into a fit of giggles. 'Did you hope it would cure me of my Scrooge-like ways?'

'Possibly,' Georgina said.

'Perhaps I am cured. But I wouldn't give credit to Dickens for the change.'

'Oh?'

'No, sweetheart.' He stared deep into her coppery brown eyes, finding the love shining in them. 'If anyone has brought Christmas into my heart, it's you.'

* * * * *

HISTORICAL

Your romantic escape to the past.

Available Next Month

The Trouble With The Daring Governess Annie Burrows
The Earl's Marriage Dilemma Sarah Mallory

....

One Waltz With The Viscount Laura Martin
When Cinderella Met The Duke Sophia Williams

Keep reading for an excerpt of a new title
from the Historical series,
COMPROMISED WITH HER FORBIDDEN VISCOUNT
by Diane Gaston

Chapter One

1819

'You can't ride to Chantry Old Hall with only a dog for company, Juno,' Lady Colby protested, '*and* the gardener says it will snow.'

Juno looked at the hazy blue sky and decided he was wrong. Just as well, as she *had* to be home in time for the worryingly early birth of her uncle's first child.

'I can join Sir Harry and Viola the rest of the way, but they will go without me if I don't hurry,' she replied, pulling on gloves as she sped down the path with Pard, her Dalmatian dog, at her heels and her godmother scurrying behind.

'It's easy to get lost in the hills, so they might go before you can get there,' Lady Colby argued.

'The innkeeper gave me good directions when I hired his best horse and Sir Harry will drive the carriage himself to get his wife there for the birth if he has to, so it's my quickest way home,' Juno said and pulled on the velvet jockey cap she wore for riding.

'He was wild to a fault until your aunt's sister and all those children tamed him, so I'm not surprised, but you're *not wed*, Juno—you can't attend a birthing.'

'I can pace outside the bedchamber with my uncle. Marianne and the Yelvertons stood by me when I needed them, so I must do the same for them. She will need all our support if the baby is too small to survive.'

When Juno's life felt shattered, just like her heart, Marianne had taken her in. She had been so kind and patient, helping Juno to pick up the pieces. At seventeen, her grandmother had planned to force Juno to marry a venal old man if he paid off the Dowager's debts, so she was left with no choice but to run away. When her uncle Alaric returned home from diplomatic duty in France, he was so furious to discover what his mother had done that he paid her debts one last time and publicly disclaimed responsibility for any more.

Juno now lived with her uncle and Marianne, but hadn't told them why she had refused another London Season. There was no point since she had loved and lost and it had hurt so much that she never wanted to experience such pain again.

'You *might* get there in time if the weather holds, but it would be so much better if you hired a carriage,' Lady Colby said.

'Not fast enough,' Juno argued and thank goodness they were in the stable yard of the inn so she could say a hasty farewell and ride away.

Uncle Alaric and Marianne were her family, but even they didn't know she had fallen in love before she ran from London. She had taken one dazed look at a handsome, dashing and hopeful Lieutenant Nathaniel Grange and lost her foolish young heart. Then he had marched back to war and taken her heart with him and the only way for her to escape a forced marriage was to run to Herefordshire where her former governess was living.

Uncle Alaric had been determined that Juno would have a better life, so he had employed Marianne as Juno's companion. He and Marianne had fallen in love, so some good had come of Juno's youthful troubles. And at least she was a strong and independent woman now and very happy to stay that way.

An hour later, Juno blinked snowflakes from her eyelashes in order to see the road ahead and Lady Colby and her gardener were proved right. It wasn't far to Sir Harry Marbeck's beloved home in the hills, but she wasn't going to get there and needed shelter from the storm. She fought panic before she saw high walls and a gate that was wide open. The lodge was shuttered, so she urged the horse into the avenue and prayed for sanctuary at the end of it.

Yes, there was a grand old house there, but it was shuttered and no smoke was issuing from its chimneys. For an awful moment she thought she was imagining it—she had heard of people losing their reason as they froze to death. She wasn't that cold yet and it looked real enough as the horse forged on to the stables. The first door she tried opened, but no reply came to her shouted greeting as she led the horse inside and Pard dashed ahead to make sure it was empty.

The place smelt of old dust rather than horses, but two stalls were strewn with clean straw for someone's return, so she led the horse into one while Pard rolled in the other and wind keened around the stout old building. They had a roof over their heads; she could snuggle in the straw of the empty stall with Pard and wait out the storm. Yet what if they were caught napping by whoever had left these stalls ready? And the deserted mansion was making her imagination run wild, so she had to be sure it was really empty before they settled down.

She shivered with nerves as much as from the cold when the back door opened easily and she stepped inside the mansion, feeling like the heroine of a Gothic novel. Best not think of the horrors waiting for them as they explored places they were not supposed to be as she crept past the dark, cold kitchens. Pard's toenails sounded loud on the flagstones as Juno pushed open the door between servants' quarters and grand state rooms, hesitating in the shuttered gloom.

'Who the devil are you?' a gruff bass voice growled at her from the shadows and she gasped in shock.

The sound of that voice had haunted her dreams for so long she felt the ground lurch under her feet as her heartbeat jarred, then galloped on in shock. *He* was here? But was he just one of those delusions she had been worried about? No, that deep, rich voice was so uniquely Nathaniel Grange's he really must be standing in the shadows waiting for her to reply and he didn't sound very pleased about her intrusion.

The echoes of his gruff demand died away in the dusty gloom and she was still silenced. A younger, freer Juno wanted to rush into his arms and feel them close around her again at long last. She wanted to feel fully alive again for the first time in so long, but then she remembered how long it had taken her to live well without him and stayed where she was.

'I thought you were abroad,' she said numbly and it was his turn for a shocked silence. Pard sensed the tension and growled belatedly, but she had no words to reassure him.

'Not now,' Nathaniel said as if that explained everything. 'And if you think he's a guard dog, best think again,' he added so coolly that she must have imagined he was as shocked as she was. Pard wagged his tail as if he thought the stranger wasn't a threat.

'Traitor,' she murmured as he sat and offered the wretch a paw. 'You have neglected this house quite shamefully,' she said as Nathaniel came closer and her heartbeat sped up again at the reality of him, here and seemingly all alone.

He had grown a great beard and his physique seemed even larger and more formidable than the youthful one she remembered so fondly. He was so unlike his old self she wished she had happened on almost anyone else. She had loved that boy so much and this man wasn't even pretending to be pleased to see her.

'You can leave if it offends you,' he said curtly and she felt tears threaten because he wasn't her Nathaniel at all. The past was dead and it wasn't safe to mourn it with him watching.

'I wish I had stayed in the stables now,' she said bleakly.

'They might be cleaner. I wish I had got my manservant to light a fire in the grooms' quarters before he took my horse to be re-shod.'

So you would have stayed there and not come bothering me, she thought up the words for him.

How she wished she had taken Lady Colby's advice and hired a carriage now. 'Give me a tinderbox and I'll light one myself,' she said with a sniff to let him know he was being a terrible host, but that was all.

'Even I am not that much of a yahoo, my lady,' he said.

'I'm not married,' she said brusquely past the mournful thought that although he had once sworn he loved her he must have lied.

'You didn't marry the fat old lord, then?'

'Of course I didn't! I ran away.'

'Nobody told me.'

'Why would they?'

'True,' he said. If she added up the hours they had once spent together, they should be strangers.

Yet five years ago she thought he was her one true love—the hero that shy Juno Defford never quite dared believe she would ever find until he found her hiding in the shadows one night in Mayfair. Now he was shrugging her off as if they had always been strangers, but she had learned to hide her feelings, too, so he wouldn't know how much it hurt.

'You have been away too long,' she said with a sharp look at the dust and cobwebs she could now see in the semi-darkness.

'I thought it was being cared for by my late uncle's land agent, but clearly I was wrong.' A pause and even he must have decided that brusque explanation wasn't one at all. 'My uncle and I argued last time I was here. He wanted me to sell out after my bill of divorce was passed in the House, but I thought it was better to remain in the army while the dust settled.

'I was an arrogant young puppy and thought I was untouchable,' he said as if talking to himself now. 'I was wrong and that stupid war with America they are now calling the War of 1812, although it went on longer, was more or less over by the time we got there. We were shipped back just in time for Waterloo so no time for home leave before the battle and then he died and I was...' He hesitated.

'Injured,' she finished the sentence for him. 'I saw your name on the list of wounded.'

And longed to dash to Brussels, but you had made me promise to wait for you to come for me, so I stayed at home and bit my nails, and you didn't come.

'Yes, then came the news of my uncle's sudden death and poor Dorinda's a few weeks later,' he said flatly.

She could weep for the bright and hopeful boy of nineteen she remembered—unbowed by his divorce from 'poor Dorinda' and three hard years at war in Spain and France. If only she had ignored his orders to stay away from him until the scandal of his failed marriage faded, how different their lives might be now. Except if it was only real love on her side it was best he had stayed away.

'Your former wife hated the military life and the country-side, but you were a soldier and your uncle's heir, so why did she marry you?' she asked boldly because she didn't have any-thing to lose and she had always wondered.

'Because we were both seventeen and too green to know the difference between love and passion. We were friends as chil-dren, so it probably felt real to her at the time.'

'I am sorry for your loss,' she said, wondering if he still loved Dorinda, despite her infidelity.

Juno would have followed him to war barefoot and unwed if he had let her, but had he mourned his unfaithful former wife so dearly he forgot her? He had stolen Juno's heart when he found her hiding from the lord she didn't want to marry and Lieu-tenant Grange was too kind to walk away from a girl fighting tears, so he stayed to joke her out of them. Then he kissed her to make it better and changed her world.

Had he been too kind to call a halt—was that how he had ended up married to his *friend*? She hated the notion history could have repeated itself, if he hadn't thought better of marry-ing Juno. She saw the closed expression on his once-open face and, once again, mourned the bright youth she remembered.

'Why were you out alone in a blizzard?' he asked and his turn to change the subject. 'And this fine boy is no protection so don't tell me you were not alone.'

'He usually is.'

'His instincts aren't working today, then,' Nathaniel mur-mured so softly she must have misheard.

'Do you have somewhere warmer where we can argue?' she

said as cold seemed to reach into her very bones and she knew it wasn't caused by the weather.

'The agent's house,' he said with another frown—maybe he didn't want her there either.

'It's very cold in here,' she said with as much dignity as she could find as her snow-wet clothes clung to her—no wonder she was shivering.

'Agreed,' he said and strode off into the gloom and she supposed he meant her to follow him. 'But where *were* you bound on such a day?' he asked without turning round.

'None of your business,' she said and scurried in his wake.

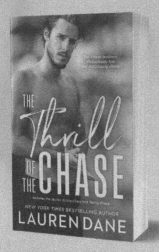 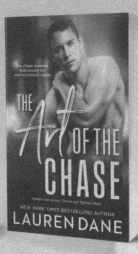